falling into LOVE with YOU

USA Today and International Bestselling Author

Lauren Rowe

BOOKS BY LAUREN ROWE

Standalone Novels

Smitten

The Reed Rivers Trilogy (to be read in order)

Bad Liar

Beautiful Liar

Beloved Liar

The Club Trilogy (to be read in order)

The Club: Obsession

The Club: Reclamation

The Club: Redemption

The Club: Culmination (A Full-Length Epilogue Book)

The Josh and Kat Trilogy (to be read in order)

Infatuation

Revelation

Consummation

The Morgan Brothers (a series of related standalones):

Hero

Captain

Ball Peen Hammer

Mister Bodyguard

ROCKSTAR

The Misadventures Series (a series of unrelated standalones):

Misadventures on the Night Shift

Misadventures of a College Girl

Misadventures on the Rebound

Standalone Psychological Thriller/Dark Comedy

Countdown to Killing Kurtis

Short Stories

The Secret Note

ONE
LAILA

As Savage leaves Reed's guest house after our stilted, awkward conversation about "Hate Sex High," I shove my earbuds back in, press play on the song, close my eyes, and listen carefully. A moment later, the makeup artist taps my arm, letting me know she's returned from outside, so I nod to her and close my eyes again, finding it hard to give my attention, even fleetingly, to anything but Savage's voice in my ears.

Presently, Savage's sexy voice is singing, *"You're falling in hate with me/I'm feeling something I don't want to feel . . ."* And I can't help wondering . . . what is the *something* Savage was feeling when he wrote this song—the *something* he didn't want to feel? A few minutes ago, Savage swore, up and down, that the entire song was "pure fiction." But then, he immediately backtracked and said the chorus was a "popcorn lie" he'd spun from various "kernels of truth" in the verses. The thing is, though, I hadn't even mentioned the chorus when Savage felt the need to vehemently deny its truth. So now, I can't help thinking the dude doth protest too much.

The song continues to the second half of the chorus, the part where Savage sings a string of "*la la's*." And, once again, I hear *my* name at the ends of those lines. *Repeatedly.* Yep, that's definitely my name! Granted, Savage's voice is buried in the mix, artfully interwoven with his bandmates' voices singing "*la la.*" Most likely to preserve deniability for Savage. But, nonetheless, anyone with the ability to hear would be able to discern *my* name at the end of those *la la's*.

A flash of energy courses through my veins. Does Savage singing my name in the song *enthrall* or *anger* me? I can't decide. All I know for certain is that hearing Savage belting out *my* name, for the entire world to hear—knowing he's explicitly identifying *me* as the muse for this raunchy song— is making my blood simmer and every hair on my body stand at full attention.

The song continues, with Savage making a big thing about his muse coming three times. "Girl, you came three times," he sings, *twice*, before speaking the line in a smug, matter-of-fact tone. Finally, Savage concludes in the bridge, "You're chasing . . . a . . . hate sex high"—and as Savage sings the titular lyrics of the song, a shiver skates across my skin. As freaked out as I am in this moment, I can't help reliving the night of the hot tub as I listen. The night I did, in fact, chase a hate sex high with Savage, all the way to three glorious orgasms that felt far more intense and electrifying than anything I'd experienced before.

I feel a tap on my shoulder and open my eyes to find the makeup artist smiling at me. She holds up a makeup brush as if to say "all done!" So, I stop the song, which is currently barreling into its final chorus, and check myself out in the mirror.

"Looks great," I say. "Thank you."

"You're welcome."

"Who's sitting in your chair next?" I ask, hoping she'll say Aloha, and when she does, I tap out a text to my darling friend, asking her to please get her ass down to Reed's guest house as soon as possible—earlier than scheduled—because I need to talk to her about something urgent.

Three minutes later, Aloha appears, her famous emerald-green eyes practically glowing. After greeting the makeup artist, Aloha asks me, "Is everything okay?"

I jut my chin toward the makeup artist, who's presently preparing her station, to let Aloha know the urgent thing I need to talk to her about is confidential, and Aloha instantly gets the message.

"Hey, Susanna," Aloha says. "Would you mind taking a quick break before we get started? I came early to chat with Laila."

"Of course," the makeup artist replies. "How's fifteen minutes?"

Aloha looks at me, her eyebrows raised. And when she sees the expression of pure panic on my face, she says, "Let's make it twenty."

The door closes behind the makeup artist, and before I've said a word, Aloha lurches at me and yells, "What did Savage do to you last night, you little freak? My room was across the hallway from Savage's and I heard every scream and moan!" She takes the chair next to mine, smiling wickedly. "And don't tell me all those noises were you barfing, and not the sounds of pure ecstasy. I know barfing when I hear it, and that wasn't it."

I roll my eyes, even as I'm blushing. "The second half of what you heard was me barfing."

"And the first half?"

I can't help smiling. "The sounds of pure ecstasy."

Aloha squeals. "Tell me *everything*."

"There's not much to tell. Savage ate me from every angle and I was too drunk to care if anyone in the house heard my reaction."

Aloha fans herself. "Girl, you never disappoint. How did you even wind up in Savage's room?"

"I was horny and drunk and didn't know which room was his, so I crept down the hallway on my tiptoes, in my undies, and went looking for him."

Aloha hoots. "Laila Fitzgerald! You little horndog!"

I snort. "I pressed my ear against a couple doors, hoping to feel some kind of 'Savage vibration' emanating from the other side. And then, lo and behold, there Savage was in *his* underwear on the far end of the hallway, on his way to find *me*."

Aloha reacts gleefully.

"But that's not the urgent thing I needed to talk to you about. I need you to listen to something that's making my head explode. Talk me off the ledge, Aloha. I'm freaking out." I grab my phone, anxiety coursing through me, and get "Hate Sex High" cued up. My heart thumping, I explain, "This morning, Kendrick gave me an early copy of Fugitive Summer's new album, so I could listen to the mixes." I hand my phone to Aloha. "Listen to the third track. 'Hate Sex High.' It's about *me*—about the night I told you about, when I screwed Savage's brains out during the tour."

"Holy crap," Aloha whispers, taking my phone and earbuds.

As she begins listening, I get up and pace back and forth in the small guest house, unable to keep my body, or mind, from spazzing out.

"Love the beat," Aloha murmurs. "Cool baseline." She pauses. "Ha! That's so Savage. It sounds like he's getting a blowjob."

"Keep listening," I say. Clearly, she's only gotten as far as the introductory "yeahs."

Suddenly, Aloha's eyebrows lift. Her eyes widen. She begins muttering things like "Whoa" and "Wow." Finally, she shouts, "He's singing *Laila*! What the fuck!" She presses pause. "He's called you out by *name*?"

"*Right?*"

"*Dude.*" She presses play again and a moment later shrieks, "You came *three* times with him that night?"

I blush and nod. "More last night."

Aloha flashes me a snarky look. "Well, damn. No wonder you don't care if he's an asshole." She snickers to herself before quieting down to listen again. And then, "Wow, he's proud of those three orgasms, huh?" She pauses. "Okay, Savage, we get it. She came *three* times." She snorts. "What a smug little shit to put this song as the *third* track on the album, as yet another nod to those three Os. That's so Savage."

My pulse lurches. I hadn't thought of that, but she's right.

Aloha continues listening for a moment before snorting and saying, "He just had to gloat, one more time, at the end. Such a cheeky bastard." She presses pause and takes out the earbuds. "So, Laila. I have a question not answered by the lyrics. Something that wasn't clear." Aloha furrows her brow, like she's trying to solve the secrets of the universe.

"Did Savage, by any chance . . . make you come *three* times?"

We both break into raucous laughter. Even in my present state of total freak-out, I can't help giggling with my good friend.

I resume my chair next to Aloha. "So, you agree he's singing my name in those 'la la' parts, right? Because Savage denied it."

"You've already talked to Savage about the song?"

I nod furiously. "He burst in here, while I was midway through listening to it. Apparently, Kendrick gave me an early copy of the album without consulting Savage first, and when Savage found out, he hightailed it straight down here to find me."

"Interesting."

"And then, when Savage realized I was already listening to 'Hate Sex High,' he had the nerve to *deny* he sang my name in the song! He *insisted* he was singing 'la la' all the way through."

Aloha scoffs, her expression making it clear she doesn't buy Savage's explanation for a minute.

I continue, "Savage insisted I was only hearing my name because I'm a 'megalomaniac' who thinks the world revolves around me."

Aloha laughs in a way that would have resulted in a spit-take if she'd taken a sip of a beverage immediately beforehand.

"Preposterous, right?" I ask.

"Utterly and totally preposterous. Not to mention, insulting to your intelligence. He's singing 'Laila,' over and over again. Plus, come on, the verses track what happened between you and Savage during the tour—the stuff with

Malik in New York and your hookup later on. So, there's no doubt, even if he didn't call you out by name, which he *did,* that the song is one thousand percent about *you.* But, yes, there's no question he *also* says your name, repeatedly, to emphasize his point."

"*But what's his point?*" I ask breathlessly. "Is his point what he sings in the chorus? The part where he says he's feeling 'something' he doesn't want to feel for his muse—for 'Laila' who's falling into hate with him?"

"You mean, Laila who's coming *three* times while chasing a hate sex high?"

I exhale loudly. "Honestly, it's the chorus that's freaking me out the most, even more than all the sex stuff. I don't know if it would be hitting me so hard if Savage hadn't raced down here with bulging eyes the minute he found out I had an early copy. But, Aloha, when Savage burst through that door, he looked like he was going to have a heart attack at the thought of me listening to *that* particular song. And then *he* brought up the chorus first, to *deny* it was true, before I'd said a word about it. So, I don't think his main worry was the sex stuff."

Aloha bites her lip, processing. "How'd you leave it with him?"

"He conceded the song was 'inspired' by me. That there were 'kernels of truth' in the verses. But he said he took those 'kernels of truth' and spun them into 'popcorn lies' in the chorus. But why would Savage feel the need to *sprint* down here, like a bat out of hell, unless he *knew* that chorus admits he caught feelings for me during the tour?" I let my mouth hang open, wide, as if to say, *Can you believe it?*

But Aloha's face reflects skepticism. "Well, I mean, he could have been worried you'd be livid to be called out, by *name*, as someone he'd screwed." Aloha pauses, waiting for a reaction from me, and whatever wilted expression she's seeing on my face makes her sigh with compassion. "Okay, let's look at this objectively, honey. Savage is the guy who had sex with you on the night of the hot tub, and then, mere hours later, turned around and screwed someone else. So, even if he *is* singing in the chorus about 'catching feelings' for you, then how much stock do you really think you should put into those supposed feelings?"

I look down at my lap, feeling embarrassed about my show of excitement.

"Aw, I'm sorry," Aloha says quickly. "Maybe you're right. I'm certainly not trying to rain on your parade here . . ."

I take a deep breath and look up, making a concerted effort to wipe all traces of disappointment off my face. Aloha is right. I'm assigning *way* too much depth and importance to that chorus, when the obvious truth is that Savage proved himself a diehard womanizer in Las Vegas. A man who'd felt nothing but lust toward me, the same thing he'd felt toward countless other women across the globe. Truly, it was the height of self-delusion for me to think the song is about Savage catching feelings for me, when the truth is that I was never anything special to him. Nothing but another conquest.

Aloha apologizes again and tries to backtrack, but I wave her off, saying, "No, no, don't apologize. I asked for your honest opinion, and you gave it to me. I'm glad you never pull any punches with me."

"But, honey, I never want to 'punch' you in any way. I just wanted—"

"No, no, stop. Like you said, even if Savage *did* catch feelings for me after the night of the hot tub, which is unlikely, his 'feelings' wouldn't be something I should rely on, based on his subsequent behavior. I need to remember the timeline of events here. There's no other conclusion to be drawn when I look at Savage's *actions*, rather than projecting some fairytale fantasy onto a few stupid lyrics in a song."

Aloha looks sympathetic. "Oh, Laila, I'd *love* for you to be the woman who brought Mr. Fuckboy to his knees. I'd *love* that for you. I just don't want you to get hurt. In the past, I've seen Savage in action, from afar, and let's just say his reputation as a lady killer is well-earned."

I nod. "Yeah, I know. I always want you to be nothing but totally honest with me. Even if the truth hurts, that's what I want to hear."

Aloha puffs out her cheeks. "Okay, well, if I'm being *totally* honest with you, it seems to me the song is a 'gloating song' about Savage having sex with you. A song written to taunt Malik, far more than to express any secret feelings he was having for you. I mean, Savage literally asks, at the end, if 'he'—meaning Malik—made you come three times, the same way Savage did. If that's not a pissing contest between two dudes—if that's not Savage running a victory lap—then I don't know what is."

My heart feels like it's lodged in my toes. Aloha is right, yet again. After his tussle with Malik in that restaurant, Savage wanted his adversary to know he'd won the game and claimed the prize. Also, that he'd done all of it exceedingly well. Savage sat down and wrote "Hate Sex High" to deride Malik, not because he felt tortured by his blossoming feelings for me. In the end, the song had very little to do with me, actually, and everything to do with his desire to flip the bird at Malik.

Suddenly, I feel like I'm standing in that hallway in Las

Vegas, all over again. An acute sensation of rejection washes over me. I feel pathetic. Foolish. *Embarrassed.* Why do I *still* want Savage to want me, more than anyone else—but especially more than some random groupie he just met? Why does he *still* have this ridiculous hold over me?

Aloha says, "Aw, Laila. I could be wrong. After the night of the hot tub, was there *any* indication Savage was feeling 'something' he didn't want to feel toward you? Think back."

Images flood me. Savage's arm slung over that groupie's shoulders. A booze bottle dangling in his free hand. The woman's obvious excitement that Savage had deigned to choose *her.* I hear her voice saying, "Let me at that famous body!" And every molecule in my body recoils and shudders at the memory. "No," I reply, my spirit heavy. "On the contrary, the only indication was that Savage felt the same thing men always feel for me: nothing but lust." I take a deep breath to regulate the pang of embarrassment twisting my core. How on earth did I hear "Hate Sex High" and turn it into a confessional about Savage catching feelings for me, when the truth is so damned obvious?

Aloha juts her lower lip in sympathy. "Aw, honey. Who cares what I think? I wasn't there, and you were. Trust your gut."

"I do. And my gut is telling me you're right. It's telling me I heard what I wanted to hear in the song, not what was actually there."

Sighing, Aloha gets up from her chair and hugs me. "Oh, sweet Laila. You and your horrible taste in men." She kisses my hair. "Why can't you ever fall for guys who aren't players and heartbreakers, girlie?"

I nuzzle into Aloha's dark hair and exhale. "It's my fatal flaw. I see a guy with multiple red flags sticking out of his hair and ears and asshole, and I run *towards* him, at full speed, rather than away."

Aloha chuckles, while I groan in misery.

"I don't even like Savage, as a person," I say softly. "He's an arrogant jerk. It's like he's cast a spell on me. Like I'm a drug addict and he's my drug. I know he's bad for me, but I can't stop wanting him."

Aloha pulls back from our embrace to level me with her green eyes. "Do you really want him—or do you want *him* to want *you*?"

"I want *him* to want *me*!" I shout, without hesitation. "*Why doesn't he want me, Aloha?*"

Aloha chuckles. "Well, it seems pretty clear, from what I heard coming out of Savage's room last night, you both want each other—physically, anyway." She smooths my hair, presses a kiss to my forehead, and resumes her chair. "Buckle up, Buttercup. It sounds like the next three months are going to be a wild ride for you. You're going to be living and working with Savage, and probably having amazing sex with him every night, too, if those sounds I heard last night were any indication. So, do yourself a favor and make sure you're not projecting feelings onto him that might not be there. Or else, the next three months could really mess with your heart."

I sigh. "Don't worry. I've got my head on straight now. Savage has no idea Malik was nothing to me. I made him think I was with Malik for weeks after I'd already kicked him to the curb in New York. Obviously, it drove Savage crazy to think there was one woman on planet earth who was resistant to his charms. That's what the song is about."

The makeup artist sticks her head inside the door. "Ready for me?"

Aloha raises her eyebrows, asking me if I'm good.

"Yeah, come in," I reply, flashing a wistful smile at Aloha. "We're done here."

"I'm always here for you," Aloha says softly.

"Thank you. I'm good. If you don't mind, I think I'll hide out here for a bit. I promised Kendrick I'd listen to the whole album, and I don't want to go out there and bump into You Know Who while I'm doing that."

"Stay as long as you like—provided you let me know if there's another song about you."

"God help me," I mutter, before leaning back and shoving my earbuds in again. But, thankfully, as I listen to the rest of the album, I don't hear another song that contains my name buried in the mix or a single lyric that feels even remotely like it was inspired by me.

TWO

SAVAGE

As I exit Reed's guest house following my conversation with Laila about "Hate Sex High," the makeup artist I'd asked to step outside on my way in is standing outside the door, looking stressed. Clearly, the poor woman has a tight schedule before the press conference and the last thing she needed was some asshole rock star showing up and asking her to step outside.

"Sorry about that," I mutter. "You can go back in now."

"No worries. Have a good one."

"You, too."

As the woman heads inside to return to Laila, I begin traipsing up the pathway toward Reed's gigantic main house, physically shaking with adrenaline. I *think* I persuaded Laila, pretty convincingly, not to put too much stock in my lyrics. In fact, by the time I left the guest house, I *think* I had Laila pretty well convinced "Hate Sex High" is mostly fiction, other than the obvious references in the verses. Obviously, there's no getting around the fact that Laila was the one who chased a hate sex high with me, all the way to three orgasms. But, thankfully, I think I persuaded Laila not to freak out about the chorus—specifically, the one lyric I didn't want her to hear the most.

If I'd had the balls to tell Laila the truth about that particular lyric a moment ago, the one in which I confessed I was feeling something I didn't want to feel for her, I would have had to tell her I was flat-out obsessed with her by the time I stumbled upon her in that hot tub. I would have had to tell her I became even more obsessed with her after finding out sex with her was hotter than my hottest fantasy. I would have had to tell her my obsession with her morphed into downright madness, once she'd started ignoring me and all my texts, in city after city, beginning in Las Vegas. And that my madness only amplified when she started showing up *everywhere* with motherfucking Charlie the Fitness Trainer, looking like she'd just finished sucking his dick. But I couldn't tell Laila any of that. Not yet, anyway. Not now.

After rounding a corner, I come upon Kendrick, sitting in the same spot on Reed's patio where I left him earlier, his MacBook open and his headphones on.

When my best friend sees me approaching, he rips off his headphones. "Well?"

I come to a stop in front of Kendrick and exhale. "When I walked in, Laila was in the middle of listening to 'Hate Sex High'—a fact I knew, instantly, because of the look on her face." I mimic Laila's expression, making the same sort of look people make during a jump-scare in a horror movie.

Kendrick grimaces. "What'd she say about the song?"

I take a chair and tell Kendrick the whole story, in great detail, concluding with, "Thankfully, by the time I left, I think I had her pretty well convinced the song is just, you know, *inspired* by her, but with *lots* of artistic license taken, especially in relation to the chorus. The part that matters the most."

Kendrick sighs. "Well, it's a relief you were able to talk to her right away, so the situation didn't spiral out of control on you."

"Mm-hmm," I say, simply because, the minute Kendrick says the word *relief*, I realize that's not the predominant emotion I'm feeling. That, in fact, I'm feeling mostly *disappointment* that Laila believed my bullshit about the song not being completely true. Did I secretly hope Laila would see right through my lies and force me to come clean and confess everything to her? No. That's a ludicrous thought, especially since I don't even know what "coming clean" and "confessing everything" would mean in this situation. What do I honestly feel for Laila? I know Laila blasted her way into my sexual fantasies when I saw her music video during the international leg of our tour, and that she cast one hell of a spell on me when I laid eyes on her at Reed's party. But like Kendrick's said to me in the past, I think it's highly possible I've only wanted what I can't have. Is Laila nothing but a sex kitten fantasy for me, and the real Laila, if I got to know her, wouldn't interest me at all? Honestly, I don't know. And until I do, I'm sticking to my story that "Hate Sex High" is only *based* on the truth.

"*No*, Savage," Kendrick says, out of nowhere, apparently, reacting to my facial expression. "We talked about this last night."

"What?"

Kendrick's jaw tightens. "Feel free to mind fuck anyone else, if that's what gets you off. Make anyone else fall for you, right before you toss them aside because they've become 'boring' to you when the chase is over. But don't you dare pull any of your usual shit with Laila, or I swear, I'll take it personally, like you've pulled that shit on *me*. You understand?"

I exhale. "You already said all this to me last night."

"But not when you were sober. I'm just making sure we're clear."

All of a sudden, it hits me like a ton of bricks: Kendrick is *in love* with Laila. Or, at least, he thinks he is. Surely, his head knows by now he can't have her, but his heart still hasn't gotten the memo. "We're clear," I reply softly. "I promise I won't pull my usual bullshit with her."

Kendrick's Adam's apple bobs. He nods, but before he's said a word, a female voice sings out, "Hey, boys!" And when we turn to look, it's Aloha, coming up the path from Reed's guest house alongside Laila, both women looking made-up and camera-ready.

"Hey, girls," Kendrick replies brightly, while I look down at my toes, feeling awkward about my earlier conversation with Laila.

The women reach Kendrick and me and Laila announces she's listened to our entire album and loves it. Kendrick thanks her, so I look up and thank her, too. But the minute our eyes meet, Laila quickly looks away.

"I had a couple notes on the mixes," Laila says to Kendrick. She itemizes them and I'm impressed by her observations.

"Awesome notes, Laila," Kendrick says, giving voice to my thoughts. "I'll send your thoughts along to Zeke and the band. I'm sure we'll make a few adjustments."

Laila responds to Kendrick, and as she talks, I can't stop staring at her, willing her look at me. But no dice. She only has eyes for Kendrick. My gaze drifts to Aloha's green eyes to find her staring at me. And the second our eyes meet, Aloha flashes me a look that reinforces everything Kendrick said to me a moment ago: *Don't fuck with my friend.*

I look away from Aloha's scowl, feeling exposed. Embarrassed. And, mostly, annoyed. It's one thing for my best friend to bitch-slap me. He has that right. But I'm not going to cower to anyone else. Least of all a Disney princess who's obviously passed judgment on me, based on something she knows nothing about. Aloha is good friends with both Colin's ex and Dax's wife. So I'm sure she's heard plenty of stories from both women about me being a player. Come to think of it, I think I might have ghosted Colin's ex after we hooked up. Maybe? So, I guess Aloha has good reason to dislike me. But, still, there's no reason for Aloha to send me that big a nonverbal "fuck you." I didn't kill anyone, for fuck's sake. I just didn't return a few texts!

I look at the ground, since that's the only safe place for me to look right now, and a moment later, a production assistant arrives to let us know we're minutes away from the press conference. "We need the full cast to get dressed and head into Reed's game room," she says.

Aloha and Kendrick head to their respective rooms to get dressed, but I touch Laila's arm and ask her if we can talk alone for a second.

"We don't have a lot of time," Laila says.

"This will only take a minute." I clear my throat. "I just want to make sure we're good."

Laila crosses her arms. "Why wouldn't we be?"

"Because of what we talked about in the guest house. The song?"

"Oh, *that,*" Laila says. But it's horseshit—yet another over-the-top performance by Miss Fitzgerald. She shrugs nonchalantly. "Honestly, I'd already forgotten all about that."

My stomach flip-flops. This should be great news. I should be feeling relieved Laila is ready to move on. But that's not how I'm feeling. "I just want to be sure you're not mad or maybe confused about some of the lyrics . . .?" I clear my throat again. "I mean, coming on the heels of that Instagrammer's video, I have to think you're pretty confused about what the hell I'm—"

"I'm not confused at all," she says flatly. "I don't believe a word that Instagrammer said, Adrian. I only said I believed her to torture you." She pats my arm. "Don't worry. I'm well aware 'Hate Sex High' was about you taunting Malik—letting him know you'd fucked me, and done it well—rather than you confessing you'd caught feelings for me." She scoffs. "I know you were pissed Malik physically attacked you in New York, and you wanted to mess with him. That's *all* that song is about. Only a fool would think otherwise."

Shit. That's what I'm thinking, even though I should be thinking, "Thank God."

"Hey, you know what?" Laila says, her blue eyes blazing. "I know I said earlier it wouldn't be necessary to rerecord those 'la la' parts, but I've changed my mind. On second thought, I don't want the whole world to know, for a fact, *I'm* the woman who came three times."

"Okay. No problem. Should be an easy fix."

"Sorry to ask you to change your art, but—"

"I'm the one who offered, remember? I think maybe I'll replace those last 'la las' with 'whoa-ohs,' so there won't be any chance of confusion."

"Perfect," she says. She stares at me for a long moment, like she's expecting me to say more. And when I don't, she says, "Well, if that's all you wanted to talk to me about, then I think we'd better get dressed and head to Reed's game room."

"Yeah."

"Don't be late, Adrian," she warns, her index finger wagging. "I'm your babysitter now. If you're late, that's on me."

"I won't be late."

"I know you had a great ol' time messing with me during the tour," she continues. "But I'm begging you not to pull that shit on me again. Being on this show is a dream come true for me and I want to do a good job."

I feel a pang of guilt for all the times I messed with Laila during the tour. Why'd I do that, again? "I promise I'll be a good boy for you, Laila," I say. And when her face plainly says, *I'll believe it when I see it*, I add, "Laila, when I give my word about something, you can take it to the bank." I shift my weight under her scornful stare. "Okay, maybe you can't take it to the bank, *every* time. But you can count on my promise *this* time."

Again, she looks unconvinced.

"Also, as a rule of thumb going forward," I continue, "I'd say you can count on my word being my bond . . ." I smile. "A solid *eight* times out of ten."

THREE

LAILA

Exactly nine minutes after my conversation with Savage on Reed's patio, I walk into Reed's game room to await Savage's imminent arrival. Or, rather, Savage's imminent *non*-arrival, so I can ask a PA to march up to his room and drag his infuriating ass down here. But to my surprise, when I enter the spacious room, Savage is already here, chatting with Kendrick. In fact, I'm the last cast member to arrive.

I head over to Savage and Kendrick, noting that Savage looks especially gorgeous. Savage often rocks edgy designer duds onstage, also when he's on-camera for an interview or awards show, so I'm used to seeing him looking like a runway model. But Savage looks especially yummy right now, like he leaped off the pages of *Gentlemen's World*.

"Hey, Fitzy," Savage says when I reach him.

"Hey, Fitzy," Kendrick echoes.

"*No*. Just *me*," Savage says sharply to Kendrick, wagging his finger to emphasize his point. Savage pauses, making sure Kendrick got the message, and then returns to me with a smile. "What took you so long, *Fitzy*? I've been waiting on you for five minutes."

I roll my eyes. "Sure, Jan."

"It's true," Savage says. "Ask Kendrick."

Kendrick nods. "It's true."

Savage looks me up and down, taking in my minidress and thigh-high boots. "I have to say, you were worth the wait. Damn, girl."

"Yeah, you look great, Laila," Kendrick concurs, his tone pointedly platonic, unlike the one used by Savage.

"Thank you. You both look very handsome, too." I address Savage. "Thank you for not making me hunt you down on Day One of my babysitting gig." I look at Kendrick. "I assume I have you to thank for that."

"Nope. Savage was already here when I arrived."

My eyebrows ride up in surprise.

Savage says, "I promised I'd be on time, so I was. Remember when I promised Reed I'd show up for Alessandra's music video shoot? My word is my bond, baby. Mostly. Sometimes. On occasion."

I can't help chuckling, along with Kendrick and Savage. Even when he's annoying, Adrian Savage is incredibly charming. There's no denying that.

"Yeah, so I guess that VIP meet and greet you barely made it to was one of the two in ten times your promise is worth nothing, huh?" I say. "If you ask me, being an *hour* late for a professional obligation is the same thing as breaking a promise."

I've intended to razz Savage, lightheartedly, with my comment. But Savage looks like I've slapped him across his chiseled face. And that's all it takes for me to realize there's been a shift between us, without me realizing it until now

—a shift that's made me seem like a petty bitch for bringing up that VIP event, yet again. Did the shift between us happen last night, when we shared our electrifying first kiss? Or did it happen while I was sitting on Savage's face, screaming in ecstasy? Did it happen when Savage held my hair to keep it from falling into the toilet? Or when Savage said yes to every stupid, ridiculous thing the producers asked of him yesterday, and then agreed to pay two million bucks out of his own pocket to seal the deal?

Whenever the shift between us happened, it's now clear that stupid VIP meet and greet is off-limits for me to bitch about, along with all the other petty stuff that pissed me off during the tour. I already reamed the guy about all of it in Atlanta, after all, in front of *everyone*. And the man is obviously trying to get off on the right foot in our new adventure by arriving here early. So, perhaps I should shut my mouth and turn the freaking page and try to get along.

"I shouldn't have said that," I blurt quickly, before Savage can reply to my barb. "That was petty of me. You've bent over backwards to get me this job, and I'm grateful to you." I bite my lip. "I think it's going to take some conscious effort to rewire my brain not to immediately switch into 'bitch mode' as my default around you. But I promise I'll try my best, starting now."

Savage swallows hard. "I don't blame you for constantly putting up your dukes around me, Laila. I was a royal prick to you, over and over again, during the tour."

My lips part in surprise. That sounded awfully close to an apology. "Well, it takes two to tango," I murmur, my heart thumping. "I reacted to you. You reacted to me. And around and around we went."

"Yeah, but I think we both know who was leading our tango."

Holy fuck. I'm floored. I stare at him in disbelief for a long moment, as palpable conciliation passes between us. Or maybe that's nothing but our usual white-hot lust. Whatever it is, it's enough to make Kendrick clear his throat and excuse himself, mumbling something about needing to talk to Fish, who's chatting with Aloha nearby in the game room.

When Kendrick is gone, Savage says, "Listen, Laila. I can't explain away all the times I was late during the tour. Sometimes, I lost track of time, which happens to me a lot. Other times, I showed up late on purpose to piss you off. But regarding that VIP meet and greet, specifically, I had good reason to be late. As I was leaving to head over there, my cousin called with some bad news about our grandmother. Mimi—that's my grandmother—had been in treatment for cancer for a while at that point, and my cousin called to say she'd taken a turn for the worse."

"Oh no."

"So, after hanging up with my cousin, it took me a while to pull myself together enough to head over to the meet and greet, where I knew I'd be expected to take selfies and smile. I'm not great at interacting with strangers, in the best of times, but—"

"Oh, Savage," I interject. My heart feels like it's exploding with sympathy, along with remorse for the way I tore into him about his lateness for that particular event. "I get it. How is your grandma doing now?"

The man shakes his head woefully, looking devastated. "Not well, unfortunately. She's decided to quit treatments altogether and let nature take its course."

I look around the large room at the other cast members

and staff milling around, and feel an overwhelming tidal
wave of regret flooding me. I can't believe I screamed at
Savage in Atlanta about his tardiness for *that* particular
event, and he never once defended himself by telling me the
situation. I ask, "Is your grandma here in LA?"

Savage shakes his head, his devastation palpable. "No,
she lives in Chicago with my cousin. I visit as much as I can.
Usually, about once a month."

Chicago.

At the mention of that city, I feel even more regretful.
That's the city Kendrick mentioned the day our tour kicked
off, when I was all bent out of shape that Savage had flown
into Philadelphia the same day as our opening show, thereby
messing up *my* schedule with his lateness. *My* interviews
and hair and makeup. As if any of those things mattered
more than Savage maximizing his time with his ailing
grandmother.

"I had no idea you were carrying such a heavy burden all
this time," I say. "Why didn't you tell me about your grandmother when I was ripping you a new asshole in Atlanta?"

Savage screws up his face, looking confused. "Why
would I tell you about my grandmother being sick?"

"To defend yourself! I went on and on about you being a
selfish and unprofessional prick for being late for that event,
and then going through the motions, halfheartedly, once you
got there. But in reality, you showing up *at all* to that event
was the epitome of selflessness and professionalism! Savage,
you were a saint to show up to that event at all, given what
you were going through that day. But you didn't tell me any
of that."

Savage shrugs. "I didn't say anything about my grandmother

because you were right about everything else you accused me of doing. Why defend myself about the *one* time I hadn't done anything wrong, when my rap sheet was long and embarrassing, regardless? Plus, I was in a particularly foul mood in Atlanta and it felt good to unload on you. That was the day my cousin called to say my grandmother had decided to stop treatments, so—"

"Oh, for the love of fuck!" I yell, palming my forehead. "No wonder you tore into me that day, after I tore into you, so cluelessly—and in front of *everyone*."

"I wasn't in my right mind in Atlanta," he says. "I was scared to death for my grandmother. Angry at God for making humans mortal creatures. So, when you read me the Riot Act in front of everyone, I just sort of used it as an excuse to get all my anger out. I mean, don't get me wrong, I was pissed at you for tearing into me in front of everyone. That was lame of you to do that, Laila. But I wasn't nearly as pissed at you, specifically, as it seemed. I was mostly just taking a whole lot of shit out on you."

I rub my forehead, feeling physically dizzy and disoriented by Savage's words. After months of casting Savage as the villain in my narrative, I suddenly feel like I was equally villainous, if not more so. At least, in relation to what happened in Atlanta. But before I've figured out what to say in response, a PA approaches and tells us it's time to line up on the far side of the game room, in order to await our cue to enter the press conference.

As the PA escorts Savage and me across the room, she tells us Sunshine Vaughn, the longtime host of *Sing Your Heart Out,* has already started making some opening remarks. The PA explains, "After Sunshine finishes her opening speech, the judges will be trotted out to answer questions for about thirty minutes, and then, at the very end, we'll invite the mentors to join the panel, too."

I feel a squeeze to my hand and realize Savage must have taken it as we walked across the room. Or did I take *his*? I don't even remember how it happened that our hands came to be joined. It happened so naturally, so easily, I don't know who made the first move.

When we reach our destination—a spot behind Aloha and Jon across Reed's large game room—Savage and I make whispered small talk with our fellow judges for a few minutes. And through it all, Savage and I never let go of each other's hands. Not only that, I can't stop sneaking peeks at Savage's striking profile, my heart squeezing and my stomach flip-flopping. Clearly, I misjudged this man during our tour. Not about *everything*, obviously. But about a lot. I turned Savage into a caricature by the end of the tour. A one-dimensional villain. A man without a shred of decency or conscience.

Well, enough of that. I wasn't faultless during the tour, either. I don't think I can forgive Savage for everything he did during the tour—at least, not for that groupie in Vegas—but I decide to wipe the slate clean, as best I can, and give our fake relationship a genuine shot.

FOUR

LAILA

As we await our cue to enter the press conference in the next room, we hear the voice of the show's longtime host, Sunshine Vaughn, as she cheerily welcomes the assembled press—the reporters and influencers who've come here today on a Sunday afternoon to interview the show's judges, and especially to hear the "shocking announcement" they've been promised is going to "rock their worlds." Although I'm sure every last one of them would have flocked here, regardless, if only to tour the legendary mansion of Reed Rivers and get to interview Hugh Delaney's buzzworthy replacement—the savagely sexy rock star whose face and abs have become as much of a perma-nent fixture on magazine covers lately as his dick has become one on Twitter. And, oh yeah, the dude also sings and plays his guitar pretty well, too.

I take a deep breath to calm my racing heart, and in reac-tion to my body language, Savage squeezes my hand, leans in, and whispers, "You're gonna be great. The world is going to fall head over heels for you."

Aloha, who's standing in front of us, turns around and says, "Amen, sister. The world is going to *love* you, Laila, every bit as much as I do."

"Thank you for everything you've done for me," I say to Aloha. "You've been my guardian angel." I look at Savage. "And thank you, too. Being on this show is a dream come true for me. I wouldn't be here if you hadn't said yes to every ridiculous demand by the producers and my agent. I'm grateful to you."

Savage shakes his head. "You saved my ass, Laila. This show is my grandma's all-time favorite, and I'd already told her I was going to be a judge when the shit hit the fan for me yesterday. You did me a huge favor by saving me from having to tell her I'd gotten myself fired."

I press my lips together. The hits just keep on coming. *Savage agreed to do the show for his ailing grandma.* How did I not know about this man's diehard devotion to his grandmother before now?

In the other room, the show's host bellows, "And now, let's welcome our panel of judges!" Excited applause rises up as Sunshine says, "First off, it's our resident Teddy Bear . . . Jon Stapleton!" A production assistant cues Jon, prompting him to head into the adjacent room. Sunshine continues, "And now, it's our beloved queen . . . *Aloha Carmichael!*" The PA waves Aloha into the room, and her entrance elicits even louder applause than Jon's. "And noooow . . ." Sunshine teases, prompting a hushed anticipation to fall over the press conference. "Please, welcome our *two* new judges! That's right, we've got not *one*, but *two* new judges this season: Savage from Fugitive Summer *and* his gorgeous and talented *girlfriend,* a superstar on the rise . . . Miss Laila Fitzgerald!"

A collective gasp rises up as Savage and I appear, our

hands clasped and happy smiles plastered on our faces—and by the time we're taking our assigned seats between Jon and Aloha at a table facing the assembled press, the room is pure pandemonium.

Once we're seated, there's a photo shoot for a long moment, as Savage and I, along with our two fellow judges, oscillate our smiling faces like sprinklers on a lawn, allowing every camera in the room to get a perfect shot of this season's judges. Although, based on the number of reporters shouting at Savage and me, specifically, it seems the lion's share of photos being snapped are of the happy couple.

"Let's get to your questions!" Sunshine calls out, before pointing at one of the reporters.

The reporter stands. "Savage and Laila, are you *really* a couple or is this a publicity stunt?"

Well, that was fast.

"We're a couple," Savage answers smoothly, sliding his arm around me, and I instinctively rest my cheek on his broad shoulder.

"In fact," I say, "we've recently moved in together."

The room titters in response to that little nugget.

A reporter shouts, "So, Laila, did you lie about Savage during your interview on *Sylvia*?"

I lift my head from Savage's shoulder and grimace at my fake boyfriend.

"Time to 'fess up, babe," he says, smirking.

Sighing dramatically, I address the room. "Yeah, I lied through my teeth!" Everyone chuckles, along with Savage. "I wanted to keep our relationship under wraps for a bit longer, so we could make sure it was rock solid before we subjected ourselves to worldwide attention."

Savage nods. "I respected where Laila was coming from

on that, even though I was ready to shout about my feelings for Laila from the rooftops. Laila said she didn't want to feel pressure to 'perform' our relationship for the world, and I understood that."

Clever boy. He just paraphrased something I said to Sylvia about why I don't like making my relationships "Instagram official."

Savage continues, "But then, when that Instagrammer made her video, broadcasting to the world everything I'd drunkenly babbled to her in private, I told Laila, 'There's no turning back now, babe. Let's make it official!' But before we'd decided how or when to do that, the producers called to say they'd decided to promote Laila from mentor to judge this season." He smiles at me. "And now, here we are."

"Ah, so this *is* a publicity stunt," a reporter yells.

"No, not at all," Savage insists. "The powers that be at the show determined Laila sitting at the judges' table would make things especially fun and interesting this season. But that doesn't make our relationship any less real. All that means is Laila and I will get to spend a whole lot more time together over the next few months." He looks at me and smiles. "Which is a great thing, as far as we're concerned. Who wouldn't leap at the chance to work with the person they're head over heels in love with?"

Whoa. The man is *good.*

"How long have you two been together?" that same reporter asks, all prior skepticism gone from his tone.

"It happened little by little during our tour," Savage explains. "But we've been glued at the hip for about the past month."

"To be clear," I interject, my finger raised, "I wasn't lying to Sylvia when I said Savage and I didn't get along during most of the tour. As a matter of fact, we couldn't stand each other for a large portion of it."

"No, *you* couldn't stand *me*," Savage corrects, making everyone chuckle. "And rightly so. I was like a kid pulling her pigtails on the playground, guys. But after we got back from the tour, I called Laila and charmed her pants off . . . *literally*." Everyone guffaws, while I bat Savage's shoulder playfully. "And then, everything took off from there, on a rocket." Savage leans forward. "That 'rocket' being the one in my pants."

As the room explodes at Savage's raunchy comment, Sunshine chokes out, "It's a family show, Savage." But by the expression on Nadine Collins' face at the back of the room, it's clear our executive producer isn't upset in the least about Savage's sexual innuendo. In fact, her expression makes it clear the head honcho is pleased as punch.

"How'd you convince Laila to board your *rocket*, Savage?" someone shouts.

"*Have you seen me?*" he says cheekily. And, again, everyone in the room rolls with laughter. Savage waves the air in front of him. "No, no. Actually, it required some good old- fashioned groveling to get things going with Laila. I called her after the tour and apologized for my bad behavior, and, thankfully, things took off from there." He looks at me. "I'm not the best at apologizing, usually. At least, not first. But, somehow, my desire to win Laila over outweighed my ego and pride." He kisses the top of my hand that's still clasped in his. "It was the best decision I've ever made."

Awwww, everyone in the room says in unison. And I must admit, I'm swooning along with them. I know, intellectually, this is all fake. A pitch-perfect performance from one of the world's best performers. But my heart and body can't resist reacting to this moment as if what Savage is saying is very, *very* real.

"What'd you think when Savage called and groveled, Laila?" someone yells.

I look at my fake boyfriend adoringly. "I thought 'Is this a prank?'"

Everyone chuckles.

"But then, Savage shocked me by letting down his guard. He told me some personal things that made me realize I'd misjudged him during the tour. And that's when he *really* turned on the charm." I grin at Savage. "He told me that, ever since we'd been home from tour, he'd been desperately missing my 'beautiful face,' and—"

"No," Savage interrupts. "I said I'd been missing your beautiful *smug* face. And I didn't use the word 'desperately.'"

"Yes, you did."

"That word isn't in my vocabulary."

"Well, it was that day." I address the crowd, rolling my eyes, and it's clear they're eating up this interaction with a spoon. "Savage told me he'd been 'desperately' missing my 'beautiful *smug* face'—I admit he used the word 'smug.' And then, he said he was sorry for being such a 'jerk' to me during the tour. He explained he'd had some personal stuff going on during that time that had been difficult for him, and my heart cracked wide open." I look into Savage's dark eyes. "After that, this man crawled right into the crack in my heart he created that day, during that first phone call, and he's never crawled back out."

Savage is blushing, which I find surprising. Humans can't fake blushing, can they?

"I feel like I should mention," Savage says, "Laila apologized to me, too, during that first phone call. Don't leave me hanging out here, looking like too big a softie, Laila."

"Yes, it's true. I apologized to him, too. Profusely. If Savage had been a kid pulling my pigtails on the playground, then I'd been the annoying girl who'd purposely tried to provoke that exact reaction. Lucky for me, Savage accepted my apology, and we both agreed to press the reset button. And we haven't looked back, ever since."

A collective swoon rises up in the room and Savage and I look away from each other again. And this time, Savage isn't the only one blushing.

"Thank you for sharing that beautiful story," Sunshine says reverently. She looks at the crowd. "I don't know about you, but I'm all aflutter here. *Wow.*" She returns to Savage and me. "Tell us about your first date."

Savage says, "At the end of our first phone call, Laila invited me to her place for pizza. And I was like, '*Pizza?* No, I'll cook for you!'"

I interject, "So, he came over to my place that night and made me a *phenomenal* meal, and"—I smirk suggestively at Savage—"we've been inseparable ever since."

The crowd applauds.

"Wonderful!" Sunshine bellows. "And now, are there any questions for Jon and Aloha?"

Nadine at the back of the room shakes her head sharply, telling our host it's not yet time to shift focus to the other judges. And Sunshine, pro that she is, instantly changes course. "Actually, the floor still belongs to Savage and Laila! Any other questions for our happy couple?"

A reporter yells, "Laila, what did you think when you found out Savage had let the cat out of the bag about your relationship to Sheree Dawson—the influencer who then made that viral video? Were you mad? Sheree's got a huge following and notoriously loves Savage and Fugitive Summer, so he must have known she'd post something."

"To be clear," Savage interjects, before I've replied, "I had no idea who she was. But I do admit I was drunk and bursting at the seams to tell the world about Laila and me by then. So, you do the math. I'm not known for making sound decisions on my best day—but particularly not when I've been drinking."

The entire room chuckles. Surely, all of them thinking of Savage's naked swan dive into that hotel pool.

"What exactly did you say to Sheree, Savage?" the reporter asks.

"I said she reminded me of Laila, which she did," Savage replies. "And I guess, once I said Laila's name to her, it was like I'd broken the seal or something—and, suddenly, I couldn't stop myself from babbling everything about us."

"Adrian's always got loose lips when he drinks," I say, pinching Savage's chiseled cheek. "But I wasn't mad at him when I saw the video. In fact, I thought it was sweet he couldn't keep our secret any longer. I mean, my boyfriend spilled the beans while turning down a woman who was flirting with him. What girlfriend could be mad about that, at the end of the day?"

After a few more questions, Sunshine steers the conversation away from Savage and me toward Aloha and Jon for a bit—although, in keeping with today's apparent theme, the first reporter called upon asks Aloha and Jon what they think of the addition of Savage and me to the show.

As Aloha and Jon talk, my mind wanders. It seemed preposterous to think Savage might have mentioned my name, at all, to that Instagrammer when I first saw the video.

I assumed she was chasing her fifteen minutes of fame. But after hearing Savage's smooth explanation of what supposedly went down—it seems logical that he might have at least commented on how much she looks like me. Could the story he told just now be based on a kernel of truth? Surely, she misheard Savage when he went on to say he had to "lay low" because of the show. But is it possible Savage thought of me when he saw that woman, and then actually said my name to her?

"Hey, Savage," a reporter says, jerking me from my thoughts. "Are there any songs about Laila on your band's upcoming album?"

"No," Savage says, and I sigh with relief. "The album was written before Laila and I got together."

Another reporter asks, "Are you two planning to release any music together, now that the world knows about you?"

To my surprise, Reed Rivers, who's been standing at the back of the room next to Nadine Collins, answers before Savage or me. "They are!" Reed calls out. "Stay tuned for details."

"They're going to premiere a song during the finale!" Nadine shouts.

And that's that. I look at Savage, as if to say, *Well, that took a turn,* and he smiles mischievously, letting me know he's on board for this brazen money grab. I don't blame him, really. If someone swooped in and unexpectedly snaked two million bucks out of my pocket, I'd be down to make some of it back with a hit song, too. Especially one advertised and performed on national TV.

A reporter stands and introduces herself to Savage and me as a writer for a popular women's magazine. She says, "I know my readers would *love* to know what you two love about each other, if you wouldn't mind speaking to that."

"Savage?" I say, feeling my heart rate spike. How can I possibly answer that question, even for pretend?

But Savage is the portrait of ease and charm. He says, "Actually, this is an easy one. Obviously, Laila is physically gorgeous. I love that she looks like she could murder me in my sleep, right after coming home from cheerleading practice."

Everyone in the room, including me, chuckles at that description.

"Also, she's incredibly talented," he continues. "I can't tell you how many times she's given me goosebumps with her voice. But, at the end of the day, it's Laila's personality that attracts me the most. I love that she's tough and fierce, but also a softie. In fact, Laila can be downright goofy, once you get to know her. Like, when she misses a shot in a game of HORSE, for example, she'll fall to the ground and writhe around like she's been shot."

My eyebrows shoot up to my hairline. *How'd Savage know about that?* He was nowhere near the basketball court when I did that at Reed's party. Or, at least, not that I saw. Wasn't he hitting on that pretty Asian woman by the pool around that time?

Savage's dark eyes locked with mine, he says, "I also love how close Laila is with her family—her mom, sister, and baby niece. How easily she makes friends. During our tour, *everyone* loved Laila. Musicians, makeup artists, roadies, caterers, bus drivers. *Everyone.* Laila even went to weekly game nights with the crew. But did they invite me, even once? *Nope.*"

"You're a huge star," I say. "It was nothing personal."

"That's not why, Laila. They invited *you* because you make every person you meet feel special. Like they're your friend. That's a rare gift—and one I certainly don't possess."

Heat is wafting between us. Without thinking about it, I lean in and give Savage a peck on the lips. Even if that speech was a load of complete crap, it's making my heart flutter and sending butterflies into my belly. Without hesitation, Savage grabs my face and turns my peck into a whopper of a kiss—a deep and passionate one that sends electricity scorching into every nerve ending of my body while setting off fireworks in my abdomen.

The assembled press in the room variously titters and whoops. Cameras begin clicking furiously, capturing every moment of our kiss.

"Wow, guys," Sunshine Vaughn says, when Savage finally releases me from his hungry lips. "I'm swooning here, right along with Laila."

I look down at the table, breathing hard, realizing Sunshine is right: I'm physically *swooning*. Literally, dizzy with adrenaline and excitement. And not only because of the passionate kiss Savage bestowed upon me, in front of the world, but also because of the speech he gave right before it. Were any parts of Savage's speech based in truth—or was *all* of it for show?

Sunshine says, "Your turn, Laila. What do you love about Savage?"

I force my blushing face to address Savage. His cheeks are flushed. His dark eyes sparkling. I take a deep breath and say, "Well, he's obviously physically gorgeous, as you can see, and incredibly talented and charismatic and charming. The whole world is in love with this man, for all of those reasons, so it shouldn't be hard to understand why I feel the same way."

There. I did it.

Sunshine says, "But what's something we don't know about him, that you do? Something you find endearing about your boyfriend, behind closed doors?"

Fuck.

Seriously?

I look into Savage's dark eyes again, and realize this question isn't all that difficult to answer, after all. A day ago, it would have been impossible. But after the conversation I had with Savage on Reed's patio a few minutes ago, I feel like there's a whole other side to Adrian Savage I didn't appreciate before.

"Well, I love how devoted Adrian is to his family," I say, looking into Savage's soulful, dark eyes. "His family is his top priority and he'd do anything for them. I don't think everyone knows that about him." Images of Savage from during the tour flash across my mind, making me realize I'd witnessed his softer side, many times. I just didn't give those aspects of his personality their proper due, up until now. I continue, "Savage will do anything for his friends." I chuckle. "Including drunkenly jumping naked into a hotel swimming pool as a friend's birthday gift."

Everyone in the room laughs with glee.

"He's also surprisingly goofy. The same as me, actually. He doesn't do it all that often—but, on occasion, Savage belly laughs with those closest to him. And when he does, it's the sweetest, most endearing sound you'll ever hear. It's like the clouds part when Adrian Savage laughs from the depths of his soul, and the entire world is bathed in glorious sunshine."

Savage's chest heaves. His nostrils flare. His body

language reflecting back to me how I'm feeling as I stare into his chocolate eyes.

I swallow hard. "Adrian is protective and supportive, too. He tells me to demand what I'm worth and not settle for anything less. He's also a thoughtful boyfriend. He knows I can't stand the smell or taste of cigarettes, so he quit smoking, just for me. When I was sick, he took care of me. Held my hair for me when I threw up." I bite my lower lip. "And, of course, it doesn't hurt that he's literally the sexiest man on Earth." I press my lips together, signaling that's all I've got, and Savage leans in and kisses me again—this time, even more passionately than before.

The crowd applauds, while Sunshine, our host, laughingly says, "Hey, it's a family show, guys."

Savage and I break apart, both of us breathing hard, and as the place explodes with raucous applause, Savage lays his palm on my thigh under the table, letting me know his arousal is most definitely *not* for show.

"Okay, before these two need a room," Sunshine says, "I think we'd better get our mentors out here. *Four* judges this season means *four* mentors! And here they are!" She motions to the side door and calls out each mentor's name, one by one, and they appear in order and stand behind their respective judge at the table.

There are a flurry of questions for the group—but, thankfully, no curveballs or surprises—and, finally, Sunshine wraps things up.

"Thank you for coming today! Full promo packages have been sent to you via email."

I look at Savage, ready to flash him a look of relief that the press conference is over, but he's eyeing my mentor behind me like he's plotting murder.

"Hey," I whisper sharply, squeezing Savage's thigh, and he turns around and smiles at the crowd again. But it's too late. His jealousy was on full display. Clearly, he's trying to figure out why the producers chose Colin, of all people—a drummer known more for his recent underwear campaign than his singing—as my mentor. And I must admit, I'm wondering the same thing. Colin and I have never been anything but friends. But there's no denying our chemistry. Also, I can't help remembering I offered up Colin on *Sylvia* as someone I've been wrongly linked with, right before I denied the rumors about Savage and me. Did the producers notice that little detail, too?

"Back to the greenroom, guys," a PA says to the cast. And, in short order, all eight of us exit the press conference and head back into Reed's game room. The minute we get to our destination, I begin walking toward Colin, intending to ask him what the producers said to him when they hired him. Did they mention what I said on *Sylvia* as one of the reasons they'd picked him? But before I've reached Colin, Nadine, the executive producer of the show, hugs me and pulls me over to Savage.

"You two are *geniuses*!" Nadine blurts, her angular face aflame. "We had *extremely* high expectations about you two this season. But now that I've seen the goosebumps you're capable of delivering, I can already tell we didn't aim nearly high enough."

FIVE
LAILA

I'm sitting next to Savage in the backseat of a large, black SUV with tinted windows, headed toward whatever home the producers have secured as our fake love nest for the next three months. The same driver and bodyguard from yesterday are seated up front. Savage is looking out the window on his side of the car. *And I'm freaking out.*

Which parts of Savage's speech during the press conference—the one where he itemized all the things he supposedly "loves" about me—were based in truth? For my part, every word I said about Savage in *my* speech was tethered to truth. I don't *love* Savage, obviously, but now that I know about his devotion to his ailing grandma—like, seriously, where did *that* come from?—I realize he's not quite the monster I'd come to believe by the end of the tour. In fact, I think he might be a whole lot more like the dude I shared a bottle of whiskey with in Providence, than the asshole who tore me a new one in Atlanta.

Also, those two kisses Savage and I shared during the press conference are messing with my head. I've never swooned so hard in my life as I did during those kisses! My *brain* knew it was all for show, but my heart exploded like a nuclear bomb. I felt urgency and *need* in Savage's lips and tongue. I felt *passion*. And now, as I sit here next to Savage, driving to who-knows-where, I'm realizing, much to my dismay, I'm in for a very confusing three months, exactly as Aloha warned.

I look at Savage sitting next to me to find him tapping on his phone with a cute little smile on his face—the kind of grin I've seen on him only when he's interacting with one of his bandmates, but especially with Kendrick or Ruby.

"Are you texting with Kendrick?" I venture, looking for any excuse to start a conversation.

Savage looks up, still looking adorable. "My cousin, Sasha. She lives with our grandmother in Chicago. They watched the press conference and now my cousin is texting in all caps." He snorts. "She's so funny. Both Sasha and my grandma are losing it about the 'amazing girlfriend' I've never bothered to tell them about."

I glance at the two men at the front of the car and lean in to whisper. Surely, our companions are bound by an ironclad non-disclosure agreement, but better safe than sorry. "What are you telling your family about our 'relationship'?"

Savage flushes a deep crimson, telegraphing the answer to my question is: *I've let them believe we're an actual couple.*

"You haven't told them the truth?" I whisper.

He shakes his head, looking sheepish. "I was going to give my cousin a heads-up about us before the press conference, but I got distracted when I ran into Kendrick and found out he'd sent you the album. And now, they're both so excited about everything . . ." He exhales. "Mimi—my grandma—she's my father's mother—she always says she wants me to settle down and find the 'great love of my life,' the kind she had with her husband, Jasper, who died young. Apparently, after watching the press conference, Mimi told Sasha she felt like she could finally stop worrying about me, now that I've found a woman who can 'see past all that silly rock star business' to the 'real *me*.'" He chuckles. "Apparently, that comment you made about my laugh 'parting the clouds,' or whatever you said, made quite an impression on Mimi."

I chuckle with him. "Honestly, I'm relieved you haven't told your family the truth about us. It makes it a whole lot easier for me to ask you to lie to my family about us for the next three months."

Savage laughs. "You haven't told your family the truth, either?"

I shake my head. "I could tell my sister, but my mom is *always* on me about my supposedly horrible taste in men. I'm hoping our 'blissful relationship' will give me a breather from constantly hearing about how I need to stop falling for jerks and find myself someone 'nice' who 'treats me right.'"

"Your *supposedly* horrible taste in men?" Savage scoffs. "If Malik is any indication, there's no 'supposedly' about it, Fitzy."

I bite back a smile. Is it wrong of me to continue letting Savage think I had an actual relationship with Malik—and even more so that said relationship lasted well beyond Malik's horrible behavior in New York? If so, I don't want to be right. Not when Savage banged that flirty waitress in New York the very same night I kicked Malik to the curb.

"Are you sure your mom wouldn't think *I'm* further

evidence of your horrible taste in men?" Savage asks, his eyebrow raised.

"Well, yes, *normally* you would be. You're exactly my type—which isn't a compliment. But after all that amazing stuff you said about me during the press conference, my mother and sister are convinced I've finally found the perfect man who totally gets the real me. So, if you don't mind, I'd be grateful for you to play along whenever I talk to my family, in exchange for me playing along when you talk to yours."

"Deal. Although I should mention, I sing Mimi to sleep on FaceTime, pretty much every night when I'm not on tour."

"Aw, that's so sweet. Don't worry. I'd love to say hi to your grandma, every single night."

Savage shoots me a smolder that flash-melts my panties. "Thank you."

"You're paying me two million bucks. It's the least I can do."

Savage grabs my hand. "Let's not talk about the money anymore, okay? I'm over it. Your agent was right—this is an equal partnership. I was an asshole to whine about it."

I look into his dark eyes, feeling my heart beating like a hummingbird's. "No, you weren't. It was a huge and unexpected pay cut for you. It was only natural for you to feel upset about it. I tell you what. To help you recoup some of the money you're paying to me, why don't you leave my name in 'Hate Sex High' and make it your leadoff single? The song is amazing, and with all the publicity swirling around us, I bet that sexy little Easter egg buried in the mix will give the song even more buzz. It might even become your biggest hit yet."

Savage looks excited. "Are you sure you don't mind your name being in there?"

"Ha! You admit you sang my name!"

"No, I'm merely adopting your crazy megalomaniacal version of reality for the purposes of my question."

He's so full of it. Any sane human would hear my name at the end of those "la la" parts, as clear as a bell. But there's no point in arguing with him. He'll obviously *never* concede the point. "Yes, I'm sure," I say. "After what you said about me at the press conference, everyone thinks you're desperately in love with me. So, in that case, I'm now thinking it'd be kind of cool for people to think I'm not only the great love of your life, I'm also the freak in the sheets you made come three times. Plus, like I said, the smartest move in terms of marketing is making that song the leadoff single, with my name all over it."

He snickers. "Reed already picked that song as the first single. He was furious when I told him I needed to rerecord the 'la la' lines to take out the part some insane megalomaniac had interpreted as her name."

"You already told Reed about rerecording those parts? That was fast."

Savage makes a face like it's not a big deal. "You said you wanted it out and the album is set to drop soon, so . . ."

"I'm sorry if I freaked everyone out about changing it. Now that I've had a minute to get used to the idea, I don't mind the world knowing the song is about me. In fact, I kind of like the idea of them knowing."

"Yeah, and I'm sure it thrills you to no end that I'm now going to look like as big a liar as you."

"Huh?"

"At the press conference, I said there are no songs on the

album about you. And now, suddenly, I'm going to release an album that *some* people *might* interpret as containing the name *Laila*?"

I snort. "You're never going to admit you're singing Laila in those parts, are you?"

"I'm simply conceding there are probably lots more nutjobs in this world than you who'll wrongly hear your name in those same parts, the way you did."

I roll my eyes. "Well, it serves you right to look like a liar, seeing as how you *are* one, for denying you're singing 'Laila.' Plus, it's only fair, since I had to admit I was a liar on *Sylvia.* But don't worry, people will think you only lied during the press conference to protect my privacy, which only makes you an even more swoonworthy boyfriend."

"*More* swoonworthy?" he says. "You admit I was *already* swoonworthy?"

"I admit nothing. I'm merely conceding there are probably plenty more nutjobs in this world than *you* who'd think so."

Savage belly laughs. "Touché, Fitzy. Too-fucking-shay."

Butterflies.

They've just now whooshed into my belly at the sound of his laughter.

With a little wink to me, Savage returns to his phone, so I look out the car window for a while, biting back a huge smile. After a few minutes of staring at the coastline, I realize our car has headed far enough north that we must be heading into Malibu. "Do you think we're going to be staying in Malibu?"

Savage looks up from his phone and looks around for a beat. "It sure looks like we're headed there."

"I hope that's where we'll be living," I say. "I *love* Malibu."

"Me, too. I love the ocean."

"So do I. I wish I could wake up every day of my life and see it, first thing."

"You can. By the end of the season, you'll have two million bucks in your bank account. Buy yourself a beach-front condo, if that's your pleasure."

I press my lips together. That's not going to happen, for several reasons. After taxes and commissions, and a few important things I want to do for my family, there won't be much left of that two million bucks. Certainly, not enough to upgrade my small condo in the Valley to something along the coast. Beachfront property isn't cheap. Plus, Savage is assuming I'll make it to the end of the season on the show. When in reality, that's not a certainty.

Unfortunately, when Daria and I finally got my contract from the show yesterday, it contained a buy-out clause that would allow the show to terminate me at any time for a payment of a hundred grand. Daria said the clause was non-negotiable. A dealbreaker. So, I signed on the dotted line. Luckily, Daria also assured me the chances the producers would exercise the buy-out were virtually nil. But, still, to be safe, I'm not going to spend a dime of my earnings from the show unless and until I'm positive I'm going to be around for the long haul. And even then, most of my salary will go toward helping my family in ways I've dreamed of doing for a while now, so a beachfront condo will have to wait.

The car makes a turn off the highway that makes it clear my Malibu guess was right, and ten minutes later, our SUV pulls to a stop in front of a large, gated home that's instantly recognizable to me—a cliffside mansion I've seen countless times on one of my favorite reality TV shows.

"Oh my gosh!" I blurt, my butt dancing on the car seat beneath me. "This is the mansion from *The Engagement Experiment!*"

SIX

SAVAGE

A s our SUV rolls to a stop in front of a large Mediterranean-style home seated on a cliff in Malibu, Laila shrieks, "My mom and sister are going to freak out we're living at the mansion from *The Engagement Experiment!*"

I've never watched the long-running reality TV dating show Laila's referenced, but I'm familiar with its basic concept, since Sasha watches it with Mimi sometimes. Also, my feed on Twitter is constantly filled with memes and tweets about that show, so I'm passively kept up to date on the gist of it.

"Is this where Savage and I will be living for the next three months?" Laila excitedly asks the driver.

"It sure is," the man replies, making Laila squeal and bop around in her seat.

The bodyguard in the passenger seat says, "Please wait here, while I do a sweep of the area."

When the bodyguard exits the car, the driver steps out,

too, leaving Laila and me alone. Laila leans back and says, "Have you ever watched *The Engagement Experiment*?"

"No, but I know the concept. A bunch of fame-hungry women live in a big house, vying to get 'selected' by some random dude who's been anointed 'Prince Charming' by the show, for no discernible reason. At the end, the 'happy couple' rides off into the sunset, only to break up as soon as their contract allows, at which point, they become influencers who can charge upwards of fifty grand per Instagram post."

Laila makes a face like she's offended.

"Oh, come on," I say. "You can't possibly think anyone actually finds true love on that show."

"Some of them do," she insists. But when I look at her like she's naive, she adds, "At least, I think *they* think they do . . . for a little while. Whatever. The only reason I asked if you've seen the show is to explain that, at the beginning of each season, before the contestants start getting the boot, *thirty* women live in this house together, and there's plenty of room for all of them. So, I think we should be able to avoid killing each other over the next three months, if only barely."

"I'll believe it when I see it."

The bodyguard returns and says we're all clear, that there are no paparazzi or stalkers to be found, and Laila and I exit the car, where we're greeted by an attractive brunette in glasses.

"Hey, guys," the woman says brightly. "I'm Rhoda, a junior producer at *Sing Your Heart Out*. I'm here to give you a tour of the house and get you settled in your new digs."

Laila jumps for joy at the woman's news and then proceeds to chatter with her excitedly as we head toward the house. Inside the front door, Laila abruptly stops chatting when she beholds the large entrance foyer. "It's *exactly* like it looks on TV!" Laila gushes. "I can't believe this is my life!"

The producer laughs. "You mentioned in a recent interview that you and your sister always watch *The Engagement Experiment*, so we thought we'd surprise you. As luck would have it, the timing was perfect and the house is empty."

"That's so lucky!" Laila exclaims. She looks at me, her blue eyes wide and sparkling. "Aren't we lucky, Savage?"

I know Laila is looking for an exuberant reaction from me, but I can't supply it. Not when I feel like I got hoodwinked into pimping out not one but *two* reality TV shows—and for *half* the salary I'd originally negotiated. "This might be a stupid question," I say, walking behind the producer and Laila as they head into the living room. "But whenever Laila and I do our required 'happy couple' social media videos every night, won't fans recognize this house and think our relationship is nothing but a set-up?"

"We've got an easy solution for that," the producer says. "In your first video tonight, you'll explain the producers of *Sing Your Heart Out* supplied this famous house to you because, one, you didn't want to show your actual home on national TV, and, two, the producers heard *The Engagement Experiment* is one of Laila's all-time favorite shows."

"*Perfect!*" Laila squeals.

The producer continues, "With you two living here and filming your behind-the-scenes videos, we'll get some fantastic cross-promotion between the two shows. Plus, the audience will adore seeing you two living in this famous house. It's a win-win-win."

More like a singular win, I think. *For the network.*

But Laila is thrilled. "Genius!" she exclaims, twirling around. And even though I'm annoyed with the producers, I can't help smiling at Laila's obvious joy. The girl is a lot of things, but jaded ain't one of them. I've seen this bubbly, sunny side of Laila many times during the tour, but never with me. Always with someone else, from afar. And I must admit, finally getting to experience Laila's happy, sweet side, up close and personal, is making me forget I'm annoyed that the show is exploiting my valuable image and name to promote a cringey-ass dating show without my consent.

"Ooooh!" Laila coos, sprinting into the next room. "I'd know this kitchen *anywhere*. Ha!" She addresses the producer. "Remember that time those two guys from Jenny's season had that food fight in here?" She snaps her fingers, like she's trying to come up with something.

"Damian and Gregory," Rhoda replies, without missing a beat.

"Yes!"

Rhoda chuckles. "I worked on *The Engagement Experiment* that season. I even got mashed potatoes in my hair during that famous food fight."

"Shut up!" Laila shrieks, clearly enthralled.

The producer nods. "True story. I worked on that show five seasons—one through five, before getting promoted to help Nadine launch a certain singing competition that turned out to be the network's biggest hit, ever."

Laila grabs the woman's arm like she's gripping a flotation device during a plane crash. "Rhoda, you have to tell me every juicy detail from your five seasons on *The Engagement Experiment*. I have to know *everything* you know!"

The producer giggles. "I can't tell you *everything*. I've signed an NDA."

"Okay, just tell me this: was the food fight *real*—or did

the show tell Damian to throw that first blob of mashed potatoes?"

"I really can't say."

"Shoot. That means it was fake?"

"I can't say."

Laila pulls at her hair comically, like she's a patient in an insane asylum. "Gah! I need to know! Please, please, Rhoda, come over here after work one night this week to hang out with me, so I can get you to spill *all* the tea. Thanks to *my* NDA, I wouldn't be able to tell a soul anything you tell me, right?—but I *have* to know *everything!*"

The woman looks thoroughly charmed by Laila, the same way everyone is when she turns on her mesmerizing charisma to full blast. "Okay, okay," the woman says, holding up her palms. "You make an excellent point about your NDA. I guess, since you're bound to secrecy, I could come over to tell you a *few* behind the scenes tidbits."

Laila hoots and dances and whoops from the depths of her soul, and I know, deep in my bones, this producer is now putty in Laila's pretty palm. *And there she goes again,* I think. *Adding to her collection of insta-friends.*

After a bit more chatter about the stupid dating show, we continue the tour. The producer opens a large, industrial-sized refrigerator, which makes Laila gasp at its neatly stocked shelves.

"As you can see," the producer says proudly, "we've stocked the fridge with everything you both mentioned you like snacking on." She looks at me. "And we got all the ingredients you requested to make tonight's meal, too, Savage."

"Tonight's meal?" Laila gasps out, her blue eyes wide. "You're cooking tonight?"

I wink. "I'm making you my grandmother's cioppino. I

figured I should replace your false memories of our first date with some real ones."

Laila raises an eyebrow, perhaps understanding my ulterior motive here. When we talked about our fictitious first date, I told Laila our meal ended midway through with me eating her out and fucking her on her kitchen table. Surely, she knows that's my plan for tonight.

"Oooh, make sure you two look at each other exactly like that in front of the cameras tomorrow," the producer says. "That's sexy, guys."

We look away from each other, our faces flushed, and the tour continues. We head into a large living space with a glorious ocean view and a baby grand in a corner. Squealing happily, Laila makes herself at home behind the piano and plays the first few bars of one of her biggest hits. And, of course, as usual, her voice sends goosebumps skating across my skin.

When she stops playing, Laila leans forward and hugs the piano. "I love you," she purrs, making the producer and me chuckle. She adds, "I've always wanted one of these. The sound is so full and rich." She sits up and sighs happily. "I feel like Anne Hathaway in *The Princess Diaries*." She looks at me. "Have you seen that one?"

"No."

"Then, put it on our list! We'll watch it after *Beauty and the Beast* and the high school one you mentioned."

"I'm not watching a movie called *The Princess Diaries,* Laila."

"Oh, yes, you are, or *else.*" She throws back her head and strikes an ominous-sounding chord on the piano, like she's the Phantom of the Opera on the warpath, and I can't help laughing at her goofiness.

"Your threats don't scare me, Fitzy," I tease. But I'm smiling like a fool.

"Well, you should be scared of me, *Adrian*. I'm a dangerous woman." She strikes another ominous chord, this time even more passionately. And this time, I not only chuckle. I belly laugh from the depths of my soul.

"Oh my gosh," the producer says. "Be sure to do this whole bit during a behind the scenes video at some point. This is pure gold."

I bristle. Is that what she thinks Laila and I are doing here—a *bit*? Because I'm certainly not. I don't think I'm even capable of laughing like that for pretend.

The tour continues upstairs. We see a home gym, an office we won't be using, and several bedrooms, before winding up in a large master.

"You can take this one," Laila says. "I'll take one of the other bedrooms down the hall."

My heart sinks. I know Laila requested separate bedrooms at Reed's house last night, but we've been getting along so well, I was kind of hoping she'd want to sleep with me during our three-month stay here. "No, you can have the master," I reply, not knowing what else to say. "I'm pretty easygoing when it comes to where I lay my head."

"No, no," Laila says. "You're the big kahuna here. I'm just the *opener*, remember?" She smiles broadly, without a hint of malice, letting me know her comment wasn't meant as a barb. But, rather, as self-deprecation. Clearly, Laila means to extend an olive branch for the tension we experienced during the tour, rather than starting yet another fight.

"No, no, we're equal partners this time," I insist. "Fifty-fifty. Honestly, I don't mind having one of the smaller rooms. I grew up sleeping in a closet, literally. And as a teen, I slept on a couch. For me, any room with an actual bed and a door feels like a palace."

Laila's face contorts with sympathy—which wasn't at all what I was going for. She says, "All the more reason for you to take this room. It's settled."

I shift my weight and say awkwardly, "Okay. Thanks."

The producer smiles broadly. "You guys are too cute. Why don't we shoot your first live video now, so I can hold the camera? We'll restart the tour, and Laila can react excitedly to the house."

"Great idea!" Laila says. She looks at me, her eyebrows raised. And it suddenly becomes clear I need to embrace this bullshit and give it my all, or I'm going to make Laila nothing but miserable for the next three months. Clearly, today is a thrilling day for her. Why drag her down by making her feel like she's dragging me along, kicking and screaming?

"Sounds good," I say, and Laila flashes me a smile that makes my heart skip a beat.

With the camera recording, we go back to the foyer and give our required speech about why we're living here. We redo our entrance to the kitchen, and then to the master bedroom we're supposedly going to share. We head into a small room we haven't already seen, and Laila is thrilled to find the producers have brought in a pottery wheel for her, much like the one she has at her own place. And, finally, we head outside and tour the large swimming pool, fire feature, and hot tub.

"Oh, man, I know that gleam in my boyfriend's eyes," Laila says suggestively when we reach the hot tub. "That's my cue to say goodbye for now, guys. We'll say hello again tomorrow when we get on-set for our first day of shooting. Until then . . . " She blows a kiss to the camera and slides her arm around my waist. "Say goodbye to the nice people, babe!"

I bristle. I've dreamed of Laila calling me babe for a very long time. *But not like this.* "Goodbye to the nice people, *babe*," I deadpan, making Laila laugh. Or, rather, making her *fake* laugh.

Finally, the producer lowers her camera and whoops happily. "Brilliant, guys. Perfect."

Laila removes her arm from my waist and exhales like she's just finished a workout. "What time will the car come for us in the morning, Rhoda?"

"Nine."

"Perfect."

We accompany the producer to the front door and say our goodbyes to her. And, suddenly, Laila and I are standing alone, in the foyer of our fake love nest—the house we're going to share for the next three months.

"So . . . are you hungry?" I ask.

"I could eat."

"Let's change into some comfortable clothes and meet in the kitchen in five."

"Cool." We start walking toward the staircase together, but Laila stops when her phone buzzes. "Oh, crap," she says, looking down. "My mom and sister saw our live video and demand I call them." She snickers. "As predicted, they're freaking out about the house."

"I'm sure my cousin showed Mimi our video, too. I tell you what, *babe*. Cioppino takes a half hour to prep and about an hour to simmer, before it's time to add a few last-minute ingredients. Why don't we get the broth simmering, and then we'll call both our families while it cooks?"

"You're a genius chef." She mimes a chef's kiss. "I'll meet

you in the kitchen in five, *babe.*" We walk up the grand stair-case together and stop at the top. "If I'm forbidden to go into the West Wing," she says, "tell me now. Or I'm going there, first thing."

I look at her blankly.

"In your enchanted castle," Laila clarifies. "In *Beauty and the Beast,* the Beast forbids Belle from entering the West Wing. That was my way of saying you remind me so much of the Beast, I can't stand it."

"I told you I haven't seen that movie."

"I know. I said that to amuse myself." She smirks. "Do me a favor. Growl at me and say, 'I forbid you to go into the West Wing!'"

I pull a face that says, *Over my dead body.*

Laila snickers. "The Beast wouldn't do that on command, either."

"Just to be clear," I say, "you're supposed to *like* the Beast, right? He's the *hero* of that movie?"

Laila surprises me by stepping forward into my personal space and pulling me toward her. "Hell yeah, we're supposed to like the Beast. In fact, I didn't understand my reaction to the Beast as a little girl—the tingle he provoked on my skin and between my legs. But now, looking back, I understand that movie was my first foray into porn."

I bite back a smile and then growl and whisper-shout, "I forbid you to go into the West Wing!"

"Oooh, baaaaby," she purrs, like she's having a little orgasm, and I can't help chuckling in reply. "Just so you know," she says, "I'm the kind of twisted bitch who thought the Beast was a five-alarm fire . . . and the prince he becomes at the end when the spell is broken was a total disap-pointment."

"Thanks for ruining the ending for me, dude."

Laila slides her hand to my package to confirm what she already suspects: I'm finding this exchange hot as hell. "Aw, come on, Adrian," she says seductively, her hand cupping the bulge in my pants. "Nobody watches porn for the plot."

My breathing hitches. *This girl.* She knows how to hook me like nobody else. In fact, she's known it since the minute I laid eyes on her at Reed's party.

"Okay, you've convinced me," I say. "We'll watch *Beauty and the Beast* tonight."

She smiles seductively. "Fair warning, Beast? I always get what I want, one way or another. You'll find that out soon enough." With that, she releases me, winks, and sashays down the hallway, pointedly walking past the door to the master bedroom and disappearing into a bedroom a few doors away.

SEVEN

LAILA

"You two are so beautiful together!" Savage's grandmother, Mimi, exclaims, beaming at Savage and me on Savage's phone. Mimi is in her bed in Chicago, while Savage and I are leaning over the island in our new kitchen. And if I thought Savage resembled the grouchy, snarling Beast during our tour of the house, he's turned into the sweet version of the Beast—the one who had the famous snowball fight with Belle—while talking to his grandmother on this call.

With his grandma, Savage is surprisingly gentle and easygoing. A man who smiles easily and chuckles often. A man who reminds his grandmother to "get plenty of rest" and "drink lots of water" and not to "overdo." Basically, he's the guy I've observed hanging out with his bandmates, with half the swearing and twice the adorableness.

"Don't take any of his crap, Laila," Mimi says.

"She never does," Savage says.

"Oh, I take *some* of his crap," I say. "But only because he's so charming."

"Yes, he is," Mimi replies wistfully. "That's why I still take some of his crap, too."

We giggle together.

"Oh, guess what, Mimi?" Savage says. "I checked the shooting schedule, and it looks like I'll be able to visit for Christmas. You'll be moved into the new house by then, so I'll get you a big ol' Christmas tree. The biggest tree you've ever had."

"How wonderful! Will you come to Chicago, too, Laila?"

I look at Savage and his eyes are saying, *Please, please, please.* "I'll be spending Christmas day with my mom and sister," I say. "But I'd love to come for a few days before then." I'm curious to find out some details about the house Savage bought his grandmother, but if I were truly his girlfriend, I'd already know all about it. So, I ask a question that seems pretty safe. "Are you excited to move into the new house, Mimi?"

"Very excited. But I feel guilty, too, that Adrian did this for me. When he told me what he did, I told him to return it. But he wouldn't do it."

"A house isn't like a pair of shoes," Savage says. "But even if I could 'return it,' I wouldn't do that. I bought the house for you, as a gift to *myself.* I want to see you in that house, Mimi. Now, please, let's not talk about this again. What's done is done."

Mimi addresses me. "See what I'm dealing with here, Laila?"

"He's incorrigible."

She flashes an adorable smile at her grandson. "Thank you, Ady."

"You're very welcome."

Mimi's dark eyes widen. "Ooh! Isn't it time to add the clams and mussels?"

Savage shrugs. "I have no idea."

"Well, what does your timer say?"

"I didn't set a timer. I forgot."

"*Adrian!*"

Savage laughs. "I got distracted." He pulls me into the frame and cups my face in his palm. "Wouldn't you get distracted, looking at this face, too?"

Mimi giggles. "Yes, I suppose if I were a young man, I most certainly would. Now, show me the pot, sweetheart. I'll be able to tell if it's time by looking at the broth."

Savage points his phone at the pot on the stove, and Mimi confirms her hunch is correct: it's time to add the shellfish to the soup.

"Okay, now what?" Savage says after completing his task.

"You tell me," Mimi says.

"Mimi, come on. It's been forever since I've made this and I've had a long day."

"Okay, okay." She gives her grandson direction, while Savage repeatedly says, "Oh, yeah!" And I must admit, the entire exchange makes me giggle and swoon. They're adorable together. Endlessly entertaining.

"Laila?" Mimi says.

I peek my head onto the screen, my eyebrows raised.

"Next time Adrian makes my cioppino for you, please remind him to set a timer at each step. It'll work out fine this time because I'm here to save the day. But next time, he might not be so lucky."

I look at Savage and, not surprisingly, sadness washes

over his handsome features at the implication of Mimi's comment—that she won't be around forever.

"I'll remind him, Mimi," I say, taking Savage's hand.

Finally, when the last ingredients are simmering, Savage says, "Okay, now that we've got everything added to the pot, let's get you to bed, Mimi. Close your eyes."

Mimi gets situated for the night, with the help of her caregiver. Sasha peeks onto the screen to say goodnight. And, finally, Savage begins to sing softly, in a hushed, soothing tone, "Mimi, Mimi, Mimi, I made you out of wishes. Mimi, Mimi, Mimi, and now I'm sending kisses. Hugs and kisses to you, I send them through the air. And when they reach you miles away, you'll feel how much I care." He sings the same refrain again, before finally whispering, "Sleep tight, sweet Mimi. I love you."

Mimi doesn't respond. Apparently, Savage's lullaby had its intended effect.

Savage whispers, "Stuart?"

Mimi's caregiver comes onto the screen, and Savage converses with him briefly before ending the call. As Savage puts his phone down onto the island, his Adam's apple bobs. He takes a moment to collect himself, and then takes a seat next to me at the kitchen table. When he doesn't speak, I rub his back in silence for a long moment, feeling the weight of his burden wafting off him. From what he said earlier today, I could tell he loves his grandmother. But watching him with her—watching his face as he sang to her—made me understand their bond in a whole new way. She's *everything* to him, clearly. A central figure in his life.

"I'm so sorry Mimi is sick," I say softly.

Without replying to my comment, Savage pulls me to him and kisses me deeply, with such depth of feeling, such passion, he takes my breath away. Without hesitation, I slide onto his lap and straddle him, kissing him sensuously. Finally, when we break free of our kiss, Savage looks flustered. Flushed. Disoriented. *Beautiful.* If he'd been born hundreds of years ago in Italy, I'd have no trouble believing he was Michelangelo's inspiration for *David*.

"I know for our first date I'm supposed to feed you first and fuck you on the kitchen table second," Savage says, his voice husky with arousal. "But I'm going to have to turn off the heat on the soup now and flip the script."

EIGHT

SAVAGE

After turning off the burner on the stove, I return to Laila at the kitchen table. Practically panting with desire, I peel off her clothes, lay her naked body onto the table, and open her smooth thighs wide, until her glorious pussy is opened to me and her pink clit is calling out to be licked like a lollipop. With my mouth watering and my cock rock-hard, I lean down and get to work, eating Laila enthusiastically, with fervent swirls and swipes of my tongue and voracious movements of my lips. And all this while stroking her with my fingers and groaning and growling like a wild animal devouring his prey.

"Savage," Laila purrs. "Adrian. Oh, God." She arches her back and comes undone against my tongue in the best possible way, screaming and howling as her orgasm throttles her.

"God, I love that you're a screamer," I choke out, enthralled by the sounds of Laila's ecstasy.

When Laila's body goes slack and her screams die down,

I grab a condom out of a nearby drawer—one of the many I stashed there while Laila was still changing her clothes earlier—and after getting myself covered, I rest Laila's calves on my shoulders, pin her wrists against the wooden table, and plunge myself inside her, balls deep. As my tip slams her farthest reaches, we both moan with relief and excitement. As I start thrusting, and my tip slams her repeatedly, Laila grunts and moans with each and every movement.

It's a special kind of bliss, fucking Laila on this table. Knowing I'm going to be fucking her every day for the next three months. Knowing she's mine, all mine, at least for now. *Finally.* It feels so good to be railing Laila, in fact, after not too long, I have to slow my thrusts, and then pause altogether, to keep myself from coming too quickly. Nobody feels as good as this woman. Nobody tastes as good. Nobody looks as good. She's in a league of her own, in every way.

I didn't know I could feel quite *this* turned on—like I'm literally under a spell. As I pause with myself inside her, I massage her clit, slowly, methodically, relentlessly—and then resume fucking her, also slowly—while whispering dirty-talk to her. I tell her she feels amazing. Tastes amazing. That her tits are incredible. Her body perfect. Until, finally, Laila comes again, this time with my entire cock buried inside her, all the way. And there's no way to describe the ecstasy I feel as her body milks mine.

Somehow, I manage to hang on by the barest of threads through Laila's orgasm. I run my palms over her splayed body as she moans and writhes, and then begin fucking her, much harder. Harder and harder, I fuck her, my thoughts spiraling along with my pleasure. Why didn't Laila come to my room in Vegas, or any other city after that? Why didn't she break up with Malik in New York, when she *knew* I wanted her? Yeah, I mentioned Kendrick on that sidewalk, but Laila's not stupid. She knew I wanted her for myself. She *knew*. And she picked Malik over me. I slam her, over and over again, angry with myself for not saying what needed to be said back then. For not saying what needs to be said *now*. Fuck! I've wanted this woman so badly, for so long, but there's always something or someone standing in my way! Well, now I'm going to make her want me, as badly as I want her, even if I have to fuck her into submission. Even if I have to make her addicted to fucking me to get what I want.

When I'm on the cusp of losing it, I pull out and turn Laila around, bend her over the kitchen table, grab a fistful of her thick, sandy hair, and with one hand lodged against her scalp and the other reaching around to massage her clit in slow circles, I fuck my woman raw, with deep, unapologetic thrusts that make it impossible for her *not* to scream.

"I'm gonna come!" she shouts, her ass jerking and jolting against me.

Through sheer force of will, I pull out and kneel behind her, sensing her climax will be a straight-up gusher. A geyser of delicious goodness. The ultimate trophy. I eat her gently for a moment, letting her come down. Teasing her. Making her beg for more. And when I feel her ramping up again, I slide my fingers inside her and stimulate her G-spot as I eat her. When I feel her inner muscles shudder and tighten, I pull back and tease her again, until she's literally whimpering and begging me to fuck her. Over and over again, I take her to the edge and then back away. Over and over again, I pull her strings, letting her know I'm in control here. That every breath she takes, every moan she makes is exactly as I'm commanding.

Finally, I finger her while eating her with gusto. And

when her body begins tightening sharply, when her moans become primal and pathetic, I let her go, pushing through those initial shudders without stopping, until I get what I want—a torrent of sweet, warm fluid gushing into my face. With a loud growl, I lick up my prize like a rabid dog, off her lips and inner thighs, the very taste of my trophy sending me to the bitter edge of ecstasy, without so much as a single touch to my cock.

When I've licked up the last drop of Laila's cum, I pick her up and carry her slack body into the living room and straight to the couch. On the night of the hot tub, Laila mentioned she likes being on top. Well, then, let the woman ride my cock until we're coming together.

I guide her on top of me as I lie on the couch and she immediately slams herself down and begins riding me like a feral animal. As she fucks me, I devour her breasts and nipples. Her neck and lips. I whisper into her ear that she's mine now. That I own her body. I tell her she's a dirty little freak who's going to come for me again. And that tonight is just the beginning of what I'm going to do to her, while we're living here together. I tell her she turns me on like nobody else. I whisper all the things I can only say out loud while fucking her. The things I can pass off as dirty talk, even though they're the things I should have said on that sidewalk in New York. Or during the last month of the tour. Or backstage at the awards show. Or today in the fucking SUV. I say it all. And she groans and moans and throws her head back and fucks me hard.

When Laila starts making her most primal sounds, the ones I now recognize as the precursor to her losing control completely, I press down on her clit with my thumb while twisting her nipple, hard, with my other hand, and grit out, "Come, baby." And I'll be damned, Little Miss Freak comes again. For the *fourth* time. Like she's a goddamned sex doll with a written pamphlet of instructions. This time, with a roar so glorious, it flash-boils the blood in my veins.

When my orgasm comes, it's unlike any other I've experienced. So pleasurable, it momentarily blinds me. I'm not merely *seeing* God right now, I'm getting my cock sucked by him. And it feels fucking amazing.

With one last groan, Laila collapses on top of me, sweaty and panting, as my body finishes convulsing underneath her. I pull her head up by her hair and kiss her deeply and she grips my face and returns my kiss like I've just given her CPR after drowning.

When we break from our kiss, we stare at each other for a long moment, both of us dazed and breathless.

"Wow," she says.

I nod. "That about covers it."

She falls on top of me, breathing hard, and I stroke her back, half crowing to myself in victory and half freaking out. *That wasn't normal.* In fact, if I'm being honest with myself, it was so damned *abnormal,* so damned good, as to be terrifying. Now that I know sex can be *that* good—now that I know the night of the hot tub wasn't a fluke, but a *preview*—how will I *ever* want to fuck anyone else, as long as I live? The very thought makes me convulse with terror. Or, shit, maybe that's just an after-shock from my insane orgasm.

"I'm hungry," Laila says, sitting up. "Starving, actually."

I exhale a long breath. I need to make this woman *mine.* I need to make it so she doesn't want anything or anyone but me. I clear my throat. "Yeah, I'm pretty hungry, too," I say calmly, trying desperately not to sound like the raving lunatic I've become. The madman hell-bent on making this woman as addicted to me as I am to her. I smile brightly. Like a sane, normal man might do, and say, "Let's dig into that cioppino, eh? We'll need to fuel up for rounds two, three, and four."

NINE

SAVAGE

"It's *soooo good*," Laila coos, like she's in the midst of slowly riding my cock, rather than merely eating a bowl of Italian fish soup. "You didn't over-promise on this at all, Adrian."

I smile at her across our fancy dining room table. "I'm glad it turned out well. You never know. As you saw, I'm not particularly 'detail oriented' when I cook."

She snickers. "Honestly, I was surprised you were such a shit show while making this. I was under the impression you make this dish frequently."

I shake my head. "I don't have a kitchen, remember? Before tonight, I've only made this one time without Mimi standing right there to help me."

"What was the one time?"

"Mimi's seventieth birthday."

"How'd it turn out?"

"Not so great."

We both laugh.

"How old were you?" she asks.

"Seventeen. I'd just gotten my first job at a grocery store as a bagger, which meant I could afford all the ingredients, thanks to my fat paycheck and employee discount. I thought I was such a baller when I got that job. I thought I was Reed fucking Rivers."

She giggles. "I bet you got flirted with a ton while bagging nice ladies' groceries."

"I did. My co-workers used to tease me that whatever register I happened to be working always had the longest line."

Laila snickers. "Of course, it did." She takes another zealous bite of food, before saying, "So, what you're telling me is you discovered at an early age you're drop-dead gorgeous."

I feel my cheeks bloom. I know she's being light-hearted, but at her comment, memories of my early years flicker across my mind—times when, to put it mildly, I didn't feel 'drop-dead gorgeous' in the slightest.

Whatever Laila sees on my face, it causes her to furrow her brow. "I was just teasing you. Sort of. You can't help that's your face."

"No offense taken. I just . . ." I don't know how to finish the sentence, so I don't.

Laila shifts in her chair, obviously trying to read me. But when she can't crack the code, she looks down and takes another bite of food.

"So . . . you said Mimi is your dad's mother?"

"Yeah."

"Did your family go to your grandma's house and cook a nice meal for her on her birthday every year, or was Mimi's seventieth birthday an extra-special thing?"

I take a sip of water. "Mimi's seventieth was the only

time I was stupid enough to try to cook a big meal for her. Like I said, I wanted to impress her, not only with my cooking skills, but with my deep pockets."

"That's so cute, Savage."

I pause. If I say this next thing, there will be no turning back. I'll open the door to talking about the real stuff. The shit I don't say in interviews. The stories I only tell Kendrick and Kai, since they were living in Mimi's apartment complex when I arrived on my grandmother's doorstep like a lost puppy.

I take another sip of water and decide: *Fuck it.* Laila's already met Mimi, and she's going to be talking to my grandmother every night for the next three months. I might as well give Laila a full picture of why Mimi means so much to me. "I didn't 'go' to Mimi's house for her birthday, by the way. I lived with Mimi. She was my only parent, beginning at age twelve."

"Oh. I didn't realize that."

"Mm-hmm." I take a bite of food.

Laila cocks her head to the side. "Why did you start living with Mimi? Did something bad happen to your parents?"

I take a long sip of water, gearing up for the conversation we're about to have. "Not in the way you mean. I'm sure if you asked my mom, she'd say *I* was the 'bad' thing that happened to *her*."

Laila's features contort with sympathy. "Oh."

"Or, at the very least," I add, "I was the 'highly inconvenient' thing that made all subsequent bad things unavoidable. You know my band's song 'Sorry for the Inconvenience'?"

She nods.

"That song is a big 'fuck you' to both my parents."

Laila puts down her spoon. "You mentioned your 'asshole father' when we drank that bottle of whiskey in Providence. But I didn't realize you have an asshole *mother*, too."

"She's not an asshole. At least, she *tried* to raise me for a while, unlike him. She's just not a person who ever should have had a kid."

"I can't imagine. My mom is so grateful to have my sister and me. And now, my niece. She always says we're the best thing that's ever happened to her."

"That's what Mimi always says about me."

"Were your parents in a relationship?"

"No. It was a one-night stand. My father knocked up the bartender—my mother—at his favorite bar. Once my mom realized she was pregnant, she tracked my father down, but he denied I was his."

"No paternity test?"

I shrug. "I've never asked her about it. My hunch is she wasn't sure who the father was. By the time I was a toddler, though, it was a moot point. I looked just like him. She said she brought me to him when I was two or three and demanded he take me for a while, so she could have some fun again."

"*She told you that?*"

"My mother hasn't been shy about her lack of attachment to me. Anyway, she brought me to him, but he didn't want me, either. So, she did her best."

Laila is visibly floored. "I'm so sorry, Savage. Growing up, did you see your father, at all?"

"I saw him, now and again. Whenever he'd started feeling guilty about ignoring my existence. He'd come over, but only when he was drunk. Usually on my birthday or

Christmas and we'd try to play happy family for a hot minute. But things always turned into a screaming match between my parents, and I'd run and hide in my closet. Which by the way, doubled as my bedroom, by choice. I've always liked small spaces. Anyway, fast-forward to Chicago, after I'd moved there and had been living with Mimi for a couple years—"

"Where did you live with your mom?"

"Phoenix."

Laila's eyebrows ride up.

"Yeah, you hate-fucked me in my hometown," I say. I wink. "It definitely made it extra special for me. Anyway, my sperm donor father got out of prison when I was fifteen or so. He showed up at Mimi's apartment, angry that she'd taken me in, when he wasn't sure I was his kid. He told her I was conning her. Planning to steal from her. So, I flattened his stupid ass." I smile. "I was fifteen and my father was three inches taller than me—and I took his ass *down*."

"Whoa."

"It felt amazing when I was standing over him. That was the moment I realized how small he truly was—and that he had zero power over me. It was a huge turning point for Mimi and me. Until then, I'd been a little asshole to her. Always testing her. Trying to prove my theory she was going to throw me out at some point. But after that, I realized I loved her and that I'd do anything for her. *Anything.* And that's when I said to myself, 'Why not give her a real chance here? Why not stop being an asshole and start listening to her?' So, that's what I did. I started following her rules, and giving her the respect she deserved. And it was the best thing I've ever done. From that point, everything started falling into place for me. I befriended Kendrick and Kai, seeing as how I was going to be sticking around, and that's when I realized I could write songs and sing. Everything came together for me after that."

"I'm so glad you decided to let Mimi love you."

"I can't imagine who I'd be right now if I hadn't."

"Is it Sasha's mom or dad who's Mimi's kid?"

"Her father, Frank. He died in an accident at work when Sasha was eleven. Apparently, he was an amazing guy. Really sweet and kind. Thanks to Frank, Mimi knew she was capable of having a normal, loving son. Poor Mimi always blamed herself for my father, her second son, being such a dickbag. But at least Frank gave her some comfort that my father's assholery wasn't her fault. Mimi once told me she felt like my father was born without a complete soul. Like, he just didn't feel things the way other people did. She said it only got worse when his dad, Mimi's husband, died."

Laila looks down at her bowl of soup, looking distraught. "I'm sorry you've had it so rough, Savage."

"Nobody has it easy in life, really. Speaking of which, tell me about your asshole father."

Laila drags her spoon through her bowl of soup, gathering her thoughts. "My parents got married when my mom got accidentally pregnant with my sister. When things became rocky in their marriage, they decided in their infinite wisdom to have a second baby to 'fix' things."

"Brilliant plan."

Laila rolls her eyes. "Yeah. Obviously, my existence didn't fix a damned thing. I remember my dad often being loud and angry when Angel and I were little. He'd punch holes in walls. Smash plates and lamps onto the ground. And then, one day, my father did the unthinkable: he punched my mom in the face during an argument and broke a bone under her eye."

"Jesus."

"My mom took Angel and me to live with my aunt in Whittier. We lived there until my mom could afford an apartment of our own."

"Did you keep in touch with your father through all that?"

"Sort of. My sister was done with him the day we moved out. But I kept in touch for a while, by phone, and listened to him tell me how sorry he was. How much he'd changed. But one day, I heard my mom crying while talking to him on the phone, so I listened in. And the way he was cussing her out . . . That's when I knew he was still the same asshole who'd broken her face. And that's when I was done with him for good, too. I grabbed the phone and told him to fuck off and never speak to any of us again. Angel got on the phone and said the same. We told our mom we'd always take care of her and not to bother trying to squeeze any child support out of him, again. It wasn't worth it. And we've been a threesome ever since."

"Until he called to ask you for money," I say.

She looks up, surprised. "How'd you know about that?"

"It's always the same story, Laila. The same thing happened to me and to so many of my friends, once they started getting any kind of success and fame. You have no idea how common it is."

"Oh."

"So, did you give him money when he asked?"

She looks sheepish. "Did you?"

I nod. "I paid my father ten grand, in exchange for a comprehensive agreement. He's prohibited from talking about me to the press and can't sue me for the time I decked him. So, it was money well spent."

"Shoot. I didn't think to get an agreement like that. He's given several interviews about me. It's so embarrassing. He acts like he's been an amazing father to me—like my success is all his doing, simply because he got me a Fisher Price keyboard as a toddler. But he's not the one who sacrificed, constantly, to keep me going to piano lessons. He's not the one who listened to every new song I wrote, even the terrible ones, and cried tears of joy and told me I had a gift."

"Don't pay him another dime, Laila. Ever."

She sniffles. "I send him money a few times a year."

"Why?"

She shrugs. "I don't know. He was a heavy smoker and now he's sick. Helping with his medical bills makes me feel less guilty, I guess."

"Guilty for *what*?"

She twists her sultry lips. "I can't abandon him. He's blood. And I've been so lucky in my career."

Anger surges inside me. "No, Laila. Fuck him. You didn't ask him to have sex with your mom without a condom. And, yes, you've been lucky in your career. But luck is only one of the factors of your success." I motion to the half-empty bowl in front of me at the dining room table. "It's like this soup. There've been a whole lot of ingredients, besides luck, to get you where you are today. Hard work. Piano lessons. And most of all, like your mom said, your *gift*. Whatever luck you've had, it wouldn't have gotten you anywhere, without the rest of the ingredients along with it."

"Thank you," she whispers, looking moved. She swallows hard. "That means a lot, coming from you. I think so highly of your talent. You're an amazing artist."

My chest heaves. "Thank you. That means a lot, coming from you. I think the same of you. Your voice gives me goosebumps. When you hit those high notes, I literally get a tear in my eye."

She exhales a slow, long breath, like her heart is beating a mile a minute, and electricity crackles between us.

"He's a douchebag, Laila," I say, my eyes locked with hers, skin on fire. "Don't send him another dime."

"I probably will," she admits. "Because sending it is my way of controlling him—keeping him away from me and my family, for good."

The full extent of my assholery toward Laila hits me like a tsunami. "I'm so sorry for all the times I was a flaming dickhead to you during the tour, Laila. I'm sorry for any time I yelled at you or made you feel uncomfortable. I'm sorry for that time I said you didn't belong on the tour. You *did*. You're a genius with incredible talent and star quality and I was an asshole to suggest otherwise. I'm sorry for the times I've smoked around you, especially the times I've purposely blown smoke in your face, solely to piss you off. Please, forgive me for all of it. There were times during the tour when I felt irrationally rejected by you, or maybe I thought I couldn't make a play for you because Kendrick had a crush on you, and my solution to all of it was to lash out and/or push you away, with all my might. It was stupid of me. And I'm so sorry."

Her chest visibly rises and falls for a moment. Her blue eyes are practically glowing. "I accept your apology," she says. "I wasn't all that nice to you, on many occasions."

"It doesn't matter. There's something wrong with me, Laila. The same way there's something wrong with my father. Sometimes, I feel like I don't have a complete soul."

"That's not true, Adrian. I saw you with Mimi. I saw you with your bandmates for three months. I saw how respectful and sweet you are with Ruby. Trust me, you've got a complete soul."

"But what if I don't?" I say, admitting my worst fear, out loud, for the first time, ever. "What if I'm my father's son, in ways I don't want to be?"

Laila gets up and strides to me at my end of the table. "Stop. You're nothing like him." She stands over me and clutches me to her, and I lay my cheek on her belly, while she runs her fingers through my hair. She whispers, "You've got a beautiful soul, Adrian. You're just scarred by the stuff that happened to you as a kid, as anyone in your shoes would be." She kisses the top of my head and takes the seat next to me at the table. "Can I ask you something? That lyric in 'Hate Sex High' about punching a hole in the wall. Was that true?"

I nod. "After my run-in with Malik at the restaurant, followed by that argument we had outside on the sidewalk, I was angry and shitfaced. Feeling rejected and confused. So, I went back to my hotel room and punched a hole in the wall."

Laila presses her lips together. "I'm going to need you to promise not to do that sort of thing while we're living here together, no matter how much I might annoy or anger you."

"Of course, I won't. Ask Mimi or Sasha or Ruby. I'm not violent." I grab her hand. "I'd never hurt you. I'd protect you, yes. But I'd never hurt you."

"I don't think you'd hurt me. I'm just telling you that holes punched in walls and plates being smashed . . . those are the kinds of things that are triggering for me."

"I understand. You have my word."

Laila squeezes my hand. "How did you wind up living

with Mimi at age twelve, given that you hardly ever saw your asshole father?"

I pause to gather my thoughts. To steady my racing heart. "When I lived with my mom, she used to run off with different guys for days at a time. She'd leave me with a few basic groceries and say, 'I'll be back soon.' So, this one time, right after I'd turned twelve, she was gone on one of her trips, and I wanted to make myself a grilled cheese sandwich on the stove. I don't know how it happened, since I'd made the same thing before, lots of times, but I somehow started a fire in the kitchen. I got it out, pretty quickly, without it spreading too much, thank God, but the fire department was called by a neighbor. And that's when they found out a twelve-year-old had been living alone in the apartment with no parent in sight for days and days—and that it was a common occurrence in my house. They sent me off to Child Protective Services while they looked for my mom. And when they couldn't find her, they contacted my dad, who was in prison at the time for assaulting someone. And that's when they found out my next of kin was one Maria Savage Wilkes of Chicago, Illinois. They called and dropped the bomb on Mimi that she had a twelve-year-old grandson in Phoenix she'd never known about. She came and got me and brought me back to her little shoebox apartment, where I slept on the couch and acted like a raving asshole for almost three years, until I finally decided to give her a chance."

"Did your mother get in trouble for leaving you alone?"

I nod. "She got charged with reckless endangerment of a child after the fire, but she only got probation. To this day, she thinks I intentionally set that fire to get her into trouble."

"Oh my gosh."

"Maybe I did, subconsciously. I've certainly amassed a

long track record since then of doing toxic, stupid shit as a backwards means of getting something I don't even know I want." I clamp my lips together, so I don't say something I'll regret. Something like, "Look at the way I treated you during the tour. Perfect example."

Laila knits her brows together. "I just realized . . . you go by Mimi's maiden name?"

"Yeah."

"So, your name is a stage name, after all."

"No, Savage has been my legal name since age fifteen. My mother gave me her name when I was born—Carter. But once I decided Mimi was my mother, I asked to change my name to hers. I didn't want Mimi's married name—Wilkes— since that's my father's name. Plus, Savage is a badass name."

"You're such a liar. You said you were 'born Savage.'"

I smile. "I was using a lower case 's.'"

Laila flashes me an adorable grin that sends a flock of butterflies into my stomach, and I can't help returning her smile with an even bigger one.

"You should copyright that smile, Fitzy," I say softly. "You'd make a mint."

She flushes. "There are no cameras here. We don't have to pretend anything."

"I'm not pretending a goddamned thing."

Laila's chest heaves. "Neither am I."

It's too much excitement for my body to handle gracefully. Physically twitching with arousal and excitement, relief that she's clearly beginning to trust me, I get up from my seat at the table, pull Laila up, and kiss her passionately. "Come on, beautiful," I whisper. "It's time for me to finally get to fuck you in a bed."

TEN
SAVAGE

As Laila rides my cock, I admire the curves of her body in the moonlight streaming through the bedroom window.

"You're gorgeous," I whisper, my pleasure ramping up and up. But I can't find the right words to convey how stunning she is to me. How perfect and addicting. Or, hell, maybe I do know the right words, but I'm too chicken to say them out loud to her. The only thing I'm sure about is that fucking Laila in this bed, in this moment, is a new level of rapture for me. I've never bared myself to a woman the way I did downstairs to Laila in the dining room. And somehow, knowing *she* knows all that shit about me, and is now riding my cock like none of it dampens her desire for me in the least, feels even hotter than the hottest hate sex.

"You feel so fucking good," I whisper, as Laila gyrates on top of me. I touch her clit and massage it round and round as she moves, and she begins snapping her hips back and forth with added enthusiasm. After a bit, Laila grips my chest and digs her nails into me, like she's hanging on by a thread. I make a guttural sound, as my eyes roll back from pleasure. She gasps out my name. My first name. Which feels amazing. That's a first during sex. And then, her interior muscles surrounding my cock release and ripple and squeeze fiercely, sending so much pleasure into my cock, I lose it, along with her.

When both our bodies have become quiet and still, Laila leans down and kisses me deeply. As her long hair falls on either side of my face, I inhale the scent of her shampoo. Revel in the taste of her lips and tongue. I run my fingertips down her bare back, feeling high. Drugged. Addicted. Gone.

"I feel high," she whispers into my lips, reading my mind.

"So do I," I admit. "Physically, like you're a drug."

We share a smile. This isn't a "hate sex high" we're feeling this time, and we both know it. Frankly, if I were to write a song about *this* kind of high, I don't know what the song would be called. This feeling is something I've never felt before. Something I can't name. Whatever it is, though, I never want it to end.

Sighing happily, Laila slides off me and lies alongside my naked body in the bed, cleaving every bit of her flesh into mine. "You really think I'm gifted as an artist?"

"One hundred percent."

"Why, exactly, did you step aside for Kendrick?"

"He had a crush on you."

"Yeah, I kinda figured. But so what? Why did you step aside for him?"

"He's my best friend. Plus, I knew he's boyfriend material, and I'm not."

"Yeah, but you don't pretend to be. Isn't that what you said in Providence, when you were bashing me for supposedly dating Malik?"

I furrow my brow. "*Supposedly* dating Malik? It sure felt like a whole lot more than 'supposedly' when he was throwing me against a wall, Laila."

Her cheeks flush. "No, yeah. I meant to say you act like you're *supposedly* not boyfriend material. You *supposedly* pretend not to be."

She's speaking gibberish all of a sudden. What am I missing? "There's no 'supposedly' about any of that, Laila. I've never pretended to be boyfriend material. I don't think anyone would make that mistake about me."

Her chest heaves. "Oh, I don't know about that. You did an awfully good impression of a guy who's grade-A 'boyfriend material' when you made me that amazing meal tonight." She swallows hard. "Listen, about Kendrick . . . I feel like I should tell you he never had a shot with me. Not with you on the tour. And probably not at all. Kendrick is the sweetest person who ever lived. But the minute I met him, I felt only platonic friendship for him. No lust. No heat."

I stroke her back. "Don't take it personally that I stepped aside for my best friend. It doesn't reflect on you. You were nothing but a vixen in a music video to me at that point. A fantasy. And Kendrick has been a better friend to me than I could ever explain to you. I wouldn't be here now without Mimi and Kendrick. They're the only reason I've got this life."

"I don't hold it against you. I think it's sweet you're a loyal friend to Kendrick."

"Plus, I hate to sound arrogant, but I knew I could have pretty much anyone else I wanted. So, why endanger my friendship with Kendrick over a girl I didn't even know, when someone else would surely catch my eye any minute?"

"Which is exactly what happened, many times over. I get it."

Fuck. That's what she still thinks? That all those groupies in her dressing rooms, that waitress in New York, all the ways I shoved my rockstar bullshit in her face, were real? Somehow, I thought she'd understood by now that I was only messing with her all those times—I thought maybe she'd understand I've only got eyes for her—and it's been that way for a very long time now—without me needing to explain it to her with words.

Fuck, fuck, fuck.

Should I come clean to her? Or would that be too big a confession on night one of our three months together? It was only yesterday that I swore I wouldn't "catch feelings" during this little charade, after all.

"Here's what I don't get," Laila says, before I've decided how much to confess to her, if anything. "Kendrick couldn't have had a crush on me when Reed first put me on the tour. I only met Kendrick at Reed's party, and the decision had already been made by then."

"Kendrick had a crush on you, even before he met you." *And so did I.* "You were his 'celebrity crush.'" *And mine, too.*

"No way." She makes an adorable face. "That's so sweet. Unfortunately, for him, though, you were *my* celebrity crush."

Hallelujah. "Well, that's convenient, because *you* were *mine.*" *There, I said it.* It's a small confession, considering what I'm holding back. But at least it's a start.

"No way," she says, her blue eyes sparkling.

"*Way.*"

Laila swats at my chest. "Okay, now I'm pissed at you for

stepping aside for Kendrick—and especially that you objected to me being on the tour!"

I groan. "Laila, I only objected to you being on the tour out of self-preservation. Because I didn't want to watch you canoodling with Kendrick for three months. Because I'm that stupid and immature and selfish. Can we *please* forget everything that happened on the tour? Let's erase the whole damned thing from our memory banks and pretend none of it happened."

She's nodding furiously.

"From now on," I say, my pulse pounding, "we'll be the Savage and Laila we were downstairs in the dining room. The Savage and Laila who told each other about our dads. We'll start fresh and erase every last memory of the tour, and agree to only look forward from now on, okay?"

Laila looks bowled over. Surprisingly emotional and relieved. With a deep exhale, she throws herself at me, and I wrap her in my arms. "That sounds amazing," she murmurs into my shoulder.

"I'm so sorry, Laila," I whisper. "I fucked up right and left on that tour. I didn't know how to handle my attraction to you. Didn't want to betray my friend. I was jealous of Malik and pissed that you'd want an asshole like him over me. I was irrational and stupid, but that's me, unfortunately —irrational and stupid, a lot of the time."

"It's okay." She wipes her eyes. "The past is completely forgotten. We'll both press the reset button and start over and not mention anything either of us did, ever again."

"Thank you so much." I hug her to me. "Thank you, Laila."

For a long moment, we lie quietly, our bodies entwined in the moonlight. Suddenly, though, she lifts her head and says, "One tiny question about the past before we leave it for good. How did you know I played HORSE at Reed's party, and writhed around on the ground when I missed my shot?"

My stomach tightens. "Huh?"

"You mentioned that at the press conference, but you were nowhere near the basketball court when I did that. In fact, right after the game, I saw you hitting on a pretty woman by the pool."

I push Laila's long hair behind her bare shoulder. "I wasn't hitting on that woman. She was a reporter for *Rock 'n' Roll* and we were talking about my interview."

"I didn't know there were two reporters at that party!"

I nod. "While I was talking to the reporter, I glanced over at the basketball court, just in time to see none other than Laila Fitzgerald miss her shot and then drop to the ground like a goofball."

She giggles. "Why didn't you come inside and watch my performance with Aloha and the Goats, after I walked past you?"

"You mean, why didn't I follow you into the house, after you walked past me, flanked by Malik and Kendrick?"

"Oh."

I chuckle. "That's when I decided, once and for all, to give Kendrick a wide berth to take his shot."

Laila twists her mouth but says nothing.

"Any other questions before we leave the past and never, ever think about it again?" I ask.

Laila pauses. "No. I think I'm good. You?"

"I'm good."

She makes a goofy, cartoonish series of expressions and sounds, which I quickly find out, based on her next words, is her version of "erasing" the hard drive in her brain. She says, in a computerized voice, "Reed's party and the tour are now officially erased from the hard drive of Laila Fitzgerald's brain. *Goodbye.*" She closes her eyes and lets her tongue hang out.

I laugh. "You dork. I can't believe they hired *you* as *my* babysitter."

"I fooled them all."

"You sure did." When she yawns, I add, "Time for bed. We've got a big day tomorrow. We need our beauty sleep. Which, by the way, is what *you* should be saying to *me*, babysitter."

"Oh, I should put on my zit cream." With that, she hops out of bed and pads out of the room, much to my disappointment. And that's it. All hope I had Laila would sleep here in this room with me—

Oh. She's back. Carrying a toiletry bag and heading into my bathroom with a little wink. I hear a commotion in there. The shower turning on. And a moment later, the sound of Laila singing "Fireflies" by 22 Goats in the shower wafts into the bedroom.

My heart thumping, I head into the bathroom, step into the shower with her, and kiss her. And, instantly, my body makes it clear I'm damned happy to see her. I wash her wet, naked skin. Kiss her breasts. And when I can't resist any longer, drop to my knees and eat her out, with hot water running down my face and back.

After she comes, she returns the favor, while I press my palms against the plexiglass of the shower and groan like a yeti. When I come, we indulge in another round of washing, kissing, and caressing. But finally, she smacks my ass and tells me we need to get our beauty sleep, and we begrudgingly drag our asses out of the shower.

After drying off, I secure a white towel around my waist and watch Laila applying cream to her face.

"It's a crying shame condoms don't work in water, don't you think?" I say, leaning my hip against the bathroom counter.

Laila stops what she's doing and looks at me. "Is that your way of asking me if I'm on birth control?"

I grin. "It sure is."

Laila smirks. "Yes, I've got an IUD. But that's only to prevent me from getting knocked up accidentally. My firm rule is 'No wrapper, no dice, unless we're in a committed relationship and I trust you *completely*.'"

I furrow my brow, as Laila resumes her nighttime routine. I think she just implied she doesn't trust me completely. That's what she meant by that, right? "I've already promised I'm only going to have sex with you for the next three months," I say. "That's basically the same thing as a 'committed relationship.' And I promise you can trust me completely."

Not stopping what she's doing in the mirror, Laila says, "How shall I put this, Adrian? Oh, I know. *I don't.*"

"Trust me?"

"Correct. Not completely. But don't be offended. My complete trust is *very* hard to get. And you've got quite a reputation."

"I thought we agreed to forget the past."

"We did. But even so, I could google you right now, in the *present,* and instantly find out you're not the best bet to let raw-dog me."

"So, is your concern that I'm not clean or that I'm going to cheat on you? Because I've already promised I won't have sex with anyone else, and that's a promise you can take to the bank, ten out of ten times. On the other hand, if you're concerned I'm not clean, then I'm sure we could arrange for a doctor to test us both tomorrow, either on the set at lunchtime or here at the house after work."

Laila considers my suggestion for a long moment, making my heart thump in my ears with anticipation. Finally, she says, "Do you swear on your love for Mimi you won't sleep with anyone else, the whole time we're living together?"

I grimace. "Can we please leave my grandmother out of this conversation about raw-dogging you?"

She laughs. "Fair enough. Do you swear on your life?"

"I do. I won't touch anyone else while we're living together. I've already promised that in writing."

"To the *show*, in order to avoid the risk of a 'cheating scandal.' What I'm asking is for you to promise *me*, personally. And then, to keep that promise, no matter what."

I walk to her, cup her face in my palms, and look into her blue eyes. "I hereby promise, Laila Fitzgerald, that I, Adrian Savage, will have sex with you, and only you, and nobody else, for the entire time we're living together, so help me God."

Laila blushes. "Okay, let's do it, then, as soon as we get the 'all clear' from a doctor. And by 'doctor' I mean a real one —not an actor who plays one on TV."

I snicker. "I'll make it happen tomorrow."

"Cool. Now, come on. Your babysitter says it's time for bed." She takes my hand and pulls me into the bedroom. And then, to my thrill and relief, she guides me into bed under the covers and crawls in right next to me, obviously intending to stay with me.

I try not to smile too big. I try to act like I knew all along Laila was going to sleep with me here in the master bedroom.

"Goodnight, Fitzy," I say casually. Like it's no big thing. But I'm smiling from ear to ear.

"Goodnight, Adrian," she replies. And even though she's now rolled onto her side, facing away from me, I can physically hear her wide, beautiful smile from here.

ELEVEN

LAILA

"Welcome to the new season of *Sing Your Heart Out!*" Sunshine Vaughn, our famous host, bellows from the large stage, and the studio audience behind the judges' table bursts into applause.

My heart thumping wildly, I clutch Savage's thigh under the table and squeeze, letting him know I'm freaking out right now, and he places his hand on top of mine, letting me know we're in this crazy thing together.

"And now, let's say hello to our *four* judges!" Sunshine booms, gesturing to the panel. She introduces each of us, one by one, and each judge waves or blows kisses—or halfheartedly smirks like they'd rather be anywhere else, in the case of Savage—as their name is called.

Sunshine says, "Before we get started with the first audition, let's take a look at the journey our contestants have traveled to get here today—to be able to audition in front of our judges and a live studio audience!"

The live cameras cut out and a pre-taped package begins

playing, and everyone at the judges' table exhales for a moment.

Savage leans into me and whispers, "You feeling okay?"

"Honestly, no. I'm suffering from major imposter syndrome right now."

"Bah." He squeezes my hand under the table. "Just pretend Sunshine is Aloha and each contestant a crew member and you'll be fine."

I pull a face of surprise. "That's great advice. Thanks."

Savage winks. "I get it right, once in a while."

"Actually, more than *once*, if last night was any indication." I wink suggestively, and that's all the invitation this horny man needs to lean in and kiss me.

Instantly, at the touch of Savage's lips to mine, the audience behind us bursts into wild whoops and cheers, and there's no doubt they're not reacting to the video.

The director peeks out from behind a monitor. "Savage and Laila!" He motions to the cameras, looking annoyed. "See how all the little red lights are *off*? We want you to make the audience react like that when one of the little red lights is *on*."

Nadine, our executive producer, appears out of nowhere, looking frazzled.

"I already told them," the director says, cutting her off at the pass. But, apparently, she feels the need to say it anyway. "Guys," Nadine says, looking at Savage and me. "The cameras have to be *on* when you whip the audience into a frenzy."

"We're sorry," I say, speaking for both of us, even though Savage's facial expression makes it clear he's not sorry in the slightest—that in fact, he's presently imagining both the director and Nadine eating a bag of dicks. I add, "We didn't mean to whip anyone into a frenzy. We simply got swept up in the moment and forgot about the audience and cameras for a second there. It won't happen again."

Nadine pauses, looking surprised by my explanation. And, suddenly, I realize I just admitted that Savage and I kissed off-camera, not because we're newbies who forgot to wait for the cameras to be trained on us, but because we kissed for real. For nothing but the sheer pleasure of it.

"Oh," Nadine says, her eyebrow raised. She smirks at the director before returning to Savage and me. "No worries at all. We know there will be a learning curve for you two, so we've folded that into the shooting schedule. We can do reshoots and edits throughout the audition shows, so it's no biggie. The problem will come later, when we switch to the 'live taping' format for the weekly singing competition. At that point, you two are going to have to be a well-oiled machine. But for now, we'll just have you redo the kiss."

Nadine and the director both leave, and the minute they're gone, Savage leans into me and says, "This is going to be even more painful than I thought."

"Nah, I'm sure it'll be lots of fun, once we get the hang of it."

He looks at me like I'm crazy. "No, it'll be flat-out torture, from beginning to end. All I can say is thank God you're here with me."

My heart skips a beat.

"Hey, everyone!" Sunshine says to the studio audience, after conferring with Nadine. "In a minute here, I'm going to chitchat with the judges. And when I get to Savage, he's going to kiss Laila again, the same way he did a moment ago.

And when he does, will you folks please whoop and cheer, the same way you did the last time?"

The audience claps enthusiastically.

"I knew I could I count on you! Let's cheer even more loudly than last time, yes?"

I look at Savage and roll my eyes and he pulls a face like he wants to bang his head against the table.

A moment later, Sunshine begins going down the line of judges, chatting with Jon, and then Aloha, followed by me, asking us if we're excited to kick things off. Yes, yes, yes. We're so excited. When she gets to Savage, however, and asks him if he's excited about the season, he smiles at me and says, "I'll say this: I'm excited to be here with Laila."

"Aw," the audience says, along with me, just as Savage leans forward and kisses me. As promised, the audience combusts when Savage's lips touch mine, which prompts me to break away and act like I'm flustered and embarrassed by the crowd's boisterous reaction. For his part, however, Savage leans back in his chair and flashes a look that says, "Yeah, I fucked her three times last night." And the audience eats it up.

There's a bit more pageantry from Sunshine, until, finally, she introduces the first audition of the season—a blue-haired cutie named Addison Swain from Madison, Wisconsin, age eighteen. At the sound of her name, Addison walks onstage, looking nervous and adorable. She greets the judges and Sunshine and says this is a dream come true. After a little chatter, she performs a bit of "Titanium" by Sia—instantly establishing, in my opinion, she's the one to beat this season. I mean, holy hell, this blue-haired pixie can *sing*!

When Addison finishes her performance, the audience

goes ballistic. As they should. On impulse, I bolt out of my chair and give Addison a standing ovation—which makes the girl burst into soggy tears. When the audience's applause dies down, Jon, Aloha, and I give Addison our effusive praise, with me being the most effusive. And, finally, all eyes turn to Savage, who's apparently already positioned himself as The Hard-to-Impress Judge.

"I agree with everyone else," Savage says calmly. "Addison, you've got some serious pipes and stage presence. You get an unreserved 'atta girl' from me."

The audience loses their collective mind. And, just this fast, it's clear Savage's opinion is going to hold more weight than anyone else's this season. Why? I don't know, exactly. All I know is that Savage's opinion has always held a whole lot of weight for me, too.

"Okay, judges," Sunshine says. "It's time to decide if you want to use one of your valuable tokens on Addison, in order to mark her as someone you want to haggle over on Draft Day!"

Jon and Aloha say they adored Addison's performance, but they're going to pass, since it's early days yet. But Savage and I both throw in our precious tokens, signifying we plan to fight over Addison, tooth and nail, when the time comes, and the audience claps and screams their approval of our choice.

And away we go, seeing audition after audition after Addison's, with varying degrees of success. Finally, the long day is over, and Nadine appears at the judges' table, bursting with enthusiasm. She tells Savage and me we "killed it" and that we should continue doing everything as we did today. I thank Nadine effusively, feeling the weight of the world lifted off my shoulders, while Savage, predictably, says nothing.

After a bit, Nadine asks Savage to come with her backstage. "My boss brought his thirteen-year-old to the taping today," she explains. "And apparently, she's a *huge* Fugitive Summer fan."

"I'm pretty tired, Nadine," Savage says, much to my shock. Dude. This woman is our boss and she's trying to impress *her* boss. Does Savage not understand workplace politics at all?

"It'll only take a few minutes," Nadine says. "I'd be grateful."

"Go on," I say in a casual tone, but my eyes are screaming, "Don't be an idiot! This woman signs the check you split with me!"

"Uh, okay," Savage says, peeling his gaze off mine. "I'd be happy to do it." He shoots me a look that says, *Happy now?* And I shoot him one that says, *Yes, I am, dumbass. Thank you.*

Savage leaves with Nadine, throwing over his shoulder as he goes, "I'll come to your dressing room when I'm done, *babe*."

"Okay, *babe*," I reply, and then giggle at the wink he shoots me, just before turning away.

"Laila."

I turn and discover Aloha standing before me, her famous green eyes sparkling.

"Hey, girl," I say. "What a day, huh? I'm exhausted."

"Every audition day is always exhausting," she says. "Hey, will you come hang out with me in my dressing room while I change? I'd love to chat with you about your first day."

"Great."

As we walk, Aloha and I talk casually about the day. Mostly, about the amazing talent we've seen. But the second we get into Aloha's dressing room, and she's closed the door behind us, she whirls around and whisper-shouts, "What the hell is going on with you and Savage?"

"What do you mean what's going on?" I say to Aloha, taken aback.

She drags me to a couch on the far side of her dressing room. "I mean you and Savage couldn't keep your hands off each other all day, even when the cameras were off. You exchanged googly-eyed looks and goofy smiles, *even when the cameras were off*. And you giggled at *everything* that man said, even when it wasn't funny, even when the cameras were off. So, I'm asking you, 'What the heck is going on between you and that man that you haven't told me,' because I know you and this is exactly how you act when you're gone, baby, gone!"

I flop onto the couch and rub my face. "You nailed it. I'm gone, baby, gone."

"Oh, girl."

"I'm in big trouble here, Aloha." I throw up my hands. "Savage is The Beast and I'm Belle and last night was our snowball fight!"

Aloha gasps. "No."

"*Yes!*"

"Holy hell, Laila. The boy gives you a few orgasms and suddenly you've got amnesia about all the times he made you cry during the tour?"

"Well, it wasn't just a *few* orgasms," I mutter, snickering. And when Aloha chastises me nonverbally, I add, "Okay, look, I know Savage was a colossal jerk to me during the tour. But I wasn't exactly a saint to him."

"You didn't deserve what he did to you, though. That tirade in Atlanta. The groupies he brought to your dressing rooms. The groupie he fucked in Vegas, mere *hours* after having sex with you."

"I know. But I found out he'd gotten some terrible news the morning of his tirade in Atlanta. And he thought I was dating Malik when he brought all those groupies into my dressing rooms. And it's not like we'd agreed to be *exclusive* when he banged that groupie in Vegas. So, all things considered—"

"He'd sent you a text, begging you to come to his room, mere minutes before banging that groupie, Laila!"

I pout. "Yes, I know, Aloha. But we've both agreed to forgive and forget all sins committed during the tour by either of us. We're going to press the reset button and see what happens and I'm excited about that."

Aloha raises her eyebrows. "You think you can do that?"

"I do. Now that I've had a chance to get to know him on a deeper level, I think I can forgive and forget and move on. I've told him that I expect and require monogamy while we're living together, and he said he totally understands and promises to be with nobody but me. And not because of his contract or the fake romance. But for *real*. And I believe him."

Aloha looks skeptical.

"What's the downside?" I blurt. "He's hot as hell and I'm stuck with him in a fancy house for three months. I might as well enjoy myself."

Aloha smirks. "Well, that's true. I just don't want you getting hurt, that's all."

"I'll be fine. Thank you."

"Regardless, I think you should bring it down a notch, on-camera, just to give yourself a little headroom, so to speak —room for the on-camera romance to grow."

I furrow my brow. "Nadine said she was thrilled with what we did today."

"Yeah, I heard. But let me offer some unsolicited advice. I've been in this industry my whole life, so trust me when I say you can't give the suits everything they want on day one, or there's nowhere for your performance to go. Trust me, they always want more, more, *more*, until their expectations feel impossible to fulfill. You and Savage should leave your-selves some room for your 'romance' to blossom each week on the show, or else, by the finale, they're going to want you to give birth on-air."

I laugh.

"I'm only half-kidding."

I process that for a moment. "Here's my predicament, though. The producers slipped a cheap buy-out clause into my contract, and I'm worried if the romance storyline isn't a ratings bonanza out of the gate, the producers will axe me from the show."

"Shoot, Laila. Daria was okay with a buy-out clause?"

"We had no choice. The producers wouldn't do the deal

without it, and I wanted to do the deal. Daria said the chances of them invoking the clause are almost nothing, because she thinks we'll pull in record ratings. But, still, just knowing that clause is in my contract like a ticking time bomb is messing with my head. It makes me not want to give anything less than a hundred percent, right out of the gate."

Aloha pats my arm. "Don't worry, Laila. Like you said, Nadine is thrilled with you and Savage. I'm probably just being paranoid. Nadine was the executive producer of *The Engagement Experiment* when it first launched, so I know for a fact she's hard-wired to wring every drop of romance she can out of every situation, at full blast."

"I'll keep that in mind and maybe try to pace myself a little bit more, on-camera."

"And also maybe try to keep your wits about you a tiny bit, off-camera, too?" She smiles. "Honey, I want you to be happy. And I want this thing with Savage to work out great for you. I'm just saying you cried a whole lot during that tour. And I don't want that boy to make you cry again, this time around."

I pat her arm. "I hear you and appreciate what you're saying. But it's going to be okay. Like I said, we're both pretending the past doesn't exist and taking each other as we are now. Trust me, that strategy absolves me of almost as many sins as Savage."

Aloha looks at me for a very long moment with nothing but kindness in her eyes. "Well, that sounds like a great thing, then. I'm happy for you."

"But you think I'm pulling a 'Laila.' Sprinting ahead with blinders on and ignoring every red flag."

Aloha pauses. "No. I mean, yes. But I don't blame you. What I think is that you're a gorgeous, passionate, horny-ass woman who's stuck for three months in the mansion from *The Engagement Experiment* with a rock star who regularly gives you multiple orgasms that make you scream in ecstasy. Frankly, I don't think you're pulling a 'Laila' this time, as much I think you're pulling a 'red-blooded human.'"

THIRTEEN

LAILA

"Cheers!" I say, holding up a glass of champagne in one hand and my phone in video mode in the other. While recording a live video, Savage and I are sitting side by side on the couch in our living room, toasting our first day of shooting with a bottle of Dom Perignon sent home with us by Nadine. Despite the sobriety clause in Savage's contract, Nadine gave us the bottle on two conditions. One, we had to promise we'd open the champagne in a live video tonight and joyfully toast on-camera to our first day as judges. And two, Savage had to promise no photos of his dick or bare ass would join his already robust collection on the internet.

"Cheers, baby," Savage says, clinking my glass with his and kissing my cheek.

We sip our champagne and talk about the day's shoot, telling everyone watching we can't wait for them to see the amazing talent we witnessed today when the first episode airs in a few weeks. We trade playful banter about who's going to wind up with the best team after Draft Day—the notorious day on *Sing Your Heart Out* when the judges haggle and jockey to wind up with the best contestants from those they've given a precious token. And, finally, we wrap up our video with a little kiss on the mouth and a joyful "See you next time!"

When I turn off my camera, I plop my phone onto the coffee table in front of us and exhale. "I think it's distinctly possible by the end of the season, these daily videos will feel like a colossal pain in the ass."

"By the *end* of the season?" Savage says, his expression making it clear he already feels that way.

A buzz simultaneously emanates from both our phones on the coffee table, and we grab them, curious to see who's texted us. It's Reed Rivers, telling us he wants us to write a "sappy, classic love song" as soon as possible—a single we'll perform in the show's finale and release that same day. Reed writes, "Send me the bones of the song within a week or so, to give us enough time to get it fully produced before the finale."

I look up from my phone and wait a beat for Savage to finish reading. When he looks up, I say, "I think a week to write one song is doable. Do you?"

"In theory, yeah. But I've never written a 'sappy, classic love song' before. I've never even written a straight-up love song."

"You've heard my songs. Sappy love songs aren't exactly in my wheelhouse, either." It's the truth. I'm known for writing breakup songs. You-did-me-wrong songs. Or, on occasion, damn-boy-you're-so-fine songs. But never the kind of song Reed has requested. "I still think we can do it, though," I say. "All we have to do is treat this like a creative writing project. We'll write the song as if we're writing it about some other couple—a perfect, sweet one who's 'couple goals.'"

Savage scowls. "'Perfect and sweet' isn't my goal, Laila."

I roll my eyes. "It's not mine, either. But you know what *is* my goal? Making a whole lot of money off this song. And 'perfect and sweet' is the world's couple goals, so that's what we'll write. God help us, if we infuse too much of our actual personalities into the lyrics, the song will be about a couple fucking in a shower."

Savage's face lights up. "And in a bathtub, a hot tub, a pool . . . a rainstorm . . ."

I snicker. True to his word, Savage arranged for a doctor to come to the set today during one of our breaks—a real one, not a dude who plays one on TV—and we both got our "all clear" results during the drive home.

"You know what I think we should do to get into the mindset to write this song?" I say. "We'll pretend we're writing the soundtrack to a romantic movie—like, you know, something unapologetically sweet. Like, I don't know, we'll pretend we've been asked to write the 'big song' for a remake of *Ghost*."

"I haven't seen that one. But I get your drift, I think."

"You haven't seen *Ghost*?" I shout incredulously.

Savage shrugs. "I think this is going to be a running theme, Laila. So I'd ration your outrage, if I were you."

"But *Ghost* is one of the greatest movies ever made! I got my pottery wheel after seeing that one. It's so romantic. A total tear-jerker."

"Yecch. I hate tear jerkers."

"Well, too bad, because we're watching it now. *Ghost* is the *perfect* movie to inspire our song!" I pick up the remote control exuberantly. "Fire up the popcorn maker, Adrian!

We're going to snuggle up and watch the most romantic movie ever made, and then sit down and write the sweetest, sappiest love song ever written in fifteen minutes flat!"

So much for writing a love song after watching *Ghost*. The only thing that movie inspired Savage to do was demand that I immediately teach him how to work my pottery wheel. And I'm such a dork for my wheel, I leaped off the couch and sprinted up here with glee to get the thing fired up. Yes, I'm well aware Savage's request was nothing but a ruse to be able to make out while using the wheel, the same way Demi and Patrick do in the movie. But I don't care. I'd never pass up the chance to watch Savage's talented fingers molding wet, spinning clay. Plus, bonus points, Savage is shirtless as he works, and his face is wearing an expression of extreme concentration. In short, he's fatally gorgeous right now.

"How are you already so good at this?" I say, mesmerized by the bowl taking shape underneath his fingertips. He's making it for Mimi, of course, as a Christmas present, he said, even though he's already bought the woman a house for Christmas.

"It took me weeks to get anything to take shape that symmetrically," I marvel as Savage slowly continues coaxing the clay into form. "You've done this before, haven't you? You lied."

Savage chuckles. "I swear I've never done this. I've always been pretty good with my hands, though. This feels intuitive to me."

Damn straight, you're good with your hands, I think. I

watch for a moment longer, before putting up my palm. "Okay, I think that's enough. You should stop now."

Savage doesn't stop.

"Adrian, seriously," I say. "Stop now. If you make the clay too thin on the edges, it'll flop over."

"I just want to make the top rim a bit thinner."

"If you overwork the clay—"

"Nooo!" Savage shouts dramatically as the edge of his creation flops over and then wobbles asymmetrically on the wheel, before abruptly turning into nothing but a marred, spinning blob. Savage lifts his bare foot from the wheel's pedal, bringing the turntable to a stop, and looks at me. He grimaces adorably. "Sorry, what were you saying?"

I giggle. "It shouldn't be too hard to fix. If it is, we'll start again. That's life. In the meantime, though . . ." I get up and move to him, spread his thighs wide, enough to accommodate me kneeling between them, and then look up at him and say, "As it turns out, watching you making pottery is a huge turn-on for me."

Savage smolders down at me, his face awash in lust. "That's a good thing, since it turns out, you watching me making pottery turns *me* on."

"What *doesn't* turn you on, Adrian?"

He touches my face, smearing clay onto my cheek. "Nothing, as long as you're nearby." He bites his lower lip. "Take off your clothes for me, unless you want me to get clay all over them. One way or another, I want those clothes off."

I rise and comply with his request, while he proceeds to peel off his own clothes, his clay-covered hands be damned.

When we're both naked, Savage resumes his chair before me, his cock straining. So, I resume my prior kneeling position and take his erection into my mouth. As his pleasure ramps up, Savage reaches behind me, and a moment later, I feel the sensation of wet clay being smeared onto my bare back. And then, my left shoulder. My skin alive and my heart racing, I stop what I'm doing, pulling my mouth off him with a loud pop—and then dip my hand into the wet clay on the wheel behind me. When I turn back around, I smear clay across the grooves and ridges of Savage's cut abs, while swirling my tongue across the tip of his cock.

When I'm finished painting his abdomen with clay, I lick him from his balls, all the way to his tip, and then purr, "Now you're a real-life version of the *David*."

"And you're my *Venus de Milo*," he replies, not missing a beat. He adds, "With arms, of course." To emphasize that last point, he smears clay down my left arm, and then my right. He grabs more clay, takes my face in his palms, and kisses me. After that, he pulls me to standing along with him and smears even more wet clay across my belly and ass. He bends down and devours my breasts and nipples for a bit, making me shudder and moan softly, before smearing those areas with wet clay, as well. "You're a work of art, Laila," he whispers, his dark eyes blazing and his tone passionate.

I feel like I've got a jackhammer in my chest, as well as one between my legs. Breathing hard, I guide Savage back to sitting, gather some wet clay onto my fingertips, and smear it onto the bridge of his perfect nose. Shaking with arousal, I straddle him in his chair—he's the hottest I've ever seen him right now, and that includes the times I've had drool running down my chin while watching him onstage—and then take Savage's big, thick, gorgeous cock inside me, all the way, making him groan loudly as I slide down. I know when Savage suggested we get tested by a doctor, he wasn't envisioning this particular scenario. But I can't imagine a better way to kick off our condom-less adventure.

As my palms cup Savage's cheeks, leaving clay all over them, Savage grips my back, leaving more clay on me. I move my body energetically on top of him, rubbing myself against him in just the right way—and soon, I find myself erupting with a delicious orgasm that causes me to scream loudly with pleasure.

As my body releases, Savage's does too. He growls as he comes and clutches me, hard. For a long moment, we remain intertwined, our clay-streaked bodies slack. Our lungs working hard. Our hearts beating in tandem.

"So . . ." he says on an exhale. "Did you get inspired to write a sappy love song while I was railing you?"

I laugh. "I believe I railed *you*, sir."

"And quite well, I might add."

Smiling, I reach behind me and grab a handful of wet clay and then caress every inch of Savage's smooth forehead, sculpted nose, chiseled cheeks, and steel chin with both sets of fingertips, like I'm a facialist at a fancy spa, and Savage is my client. "You're so freaking beautiful," I whisper, and his body underneath me physically shudders in reply. I nuzzle his nose with mine, stealing some of the clay I've wiped on him. "I feel drugged by you, Adrian," I whisper. "I feel high as a kite when I'm around you."

"Laila," he whispers. And for a long moment, we stare into each other's eyes, neither of us moving.

"Wait here," I say. "Before this moment ends, I want to get a photo of you."

He grabs my forearm. "No, Laila. Don't go."

"I'll be right back."

"Don't take a photo."

I knit my brows. "But you look so beautiful—like a statue. I want to remember this moment."

Savage's usual swagger is nowhere to be found. He's earnest now. *Vulnerable.* And breathtakingly beautiful. "For your own memories?" he asks. "Not to post? Because I don't want you to post a photo of me like this with some cringey caption that says, 'Look what happens when I try to teach my boyfriend to use my pottery wheel!'"

Oh, my heart. The look on his gorgeous face is making my heart feel like it's physically twisting. "I only want a photo for *me*," I assure him. "Not to post. Not to brag. Just to remember."

Savage exhales and shoots me a lopsided smile that says more than a thousand words ever could. He drops his hand from my arm, freeing me to go, and whispers, "Only if you'll let me take a photo of you, too, for the exact same reason."

FOURTEEN

LAILA

"Can you believe we're heading into the final day of auditions?" Sunshine Vaughn says into the camera. We've been shooting auditions for the past two weeks now, assembling enough footage for the show's editors to cobble together the first four episodes. Throughout the shoot thus far, Savage and I have been sitting side by side at the judges' table, barely able to keep our hands off each other. If we're not physically touching, we're shooting each other lascivious looks and flirtatious smiles. When we're offering our feedback to whichever contestant onstage, we almost always wind up playfully teasing each other or laughing at each other's jokes. Basically, we've behaved on-camera the same way we do when we're home alone. We act addicted and head over heels *on*-camera because that's exactly how we're both feeling, in real life.

As a matter of fact, real life with Savage has been the most fun I've ever had. When we get home from work, we eat whatever fancy meal our private chef has made for us. And then, after doing our required live video for fans, we call our families and say hello, and then plug our phones onto their chargers and leave them there for the rest of the night. After that, we attack each other, basically. Usually, in order to check off another box on our proverbial bingo card by having sex in yet another room or area of our massive house. So far, we've been making incredible progress in our game. Thank God, "Let's Have Sex in Every Room of the House" isn't a drinking game, or Savage and I would be blitzed out of our minds every night.

Amazingly, though, sex isn't even the best thing Savage and I do together, as great as it is. The best thing is just . . . hanging out. We work out together in our home gym. We watch movies while snuggled on our couch. Besides watching *Ghost*, we've watched *Fast Times at Ridgemont High*, too, which was hilarious. We've also watched some fabulous porn. And by that, I mean we watched *Beauty and the Beast* for me and *Mean Girls* for Savage. Oh, and we've played cards, as silly as that sounds. The games Mimi taught Savage as a boy and loves to play with him whenever he visits her.

The only thing not going amazingly well for Savage and me? Writing the duet. Try as we might, we can't write that damned love song. I thought it'd be easy to do, considering how prolific Savage and I usually are as songwriters, but, for some reason, we can't come up with an idea that leads to anything good. It's frustrating, to say the least. Not to mention, anxiety-producing, since we're now a full week past the deadline Reed initially gave.

Speaking for myself, I haven't been able to write the damned song because, every time I look into Savage's dark eyes, I feel anxious that whatever idea I might be thinking about, whatever sappy and sweet suggestion I might make, will hit too close to home. Be too honest. Too vulnerable. Something Savage will know is the truth, rather than part of a "creative writing assignment," which is what we've both agreed the song should be. And, just like that, I can't come up with an idea I'm willing to speak out loud to save my life.

I have no idea why *Savage* has had writer's block, as well, but I admit I'm hoping he's been running up against the same dilemma as me. Or maybe that's just wishful thinking. He said, right from the start, sappy loves songs aren't his thing. So, more likely than not, he's simply waiting for me to take the lead.

Sunshine's cheery voice yanks me from my reverie. Looking into a camera, she says, "Another batch of auditions, and then we'll move on to Draft Day, when our judges will get to finalize their teams. After that, we'll have Mentor Day, and then . . . *finally* . . . our live weekly singing competition will begin!"

The audience roars with excitement.

Sunshine looks at the judges' table. "Are you excited for everything that's coming, judges?"

The first three judges reply, like good soldiers, that we're excited and raring to go. Whoop-de-doo! But Savage being Savage, he gives Sunshine nothing but a half-hearted thumbs up and an expression that says, "If I must." Of course, the studio audience is enthralled by Savage's disdain, since by now, that's become his *thing* on the show—acting like the whole exercise causes him physical pain. It works so well for him, I think, only because, on occasion, he unexpectedly breaks free from his usual disdain to grace the world with a beaming smile or effusive praise, usually saying something so perfect on those rare occasions, he makes whatever contestant he's speaking to burst into tears and the entire audience swoon.

Our host returns with a huge smile to the camera aimed at her. "Until next time, I'm Sunshine Vaughn, reminding you to . . ." The studio audience joins in on the show's famous sign-off: "*Sing. Your. Heart out!*" And then, as the audience applauds, we four judges do what we always do at this point—we stand and applaud and dance to the theme song blaring in the studio.

Finally, when the theme song ends, we four judges stop celebrating and swiftly head backstage with some body-guards, so we won't get mobbed with requests for selfies and autographs from the studio audience. But as our foursome makes our way backstage, Nadine approaches the group, stopping our movement.

"Savage and Laila?" Nadine says. "Can I talk to you for a moment—perhaps in Savage's dressing room?"

My stomach drops into my toes. When the big boss says she wants to talk to you, in private, it's probably not a good thing, no matter how well the past two weeks of shooting have gone. I have to think that's especially true when you're a newbie cast member who strong-armed her way onto the show in the first place, and the producers insisted on reserving an early termination clause in her contract that's not in anybody else's.

When we get to Savage's dressing room, Nadine closes the door behind us and gestures to the couch. "Please."

Savage and I take the couch, our body language stiff, while Nadine sits in an armchair across from us, her body language confident and unapologetic. This woman has been the big boss on this show since its inception, and *The Engagement Experiment* before that, so her demeanor not surprisingly communicates power and confidence in no uncertain terms.

"So, guys," Nadine says on an exhale, clasping her manicured hands in her lap. "First off, I want to compliment you on your performance these past two weeks. You've both *far* exceeded our expectations."

I sigh with relief and grab Savage's hand. "Thank you. I'm so glad you're happy."

"We're *thrilled*. You've been selling the romance beyond our wildest dreams. You're either amazing actors, or . . ." She raises her eyebrow and lets her facial expression finish the sentence: *Or you're not acting at all.*

I look at Savage, who isn't looking at me, and can't help noticing his breathing has become noticeably stilted and his jaw tight. I return my gaze to Nadine, my cheeks radiating with heat.

"Either way," Nadine continues, "we've been blown away by how convincing and authentic you two have seemed, both here on-set and in your behind-the-scenes videos from home. When the first episodes begin airing in a few weeks, nobody could possibly doubt the authenticity of your relationship. Which, of course, was *initially* our primary goal."

Initially.

Oh, fuck.

Something about the way she emphasized that word unsettles me. If that was only the *initial* goal, then what's the goal . . . *now?*

"Now that we've got our *initial* bases covered so well," Nadine continues, once again emphasizing that same word, "we're going to shift course. Add a little conflict to the love story, to make all the sweetness and happiness feel all the more special for the audience."

Fuck.

Fuck.

Fuck!

In a flash, I know Aloha was right. We've given the suits too good a love story, right out of the gate, with nowhere to go but a live birth in the finale . . . or, in the alternative, a little trouble in paradise.

Nadine leans forward in her armchair. "Remember how you two were at each other's throats during our very first conference call? That's the dynamic we want to see during the last batch of auditions tomorrow, and then during Draft Day and Mentor Day, too. Sound good?" Her question is rhetorical. She barrels ahead without pausing. "During our break for the holidays, my team and I will pour over all the footage while editing together the first batch of episodes, and at that point, we'll decide what direction we want to go next during the 'live' singing competition."

I look at Savage, my heart crashing and my eyes wide with panic, and discover he's every bit as poker-faced and cool as a cucumber as I am freaking out. Which makes sense, I suppose, since he has no idea about the early termination clause in my contract. To him, this is all white noise. A request he isn't going to grant. While to me, this is catastrophic. Plainly, the producers are trying to figure out the best storyline for The Savage and Laila Show—which actually means, when you boil it down, they're trying to figure out if maybe The Savage and Laila Show should become The Savage Show, sans Laila, like they'd initially wanted in the first place.

Nadine says, "We want to see 'hate-lust' from you guys!

We want to see the same 'I want to fuck you to death!' energy that was in your famous meme! Bring us some of the fire from that viral video of you two fighting on the sidewalk. Bring us *heat*. Anger. *Danger!*" She chuckles with glee. "We want sniping, banter, and combativeness—the kind of hostility that'll make our audience imagine you fighting at the judges' table by *day* . . . and having angry but amazing hate-sex by *night*!"

My mouth hangs open. "But . . . Nadine, we don't hate each other anymore. We did all that stuff when we did."

"I never hated you, Laila," Savage says, speaking for the first time during this conversation.

"It doesn't matter what you feel. Fake it! The truth is that every passionate relationship straddles a thin line between love and hate. Or *lust* and hate." She raises an eyebrow, letting us know she thinks the word "lust" is a far more appropriate descriptor than "love," when it comes to Savage and me.

"But . . ." I say. I look at Savage again, but he's no help. So, I return to Nadine. "Are you *sure* that's what the audience will want to see from us? During that first conference call, you said it was your top priority to make sure our romance was *totally* believable. You wanted something that would make the audience 'swoon.' And I think we can agree that's what we've delivered."

"Absolutely. Although, to be clear, our top priority was never making the romance believable. That was a means to an end. Our actual top priority was, and still is, and always will be, supplying a show that captures maximum ratings. Now that we're confident the initial footage we've gotten will convince everyone your relationship is real, we feel the next batch of episodes should offer a plot twist that will keep viewers glued to their TVs and coming back for more. We want the audience to worry a bit that your relationship might be on the rocks. We want them rooting for you to find your way back to each other—and tuning in, breathlessly, each week, to see if, in the end, you two make it to a happily ever after."

I press my lips together, feeling flabbergasted.

In the face of my silence, Nadine addresses Savage. "Do you understand what we want?"

Savage snakes his arm behind me on the couch in an apparent show of solidarity. His jaw muscles pulse briefly, before he licks his lips and says, "I understand the meaning of your words, yes. But as far as I'm concerned, Nadine, I'm contractually obligated to be a judge on a reality TV singing competition and Laila's devoted boyfriend. I'm *not,* however, contractually obligated to become, nor am I interested in becoming, a pawn on a dating show. I'm not a contestant on *The Engagement Experiment*, Nadine. That was never the deal."

Nadine's dark eyes flicker. "You both signed on to 'sell' the romance to a television audience. And, trust me, I know better than anyone on this planet, literally, how to do that. Based on my expertise, I've determined the audience will enjoy a bit more 'Vintage Savage and Laila' for a few episodes, as a foil to the 'Blissfully Happy and In Love Savage and Laila' we've come to know and love these past few weeks." She flashes me a pointed look that telepathically screams at me to convince Savage to pivot with me. "You get it, don't you, Laila? This is reality TV, not reality. We need to keep the audience entertained."

"I understand the meaning of your words, yes," I reply, echoing Savage's comment a moment ago. His arm is still around my shoulders and I want to show him the solidarity he clearly thinks he's showing me. But when Nadine's eyes harden, I can't help adding, "I'm willing to do my best to deliver what you want, if I can. I'm just not sure, at this point, that I can."

"Oh, I have faith in you," Nadine replies, and her tone makes me feel like there's a subtextual "or else" hidden in her statement. With a plastic smile, she slaps her thighs and rises from her armchair. "Show us 'Vintage Savage and Laila' tomorrow, during the last round of auditions, and then during Draft Day and Mentor Day, too. After that, we'll take the long holiday break to regroup and figure out where we want to take things from there."

"Mm-hmm," I say, as my stomach twists and clenches.

I look at Savage to find him silently staring Nadine down.

"So," Nadine says brightly, "do either of you have any fun plans for the holidays?"

As a matter of fact, during our three weeks off, Savage and I have lots of fun plans. The morning after shooting ends, Savage and I will head to Chicago to visit Mimi and Sasha. After spending three days with Savage's family, I'll fly back to California to spend Christmas day with my family, while Savage remains in Chicago with his. A few days after that, Savage and I will reunite in LA for a couple days before flying to Cabo to relax and celebrate the new year. The trip is Savage's generous Christmas gift to me, and I can't wait. After that, as the first episodes of the show begin airing, Savage and I will return to our fake love nest in LA to relax and gear up for the weekly singing competition to come. But sitting here now, I don't know if Savage would want me to mention any of that to Nadine. In fact, based on the way

Savage has reacted to Nadine during this conversation, I'm quite certain he wouldn't want me telling her a damned thing about our private life.

"We're just going to relax and spend the holidays with our families," I reply.

Nadine looks at Savage and he nods.

"Sounds fun," Nadine says. She tells us about her holiday plans—she's taking her family to Hawaii. She's getting her daughter a puppy for Christmas. Blah, blah. As Nadine speaks, I can barely breathe, as my mind races along with my pulse. Finally, Nadine bids us a good evening and heads toward the door of Savage's dressing room. Before exiting, though, she turns around and shoots us a smile that doesn't reach her eyes. "Thanks again for doing such a great job, guys." She looks at Savage. "Especially you, Savage. The audience is going to fall even more in love with you when these audition episodes air." With that, she turns and leaves. And I'm suddenly positive my days on the show are numbered, if I don't deliver precisely what Nadine has requested. Maybe even if I do.

"This is a disaster!" Laila whisper-shouts as we tumble into the backseat of our SUV. We shot the final batch of auditions today, during which there's no doubt we didn't deliver "Vintage Savage and Laila," as requested by Nadine yesterday. Not even close. On the contrary, we were every bit as enamored and enthralled with each other, as ever. And now, Laila is freaking the fuck out.

If I'm being honest, I didn't actually *try* to change course or deliver any semblance of what Nadine asked for yesterday. Why would I? I have no desire to return to any sort of toxic, angry dynamic with Laila—to mess with the blissful happiness I've found with her these past weeks. Not for any reason. But certainly not to please the executive producer of some reality TV singing competition that's contractually obligated to pay me, regardless.

Even if I were only "pretending" to be a dick to Laila again, I worry I might genuinely hurt her feelings somehow. And I don't want to risk that. So, all day long, I've sat back and let Laila take the lead in delivering the "hate-lust" dynamic Nadine requested yesterday. And guess what? Laila has followed *my* lead. She's returned my every smile, laughed at my jokes, and squeezed my hand every time I've squeezed hers. And before I knew it, the shooting day was done, and Laila and I had given the audience a whole lot more of the same—a blissfully happy couple that adores each other, can't keep their hands off each other, and laughs at each other's jokes. Even the stupid ones. And I'm not sorry about it. Not even a little bit.

Our usual bodyguard closes the door behind Laila as she gets settled into the back seat of the SUV next to me. "It's a disaster," Laila mutters, repeating her earlier refrain. "A total and complete *disaster!*"

I chuckle and pull her to me. "I think you should pick another word besides 'disaster,' babe. Repeating the same word, over and over, makes it lose its punch."

"Catastrophe. Calamity. Crisis. Any word you want to use, today wasn't good."

"Fuck Nadine. The audience will love seeing us happy and the ratings will reflect that. And if not, oh well. You and I will get paid the same amount, either way. We'll flip Nadine the bird on our way to the bank, baby."

The car heads toward the exit of the studio's parking lot, and Laila looks out her window, her body language stiff and encumbered. In fact, she looks like she's carrying the weight of the world on her shoulders.

"You worry too much, Fitzy," I say. "I'm telling you, the audience will *love* us being happy."

I wait for her to reply, to smile and exhale and say I'm right. And when she doesn't, I sigh and pick up my phone to reply to some texts from throughout the day. I deal with a group chat from Reed Rivers about my band's imminent album release. I text Sasha to confirm my upcoming travel plans and shoot a quick selfie video for Sasha to show Mimi when she wakes up in the morning, since I've unfortunately missed singing Mimi to sleep again, the same thing that's happened the past few nights, thanks to Mimi's exhaustion from the move into the new house, my busy shooting schedule with the show, and the time difference between Chicago and LA. And, finally, last but not least, I reply to a text from my best friend, who's expressed excitement about joining the show tomorrow afternoon for Mentor Day.

Me: I can't wait for you to see the bullshit dog and pony show for yourself, KC. This show is everything I hate, all rolled into one. Thank God for Laila sitting there with me.

Kendrick: Speaking of Laila, I've acquired some fascinating information that relates to her supposed fling with Charlie the Fitness Trainer during the tour.

Me: It's not a supposed fling. Laila confirmed it herself when I saw her at the awards show.

Kendrick: She lied. In the middle of our training session today, Charlie got a phone call from his HUSBAND. I guess it's possible Charlie is a bisexual adulterer, but I think the more likely scenario is that you're a paranoid nut job and Laila is a liar who knows how to push your buttons to maximum effect. LMFAO!

My heart lurching into my throat, I look at Laila sitting

next to me in the car, to find her texting away on her phone, and an unexpected torrent of conflicting emotions floods me. Anger, relief, *rejection*. Anger that Laila took my jealousy and paranoia and stoked it, solely to mess with me. Relief that Laila didn't fuck Charlie on the tour, as I've thought for so long.

But, mostly, I'm feeling acute *rejection* in this moment. As jealous as I was to think of Laila choosing Charlie over me during the last month of the tour, a piece of me found weird solace in that idea. If Laila hadn't jumped into something with me after the amazing night of the hot tub, then I had to come up with some reason for that. Someone else had caught her eye. Someone else had stolen her away from me. Someone else had made it possible for her to resist me. Well, why not Charlie? He's handsome and buff. A good guy, from what I can tell. And Laila made it clear, every time she was near him in my vicinity, that she liked him.

So, if Charlie isn't the reason Laila didn't come to my room, not even once, then what the fuck! I'm right back to feeling literal madness at trying to figure that woman out! How and why did she stay away from me for so long after Phoenix? If Laila didn't start fucking Charlie after the night of the hot tub, then . . . does that mean she stayed away from me . . . simply because she'd lost interest in me? Because I hadn't rocked her world, the way she'd rocked mine? Because she simply didn't *want* me, the way I so desperately wanted her? Every single thought I'm having in this moment feels like a dagger not only to my ego, but to my heart.

With my pulse thumping loudly in my ears, I tap out a reply to Kendrick:

Me: I didn't see that one coming. Gotta go. See you at the studio tomorrow.

Kendrick: Hold up. Call me now.

Me: Can't. Sitting next to Laila in a car.

Kendrick: Don't do it.

Me: Don't do what?

Kendrick: Whatever scheme is already taking root inside your twisted brain. I only told you about Charlie's husband to free you from the batshit jealousy you've been holding onto since the tour. Don't turn around and throw this in Laila's face. Don't try to coax her into a conversation about Charlie so you can catch her in another round of lies. Let bygones be bygones, Savage. You're happy now. BE HAPPY.

Me: I'm not going to throw this in Laila's face. I'm not even going to mention it to her.

Kendrick: You lied to Laila, too, remember? In fact, you lied first about that waitress in NYC, and then about all those women you brought into her dressing rooms. Call it even and let it go. Otherwise, if you bring this up to her, you'd better be ready to tell her all the shit you lied about, too. And WHY you lied to her. The FEELINGS you were having when you did all that. Are you ready to open up about how obsessed and crazy you were, behind the scenes?

Me: Not even a little bit.

Kendrick: That's what I thought. So, keep your big mouth shut.

Me: I will. Thanks for the info. Gotta go.

I plop my phone down onto the seat, facedown, between Laila and me, while Laila keeps tapping away on her phone. Why didn't she want me the way I wanted her, during that last month of the tour? I just don't get it.

"Who are you texting with?" I ask, when she still hasn't looked up.

"Aloha."

"You were with her all day."

Laila calls up to our driver. "Hey, Mike, could you turn up the music, please?" When music starts blaring loudly, Laila looks sheepishly at me. She says, "I have something I need to tell you. It's something I'm contractually not supposed to tell you or anyone else. But, screw it. I've already told Aloha and I don't want to keep this from you any longer."

My stomach twists. "Okay."

Laila takes a deep breath. "I kept this from you because I didn't want to burden you with it, or make you change the way you acted on-camera. I thought if you knew what I'm about to tell you, you might act differently on-camera, in a way that didn't seem natural."

"Spit it out, Laila."

She bites her lip and exhales. "There's a termination clause in my contract. A buy-out clause, by which the show can send me packing, at their sole discretion, at any time, without prior notice, by paying me a hundred grand."

"A hundred grand? Jesus, Laila. *No*."

She nods.

"A hundred grand is *peanuts* to them!" I whisper-shout,

running my hand through my hair. "No wonder you've been so stressed out about what Nadine said yesterday."

"I'm obviously on the chopping block, especially after we didn't deliver today."

"You should have told me about this the minute Nadine left my dressing room last night, Laila!"

"I didn't want to force you to do anything you didn't want to do. Plus, I thought I could handle this on my own. But after today, when you were so sweet to me and I didn't have the heart to be anything but sweet back to you, I realized I can't do this alone. Everything depends on me delivering 'Vintage Savage and Laila' tomorrow. It's my last chance to hit a homerun before the long break. After shooting was over for today, Nadine popped into my dressing room while I was changing and made it clear she was pissed about our 'happy couple' routine today. She didn't say this, explicitly, but her demeanor made me think they're going to fire me during the break if we don't hit it out of the ballpark tomorrow, exactly like she's requested."

My heart feels like it's exploding. "They can't fire you. They're contractually obligated to let you perform in the finale, remember?"

"Okay, so maybe they'll invite me back to let me sing. Yet another chance for huge ratings."

"But we're picking *four* teams tomorrow. The whole audition process has been built around you being one of the judges."

"That'd be an easy fix. They could fire me during the break, say we broke up and I didn't want to return to the show. And then, they'd parcel off the contestants on my team to the three remaining judges and finish out the season with three judges, like always. Just think about the ratings if they did all that, Savage! They'd have a self-created 'scandal.' A big 'mess' they'd have to scramble to fix. Don't you think everyone would tune in to see that? Not to mention, to see how poor Savage is doing after his breakup with Laila? I haven't slept a wink since Nadine talked to us in your dressing room, and I've looked at it from every angle. I've decided I'm not paranoid. They're going to fire me during the break, Savage. I can feel it. Unless we deliver what Nadine asked. And even then, I might be toast, regardless."

"Well, fuck that. I won't let them fire you," I say, my jaw tight. "If that's what they ultimately decide to do, then I'll tell them I won't do the show without you."

Laila's face melts with affection for me. She touches my cheek gently and smiles ruefully. "Thank you, but I'd never let you do that. You're contractually obligated to do the show. You'd have a lawsuit on your hands."

"I don't care. I'm not doing the show without you, Laila. That was a basic condition of me doing the show. Doing it with you."

"No, it wasn't. You agreed to do it, long before you knew I'd be anything but Aloha's one-episode mentor. Plus, the whole reason you signed onto the show was for *Mimi*. And that reason still stands today, more than ever."

I feel flooded with panic. But I manage to say, "Okay, let's not panic here. I'm not supposed to tell you this, but I know something you don't. Something that proves, beyond a shadow of a doubt, they won't fire you, whether we deliver 'Vintage Savage and Laila' tomorrow or not."

She looks at me hopefully, her blue eyes wide and brimming with hope.

I glance toward the front of the vehicle, to make sure our driver and bodyguard can't overhear me, despite the loud music. And when it's clear they're enmeshed in their own conversation, I return to Laila and grab her hand. "There's a dangling carrot in my contract, baby. They'll pay me a fat bonus—a quarter mill—if I get down on bended knee and propose to you, right after we perform our duet in the finale."

Laila gasps. "*No.*"

I nod. "They didn't want me telling you about it, to ensure you had an 'authentic reaction' on-camera. And, honestly, I've never told you about it, anyway, because there's no way I'm going to do it. But the mere fact the bonus is hanging out there proves you've got nothing to worry about. Why would they offer me a bonus to propose to you in the *finale*, if they're not planning to keep you around until the finale?"

Laila's shoulders slump. The hope in her eyes a moment ago fades. Clearly, she doesn't find my logic as compelling as I do. "I don't think we can rely on that clause to protect me, honey. I think they're preserving themselves all sorts of potential storylines, depending on what happens, from week to week. You know, hedging their bets. *If* I'm still around for the finale, then *maybe* you'd choose to earn that bonus. But *if* they don't keep me around, then that's fine, because they've got a Plan B that will work, too. That's what Rhoda told me they do on *The Engagement Experiment*, all the time. She worked on that show with Nadine for five seasons, remember? When she came to the house and spilled all the tea, her stories made it clear the producers of that show always hedge their bets. They manipulate the contestants in lots of different ways, and then run with whatever storyline begins taking shape. Savage, you wouldn't believe the stuff they do to people to manipulate their emotions and actions on that show. I think Nadine has taken a page out of her old playbook."

I process that for a moment. "Okay, then. If you're genuinely worried about this, then I'll do my best to be more of a dick to you tomorrow, so you can fight fire with fire, and we can deliver 'Vintage Savage and Laila,' like Nadine wants."

Laila sighs with relief. "Thank you. I don't know if I'm capable of scowling at you anymore, let alone being a bitch to you. I'm sorry, but you're going to have to pick a fight with me tomorrow to get the ball rolling."

"Hell no! You'll have to be a bitch to me *first,* or I'll come off like a misogynistic asshole. Like I'm punching *down.* I'll play along and give *almost* as good as I get, but you're going to have to be the one to get the ball rolling." Laila snuggles into me and I put my arm around her. "It'll be fine, baby," I coo softly. "You'll be a bitch to me and I'll fight fire with fire, and we'll be everything Nadine wants and more."

She sighs like there's a hundred-pound weight resting on her chest, and my heart pangs in reply.

"I don't know if I'm capable of being a bitch to you anymore, Adrian. You fucking bastard. You've tamed the shrew."

I can't help chuckling. "You say that like it's a bad thing."

"It *is.* I can't even imagine how mortified I'd be if I got fired from the show. The list of fired judges, forevermore, would be me and Hugh Delaney." She makes a guttural, disgusted sound. "Let's face it. The word 'disaster' really does say it best."

We sit without speaking for a long moment, listening to the loud music in the car. The song, by chance, is "Fireflies," by our friends 22 Goats. Finally, Laila sits up and breaks the silence. "What if you told them you're planning to propose to me in the finale? Maybe that would make them want to keep me around!"

My heart explodes. "I . . . I don't think I could do that convincingly, Laila."

She pauses. "You couldn't *tell* them convincingly . . . or fake-*propose* to me convincingly?"

"I couldn't fake-propose convincingly. I've never once imagined myself proposing to someone. Never once imagined myself even wanting to get married. I think I'd stumble through it, red-faced and stammering, and wind up doing more harm than good."

Laila's chest heaves. "You don't think you could do it convincingly for a quarter million bucks? That's a lot of money, especially when you're already paying half your salary to me."

"We've agreed not to talk about the money anymore, remember?"

"No, you asked me not to talk about it. But I never said I wouldn't."

"I'm over it, Laila. You negotiated for an equal partnership, fair and square. And that's exactly what we are."

Boom.

For some reason, saying those words out loud—acknowledging the now-obvious fact that Laila and I truly are an equal partnership—makes me think maybe I *could* convincingly perform a fake proposal in the finale, after all. Not for the money, as Laila's suggested. But because Mimi would be thrilled to see it. That's all she's ever wanted for me—to see me settle down with a woman who loves me for *me*. So, why not give my grandmother all the bells and whistles, and also save Laila's job on the show while I'm at it? I think, up until now, I've been dismissing the idea of ambushing Laila with an on-air proposal, partly because I was scared she'd turn me down on national TV. Talk about public humiliation. And by the same token, I didn't want to risk ambushing Laila and having her say *yes* to me on national TV . . . only to find out afterwards the proposal wasn't real —that it was made by me, solely in exchange for a quarter-million bucks.

As if reading my mind, Laila says, "Now that you've told me about the bonus provision in your contract, I don't see why you wouldn't do it. Why not take their money? I promise I'll act totally surprised when you kneel down and ask me. I'll make this face." She gasps, widens her eyes, and brings a shaky hand to her mouth, like she's a newly minted beauty queen who's just heard the good news. In a heartbeat, she drops the beauty queen act, and flashes a mischievous smile. "Pretty convincing, huh?"

"Masterful," I concede.

"So . . .? I'd be thrilled for you to get a little extra money out of this gig, after I've taken half your salary. All I ask is that you give me a heads up the day before you 'propose,' to confirm you're going ahead with it, so I can warn my mom and sister it's coming. If they saw you pop the question on TV, without me telling them the real deal beforehand, they'd crap their panties with excitement, and I wouldn't want to do that to them. Telling them after the fact it was all a money grab would break their poor little hearts."

Fuck. My heart squeezes. In a flash, I have the preposterous impulse to propose to Laila for real. It's a stupid thought and I chastise myself for having it the moment I do. I'm not husband material, any more than I'm boyfriend material. But, man, it would be fun to give the Fitzgerald women that kind of thrill. A happily ever after, after all the shit they've been through with Laila's father.

"It's okay," Laila says, apparently reacting to my facial expression. "I'm sure the idea of fake-proposing to me gives you hives. It was just an idea to make some money for *you* and give *me* an insurance policy. But don't give it another thought."

I don't know what Laila saw on my face to make her say that. Yes, I'm feeling conflicted and confused about the idea of fake-proposing to Laila. But in the end, the thing that doesn't feel confusing at all is the notion that Mimi would love to see that.

"You know what?" I say. "Now that I've told you about the bonus provision in my contract, I think the proposal is probably doable."

Laila's blue eyes ignite.

"For Mimi," I clarify quickly. "Not for the money. More than anything, Mimi wants to see me settle down with the great love of my life, the way she did with her husband, Jasper. If, incidentally, me doing this silly thing for Mimi would *also* help you, then why wouldn't I do it?"

Laila's face is glowing with excitement. "Are you sure?"

My heart is racing. "Pretty sure. Can I have a little time to think about it? My contract says I don't have to give them advance warning to earn the bonus. The clause states I can decide, right up until the last possible moment. So, maybe, let's see how things shake down tomorrow with our newfound commitment to being dicks to each other again. If things look like they're going well for you after that, it'll be a moot point. But if it looks like you're still on the chopping block, then I can always swoop in and make it known that I'm planning to propose in the finale."

"Fantastic plan. Thank you so much."

"Of course."

I kiss her, and as I do, our phones buzz in unison with an incoming text. We break apart and pick them up to find we've both got the same message from Reed Rivers:

Reed: Due to time constraints, I've asked Fish and Alessandra to help you write the duet. I know you're both heading out of town for the holidays on Saturday, so I've asked them to meet at your house tomorrow night at 7. I'll take the lead on getting the song produced during the holidays, and you can add your vocals to the track in the new year. RR

"What do you think?" Laila says, putting down her phone.

"It doesn't matter what I think. The all-powerful Oz has spoken. Reed always does whatever he wants, no matter what I, or anyone else, wants."

"Yes, I know, but that doesn't mean you don't have an opinion. What do you think of Fish and Alessandra helping us get the song written? That's two more people earning royalties, at the end of the day."

"True, but what's the alternative? We've tried, many times, and we can't write this damned song to save our lives. Honestly, I think Reed is a genius for putting Fish and Alessandra on the project. Fish let me hear some of the rough cuts from the album he's co-writing with Alessandra, and every song they've written for her is the sweetest, purest, most classic little love song you've ever heard. I'm confident whatever they help us write will be perfect for what we're trying to accomplish here."

Laila nods. "Okay, so this is good news, then. Once again, Mr. Rivers knows exactly what he's doing."

"Yeah, I'm no fan of Reed's. But I have to admit this is a good call, even if it means you and I will get a smaller percentage of royalties. If you ask me, it's better to have a smash hit, with four co-writers, than to have only two writers on a shitty attempt at a love song that doesn't even make the charts."

"Great point. So, I'll tell Reed we're in agreement, then?"

"Not that he'd care. But, sure."

Laila taps on her phone and sets it down, and then looks out her side of the car like she's in deep thought again. And, suddenly, I know what I need to do. I pull out my phone and tap out a quick text, and then pull Laila to me after pressing send.

I kiss the side of Laila's head. "Stop worrying, baby. Everything is going to work out fine."

"I hope so."

"When we get home, we're going to open a contraband bottle of wine. And you're going to drink a glass or two or three."

"I promised I wouldn't drink, while you're not allowed to drink."

"Desperate times call for desperate measures. You're going to drink some wine and relax. You're going to get nice and horny and loose, while we eat whatever the chef left for us. And when you're feeling really good, and *really* naughty, I'm going to take you upstairs and fuck you like I *hate* you."

She giggles. "Oooh. You're going to help me 'get into character' for tomorrow, are you?"

"You've already figured me out. Yep, I'm gonna fuck you so hard, you'll remember what it feels like to want to fuck me to death. And tomorrow, when it's time for you to tap into your inner bitch, all you'll need to do is remember the way I fucked you like a dirty little whore the night before, and you'll be off to the races."

SIXTEEN

LAILA

With "Hate Sex High" blaring—which is creating a kinky kind of "life imitating art imitating life" energy between Savage and me —Savage is fucking me hard, doggie style, in our bed. So damned hard, I feel like the tip of his cock is going to poke out my mouth with the next beastly thrust. I grip the sheet beneath me, as the top of my head bangs against the head-board, and do everything in my power not to come. Throughout this entire, raucous session of sex with Savage, which has involved multiple positions thus far and a whole lot of groaning and screaming by me, Savage has repeatedly forbidden me from coming. "Not unless I've given you permission," he keeps saying. And, holy hell, it's been a tall order, thanks not only to the wine I had earlier with our meal, but the way Savage has been fucking and eating and fingering me, masterfully, for the past hour. Time after time, he's gotten me right to the edge. And then, he backs off and switches things up. Time after time, I've cried out with plea-sure, and begged him to say the word. But each time, he's pulled out, or stopped whatever he was doing and told me to shut up and do as I'm told.

"Please," I beg, feeling myself, yet again, on the bitter cusp of release.

"Not yet," he barks, making me moan. Without warning, he pulls my head back by my hair and growls into my ear. "Now put your vibrator against your clit again on low. *And don't come.*"

We've been playing with my toy, now and again, all night. I packed it in my suitcase in the first place, thinking I might need it, occasionally. But this is the first time I've used it since moving in. And what a way to reconnect with my loyal and efficient "ex-boyfriend"—by having a threesome with it and the best lover I've ever had, by a long mile.

"I'm gonna come," I announce. "Oh, God."

"Nope."

Savage pulls me upright, onto my knees. His frontside pressed against my backside, he roughly spreads my thighs apart and orders me to return the vibrator to my tip. "On low again. *Now.*"

Trembling, I press the vibrator between my legs, as instructed, while Savage runs his palms greedily over my torso. He gropes my breasts and nipples. Bites and licks and kisses my neck. I feel his dick against my ass and feel the quiver of his body as he holds back his own release.

I let out a garbled sound. "I'm gonna come," I choke out.

"Not yet."

With a loud growl, he flips me over, throws my legs up, and enters me. He rolls his hips as he thrusts, making my eyes roll back into my head so hard, I feel like they're rubbing against my brain.

"You're mine, Laila," Savage says, as his body plunges

into mine, over and over again. As his large dick impales me. "I own this body," he says. "It's all mine."

"*Savage.*"

"Not yet."

I feel my inside walls clench. My eyelids flutter. I make an inhuman sound.

"You can come now, baby," he coos, almost inaudibly. And that's it. I immediately come undone. With a loud scream, I come harder than I ever have in my life. As I writhe and moan in ecstasy, Savage pulls out of me . . . and a second later, I feel the sensation of warm wetness splattering across my face.

As I lie there, processing the fact that Savage just shot his load into my face, he crawls between my legs and does the same thing he always does after I've had a gushing orgasm. He licks up every drop of his trophy.

"You're delicious," he murmurs, after finishing his work. With a wink, he leaps off the bed and pads into the bathroom, leaving me cum-streaked and exhausted and staring at his hot backside in retreat. When Savage returns to the bed, he's not only got a towel in his hand, but a huge smile on his face. In fact, the boy is grinning as big and wide as a Cheshire cat. He slides his fingertip through the warm streak on my face and offers it to my lips, so I take his finger into my mouth and suck.

"Good girl," Savage says softly, like he's talking to a baby bird. With another wide smile, he wipes my face with the towel. "Are you feeling ready for tomorrow now?"

"You can't possibly think what we just did has helped me remember how to hate you. It was *incredible*."

Savage's smile broadens, even more. "Aw, come on. It had to have helped you get into character for tomorrow a *little*." He sits on the edge of the bed and counts off his supposed sins on his fingers. "I wouldn't let you come. I bossed you around and pulled your hair. And then, I topped it all off with a sperm facial." He smirks. "How rude of me. How *degrading*. How *infuriating*." His expression is pure snarkiness. He knows full well what he did to me was hot as hell, top to bottom, and that I loved every minute of it.

"This is so classic you," I say. "The same thing as when you sang my name in 'Hate Sex High,' but buried it slightly in the mix, just enough to preserve yourself some deniability. You wanted to have dirty sex and come in my face. Period. But you *said* you were doing it to help me 'get into character,' so you could hide behind your suit of armor, if it turned out I didn't like it. *Classic Savage*."

Savage smiles wickedly. "Well," he says. "Even if I haven't made you remember to hate me, at least we had a damned good time."

"We sure did." I peck his cheek and then hop out of bed and head into the bathroom. I wash my face and brush my teeth, and soon, Savage joins me for his usual bedtime routine.

"Don't worry too much about tomorrow," he says, his toothbrush sticking out of his mouth and his naked, massive dong hanging low. "I have faith you'll figure out a way to convince yourself you're highly annoyed with me tomorrow —if not downright infuriated."

"I don't know," I say. "It's a tall order these days. Look at you. You're perfect. Gorgeous. Talented. Sweet. How could I possibly remember what it feels like to be annoyed with you—let alone *infuriated*?"

Savage lifts an eyebrow, his expression practically screaming, *I've got a secret.*

"What?" I ask.

"What *what*?"

"That look."

"What look?"

"You just did it again. It's full of mischief. Like you know something I don't."

Savage spits his mouthful of toothpaste into the sink and grins adorably. "You're a drunken, paranoid lunatic. Now, come on, baby. It's time for bed. You need to sleep off all that contraband wine, so you can wake up tomorrow and, against all odds, remember how to tap into your inner bitch with me."

SEVENTEEN
SAVAGE

"Wake up, Fitzy," I say. As I say the words, I tap Laila's forehead repeatedly, like a woodpecker pecking holes into a dead pine tree. Today's mission? Operation Annoy Laila, with the higher goal of helping her recall, vividly, the sensation of hating my guts, so she can take the lead on delivering the combativeness Nadine has demanded. Obviously, I don't want to push Laila so hard as to make her *genuinely* hate me again. The very thought of regressing to those dark days with this gorgeous woman makes me physically recoil. But, for the greater good, I'm more than willing to aggravate the crap out of Laila today, in ways big and small, if it will help her get into character for today's long shooting day.

Tap, tap, tap. "Wake up!" I bellow into Laila's beautiful, sleeping face. "Up and at 'em, baby!"

All things considered, this ought to annoy her pretty well, right out of the gate. Laila isn't a morning person on a good day, the same as me, and I'm waking her up a full two hours before her alarm. Plus, Laila drank three goblets of wine last night, before we headed upstairs to screw, so I'm betting she's feeling a particular need for some extra sleep this morning.

Without opening her eyes, Laila bats at my hand as it continues tapping her forehead. "Stop it," she murmurs.

Tap, tap, tap. "There shall be no stopping!" I boom. "I've got a big surprise for you! Wake up!"

Laila squints at me. "My alarm hasn't gone off, has it?"

Tap, tap, tap. "No. It. Has. *Not!* It's only six!"

"*Six?* What the fuck!"

"Six is the time for my big surprise!" *Tap, tap, tap.*

Laila swats at my hand again. "What's wrong with you?"

Tap, tap, tap. "Nothing's wrong with me, baby! I'm all kinds of right. We're going to work out this morning before heading into work."

"Have fun with that. Bye now."

I laugh with glee. "Get dressed and meet me in the gym in five, or I'll physically drag you." *Tap, tap, tap.*

Laila's fully awake now. Scowling, she pulls the covers to her chin and rolls onto her side. "I'll work out tonight after work. I drank too much last night."

"Fish and Alessandra are coming over tonight, remember? It's now or never."

"Never, then."

Without warning, I yank the covers off Laila's near-naked body, subjecting her to the brisk early-morning air in the room, and she shrieks and curls into the fetal position. I pull out my phone and aim it at her. "Say good morning to everyone, babe. We're *live.*"

Laila shrieks and covers her face with her hands. "Please, tell me you're joking."

I don't blame her for second-guessing me. In all the time

we've been posting daily "happy couple at home" videos, it's *always* been Laila, not me, who's initiated our videos. And only when Laila is good and ready and has checked her makeup in the mirror.

"Not joking. Look." As she peeks out from behind her hands, I turn my phone around to show her the screen. "See? Now, say hi to the nice people."

She waves halfheartedly and says hello. "Sorry, guys," she says. "We'll come back after I've had my coffee. Say goodbye, Savage."

I turn the camera lens on myself. "Isn't Laila adorable when she first wakes up? So cranky! Ha! So, here's the deal, guys. I woke Laila up *way* earlier than her alarm, so we could squeeze in a workout before heading off to work today, since we've got plans with friends tonight. So, would you guys do me a big favor in the comments and help me convince Laila to work out with me? Only positive comments, please. Give her a pep talk. No trolling. And if it works, we'll come back later and show you part of our workout." I return the camera to Laila's angry face. "Say goodbye to everyone, babe."

She waves. "When you guys leave your comments, be sure to tell Savage he's annoying as hell."

Ha. Operation Annoy Laila is already off to a fantastic start.

I turn off my camera and spank Laila's ass. "Now, get dressed and meet me in the gym to see your surprise." With that, I exit the room, and head back to Charlie the Fitness Trainer, who's waiting for me in the gym.

"Charlie," Laila gasps out, freezing just inside the doorway of the gym. Her blue eyes shift to me. Confusion. Anger. *Betrayal.* Those are the emotions flickering across Laila's frozen face as she stares at me in disbelief.

Charlie reaches Laila and gives her a warm bear hug, unaware of his status as my unwitting pawn, and Laila peeks over his broad shoulder to shoot me the kind of scathing look I haven't seen from her in a very long time. Well, that's weird. I haven't even gotten to the annoying part yet—the part where I supposedly find out, in front of Laila, that Charlie is gay and married. And she's already shooting me murderous daggers? Well, that feels a bit premature . . . and vaguely worrisome. But, oh well. I've got a job to do. And I'm going to do it.

"It's great to see you again, Laila," Charlie says.

Laila returns the compliment, her face flushed.

Charlie says, "I've been following you and Savage on Instagram. Looks like you two are having a blast, living together and shooting the show. Emma can't wait to see you as a judge. When will the first episode air?"

"Right after New Year's," Laila replies.

"Sorry, who's Emma?" I ask. "Your daughter?"

"My stepdaughter. She and my husband came to visit me during the tour—and when Emma met Laila, she was starry-eyed. And then, when Emma saw Laila perform, forget about it. An obsession was born."

"Tell Emma to join the club," I say. But my eyes are on Laila's, letting her know the full implication of Charlie's story hasn't escaped me. *Charlie is married. And not only that, he's married to a dude.* Frankly, it was a lot easier than I thought it'd be to pull that information out of Charlie. I thought I'd have to ask him all sorts of awkward, uncharacteristically personal questions to get him to mention any of what he just said. But, no, right off the bat, I've hit a grand slam homerun.

Laila's plainly furious with me. It's not hard to see. Which makes sense, since I've just outed her as a liar, unless, I suppose, Charlie is a bisexual adulterer and Laila the kind of girl who'd have a tour fling with a married man. But, come on, I think we both know, in this moment, the jig is up. Her lie revealed. Yes, I was the one who jumped to the wrong conclusion in the first place about Charlie and then went on and on about my theory backstage at the awards show. But Laila confirmed her fling with Charlie and stoked my jealousy, mercilessly. So now, as far as she's concerned, I've just figured out the truth about all of it.

"Hey, you know what, Charlie?" Laila says, peeling her blazing blue eyes off my smug face. "Savage didn't know this when he invited you here to surprise me, but I've got plans this morning I can't reschedule."

"Oh, no," Charlie says.

"Yeah, it's a bummer. Hopefully, we can do this another time. But you two go ahead." She looks at me, her blue eyes homicidal. "I'll have Mike come get me now and come back for you later."

And that's it. Before I've replied, Laila turns on her heel and strides toward the exit of the gym.

"Wait!" I shout, my heart thrumming wildly in my chest. I feel panicky. Like I've made a misstep. Something is off. Laila was pissed the *minute* she saw Charlie. Yes, her anger seemed to escalate when Charlie mentioned his step-daughter and husband, thereby proving her a liar. But I can't shake the feeling there's something I don't know at play here. Some land mine I've stumbled into that just blew my arms and legs off, without me realizing it. "Laila, wait!"

To my surprise, she turns around in the doorway, her blue eyes blazing and her cheeks on fire. "What?" she says.

"Maybe we should . . . do another live video to let people know you made it into the gym."

She smiles, making my stomach twist. That wasn't a happy smile. That was a murderous one. "Great idea," she says. "Record it now. We'll tell everyone you got exactly what you wanted this morning."

I grimace, unsure what to do.

"Go on," she prompts, motioning. "Wouldn't want to keep everyone in suspense."

Fuck. She looks genuinely enraged. Capable of murder. And not for show.

"Uhh . . ."

"I'll do it myself." She grabs her phone out of a side pocket in her leggings, trains the camera on herself, and plasters a huge, fake smile on her face. She says, "Hey, guys! You did it! You convinced me to get in here and work out! I'm in the gym with my boyfriend now. He's right there. Say hi, Savage."

I wave feebly, feeling the hair on the back of my neck standing up.

"And that's Charlie Ford right there. The world's most amazing personal trainer. Say hi, Charlie!"

"Hey, everyone!"

Laila returns the camera to herself. "I'll put Charlie's links below so you can follow him. He's *amazing*, guys. And easy on the eyes, too. I can honestly tell you there's not a mean, selfish, self-centered, thoughtless, *hypocritical* bone in Charlie's body. Which is more than I can say about the other guy in this room. Man, don't you hate hypocrisy? When someone says one thing and does another? I especially hate it when the thing that person said was deeply meaningful to me. When I relied on it, totally. And in fact, *needed* it to be the truth, or everything else would fall apart." With that, she trains the camera on my astonished face and shouts, "That's the face of a hypocrite, guys! Not so pretty, is it?" With that, she lowers her phone, flips me off, and stalks out of the room.

"*Whoa,*" Charlie says, obviously taken aback by what just transpired. "What just happened?"

My heart is crashing. "Hell if I know," I say. And, unfortunately, it's the truth. For a second there, I thought Laila figured out what I was trying to do and played along, a little *too* well. But the look in her eye at the end there felt all too real. Like genuine white-hot *rage,* the likes of which I haven't seen from Laila since the tour. "That had nothing to do with you, Charlie," I choke out. "Laila and I were having an argument before you got here, and I guess I didn't read the situation right."

"You should go."

I take a deep breath. "No. Let's work out. She obviously needs a little 'alone time.'"

Charlie shakes his head. "No, I think you should follow her, Savage."

My heart wants to run after her. To take her into my arms and tell her I did this for her—to get her into character for today's shooting day. But my head tells me that's exactly what I *shouldn't* do. "No, trust me," I say, "it's for the best if I leave her alone to stew and get as angry as possible at me. Let's work out. I'll talk to Laila about everything tonight, when we get home from work."

Charlie looks at me like I'm crazy. "I realize I don't know

Laila nearly as well as you do, but we got to be pretty good friends during the tour. And I think she wanted you to follow her, Savage. Did you see the way she lingered in the doorway for a minute? It seemed like—"

"You need to trust me on this, Charlie. The best thing I can do for Laila is leave her alone, let her get pissed as hell, and throw myself on her mercy later tonight after all shooting has wrapped for the day. Now come on. I want you to really make me sweat."

EIGHTEEN

LAILA

"Where the hell is Savage?" Nadine barks at no one in particular.

It's Draft Day at *Sing Your Heart Out*. And all the judges, minus Savage, are seated at a large, round table, surrounded by the entire crew and staff, ready to start shooting. Savage's ass should have been sitting in the empty seat next to mine a full fifteen minutes ago, but he's nowhere to be found.

Nadine looks at me, her dark eyes fierce. "Where's your boyfriend, Laila? He's *your* responsibility, remember?"

"He'll be here any minute . . ." I say reflexively, even though I haven't heard from my ward all morning. Not since I left him in our home gym with Charlie. I've texted Savage, repeatedly, in the last few minutes, asking him where the heck he is, but he hasn't answered. I look beyond the nearest camera, toward the backstage area, praying I'll see Savage walking toward the set at the last minute, the way he always does in situations like this. But, no. There's no sign of him.

"I'll give him a quick call from my dressing room," I say. "Be right back."

Before anyone can reply, I bolt away and sprint down the hallway leading to my dressing room. How could Savage do this to me—*today*, of all days, when he knows I'm freaking out about my head being on the chopping block? Savage promised to help me today, and so far—

Oh, Jesus.

That fucking idiot.

Savage thought he was *helping* me this morning by inviting Charlie over, didn't he? And yet, as I know full well, inviting Charlie to the house to interrogate him, and find out the truth, once and for all, about my supposed tour fling with Charlie, was actually something Savage needed to do for *himself*. Yes, I'm sure Savage told himself he invited Charlie for my benefit. But in reality, whether Savage realizes it or not, he was pretending to wear a suit of armor for me, in order to get something he desperately wanted for himself, all along.

I poke my head into Savage's dressing room, and when he's not there, I head to mine, figuring I'll do what I said I'd do—give him a call. But when I swing open the door of my dressing room, there he is. Adrian Savage. Languidly lounging on the couch, like he doesn't have a care in the world.

"What the hell is wrong with you?" I bellow. "Everyone is waiting for you!"

"Oh, hey, Fitzy," he says. He puts his arms behind his head. "Turns out you *didn't* fuck Charlie during the tour! I wonder why you didn't tell me that."

"We'll talk about it later," I grit out through my teeth. "As your babysitter, I *order* you to head to the set now. I told you I'm on the chopping block today. How could this possibly help me, when the producers consider your misbehavior as *mine*?"

Savage stands and winks at me. "Don't worry about today. I've got a good feeling we'll deliver everything Nadine asked for, and more."

So, that's it. Savage has convinced himself he's helping me out—being an asshole in order to inspire me to slap the shit out of him on-camera today—when in reality, he's been dying to scratch this particular itch for months. That's so Savage, it makes me want to punch his gorgeous face. "I'm not *faking* my anger toward you, if that's what you think," I say. "I'm not 'playing along.' I'm genuinely pissed and *hurt* about the stunt you pulled this morning."

He looks shocked by my word choice. "*Hurt?*"

"We'll talk about it later. Right now, I need you to act like a professional."

"What do you mean you're *hurt*? You mean you're *annoyed*. Pissed off. Miffed. Frustrated. Maybe even embarrassed I caught you red-handed in a lie. But *hurt*?"

"Don't tell me what I'm allowed to feel, Adrian. Trust me, I'll be happy to explain my emotions to you, in full, later. Unfortunately, if I start explaining myself to you now, I won't be able to stop. In fact, it's fifty-fifty I'll burst into tears."

"*Tears?*" Savage blurts, looking horrified. "*Why?* Laila, what's going on?"

"I can't, Savage. Not with everyone waiting on us and my makeup done and a fucking buy-out clause hanging over me." I point. "Just, please, get your clueless ass in there and don't say another word about this morning until the cameras are off for the last time tonight."

Savage stands, looking uncertain. "I was trying to help you by inviting Charlie to the house. Surely, you've figured that out."

"Go."

His brow furrowed, he walks past me, out of the room, and I follow him into the hallway. When he stops and inhales like he's about to speak, I cut him off.

"No," I say. "Don't talk about it. Just *go*."

"I don't understand you," Savage mutters. "No good deed goes unpunished."

"Shut the fuck up and *go*."

He takes a few steps, his body language reflecting confusion . . . and then stops in the hallway, turns around, and flashes me a huge smile. "You're fucking with me. Ha! Okay. Good. This is good."

"*Go*."

He winks. "You got it, Fitzy. Bring it, baby. I can take it."

As he turns around, his demeanor shifts. He's lighter now. Unencumbered. Clearly, he's convinced himself on a dime I couldn't possibly be genuinely upset with him. But he's wrong about that. Very, very wrong.

We reach the sound stage and Savage whoops out a big hello to the crowd, like he's just waltzed onstage at Madison Square Garden.

"Thank God," Nadine mutters. She claps her hands as Savage and I take our assigned seats at the round table. "Okay, folks, we've got *two* episodes to shoot today, back to back, as you know, and time is tight." She glares at Savage and then me. "We're already running late today, so let's try to be as efficient as possible."

I lean sharply into Mr. Rockstar Cliché next to me and command, "Apologize to everyone for being late."

"Nah," Savage says, leaning back into his chair and spreading his thighs. "I think I'll let my babysitter do that for me. She's the one being paid half my salary to make sure I'm on time."

"Asshole," I whisper, before saying loudly to Nadine and the crowd, "Hey, everyone. Sorry about that. Savage was on a phone call with his grandmother." I glare at Savage, who's smirking infuriatingly at me. "We're very sorry and both promise, it won't happen again."

NINETEEN
SAVAGE

"Draft Day is a wrap, folks!" the director shouts, and in response, everyone around me on the stage—the three other judges, crew, and staff—sigh with relief and/or applaud. It's only lunchtime and we've still got Mentor Day left to shoot this afternoon. But, at least, after hours of bantering, bartering, haggling and fighting—that last one being mostly between Laila and me—all four judges now have their final teams. I didn't want to be the one to pick a fight with Laila today, but once she started giving me hell about that blue-haired pixie she wanted the most, Addison Swain, I actually enjoyed giving Laila as good as I got.

And it worked. Midway through the morning, Nadine came over to Laila and me and flashed us a huge smile and thumbs up. Which means, if Laila ever had cause to worry that her job was on the line today—which I'm not convinced was ever the case—I'm now positive she's in the clear. And that means whatever genuine anger my stunt this morning might have provoked in Laila, all will be forgiven by the time we leave the studio tonight. In fact, I'd bet dollars to doughnuts Laila will give me the blowjob of my life when we get home to thank me for knowing her better than she knows herself.

"Hey, everyone, before we break for lunch," the director says, and the room quiets down. "Why don't we get all four mentors out here real quick to shoot the full-cast round table discussion. We'll do some trash-talking about the teams and then break for lunch."

"Sounds great," Nadine says. She addresses a production assistant. "Wrangle the mentors from the greenroom, Gina."

"Yes, ma'am."

As crew members hustle-bustle around me, setting up whatever is coming next, I lean back in my chair and wink at Laila, who's sitting next to me at the table. "What'd I tell you, Fitzy? *We nailed it.*" I hold up my hand for a high-five, but she leaves me hanging. "Aw, come on. You can drop the act now. Our scenes together are almost done. After this little round-table thing, you'll be shooting with Colin and your team for the rest of the day." I hold up my palm again. But, again, Laila leaves me hanging. Chuckling, I grab her limp hand and thwap her palm against mine, like a parent showing a toddler how to high-five. "'Thank you, Savage,'" I say on her behalf. "'You're a genius and I'm grateful to you.'"

Laila yanks her hand from mine. "I told you not to talk about this until we're done for the day. I can't get into this right now."

"Into *what*? You know why I invited Charlie over this morning."

She leans forward and whisper-shouts, "*Stop. Talking. Now!* Somehow, I need to get through the rest of the day without screaming at you, bursting into tears, or murdering you."

I'm flabbergasted. "Bursting into *tears*? There you go again. What the hell is wrong with you?"

Her nostrils flare. "Trust me, I plan to enlighten you, in great detail, when my job is done and we're alone. For now, however, I'd appreciate you kindly pretending I'm not here."

"Laila, the only reason I invited Charlie to the house was to help you get into character today. Surely, you've figured that out by now."

"You want to know what I've 'figured out'? You're a hypocrite and a liar. Which I knew, of course. But I thought I could overlook the red flags and learn to trust you completely. I thought you'd changed. But now I know I was deluding myself."

My heart explodes with panic. "What are you talking about?"

"Quiet on the set!" the director yells, glaring at me. "Okay, let's cue the mentors! And . . . roll cameras! Mentors?"

After flashing me a little snarl, Laila plasters a fake smile on her face and turns her attention toward the entrance of the stage, where two seconds later, the show's four mentors enter.

My heart racing, I look down at the table. How does Laila not understand my ulterior motives here? Obviously, I pulled this morning's stunt to *help* her. But even if I didn't, even if there was no early-termination clause in her contract and I invited Charlie to the house this morning to find out if Laila did, in fact, screw him during the tour, then so what? Would that have been such a horrendous crime? Yes, it would have been a bit immature of me. Obsessive, maybe. But would it have been enough of a misstep to undo all the goodwill and trust I've built with Laila since living with her?

If so, then I guess what we've been building is a whole lot less sturdy then I've been thinking.

"Okay, judges, let's have you get up and greet your respective mentors," the director calls out. And we four judges dutifully spring into action.

When I reach Kendrick, he grips my palm in a sideways handshake, the same greeting he usually gives me, and I can't help sneaking a peek at Laila to find out how she's greeting Colin. Well, that figures. She's kissing Colin's cheek. Probably trying to get a rise out of me. Classic Laila.

I look away, and by chance, discover Aloha greeting Fish with a kiss to his cheek. *See?* I say to myself. *There's no reason to panic. Laila doesn't want to jump Colin's bones any more than Aloha wants to jump Fish's.*

"Okay, got it," the director says. "Now, everyone take seats at the round table, with judges and mentors next to each other, and we'll do a few minutes of trash-talking about the teams before breaking for lunch."

All eight of us take seats, as instructed, and proceed to banter and hype up our teams for the next fifteen minutes or so. Until, finally, the director yells cut. "Before I release you for lunch," he says, "let's get some pickups and close-ups with each judge-mentor duo. Laila and Colin, you're up first!" The director points toward a mark on the other side of the soundstage, and Laila and Colin get up and head to where he's indicated, with Laila not even bothering to look at me before she leaves.

"You're freaking out about Colin again, huh?" Kendrick says in a whisper, the minute Laila and Colin are gone. "Dude, Laila's only doing what the director tells her to do. The same as the photographer during that photo shoot."

I run my palm down my face. "I messed up today, KC." I

tell him the gist of this morning's stunt involving Charlie, and then add, "I thought I was helping Laila and now she's pissed at me in a way that feels disproportionate. For a while, I thought she had to be playing along, but now it seems she's genuinely pissed at me. She keeps saying she's 'hurt' and that she's trying not to burst into 'tears.' And I'm like, '*What the fuck is going on?*'"

Kendrick shakes his head. "I told you not to do anything with that information about Charlie. I told you to let bygones be bygones, Savage! But did you listen to me? *No.*"

"I was *helping* her, man."

"No, you were being a vindictive dick."

"Not this time! I swear to God."

The director yells, "Okay, let's have Kendrick and Savage over here next!"

With a long exhale, I get up with Kendrick and walk to the middle of the soundstage, passing Laila and Colin as they return to the table. Of course, Laila doesn't look at me as she passes. On the contrary, she pretends to be deep in conversation with her assigned mentor who just so happens to be an underwear model, as well as a kickass, tatted drummer. And suddenly, I feel like everything I've ever done to show Laila who I really am doesn't matter. I'm right back at square one with her. So why even bother to try?

When we reach our mark, the director tells Kendrick and me what to do, and we go through the motions, after which the director moves on to shooting the other two remaining judge-mentor duos while I resume my seat next to Laila. Finally, lunchtime is called. The director shouts, "After lunch, let's start with Laila and Colin and Laila's team, while the other judges and mentors rotate through some B-roll with their teams. Take forty-five, people!"

There's a commotion around us, as people begin scattering, and Aloha and Fish head over to Colin and Laila sitting to my right. There's a brief conversation I can't make out because that Penelope fucker—Jon's mentor—has waltzed over to Kendrick on my left and is talking way too loudly to him in my ear.

"Yeah, sounds good," I hear Laila saying, just before she and Colin rise from the table.

"Oh, is everyone headed to lunch together?" I ask, thinking I'll invite myself and Kendrick to join Laila and her group, whether Laila likes it or not.

"No, Colin and I are going to grab box lunches and eat in my dressing room, instead of joining Fish and Aloha in the cafeteria. Colin wants me to give him the 4-1-1 about each of my contestants before he meets them after lunch. Hi, Kendrick."

"Hi, Laila."

"I'm so happy to see you. Let's catch up later."

"Sounds good."

Without a word to me, Laila heads off with Colin, leaving me watching her departing frame like a dog pressing his nose against a window as his owner heads off to work.

"Ooph, she's definitely pissed at you," Kendrick whispers once Laila is out of earshot.

"I told you. I thought she'd understand what I was trying to do for her. I actually thought she'd be *grateful* for what I did, but she's gone off the deep end."

"Well, it's not like you came into today with a clean slate."

I turn my head sharply to scowl at Kendrick. "What the hell does that mean?"

Kendrick looks unfazed by my death glare. "It means the

stunt you pulled this morning was the same kind of shit you pulled throughout the tour. Maybe she's thinking the past weeks were a blip—an act—and now you've reverted back to true form."

I roll my eyes. "That can't be it. Laila's been living with me, night and day, Kendrick. She's seen me sing Mimi to sleep. We've had deep conversations and watched movies and eaten meals together. She knows who I am. She knows what I'm really about. Or, at least, I thought she did."

Kendrick shrugs. "That was my best guess. I mean, Laila's not crazy. Passionate, yes. Does she have a bit of a temper? Yes. But she's not legit *nuts*. So there's got to be *something* logical behind her reaction."

I look toward the exit again and exhale, feeling every cell in my body vibrating with the need to understand what's going on. To fix it, whatever it is. "I'll go to her dressing room now, and ask her—"

"No, no, not now." Kendrick sighs from the depths of his soul. "I wish I had a recording of me saying that to you, so I could press a button and save my vocal cords."

"I can't sit here and play it cool, KC. Laila is in her dressing room with Colin, feeling far more pissed off at me for what I did than is logical. God only knows what that crazy woman is thinking—what she'd do to torture me, if she thinks I've got it coming. For all I know, she's blowing Colin in there, as we speak!"

Kendrick rolls his eyes. "Would you stop being a jealous lunatic for a minute and listen to me? I swear, when it comes to Laila, you're a madman."

"Yes, I am," I admit. "That goddamned woman turns me into a *madman*. But even so, I'm not crazy this time. I can feel in my bones Colin wants her. He didn't suggest they eat lunch in Laila's dressing room, alone, to talk about Laila's contestants. He asked her in there so he could finally make his move."

"Oh, for the love of fuck. Even if you're right about that, don't you trust Laila? She wants *you,* man. Not *him.* You."

I run my hand through my hair. "But does she, though? Right now, I feel the same way I did when Laila didn't come to my room during the tour! I thought she wanted me then, too, Kendrick. I would have bet any amount of money. But she never came to me and ignored me and blocked my number, and to this day, I can't understand why! And now, here I am wondering why she's spinning out of control, simply because I invited Charlie to our house—"

"To prove she's a liar."

"To help her get into character!"

"Okay, calm down." Kendrick sighs. "I'm sure she'll explain herself tonight. But for now, let's get some lunch and let the girl do her job, okay? She and Colin are up first after lunch, so they really do have work to do before then. Let's let them do it."

I place my elbows on the table and my head in my hands. "I swear, that woman has taken *years* off my life."

Kendrick pats my back. "At some point, you've got to decide to trust her, Savage. That's what this all boils down to —you finally deciding to trust a woman, completely. To let your guard down with Laila, once and for all, and *trust.*"

Emotion surges inside of me. "How can I trust Laila when she didn't come to my room, when I was *so* sure she would? How can I trust a woman who wanted to be with Malik fucking Wallace after he so *clearly* showed her and everyone at that restaurant what a flaming asshole he is? How, how, how, Kendrick?"

"And how can *Laila* trust *you* when she thinks you're the guy who fucked that waitress and all those groupies? You weren't her boyfriend at the time, true, but she thinks she knows how you roll, man."

"She has to know I was full of shit about all that stuff by now!"

"But does she, though? Have you come clean to her about everything yet?"

I rub my forehead. "No. Once I get started talking, it's gonna be a *lot*. I want to be sure I'm all-in before I head down that road."

"Well, then, if you ask me, you can't be too surprised when she doesn't trust you any more than you trust her. My advice? You two need to sit down and talk this out, from top to bottom. Just talk to her and tell her everything."

I throw up my hands. "You specifically told me *not* to tell her a goddamned thing until I was positive of my feelings for her, or else you'd beat me up."

"That's still true." He smiles sympathetically. "But it seems to me you're pretty fucking sure about your feelings at this point, man."

I process that for a beat, and then lean back in my seat, feeling overwhelmed. "Kendrick, I'd crawl over a hundred miles of broken glass for that woman. I'd do *anything* for her. Literally *anything*. And yet, clearly, no matter what I do, she doesn't trust me as far as she can throw me. *And I don't understand why.*"

I take a seat next to Colin on the couch in my dressing room and begin opening my box lunch. "Thanks so much for meeting with me about my team," I say excitedly. "I can't wait to hear your thoughts about—"

"I didn't ask you here to talk about your team," Colin interrupts. "Sorry. I only said that to get you away from Savage."

My eyebrows shoot up. "Oh?"

"There's something I need to talk to you about, Laila. Something confidential." Colin places his box lunch on the coffee table in front of us. "I'm breaching my NDA with the show to tell you about this, but, as your friend, I can't keep it from you. Please, don't tell the producers I told you. Also, don't tell Savage. That guy's a loose cannon."

I nod and wait, my stomach tight with dread. I'm not sure I won't tell Savage whatever Colin is about to tell me, but I'm too nervous to speak, one way or the other.

Colin runs an anxious hand through his dark hair. "I found out yesterday the producers want me here to create the potential for a love triangle with you and Savage. They want me to create the impression that I'm your ex during our scenes together. I guess there's some chatter about that, online, and they don't want me to dispel it."

"Well, it's not true, obviously, so we'll just be ourselves, and—"

"That's not the part that made me feel like I needed to talk to you. I'm just giving you background." He sighs. "The big thing is the bonus they've offered me. During a break this afternoon, they want me to lure you to that patio in the back of the studio and make a move on you. They said they'll pay me a hundred grand if I do it today. Fifty grand if you're seen leaving my place in the early morning hours over the next two weeks. They didn't say it, but the implication was they'd arrange a photographer, who'd then 'leak' the photo to a click-bait farm. Or maybe they have faith someone out there in the world would organically take a photo of us. I guess that's pretty realistic, considering how much press you and Savage get. Basically, they want it to look like it's at least *possible* you're cheating on Savage with me. Or that you're tempted. Or maybe I'm your ex and you're not totally over me. They hit me with a lot of weird shit, Laila. I don't even know if *they* know what they want. All I know is they're looking to screw you over, and I'm not going to be a party to that or let it happen on my watch."

I touch his arm, trembling with adrenaline. "I can't thank you enough for telling me about this, Colin."

"Of course. I couldn't believe my ears."

"Who talked to you about this?"

"Nadine. She's the mastermind here. And she's ruthless."

I exhale. "I should have known this job was too good to

be true. They never wanted me here. They wanted their usual three judges for the live shows—the same format they've always had. In fact, when that Instagrammer's video first hit, they only wanted me as Savage's mentor and fake girlfriend for three episodes. They never wanted me as a judge, but my agent strong-armed them. I guess they've figured out a way to make lemonade out of the Laila lemons they never wanted in the first place."

"They're idiots," Colin says. "You're incredible, Laila. So talented and beautiful. Funny and witty. I watched you guys shooting Draft Day on the monitors while I was waiting in the greenroom, and I was so impressed with how natural and charismatic you're able to be on-camera. You're totally yourself, other than pretending you give a shit about Savage."

My heart pangs sharply. "I'm not pretending anything when it comes to Savage," I confess. "Our relationship was fake when I first told you about it at Reed's. But it's not anymore. It's as real as it gets." Colin looks skeptical, so I add, "At least, it's real for me."

Colin looks sympathetic. Like he thinks I'm a fool. And that's all it takes for the image of Savage walking down that hallway in Las Vegas with that groupie, one arm around her shoulders and the other holding a bottle of booze, to pop into my head and make me realize Colin is right: *I'm a fool.*

Colin assesses me for a long moment. "You're in love with him?"

My breathing hitches. Savage and I have never labeled what we feel, and I don't think I've admitted the full depths of my feelings for Savage, even to myself. I blink and a tear leaks out of my eye and streaks down my cheek. "Before today, I would have answered that question, yes, without a doubt. But today, he did something that made me realize it's probably not going to work out between us." I sniffle and wipe my cheek. "It's too bad, honestly. I've had the time of my life with him. I was feeling pretty swept away."

"Aw, Laila. Come here. Cry on my shoulder."

"Thank you."

Colin opens his muscled arms and I scooch over to him on the couch and let him wrap me in a warm hug, just as soggy tears begin falling down my cheeks.

"What'd he do?"

"It's too much to explain. Bottom line, Savage can't handle being happy. If he's feeling too happy, he has this weird compulsion to mess it up, one way or another, even against his own interests."

There's a knock at the door and I lurch away from Colin, worried someone is going to burst in with a camera and snap a photo that makes me look like I'm doing something I'm not. But thank God, it's only one of the PA's calling to me from behind the closed door. "Fifteen minutes, guys!"

"Thank you!" I call toward the door. And when I hear receding footsteps, I smile with relief at Colin. "For a split-second, I thought someone was going to barge in here and snap a photo of me crying on your shoulder."

"Aw, Laila, you poor thing," he says. And there's no doubt in my mind he's being sincere . . . but also, semi-hitting on me. Thankfully, however, Colin has the emotional intelligence not to do anything too overt in this moment.

"It's interesting they offered you a hundred grand to 'lead me astray' today," I say. "That's the same amount they'd have to pay to buy me out of my contract. Sounds like they want me gone, one way or another, for a hundred grand. I'm sure if they're not successful convincing you to do their bidding, they'll move on to Plan B and get rid of me in a much less exciting way. Either way, I'm guessing I'll be gone during the break."

"That sucks."

I shrug. "It was fun while it lasted."

"So . . . are you planning to stay with Savage when the show is over for you, or is this more like a tour fling—the show ends, and the relationship ends?"

"I don't know what the future holds for Savage and me," I admit. "But I feel like I should tell you . . . either way, you and I probably aren't destined to be more than friends, Colin."

He grins. "I'm that transparent, huh?"

"I had a hunch."

"Thanks for letting me know. I appreciate that."

"I appreciate you thinking I'm worthy of you. You're an amazing guy."

He pauses. "Are you turning me down because of your feelings for Savage, or because you're not attracted to me, regardless?"

I consider my answer for a moment and realize I like and respect Colin too much not to answer him with complete honesty. "I don't think the word 'regardless' is in my vocabulary anymore, in this context, because I can't imagine a world where I wouldn't want Savage. Even though he did something today that pissed me off and made me think I'm an idiot to want him, I still do. In fact, it's impossible for me to imagine wanting anyone else. So, given that, it's pretty hard for me to tell you if I'd be attracted to you, *regardless* of my feelings for Savage, when the truth is my heart and soul and body belong to him."

"Wow," Colin says, looking shocked.

"Before you tell me I'm a fool," I add quickly, "I already

FALLING INTO LOVE WITH YOU   171

know that. My brain knows this won't end well for me, but I guess I need to let it run its course, or my heart will never give up on him. Never get over him." Tears prick my eyes again and I wipe them. "Shit. My makeup is going to be a mess."

Colin pats the couch next to him and I scootch over again, grateful to let him comfort me. I lean into Colin's open arms, saying, "Thank you for telling me everything, Colin." But midsentence, as the second half of my comment falls out of my mouth and my body falls into Colin's waiting arms, Savage bursts into the room, his dark eyes blazing and bugging out.

"Savage," I blurt, leaping off the couch to standing.

"What the fuck?" he blurts. He looks between Colin and me. "*Laila?*"

"Nothing happened! I was upset. Colin is a friend who offered a shoulder to cry on."

"*Yeah, he did,*" Savage spits out, looking murderous. He marches toward Colin, looking homicidal, his fists clenched. And in reply, Colin leaps to standing next to me, ready to defend himself. I lurch in front of Savage, blocking his progress, and, thankfully, he stops and shifts his weight from foot to foot, his energy like a live wire that's come loose and is now zapping wildly on the ground.

"You hit on her," Savage barks at Colin. "When you *knew* she was with me!"

"I thought your relationship was *fake,*" Colin says. "And by the way, she turned me down. So now what, Savage? You're gonna beat the shit out of me for taking my shot? I didn't beat the shit out of *you* when you *fucked* my woman, but you're gonna throw down when I've done nothing but give yours a shoulder to cry on?" Savage's dark eyes shift to mine, looking guilty as hell, as Colin adds, "Maybe you should be more worried about *why* Laila needed a shoulder to cry on, than about who offered her that shoulder, you dumbass."

Savage looks like a caged animal as I flash him an enraged look. *He fucked Colin's girlfriend?* And the man has the nerve to freak out about me *talking* to Colin?

"There you are!" a male voice says, as Savage opens his mouth to say God-knows-what, and thank God, Kendrick appears a second later and grabs Savage's tense shoulders. "Come on, man. Don't do this."

Savage shakes off Kendrick's grip and looks at me plaintively, like he's on the cusp of a total and complete breakdown. "Do you want him?" he rasps out, motioning to Colin. "Is that why you didn't want me? Have you wanted Colin all along?"

"No!" I yell. "Colin is my *friend,* as I've told you many times—the same way *Ruby* is yours!"

"Yeah, well, I've never dragged Ruby into a room alone so I could hit on her!"

"Fuck you," Colin says. "I didn't do anything wrong."

"And neither did I!" Savage booms. He returns to me. "I was trying to *help* you this morning by inviting Charlie over. I don't understand why you're—"

"Of course, you don't understand!" I shout, anger flashing through my nerve endings. "Because you have the emotional intelligence of an amoeba and the impulse control of a gnat! Now, please, go, Savage. I need to wash my face and touch up my makeup before Colin and I start shooting with my team in five minutes. Kendrick, please." I point toward the door, nonverbally begging Kendrick to drag his best friend out. "I'm in charge of babysitting this boy's stupid ass, so if he disrupts the shooting schedule again, that's on *me*."

"Come on, Savage," Kendrick says, gripping Savage's arm. "Leave her alone to do her job."

Thankfully, Savage lets Kendrick guide him toward the door. But before Savage exits, he shakes off Kendrick's grip, turns around, and flashes me one last tortured look, followed by a white-hot, murderous one at Colin. And then, Adrian Savage, the man who can't get out of his own fucking way, turns around and stalks out the door . . . but not before leaving a lovely parting gift for me: *a fist-sized hole in the wall next to the doorframe.*

"You had sex with Colin's girlfriend?" Laila shouts, the minute the door closes behind us in the SUV. Draft Day is in the can. Mentor Day is in the can. And now, finally, we're alone and headed home to our fake love nest to begin a much-needed three-week break from shooting—time I've been eager to spend with Laila. First, in Chicago, then, in Cabo, and finally, back at home in LA for a week of relaxation while the show begins airing. But after today, I'm not sure Laila is still planning to spend a minute of the break with me, let alone travel to see my family or drink piña coladas with me on a Mexican beach. I'm not even sure if Laila is planning to continue living with me for the remainder of the season, even for the sake of our written contracts.

In response to Laila's angry question about Colin's "girlfriend," I call out to our two usual escorts at the front of the car and ask them to turn up the music—and the minute the volume in the car ratchets up enough to swallow my voice, I reply to Laila. "No, I didn't have sex with Colin's *girlfriend*. I had sex with Colin's *ex*-girlfriend."

Laila scoffs. "Gee, I wonder why they broke up."

"It had nothing to do with me. They'd already broken up when I got with her."

"Colin said 'I didn't beat you up when you fucked my *girlfriend*.'"

"No, he said, 'when you fucked my *woman*.' Which means, apparently, Colin thinks his *single* ex was off-limits to me and every man on the planet—a concept I'm sure you strongly disagree with, as an independent, sex-positive woman."

"He didn't mean 'every man on the planet,' Savage. He meant *you*. I'm sure Colin considered you a *friend* when you nailed his girlfriend."

"*Ex*-girlfriend. And no. Colin and I travel in the same circles, but we've never been anything more than acquaintances. Ask any of my *actual* friends, Kendrick or Kai or Titus, ask Fish or C-Bomb, and they'll *all* tell you I'm as loyal as the day is long. Laila, I stepped aside from hitting on *you*—despite my *huge* crush on you—for a *friend*. But with Colin's *ex*, I was supposed to say, 'No, no, sorry, I can't have sex with you because you dated a guy whose band is *also* signed to my label?' Give me a break."

Laila pouts but doesn't reply.

"They'd been broken up for a full week," I mutter. "She was a free woman."

"A week?" Laila shouts. "Savage! You were her rebound fuck? No wonder Colin is pissed at you."

"Aaah. I see what this is about. You're jealous you're not the only woman who's enjoyed my services as a rebound fuck. You wanted to be the only one, eh?"

Laila grunts with anger. "No, Adrian, this isn't about me being jealous of Colin's ex. This is about me realizing I've ignored way too many red flags with you. This is about me realizing I can't trust a word you say!"

"What the hell are you talking about?"

"You looked me dead in the eye at Reed's house and told me Colin didn't like you because you're buddies with C-Bomb! You said Colin must be taking Dax's side in their beef. And then you had the audacity to chew me out in Reed's laundry room for supposedly *flirting* with Colin, while not bothering to mention to me, 'Oh, gee, come to think of it, Colin *might* be pissed at me because I banged his ex-girlfriend, rather than because he's siding with his best friend in a stupid beef with C-Bomb'!"

"I didn't *lie* to you. I just didn't tell you the whole truth because I didn't want you thinking Colin was flirting with you to retaliate against *me*."

"Oooooh, so let me get this straight. You *lied* to my face—oh, sorry, 'didn't tell me the whole truth' to my face—in order to protect my sensitive feelings?"

"I shaved the truth a bit to protect your feelings, yes."

"And once again, you prove, without a doubt, you're a liar. The truth is you wanted to get laid that night, and you figured telling me about the time you railed Colin's ex a week after they'd broken up wasn't going to help your cause."

I pull a face that concedes she's got a point. "I suppose it could've been that, at least in part."

Laila throws up her hands. "See what I mean? I can't believe a word out of your mouth!"

"I just copped to wanting to get laid that night!" I shout. "Jesus, Laila! I feel like you're looking for things to be mad at me about, when what you're really mad about is Charlie, for reasons I can't comprehend, since I only invited him over to help you tap into your inner bitch! Which, by the way, you *did*—briliantly, all day long. *You're welcome.* But guess what? You can stop being a bitch now, Laila, now that the cameras are off!"

Laila gasps, and I immediately regret my comment. *Come on, Savage. You're trying to make amends here. Not fan the flames.*

"You 'can't *comprehend*' the reason I'm mad about *Charlie?*" Laila booms. "Okay, then, amoeba boy, let me explain it to you in terms your amoeba-sized brain can understand. *You're* the one who said we should put the past behind us and press the reset button. *You're* the one who said we should forget the past and move forward—so, that's what I've tried to do, with all my might. And you have no idea the mental gymnastics it took to do that! But I did! And then, what did you do? The boy who can't help self-sabotaging couldn't resist dredging up the past this morning, despite what *he* suggested we do, because he couldn't resist finding out, once and for all, if I'd let Charlie plow me during the tour!"

"Oh, my fucking God. Laila, I already knew about Charlie's family situation when I asked him to come to the house. Kendrick told me about Charlie's husband *yesterday*. I only invited Charlie over when you started freaking out about your job being on the line. I thought me supposedly finding out that Charlie is married and gay, right in front of you, would give you something to chew on during today's shoot. *And I was right about that!*"

Laila shakes her head. "Don't you see? You bringing Charlie into our *new* life, after we explicitly agreed to forgive and forget the past, made me realize you're still that guy from the tour, the one who wanted groupies more than *me*, no matter how much I try to—"

"I didn't want groupies, Laila! I only wanted *you*. All those groupies were a set-up! I thought you knew that. The same with that waitress in New York. I never even called her, Laila! I only got her number to piss you off, because I was so jealous of watching you and Malik!"

To my shock, tears prick Laila's eyes. "I saw you bringing a groupie to your room—and that was most definitely *not* a set-up."

"What? Where?"

"The fact that you don't even know which city I'm referring to isn't a good sign, Savage."

My heart is stampeding. "Laila, no. Whatever you saw, it wasn't what you thought. Women throw themselves at me, all the time, but that doesn't mean I *catch* them. I wasn't with anyone but you on that tour, Laila. Nobody but you."

She scoffs and a dam of panic and despair breaks inside me. I've been so happy with this girl. So fucking happy. How is everything falling apart so fast and suddenly?

"What happened today?" I shout, my frustration and panic boiling over. "Do you want Colin, so you're trying to get me to break up with you? Is that it?"

She wipes away a tear. "No. I've just realized I'm in way too deep with you. At your core, you're still the same guy from the tour. The Beast from *before* the snowball fight. I've realized I need to slow this thing down before I get myself really, really hurt."

"I'm not going to hurt you, Laila."

I try to grab her hand, but she yanks it away.

"You already did!" she screams. "I told you about my

father! I told you how scary and horrible he was! I asked you not to punch holes in walls or—"

"Oh, God, Laila. I'm so sorry. Please forgive me. That was so stupid of me."

"How could you do that, when I told you how much that kind of thing triggers me?"

I open and close my mouth. But there's no excuse. No words I could possibly say to make it better.

"You did it to *hurt* me!" she says. "Plain and simple. So, tell me, Savage, why would I want to be with a man who *wants* to hurt me?"

My heart feels like it's physically shattering. I didn't plan to punch that wall. I didn't make a conscious decision to do it. But I suppose it's only fair to say I knew, deep down, somewhere inside me, that punching that wall would scare the shit out of Laila. And I did it, anyway. Did I punch that wall to push her away, to make her leave me *now*, rather than later, when losing her would wreck me all that much more? Did I subconsciously do it to see if doing the unthinkable would make Laila finally leave me, the same way I did horrible shit at first with Mimi, to see if there was something, anything, that would make *her* leave me, too? For fuck's sake, did I set that kitchen fire at my apartment in Phoenix on purpose, like my mother always says I did? Despite everything, despite all the love Mimi has given to me, all the lessons she's tried to teach me, was it all for nothing because, at my core, I'm my father's son—*and always will be?*

"I'm sorry, Laila," I choke out, my emotions hanging on by a thread. "I'd never harm a hair on your head. I'd die to protect you. I'd do *anything* for you. But you're right: punching that hole in the wall was unforgivable."

Her lower lip trembles. "I don't feel physically threatened by you, Adrian. But I do think you need some sort of therapy. Anger management, maybe. You made a promise to me and you should have been able to control yourself and keep it."

I clench my jaw. My knee-jerk reaction is to reply, "Well, if I need therapy, then you do, too, sweetheart, because you're definitely a few bricks shy of a load." But, luckily, I'm not stupid enough to give voice to my honest thoughts. My next thought is, "Please forgive me, Laila. I'll do whatever it takes to make you stay with me. To make you happy. *To make you love me.*" But those words don't come out, either.

"For what it's worth," I mumble. "I think my brain didn't connect the promise I made to you at the house to your dressing room. It's stupid, I know, but I think maybe not being at the house made me forget . . ." I stop talking, based on the incredulity I'm seeing on Laila's face, and whisper, "Regardless, I made a promise to you and I broke it. I'm sorry."

Laila holds my gaze for a long beat and then looks out the window on her side of the car at passing traffic, effectively letting me know this conversation is over, and that she emphatically does *not* forgive me.

I pick up my phone and murmur, "I need to call Mimi, before it gets too late. I've missed bedtime the last three nights." I pause, hoping the mention of Mimi's name will prompt Laila to tell me if she's still planning to come to Chicago with me tomorrow. But when Laila doesn't say a word, but continues silently staring out her side of the car, I add, "While I'm talking to Mimi, I'd appreciate you pretending you still like me. My grandma still thinks we're blissfully happy and I'd like her to keep thinking it for Christmas—and for however long she's got."

Laila looks away from the window, rolling her eyes. "I won't scream at you or flip you off while you're speaking to your ailing grandmother, Adrian, if that's what you think. And you know why? Because I've got this weird thing called *impulse control*. Ask a therapist about it sometime."

Annoyance floods me. I think, "Yeah, Laila. You're a paragon of maturity." But thanks to *my* impulse control, I don't say it. After taking a few deep breaths, I press the button to FaceTime my cousin—and the minute Sasha picks up, even before saying hello, she says, "What's wrong?"

"Nothing," I reply. "We just got done with a long shooting day. Can you put Mimi on, so I can sing to her? I'm in a bad mood and not wanting to chat."

"Mimi's already asleep. I texted you an hour ago to let you know it was now or never."

I rub my face with my palm. "I didn't see your text. I was shooting and didn't have my phone."

"It's okay. You'll be here tomorrow."

I glance at the time on the dashboard of the SUV. "She fell asleep an *hour* ago? That's awfully early, Sasha."

"The move has been exhausting for her."

I furrow my brow with concern. "But she likes the house, right?"

My cousin smiles broadly. "She *loves* the house. Of course, she does, Adrian. You gave her an incredible gift. Mimi says she sees Jasper in every nook and cranny."

My heart skips a beat. "I can't wait to carry her around from room to room and hear all her stories."

"Mimi is so excited you're coming. That's all she's been talking about—getting to see you and Laila, in person."

I glance at my fake girlfriend next to me to gauge her reaction to Sasha's comment, and instantly surmise Laila is feeling conflicted. "Hey, I need to put you on hold for a sec, Cuz," I say, before muting the call. I look at Laila. "Are you still coming to Chicago tomorrow? If not, I need to give Sasha a heads-up so she can break the bad news to Mimi when she wakes up in the morning."

Laila pauses and I hold my breath, bracing myself. "I'll come," she finally decides. "*Mimi* didn't say we should leave the past behind us and then turn around and invite Charlie to the house, and *Mimi* didn't punch a hole in the wall, after promising she wouldn't."

"Thank you."

"I'm not doing it for you."

"Any drop of happiness you bring to my grandmother is a huge gift to me. So, thank you." With that, I unmute the call with my cousin. "Sorry about that. Laila and I will be landing around five tomorrow. I'll text you when we're driving to the house."

"Perfect. See you soon."

"Oh, hey. I ordered a bunch of groceries to be delivered to the house tomorrow morning—everything for Mimi's famous raviolis. I thought Mimi could show Laila and me how an expert makes pasta from scratch tomorrow."

Sasha pauses, ever so briefly. But it's long enough to make the hair on the back of my neck stand up.

"What?" I ask.

"I wouldn't get your hopes up too high about Mimi cooking with you during your visit, Ady. Mimi's been really tired lately."

My breathing catches. "I'll make sure Mimi gets plenty of rest, I promise. But I have to see her cooking like a boss in that huge gourmet kitchen."

Sasha smiles thinly, but says nothing.

I take a shallow breath. "Okay, well. Gotta go. See you tomorrow."

"Sleep tight and travel safe," Sasha says. "Is Laila there?"

"Right here."

I shift the camera to capture Laila and she waves.

"I can't wait to see you in person," Sasha says.

"Same here," Laila replies. "Thank you for taking such good care of Mimi."

"Thank you for taking such good care of Adrian."

"Okay, bye now," I say, abruptly shifting the camera back to myself. "Love you, Sash."

I hang up the call, feeling physically ill. If I hadn't messed up today, that call would have been one of the most exciting of my life. If I hadn't messed up, I'd be on the cusp of taking a girl home to meet my family, for the first time in my life. For *real*. And, man, I would have been excited about that. Proud to show Laila off, as my gorgeous, talented, brilliant girlfriend. As it is, however, for reasons I still don't fully understand, it seems like we're hanging on by the barest of threads, if at all.

Our SUV reaches the iron gate in front of our reality TV mansion and our driver punches in the code—and when we roll into our driveway, we see a car already parked in front of the house.

"Fuck," I say, suddenly remembering. "Fish and Alessandra. We're writing our sappy love song tonight, remember?"

"Fuck," Laila replies. She shakes her head. "Well, all I can say is thank God for Fish and Alessandra. Because as hard as it's been to write a song about our 'undying love' the past few weeks, it'd be fucking impossible now."

TWENTY-TWO

LAILA

When Savage and I enter our large kitchen, Fish and Alessandra are already there, seated on stools at the island while our private chef prepares something on the stove.

Savage and I greet Fish and Alessandra and the chef. We thank our friends for coming here to save our asses and chat about today's long shoot, since three out of four of us were there. And through it all, I can't bring myself to look at Savage, even once.

After some more small talk, we sit down at the kitchen table and eat the meal our chef has prepared. As we eat, I keep catching Savage staring at me, his eyes begging for forgiveness. And I must admit, despite everything, my anger thaws a bit every time I look into his dark, tormented eyes. My solution? I try to avoid looking into Savage's eyes, as much as possible. However much living with Savage in this TV mansion has made me swoon, today made me realize there's too much baggage between us, too much jealousy and hypocrisy and popcorn lies, for us to move forward together, as a real couple, outside of this carefully curated bubble. Which means I'd better get my heart extricated *now* from this situation, before it's too late.

After our meal ends, our foursome heads into the living room to get to work, with Savage and Fish grabbing acoustic guitars, Alessandra taking an armchair with her laptop, and me taking a seat behind the baby grand.

"Okay," Fish says on an exhale, tuning the guitar in his lap. "Reed said this song should be a 'classic love song.' He said he wants it 'sweet and romantic.'"

"Pure, gooey goodness," Alessandra chimes in.

Fish looks at Savage and me. "Is that your understanding, too?"

"Yep," Savage says.

"Cool," Fish replies. "Let's write a hit love song, guys."

"Thank God you and Alessandra came over to help us out," I say. "Left to our own devices, Savage and I couldn't write 'pure, gooey goodness' to save our lives."

Savage looks like I've slapped him in the face. "Well, I wouldn't go *that* far," he mutters, and I quickly look away from his pained expression.

"It shouldn't be too hard for the four of us geniuses to write something, on-brand, if we put our heads together," Fish says. And Alessandra concurs. But when the pair looks at Savage and me for confirmation . . . they get crickets. Nothing. In fact, with each passing second of silence, the air in the room is becoming increasingly thick and stilted.

Alessandra clears her throat. "So, have you two worked up any ideas to get us started, or . . . ?"

"We've got nothing," I reply, letting my eyes return to Savage's. And when the words leave my lips, he physically winces in reply, like I've lashed him with a whip. Crap.

Maybe that was a bit harsh of me. My heart aching, I peel my eyes off Savage's tormented face and return to Fish and Alessandra. "We've tried to write this song, over and over again. But everything we've come up with has been all wrong. Way too intense and passionate and angsty for the assignment."

"I think a little angst would be okay, here and there," Alessandra says.

"Yeah, well, angst is all we've got, unfortunately."

Alessandra looks at Fish. And then back at me. "I do think the song should feel authentic to you two, regardless of the assignment, since you're the ones who'll be singing it. And you're both extremely intense and passionate people. Why don't you guys let Fish and me get the ball rolling, to lay the groundwork for something on the lighter side, and then we'll let you two sprinkle in some details in the verses that are more personal to you. Little details here and there that will make the song feel tailored to you?"

"Love it, babe," Fish says. He looks at Savage and me, but we say nothing. "Is that approach cool with you guys?"

"Great," I say, while Savage strums his guitar and mutters, "Whatever you want to do."

Alessandra and Fish look at each other again for a long beat, their expressions clearly saying, "What the heck?" But after her nonverbal conversation with Fish, Alessandra turns to the group and suggests everyone think about a person we love unconditionally and without complication. "Not necessarily in a romantic way," Alessandra prompts. "I want you to think about the purest, easiest form of love in your life and meditate on the way that kind of love makes you feel, deep in your soul."

I quiet my mind and think about my infant niece, Everly,

who's already the light of my life in the most uncomplicated way possible. I look at Savage and instantly know who he's thinking about. *Mimi*. And, damn it, despite everything, my heart swells for him, as I think about how much that poor man loves his grandmother and can't stand the thought of losing her.

I lay my fingers on the piano keys and play the little melody Savage always sings to his grandmother at bedtime and Savage's attention snaps to me, his face as beautiful and heartbreaking as I've ever seen it.

"I love that!" Alessandra says. "Let's build on that!"

"Yeah, that's a perfect riff for the chorus," Fish agrees. "It feels like a lullaby."

"Exactly!" Alessandra says excitedly.

And that's all it takes. The minute we've got some mutual inspiration going, the song basically writes itself. In a flurry, we brainstorm some themes for our lyrics, based on our ideas about uncomplicated love. We shout out words like unconditional and endless. Eternal and infinite. And Alessandra notes everything on her laptop. We jam for a bit, building on that little lullaby sequence, and faster than I would have thought possible, the musical structure for the song and vocal melody begin taking shape.

As suggested by Alessandra earlier, Savage and I throw in a few angsty lyrics to complement the gooey-sweet ones we've already written. But, nonetheless, in the end, the song the group creates feels far more about the sweet love shared by Fish and Alessandra than about anything felt by Savage and me. But that's okay. The assignment was to write a classic love song that will make us truckloads of money after we perform it on *Sing Your Heart Out*. And I'm pretty confident we've done exactly that.

We run through the song several times, making tweaks, here and there, until, finally, everybody agrees we wouldn't change a thing.

"Let's record a quick demo and send it off to Reed for his feedback," Fish suggests. "If we need to change anything after Reed's notes, we can do that remotely while you guys are out of town."

"Sounds like a plan," I say. And when my eyes flicker to Savage, it's clear he's deeply relieved by the implication of my comment: I'm still planning to travel with him to Chicago, like I assured him earlier in the car.

We record a rough demo of the song on Fish's iPad, with me playing piano and the guys on their guitars—and Savage and I barely look at each other as we sing our parts. Fish says he'll add a few bells and whistles to the demo—stuff like programmed drums and a bassline—in order to give Reed an idea of the general vibe we're envisioning for the full production. And, finally, after Fish and Alessandra have gathered up their stuff, Savage and I walk them to the front door.

We say our goodbyes to our friends. Give them high-fives about the song. And, finally, Fish and Alessandra head out the door and into the starry night, to drive to the home they share together on the beach—to enjoy the sweet, uncomplicated, gooey goodness that is their love story.

I close the front door behind our friends and lean against it, exhaling. "What time is our flight?"

"Noon."

"Thank goodness it's not at the crack of dawn. Today was a long day." I press my lips together and wait. Savage looks like he's going to say something—something important. But in the end, he closes his mouth, bites the inside of his cheek, and sighs.

"Okay, well, goodnight," I say. "I'll wake you up when I get up, so don't worry about setting an alarm."

"Laila."

I turn around.

Savage's Adam's apple bobs. He clears his throat. "I'm so sorry I punched a hole in that wall. I can't believe I did that. I hope you can find your way to forgiving me for that, at some point. I promise on my love for Mimi I'll never, *ever* do that again, or anything else that would scare you. I'll never break a promise to you again, Laila. I'm giving you my solemn word on that."

I twist my mouth. His promises don't mean a whole lot to me. But I don't feel like fighting right now. I just want to go to sleep. "Thank you for that," I say calmly. "I need to get some sleep now. We can talk some more about that another time, maybe."

He nods. "Any time you want."

"Goodnight, Adrian."

"Goodnight, Laila."

As I walk away, I bite my lip, and somehow keep myself from crying until I get safely into one of the bedrooms down the hallway from the master. Which is where I throw myself onto the bed and cry myself to sleep.

Evanston, Illinois

"Is this still Chicago?" I ask Savage, looking out the window of our limo. After pulling away from the curbside at O'Hare, we've been driving about thirty minutes now, and the view out my window has become decidedly suburban and upscale.

"No, we're in Evanston now," Savage replies. "Mimi's house is a few blocks away."

"It's so pretty here."

"This is where Mimi lived as a teenager."

"Oh, I thought you lived with Mimi in the City."

"I did. In an apartment. But Mimi lived here with her mom when she was young."

I return to the window on my side of the car. "Was Mimi's family wealthy, or did this neighborhood become posh more recently?"

"Mimi grew up poor. Her dad died when she was twelve or thirteen, so her mom got work as a housekeeper in this neighborhood."

"Ah."

"I'll let Mimi tell you the whole story, but, basically, Mimi's mom went to work for a rich family in Evanston, and that's where Mimi met her husband, Jasper, a teenager. He was one of the rich family's teenaged sons."

It's the longest, and most relaxed, conversation Savage and I have had all day. We didn't speak at all during the drive to the airport this morning, though Savage's dark eyes pleaded with me to speak first. We barely spoke during our flight, other than to ask polite questions about legroom and the shows we were separately watching. But now that we're here, and on our way to Mimi's new house, the cold air feels too super-charged with excitement and adventure for my heart to remember to be closed off.

The limo turns onto a residential street lined with stunning mini-mansions. And when the car makes another turn, the passing homes turn from mini-mansions to actual ones—massive homes with meticulously sheared hedges and tidy walkways and iron gates. Stunning homes that look straight out of a bygone era.

"Whoa," I breathe. "These homes are gorgeous." I gasp and point. "Look at that one!"

To my shock, I've no sooner said the words than the car comes to a stop in front of the very house I'm indicating—a breathtaking mansion with countless windows framed by green-painted shutters, sprawling gardens, and brickwork walkways.

I open my mouth wide in shock. "*This* is the house you got for Mimi?"

"This is it," Savage confirms, his beautiful face radiating with pride.

As the driver exits the car and begins unloading our luggage from the back, Savage and I start bundling up for the short walk from the street to the front door. I don't know anything about architecture, so my brain can't conjure the right words to describe this home. All I can say is it looks like a "Victorian mansion" to me. Or maybe a Civil war era house? Yeah, I don't know what I'm talking about. All I know is it looks old, but painstakingly restored, and gorgeous. No wonder Savage wanted to keep his full salary from the show! I don't know how much this fancy house cost him, but I have to think Savage was depending on his full salary from the show when he decided to buy it.

"Who lives here with Mimi?" I ask, as we begin walking up the front pathway with our luggage.

"Sasha is staying here, for the time being, and Mimi's got a rotation of caregivers who stay here, too."

"I'm not sure there's enough room for everyone," I joke.

"Just barely," he replies.

"It must take a day just to vacuum the downstairs."

"I've got a maid service coming, twice a week, to keep it from getting dusty."

"Wow. I would have given anything to play hide and seek in a house like this as a kid."

Savage flashes a crooked smile. "I'd be happy to play with you during our stay, if you'd like." There's sexual innuendo buried in his tone. Knowing him, he's probably imagining himself nailing me, wherever he finds me.

"Let's not get ahead of ourselves," I say. "We're here for Mimi."

His face falls. "Yeah. Okay. Thanks again for that." He reaches for the doorknob, but stops and takes a deep breath, like he's gearing up for something.

"What?" I ask.

He bites his lip. "I know intellectually you're only here for Mimi's sake. But, still, my heart is racing. Even if this is fake, it's still a first for me—bringing a girl home to meet my family. I've never done that before, and it's kind of exciting."

Oh, crap. In a torrent, I feel the urge to throw myself into Savage's arms and kiss the hell out of him. I want to tell him to forget yesterday—to say we'll press the 'reset' button, *again*. But, this time, as much as my heart wants to ignore the red flags and bury my head in the sand and enjoy the ride, my head won't allow such foolishness.

"Just so you know," Savage says. "When we walk through this door, Mimi is going to fling her little hummingbird body at you like a missile." He chuckles. "I'm sure she's sitting on the couch, watching TV right now. And the minute she hears our voices in the foyer, she's going to hobble over to us and lose her ever-loving mind."

I giggle. "Sounds amazing. I think I can handle being attacked by a hummingbird. Bring it, Mimi."

With a huge smile, Savage takes a deep breath and opens the front door. We walk inside the house and into a beautiful foyer, where we're surrounded on all sides by splendor—a huge wooden staircase directly in front of us, and two well-appointed rooms to either side.

"Whoa," I say. "It looks straight out of a movie! Did you hire a designer?"

"No, I bought it this way. It's amazing, isn't it?"

"It's perfect."

"Hello?" Savage booms. "We're here!" He pauses, a huge smile on his face. And then, when the house remains quiet as a mouse, he yells, "Sasha? Mimi? We're here!" We wait. But nothing happens. "She must be watching TV in the family room. It's hard to hear back there. Come on." He grabs my hand, and off we go through a fancy living room into another room appointed with more modern-looking, comfy furniture and a large-screen TV. But it's empty. We head into the next room—a huge, modern kitchen. And, again, there's nobody here.

"Where the hell is everyone?" Savage mutters. "Mimi always watches TV around this time—and never in bed. Mimi says it makes her sleep better at night if she spends most of the day outside her bedroom."

"Adrian," a voice says behind us. And when we turn around, it's Savage's pretty cousin, Sasha Wilkes—a Mother Earth type I've spoken to several times on FaceTime. Not surprisingly, given that she shares genes with Savage, Sasha is a beauty with dark hair and eyes. Also, from what I've seen, she's someone who's earned Savage's full trust and admiration.

"Sasha! Whew. I was getting nervous." He bounds across the room toward his cousin and hugs her. "Is Mimi watching TV upstairs?"

Sasha swallows hard. "Yeah, she's in her room. Sit down, sweetie."

Savage's body stiffens. "What's wrong?"

"Sit down."

His chest heaves. "Just tell me, Sasha."

"Sit down. Hello, Laila. It's so good to see you."

"You, too." I hug her and take a seat on a couch next to

Savage, who looks like he's suddenly having trouble breathing.

After taking a chair across from us, Sasha says, "Adrian, Mimi hasn't gotten out of bed in over a week."

"*What?*" Savage whisper-shouts.

Sasha's face contorts, like she's holding back tears. "She hasn't been doing well, Ady. Even before the move, she was in a state of rapid decline. But now that she's here, it's like she's exhaling with relief. It's like she thinks she's reached the finish line."

"*No,*" Savage says, his voice tight. "No, Sasha. That's not why I bought Mimi the house—for her to give up! I bought it so she'd have a reason to keep going!"

"It doesn't work that way, honey. She says she's ready to go now."

"No!" he shouts, this time not whispering. "No! We'll tell her *no*. Have you told her no?"

Sasha smiles through tears. "Actually, I've been telling her *yes*. I've told her she's free to go, whenever she wants. I've told her we'll be okay and she'll always be with us."

"No, Sasha!" Savage pulls on his hair, his body convulsing. "Why the fuck did you tell her that shit, without asking me first? I never agreed to you telling her that! You should have consulted me!"

"She's in pain. I don't want her to feel pain anymore."

"Well, neither do I, obviously! But Mimi can't go yet." He chokes up. Pauses. Pulls himself together. And finally says, "I still need her, Sasha. You don't. *But I do.*"

I scooch over to Savage on the couch and put my arms around him and he pulls me fiercely into him, his body wracked with tremors.

Tears spill down my cheeks as I hold him.

"Why didn't you at least tell me she hasn't been getting out of bed?" Savage chokes out, his voice tight and pained. "You let me think everything's been fine. You said she was tired because of the move. You didn't say she's ready to go!"

"I didn't want to worry you. I knew you were coming today. So, why worry you before then?"

"Because you promised you'd tell me when it was time for me to drop everything and come! You swore to tell me that, Sasha!"

"I'm telling you now. You both have had a busy shooting schedule for the show and I didn't want you dropping everything for nothing. I knew Mimi was determined to hang on to see you both, in person. I knew that."

"But I would have had more time with her, Sasha! Fuck the show! I only signed on to do the goddamned show in the first place for Mimi—so she could watch me on her favorite show while lying in bed in the master bedroom of *this* house." He's shaking. Fighting tears. "Are you telling me she won't even make it to see the first episode?"

Sasha swallows hard. "I doubt she'll still be here by then."

Savage makes a garbled sound that breaks my heart. His body quaking, he pulls out his phone, pushes a button, and brings the phone to his ear. His chest heaves. His Adam's apple bobs. And then, "Nadine Collins, please. This is Adrian Savage. It's an emergency. Thanks." He waits. And as he does, Sasha and I look at each other, both of our cheeks wet with tears. Savage inhales sharply before saying, "Hi, Nadine. Thanks for taking my call. Listen, I've got a family emergency on my hands. I'm in Chicago with my sick grandma. She's like a mother to me. The only mother I've ever known. And I've just been told her time is a whole lot shorter than I realized. *Sing Your Heart Out* has been her favorite show since the beginning. She's never missed an episode. So, I'm calling to beg you, literally, *beg* you, to please send me the first episode, so I can sit down and watch it with her right away. I'll sign whatever you need and promise whatever you want. But I need this favor from you, Nadine." His chin trembles as he listens to whatever Nadine is saying on her end of the line. His shoulders soften. His chest lurches. He whispers, "Thank you. I appreciate that. Thank you. Bye."

Savage hangs up and takes a deep breath. "She's sending it now."

"That's good," Sasha says. "Mimi will be so happy to share that with you."

Savage opens his mouth, but whatever he was planning to say gets lodged in his throat. He hangs his head and breathes fitfully for a moment, while I rub his back and look at Sasha through tears.

"Ady, she's at peace," Sasha says. "She wants to see you and Laila together. She wants to hear you sing to her. She wants to kiss you and hug you. But then, she's excited to get to see Jasper and my dad again. So, please, don't make a tearful plea for her to stick around. This isn't about you. It's about *her*."

Savage inhales a deep breath and raises his head. "I understand," he says softly, resolve settling in his jawline. "I'll make sure Mimi knows I'll be okay."

"Good. Thank you." Sasha rises and extends her hand to her cousin. "Come on, sweetie. Maybe you can carry her around the house, so she can point out all the little nooks and crannies where she and Jasper fell in love." She looks at me.

"Did Adrian tell you this is where Mimi met her husband, Jasper—when Mimi's mom worked here as a live-in housekeeper?"

"He told me a little bit," I say. "But no details."

Sasha says, "Mimi and Jasper were both sixteen when they fell in love here, in this house. She got pregnant with my father, so they ran off together to get married, against the wishes of Jasper's family. In fact, Jasper's family disowned him."

"Oh, no. Did they ever come around and accept Mimi and their baby?"

Sasha shakes her head. "They never did. They acted like Jasper, and his family, were dead to them."

"Oh my gosh."

"Even after Jasper died, way too young, they didn't help his young widow with her two young sons—my father and Adrian's. They pretended Mimi and her two little boys didn't even exist."

"That's terrible." I look at Savage, suddenly understanding his motivation to purchase this sprawling house for Mimi, during the last weeks of her life. He wanted revenge against Jasper's family, obviously. He wanted Mimi to get the last laugh against her cruel in-laws. He wanted Mimi to be the mistress of this grand home, if only briefly, and perhaps get to enjoy a torrent of memories, too, about the beginning days of her love story with Jasper.

"Jasper's family tried to pay Mimi off to ditch Jasper," Sasha says. "But when she refused, they tried to pay off Jasper to leave Mimi and deny the baby was his. Jasper was their first-born son, and, apparently, they'd had an heiress in mind for him, ever since birth. But Jasper and Mimi said they'd rather be poor, but happy together, and that's precisely what they were."

Savage motions to the grandeur around us. "And now, fuck 'em all. Mimi owns their fancy fucking house. She sleeps in their fancy fucking bedroom. She's queen of this entire fucking castle, and they can all rot in hell."

TWENTY-FOUR

SAVAGE

"Mimi," I whisper, plastering a smile on my face as I race to her bedside, past her caregiver, Stuart. How did I not realize how much my grandmother has been deteriorating during our recent phone calls? Now that I'm seeing Mimi in person, it's clear how pale and whittled away she's become. No wonder Sasha looked downright pained when I talked cluelessly last night about my plan to cook raviolis with Mimi in her fancy kitchen tonight. Based on the way Mimi looks right now, it's clear I've been willfully blind these past few weeks. Seeing what I wanted to see.

"Ady," Mimi breathes with an exhausted smile, as I lean down to hug her.

"Merry Christmas," I whisper into her white hair. "I love you so much, Mimi."

"I love you, too," she whispers. "Forever and always, my sweet boy."

When we disengage, Mimi's dark eyes find Laila, who's

standing tentatively a few feet away, her body language suggesting she doesn't want to intrude.

"Come," Mimi says. "Sweet Laila. Welcome."

Laila steps forward, swallowing hard. Somehow, she manages to squeak out a heartfelt little "Merry Christmas, Mimi," before bending down and taking my beloved hummingbird into her warm embrace. "I'm so happy to be here," Laila whispers. "I love you so much, Mimi. I already do."

It's more than my already beleaguered heart can take. I turn away and breathe deeply, determined to stuff my emotions down. But when I see the faces of Sasha and Mimi's favorite caregiver, Stuart, reflecting my own heartbreak back to me, I lose it. With my back to Mimi, as Laila continues chatting with her, I put my hands over my face and try to regain control.

"Are you and Adrian happy?" Mimi says behind me.

"We're so happy," Laila replies. "We couldn't be happier."

Mimi exhales, like the weight of the world has been lifted from her tiny shoulders. "Ady?"

I take a deep breath and turn around. "I'm right here. And I've got great news for you." I pull a second chair to Mimi's bedside, next to the one Laila is now sitting in. "Mimi, I was able to get a copy of the first episode of *Sing Your Heart Out*, so we can watch it together."

"Oh, how exciting."

"Oh, come on, honey, tell Mimi our *really* good news," Laila says, her eyebrows raised. And when I look at her blankly, she leans into my ear and whispers, "Tell her we're engaged."

My heart lurches. "Ooooh, yes. Of course." I shoot Laila

a grateful smile and she winks at me. And then, I take my grandmother's hand in mine and say, "We were going to wait to tell you this on Christmas, but I think Laila's right—we shouldn't wait." I smile broadly. "Laila and I are engaged, Mimi."

Mimi gasps and her eyes prick with tears, as Sasha behind me whispers, "Oh my God."

I continue, "I asked Laila to marry me three nights ago at our house. We were having a nice dinner and, suddenly, I realized I don't want her to be my girlfriend. I want her to be my *wife*. So I asked, and she said *yes*."

"Of course, I did," Laila says, gripping my free hand. "And it was the easiest decision I've made in my life."

Tears flood Mimi's dark eyes. "Praise God," she whispers. Her eyes drift to Laila's hand, presumably looking for a ring, so I say, "We don't have a ring yet. We're going to get one when we get back home."

"Adrian figured I'd want to help pick the ring out," Laila explains.

"Well, that and I asked Laila, spur of the moment, without a plan. You know me, Mimi."

The skin around Mimi's eyes crinkles, letting me know she's thinking, *Yes, I do.*

And just like that, it hits me like a ton of bricks I wish this story were real. I wish I'd asked Laila to marry me, spur of the moment, over dinner the other night. I wish I'd been smart enough to realize, back then, that I can't live without her. That I don't want her to be my girlfriend—I want her to be my *wife*.

"I did have one condition for Adrian," Laila says. "One thing I told him he'll need to do before we say 'I do.'" She looks at me. "I told him, 'You're the most amazing man I've ever met and I don't want anyone else, ever. But if we're going to have a shot at living happily ever after, without some of the traumas of our childhoods getting in our way, then I think we should both agree to go to therapy.' I think Adrian could use some help with anger management, honestly. And I could certainly use some help dealing with a few things from my childhood, as well."

My heart is galloping. "I had no problem saying yes to that, Mimi." I look at Laila. "I told her, 'No problem. I'll do anything to make this work.' I wanted Laila to know she can always trust me—that I'd never hurt her or do anything to push her away or scare her. I wanted her to know I screw up sometimes, yes, but I want this more than I've ever wanted anything, ever, so I'll do whatever it takes."

"Holy fuck," Sasha whispers.

Laila's flushed. She says, "When Adrian said all that, I told him, 'Well, it's not like I'm perfect or anything. I've got some major hang-ups and insecurities I haven't dealt with very well. So, I think this idea would be good for both of us.'"

"I'm so proud of you both," Mimi says, patting Savage's hand. "Don't let the past rob you of the future you both deserve."

"We won't, Mimi," I say.

"Good." Mimi looks at Laila. "I'm guessing you've started to figure this out, sweetheart, but, still, it's worth mentioning. When Adrian promises something, he sometimes messes up and breaks his promise. But once he does that, if he promises *again*, that's when his word becomes unbreakable. He sometimes needs to make a mistake, *once*, to figure himself out."

Laila looks at me and says softly, "Yeah, I'm starting to realize that about him."

"Don't put up with his crap, Laila," Mimi says quietly. "But when you can, show him patience and grace, and you'll be greatly rewarded." With that, Mimi's eyelids flutter, and it's clear she's exhausted her energy for now.

"Sleep now," I say, gently caressing her cheek. "When you wake up, we'll watch the first episode of the show." I sing softly to her—the little lullaby I always sing to her—and soon, it's clear Mimi has already drifted off to sleep.

I address Stuart, Mimi's caregiver. "She's gonna wake up, right?"

"I'm sure she will," Stuart replies.

I exhale a long breath and look at Laila and my cousin. "Do you two ladies want to go downstairs, drink some whiskey, and smoke a big, fat blunt with me? Because fuck me, I need to unwind."

"Hell yeah," Sasha says.

I look at Laila. "You're not gonna rat me out to the producers for breaching the sobriety clause in my contract, are you, babysitter?"

"Dude, fiancée trumps babysitter."

Smiling, I pull Laila to me and plant a little peck on her lips, and, to my relief, she puckers and returns my kiss. With a deep exhale, I rise along with Laila, and accept a big hug from my cousin. When Sasha releases me, I walk out of the room with her, my arm around my cousin's shoulders, and with Laila trailing behind. As we head down the grand staircase, I tell Sasha how much I've missed her. I thank her for taking such good care of our grandmother and apologize for my initial reaction when I first heard the news about Mimi's decline.

"It was a lot to process," Sasha replies. She squeezes my trapezius muscle, the one near my neck that always tightens up the most, and says, "Ooph. You're knotted-up like crazy."

"This is the worst I've been in forever. The show is killing me."

"Well, let me at that famous body!" Sasha says, like she always does. "And I'll fix you right up!"

I chuckle and reply the way I always do: "Knock yourself out, Sasha."

When we get to the base of the staircase, I turn around to say something to Laila. But she's not there. On the contrary, she's frozen in the middle of the staircase, looking like she's just seen a ghost.

"Laila?" I say, my heart in my throat. "What's wrong?"

Laila's mouth is hanging open. Her face is pale. For a long moment, she doesn't reply. "*Sasha*," she finally whispers. "It was *Sasha*."

"What?" I say.

"Sasha is a massage therapist," she murmurs.

"Right," I say. "I told you that."

"I'd be happy to massage you first," Sasha says. "Fuck Adrian. He gets enough attention, right?"

"You'll be in good hands," I say. "Sasha is the best."

Laila remains frozen and pale on the staircase, not moving a muscle.

"I know it's weird," Sasha says, filling the awkward silence, "but my favorite thing in the world is working out knots."

Laila blinks a few times in rapid succession, exhales, and slowly begins descending the steps. As she walks, I disengage from Sasha to meet her in the middle, perplexed by the expression of pure shock on her face.

"What is it?" I ask.

Rather than replying to my question, Laila takes my face in her hands, pulls me to her, and kisses me deeply. Passionately. Without holding back. Like she's kissing her actual fiancé. The great love of her life.

I have no idea what's prompted this reaction, especially on a day when Laila has barely spoken to me. Was it something Mimi said? Maybe that thing about me tending to fuck up once, but not twice? Or did Mimi's frail condition remind Laila that life is short—that we're all mortal and imperfect and flawed—and should therefore not sweat the small stuff, but, instead, grab happiness, wherever we can find it?

There's no way to know, in this moment, what's inspired Laila to kiss me like she forgives me. Like she *loves* me. And, honestly, I don't need to know. All that matters is I've realized I've found the great love of my life, exactly as Mimi's always wanted for me. And this kiss tells me Laila believes she's found hers. And so, without asking why, or how long it'll last, I take Laila, the woman I love, into my arms and kiss her in return with everything I've got. Everything I am. And everything I can't wait to become, with her by my side.

TWENTY-FIVE
LAILA

Sasha blows out a plume of smoke from the joint she's sharing with Savage and me and says, "I'm so glad you're here."

The three of us are chatting while smoking pot and drinking booze in Mimi's comfortable family room. I'm sitting next to Savage on a couch, my legs draped across his lap, while Sasha is sprawled across a nearby armchair. And it's blowing my mind to realize, the whole time I'd been certain Savage was some kind of sex addict player, his cousin was the "groupie" I saw him with that fateful day in Las Vegas. *Sasha* was the one walking arm-in-arm with Savage, saying she was thrilled to be there with him. *Sasha* was the girl who wanted to get her hands on his famous body. *Because Sasha is a massage therapist.* Holy hell. If I hadn't seen Savage with his cousin that day, and hadn't misinterpreted their conversation, where would I be right now? Would I be sitting here with Savage and his cousin, feeling swept away by my feelings for Savage? Or would our tour fling have ended when the tour did?

"So, tell me the truth, guys," Sasha says, putting down her wine glass. "Are you two really engaged or did you tell Mimi a beautiful lie?"

Savage takes the joint from me. "The engagement part was a beautiful lie, but we really are together and totally committed." He looks at me, his expression saying, *Please, let that be a true statement.* And when I smile and nod, Savage grins and exhales in relief.

Sasha takes the joint from Savage and sucks on it. "I figured the engagement had to be a lie for Mimi's sake. If you'd actually proposed to Laila, you would have spammed me beforehand with a thousand texts. 'Sasha, how should I ask her?' 'Sasha, where should I ask her?' 'Sasha, what should I *wear* when I ask her?'"

Savage chuckles. "I was *sixteen* and had never asked a girl on an actual date before, dude. You always give me hell about that."

"It was cute the first *ten* times."

"It wasn't ten times. Three or four, tops. And that was back in high school when I had no game. I'm a grown-ass man now. A rock god, if you haven't heard."

"Wait, *what*?" Sasha deadpans.

"I'm on magazine covers and everything."

"Wow."

"I'm also a judge on *Sing Your Heart Out*."

"No."

"True story."

"Impressive."

"If I wanted to propose nowadays," Savage continues, "I wouldn't need to ask for your or anyone else's help to do it, any more than I need help walking onstage and performing for *tens* of thousands of people who've paid good money to come see *me*."

"Gosh, you're so fancy."

"I am. If I wanted to propose, I'd slay that shit, dude, all by myself."

"Well, pardon me, Mr. Famous. My bad." Sasha looks at me, her dark eyes sparkling. Clearly, bantering with her cousin is one of the great joys of Sasha's life. But I can barely function in this moment. Does the cheeky speech Savage just gave signal he's thinking about proposing to me in the finale, in order to grab that bonus the producers offered him? I mean, assuming I'm still around by then. Frankly, I wouldn't blame him if he did it. In fact, I *want* him to do it to earn himself some easy money. Plus, I can't deny the idea that I might get to look into The Beast's eyes and hear him say those magical words—"Will you marry me, Belle?"—is incredibly exciting to me. Even though my brain would understand the fakeness of the moment, my heart would nonetheless enjoy getting to feel, if only fleetingly, like a princess in a fairytale.

Sasha picks up her wine glass again, while I pick up my whiskey. "Well, I'm glad you told Mimi such a lovely lie. I can't remember the last time I saw her smiling that big."

Savage replies to his cousin, and an entire conversation ensues, but my attention is flickering in and out. I'm bursting at the seams to tell Savage about my epiphany on the staircase—namely, that I saw him with *Sasha* in Las Vegas, and every action and reaction of mine since then has been tainted by that misunderstanding. I should wait to tell him everything in private, I decide, since my revelation about Sasha will undoubtedly make a whole lot of other dominos fall—dominos that will surely whip up quite a bit of emotion inside me. But, still, I can't resist asking Sasha a few pointed questions about that fateful day.

I wait for a lull in the conversation between Savage and his cousin, and then ask, "Sasha, did you ever visit Adrian during our tour?"

She nods. "Once. Your show was brilliant, Laila."

"Thank you. Which show did you see?"

"Las Vegas. It was Adrian's birthday weekend. Our birthdays are five days apart, so he flew me and a couple of my friends to Las Vegas to celebrate, as a birthday gift to me."

"No, flying you to Vegas was my birthday gift to *me*," Savage corrects.

Sasha rolls her eyes. "See what I'm dealing with here? This year, he flew me and my friends to Vegas. Last year, he bought me a *house* for my birthday. And all I ever give him as a birthday present is the same thing, every year: a bottle of his favorite whiskey and an extra-long massage."

"That's all I ever want," Savage says.

"Speaking of me giving you a massage," Sasha replies. She raises her palms and kneads the air, like she's massaging invisible shoulders. "Let me at that famous body!"

Savage chuckles. "I think I'll take a rain check, actually." He looks at me and his dark eyes flicker with heat. "No offense, but I'd rather get my knots out a different way tonight."

"*Oh*," Sasha and I say at the same time.

Savage stands and extends his hand to me. "Come on, Fitzy. Time for bed." As I take his hand and rise from the couch, Savage says to his cousin, "I don't care what time it is, or what X-rated noises you might hear coming out of my room, if Mimi takes a turn or wakes up and needs me—"

"I'll get you," Sasha interrupts. "I've already told Stuart

the same thing. If Stuarts knocks on my door, then I'll immediately knock on yours."

"Thanks." Savage grips my hand. "Goodnight, Sasha."

"Goodnight. Thank you for coming, Laila. Mimi was so excited to hug you."

"There's no place I'd rather be," I say. I smile at Savage, letting him know my words are sincere, and then we walk hand in hand through the large house to the bedroom where Savage stowed his suitcase earlier.

"Wait here," he commands, guiding me to sit on the end of the bed. When I'm situated, he wordlessly leaves the room, leaving me whispering to myself, "Okay, then, goodbye." But a moment later, Savage returns, carrying my suitcase, which he pointedly sets down in a corner. It's his way of telling me I'm staying with him during this trip, obviously. And he'll get no argument from me.

"Thank you," I say.

"No. Thank *you*," he replies, taking a seat next to me.

He reaches for me, obviously intending to kiss me. But I stop him with my palm.

"You're not going to ask me why I'm not mad at you anymore?"

"No," he says flatly. "I don't want to look a gift horse in the mouth."

With burning eyes, he begins fiddling with my shirt, clearly intending to remove it, but I touch his hand, stopping him.

"Hang on," I say softly. "I need to explain myself to you. There's something important I figured out when I saw you walking down the staircase with Sasha."

Savage looks confused by that comment, but he whispers "okay" and waits for whatever is coming next.

I clear my throat. My heart is racing. "When you texted me your room number in Las Vegas and asked me to come to your room after the show—"

"More like I *begged* you to come."

"I did, Savage. I came to your room. And not after the show, but within *minutes* of receiving your text. In fact, I practically sprinted to your room."

"*What?*"

"When I got to your floor and started walking down the hallway toward your room, you happened to get off an elevator in front of me. You had your arm around a beautiful brunette, who I thought was a groupie—"

"*Sasha*," he whispers.

I nod. "I assumed you were bringing her to your room for sex, the same way you'd brought those groupies to my dressing rooms."

He palms his forehead. "Oh, God."

"Only this time, you couldn't possibly be flaunting her in my face to get a rise out of me. This time, there was no mistaking your intentions. It was the real deal. Or so I thought. In my mind, you were taking a woman to your room for sex, mere *hours* after having amazing sex with me, and mere *minutes* after you'd begged me to come to your room."

Savage exhales loudly and groans out, "I can't believe it."

"I wanted to believe it was some kind of misunderstanding," I say. "So, I tiptoed closer and eavesdropped on your conversation. And that's when Sasha said, 'Let me get my hands on that body!' Or something along those lines. And I lost it. I sprinted away and texted Charlie to meet me in the gym. And then, during my workout with Charlie, I got a second text from you, telling me you couldn't stop thinking about me—that you were lying there thinking about me."

"I was! I sent that right after my birthday massage!"

I groan. "When I got that second text, I was so grossed out. I thought, 'Okay, this guy is a sex addict or a sociopath or both. Did he text me while that groupie was riding his cock, or did he have the decency to wait for her to go into the bathroom?'"

"Oh my God. Finally, everything makes sense!"

"I blocked your number after I got that second text, and I promised myself I'd never speak to you again. That's why I got so mad about Charlie yesterday. I've been turning myself into a pretzel, trying to forgive and forget about that 'groupie' in Las Vegas. Trying to reconcile the Savage I've come to know with the asshole who brought a groupie to his room, mere minutes after begging *me* to come there. I was angry you—a hypocrite who'd fucked a multitude of groupies on tour—couldn't handle the thought of me having a nice little tour fling with the fitness trainer on tour!"

Savage looks absolutely floored. "Everything would have been so different, if only you'd come to my room two minutes later. I would have already been in there with Sasha. I would have introduced you. I would have told Sasha to leave."

"She said she wanted to get her hands on you! She squealed and said she was excited to be there. After all the groupies I'd caught you with prior to that, there wasn't a shred of doubt in my mind what I was seeing."

Savage runs his hand over his chin. "Laila, I waited up all night after that Vegas show, positive you'd come to your senses and come to me. Every noise I heard in the hallway made me leap out of bed and peek through the peephole. Every time, I was positive you'd be standing there. But you never were. Rinse and repeat, in each new city. I'd lie awake in bed, alone, every night, praying you'd finally show up.

When you seemed so cozy with Charlie, I figured that had to be the reason you didn't want me. Otherwise, I couldn't understand. How was it possible that night in Phoenix hadn't rocked your world the way it'd rocked mine?"

My heart is crashing my chest. "I'm so sorry."

"I've been a madman, Laila. Totally and completely obsessed with you, and trying to understand the enigma that is your brain. I've been so confused. Feeling so rejected."

"Oh, baby." I touch his face. "You sat alone in your room every night for the entire last month of the tour?"

"Not only the last month. I did the same thing the first two months of the tour, as well." He smiles. "Sweetheart, I haven't been with anyone but you since I laid eyes on you at Reed's party."

I gasp. "But . . . what about that waitress in New York?"

"I didn't even call her. And all those groupies were a set-up, too. I sent them packing right after you caught me with them. I was an asshole, Laila. Pissed I'd decided to step aside for Kendrick. Jealous you wanted an asshole like Malik, instead of me."

"No. I only wanted you, from the second I saw you at Reed's. I lied about Malik. We never had an actual relationship. Just one date before the tour and some texting. We never even came close to having sex. You're the only one I've been with since I first laid eyes on you at Reed's. The only one I've wanted for so long."

Savage looks like his brain is melting. "But . . . you and Malik couldn't keep your hands off each other in New York —and you were constantly on the phone with him after that."

I shake my head. "My 'relationship' with Malik was a lie that kept snowballing on me. On day one of the tour, I could tell Kendrick was interested in me, but I already had my sights set on you. So, when he mentioned he'd seen a photo of me at Malik's game, I went with it. I said Malik was my boyfriend. But it wasn't true. That game was our only date. During the tour, Malik texted me pretty persistently, but I wasn't interested. And then, he told me he was coming to the show in New York—and not because I'd invited him, by the way. So, I said he could be my plus-one at Reed's dinner party afterward. But I only brought him there to get a rise out of *you*. I couldn't understand why you always ignored me. Why you *never* hit on me. I thought maybe if you saw a guy like Malik all over me, it'd *finally* spur you into action. But all you did was get that waitress's number and scream at me to give *Kendrick* a shot."

"Oh, fuck."

"Babe, I kicked Malik to the curb right after dinner— literally, during the car ride from the restaurant to our hotel."

"No!"

I nod furiously. "I told Malik to fuck off and never contact me again. And I haven't spoken to him since."

"You faked *all* those phone calls with Malik after New York?"

"Every single one. The same way you faked *all* those groupies, apparently."

"Holy fuck," he whispers. "Kendrick said we're the same person in male and female forms . . ."

"I thought for sure you had sex with that waitress in New York!"

"Nah, I only got her number to piss you off. After our fight on the sidewalk, I stumbled back to my hotel room, punched a hole in the wall, barfed my guts out, and passed out."

"And then dragged your sorry ass to Alessandra's music video shoot the next day."

"Only because I knew you'd be there, without your asshole boyfriend. That's the only reason I showed up, Laila. Not for Reed. Not for Alessandra or Fish. But to see *you*, without Malik hanging all over you. I kept my word and showed up because I wanted you to like me."

"How was I supposed to like you when all you talked about when you got there was the hot sex you'd had all night and day with the waitress?"

"I was fighting fire with fire! You went on and on about your hot night with Malik!"

"Because I was jealous about the waitress!"

"Well, I was jealous about Malik."

"I'm positive you bragged about the waitress first."

"No, it was the other way around."

We both burst out laughing.

"Wait, what were you doing in that hot tub in Phoenix at three in the morning? I assumed you were drowning your sorrows about that video of Malik getting head."

"I *was* drowning my sorrows," I admit, "but not about *Malik*. I mean, yes, that video of him did embarrass me. I'd been romantically linked to Malik online, thanks to that photo of me cheering him on at his game. So, yes, it was embarrassing to think the world was wondering if he'd cheated on me. But, mostly, I was sitting there thinking about *you*. Kendrick had invited me to your birthday party earlier that night, and I was sitting there feeling bummed that things had gotten so bad between us, I didn't even feel like I could come to your birthday party. I was drowning my sorrows that my hot crush had turned out to be a rockstar cliché asshole who hated me, and I couldn't understand why."

Savage smiles wickedly. "You sneaky little freak. You let me think we had *revenge* sex that night."

I return his smile. "That was your assumption, so I let you keep thinking it. It made the sex extra hot, didn't it?"

His dark eyes flash with heat. "It sure did. Hot as hell."

I run my fingertip up his forearm. "If it makes you feel better, we really did have *hate* sex that night. I didn't fake that part." I wink. "Or any of my *three* orgasms."

"Well, duh." He bites his lip. "I'm so hard right now, baby. I feel like a five-hundred-pound elephant has finally gotten off my chest."

"Me, too."

"Laila, I'm so sorry I punched a hole in the wall in your dressing room. It's no excuse, but I've been slowly going insane since the tour, trying to understand why you didn't want me the way I wanted you. Trying to understand pieces of a puzzle that just didn't fit together. When I saw you with Colin, I thought I'd lost you for good. I promise I'll never do that again, or anything else to scare or hurt you."

"I know you won't. I trust you, Adrian. But I do think you should get some therapy, like I said to Mimi. There's no shame in that. You've been through a lot. Maybe a professional could help you work through some stuff."

"I'll do whatever it takes to make this work."

"So will I."

"Please forgive me for all the ways I've screwed up," he says.

"We've both screwed up. Please forgive me."

"You were fighting fire with fire. I was the bigger asshole."

"We were both assholes," I say. "Can we please press the reset button, for real now?"

Savage nods and leans in and kisses me. And that's all it takes to light our fuse. In a frenzy, we begin pulling our clothes off, both of us desperate to consummate our new beginning by fusing our bodies. Once naked, we tumble onto the bed and kiss passionately. We grope and grab and caress and stroke. Until, finally, Savage sinks himself inside me, all the way, and begins gyrating enthusiastically on top of me in a way that feels totally new. Now that we're finally *free* of the past, it's clear to me how much it was weighing us both down. How much it was holding us back. Speaking for myself, all my walls are down now. I'm no longer protecting my heart. In fact, I'm giving it to Savage in this moment, with both hands. *Take my heart, Savage. Take me. I'm all yours.*

"You're the only one I want, Laila," he whispers into my ear, as his body invades mine, over and over again. As our chests rub together with each thrust.

"I'm all yours, Adrian," I whisper back. I grip his face and kiss him deeply as he comes. He's the only one I want. The one I've wanted for so long. In fact, I can't imagine wanting anyone else, ever again.

TWENTY-SIX

SAVAGE

Even before opening my eyes, I sense sunlight on my face. Yawning, I roll onto my side and reach out next to me on the mattress, thinking Laila must have scooted to the edge of the bed in her sleep. But I feel nothing there—not even a warm spot.

I open my eyes. "Laila?" I look toward the bathroom, figuring she's in there. But when I say her name again, silence answers me. I look at the time to find it's a few minutes past seven. And that's *Chicago* time. Laila's body clock still thinks she's in LA. So, what's a night owl like her doing up so early, with nowhere she needs to be?

Mimi.

The thought hits me like a ton of bricks. Did Sasha knock on our door and I didn't hear it? *Shit.* I leap out of bed, quickly brush my teeth, wash my face, and throw on a pair of sweats and a hoodie—fuck, it's cold in this old house!—and then bolt out of the room. But when I enter Mimi's room, what I find there makes me exhale from the depths of my soul. *Calm. Quiet. Peace.* That's what I find in Mimi's room, along with Laila holding Mimi's hand at her bedside.

"Good morning, ladies," I say brightly, determined not to let my tone betray the near-panic I was feeling a moment ago. As my pulse comes down, I give both women a kiss on their foreheads and begin pulling up a chair next to Laila's. But when I notice Mimi's facial expression as I take my seat, I get the distinct impression I've interrupted something.

"Oh. Would you two like me to step out while you finish your conversation?"

To my surprise, Mimi nods, while Laila looks sheepish and apologetic.

"Not a problem," I say quickly. I address the caregiver on duty now—a sweetheart of a woman named Felicia—the one who always relieves Stuart in the early morning hours. "Let me know whenever Mimi is ready for me to come back. I'll be in my room."

"Yes, sir."

My heart thumping, I return to my room and jump in the shower. And that's where I let myself wallow in the full extent of the dread and pain I've been feeling since my conversation with Sasha last night—the one in which my cousin told me Mimi is ready to go. I didn't want to believe it when Sasha said that, but, just now, I could see it in Mimi's eyes when she told me to leave. *Sasha was right.* Mimi would never tell me to leave any room, ever, unless she felt she was saying something urgent and confidential. Which, in this instance, must have been Mimi giving Laila some sort of advice about *me.*

Finally, after I've stayed in the shower for far too long, I get out, dry off, and get dressed. Grabbing my phone off the dresser, I head to my bed, intending to text Kendrick the latest about Mimi. But when I pick up my phone, I've got a missed call from Nadine Collins, the executive producer of the show. Damn. What's she doing up so early in LA, during the break—and why the hell is she calling *me*?

"Savage!" Nadine says, answering my call. "Thanks for calling."

"You're up early on a day off."

"No rest for the wicked," she says brightly. "I've got a conference call with the entire team in an hour, so I'm getting ready for that. Oh, how's your grandmother?"

"Hanging in there. Thanks for sending that link. I'm going to watch the show with her today."

"Wonderful. Enjoy. Listen, Savage, there's something important I'd like to talk to you about. We've got a couple options, in terms of the direction we want to go for the remainder of the season. A few storylines we're considering. Some of which depend on *you*." She pauses. "Can you tell me if you're planning to earn that bonus with a proposal in the finale? Have you come to a decision on that yet?"

I don't hesitate, even though I'm not technically required by my contract to give Nadine a firm answer on that, in advance. "I'm not going to propose in the finale," I reply flatly. And I have no doubt it's the right decision as I say it. Mimi was the primary reason I was considering doing it. But now that Laila and I have already told Mimi we're engaged, what would be the point? In fact, I can't imagine anything more cringey-ass and embarrassing to me than getting down on bended knee in front of my actual girlfriend and fake-proposing to her on a reality TV show.

"Is there any way I can entice you to change your mind about that?" Nadine asks. "Maybe sweeten the pot to get an affirmative commitment from you right now?"

There's nothing Nadine could say to change my mind, but, still, I figure I'll hear the woman out. "What do you have in mind, Nadine?"

"What if I told you there's a jeweler who's willing to supply a ring to you, in a value up to half a million bucks, in exchange for a sparkling shot of the ring during the proposal and a post on Instagram afterwards by you and Laila. All you have to do is remain 'engaged' to Laila for six months after the finale, and the ring is yours. When you and Laila 'break up,' you can sell the ring and keep the proceeds! Split them with Laila, if you like, or keep them for yourself. Totally up to you."

She's high if she thinks this scenario sounds even remotely attractive to me. "Not interested," I say simply.

"Okay, then. I've got authority to add another quarter mill to the bonus we've already put on the table—which brings our offer to a half-million bucks, if only you'll agree *now,* in writing, to commit to making the proposal in the finale. All we'd require is that you and Laila continue playing happy couple for six months after the finale, including making daily social media posts, and after that, you two can do whatever you want. Date whoever else. Or ride off into the sunset for real, if that's how you're feeling. At which point, you'll have a ring to keep or sell and half a million bucks."

Listening to Nadine talk, it dawns on me there's no amount of money, no dangling carrot, no free diamond ring, that would ever make me fake-propose to Laila. And not because the moment would be cringey-ass, which it would be. But because I love Laila. Because after all the puzzle pieces have *finally* snapped into place for me, thanks to our amazing conversation last night, a dam has broken inside me and there's no turning back. I love that girl, with all my heart and soul, and I'm one hundred percent sure of it. And guess what? I'm positive getting down on bended knee, looking up at Laila with a ring in my hand, and saying those sacred words to her, without truly meaning them, will fuck things up for us beyond repair. Maybe not that same day. But down the line.

Likewise, if I get down on bended knee, ring in hand, and ask Laila to be my wife—and actually *do* mean those sacred words—then blowing that once in a lifetime memory by doing it on reality TV would haunt me for the rest of my days. I don't know if I want to get married one day. I don't know if I'm capable of being anyone's husband. Not even Laila's. But if I decide to propose to Laila in the future, then I'm going to do it right. And not because Nadine Collins wants me to do it, as some sort of ratings grab.

"I tell you what," Nadine says, apparently interpreting my silence as a "no." "We'll let you tell Laila about the proposal in advance. That's what's concerning you the most, right? That you'd propose to Laila and she'd think it's real—and then, you'd have to tell her the truth afterwards?"

Yet again, Nadine's words are helping me understand my feelings. Contrary to what Nadine thinks, I'm not worried about Laila thinking my proposal is *real*. I'm worried about her thinking it's *fake*. I'm worried about having to tell Laila, after the fact, "Oh, no, that was really me asking you to marry me." Obviously, telling Laila about the proposal in advance wouldn't solve that problem. If I told Laila in advance about my plan to get down on bended knee, Laila would assume the proposal would be fake. And then, wouldn't she feel at least a little bit disappointed about that, after everything that passed between us last night? On the other hand, if, somehow, I got to the point two months from now where I felt certain I *genuinely* wanted to propose to Laila, then I sure as hell wouldn't tell her that in advance. Not for all the money in the world. So, really, how could a proposal in the finale, real or fake, *not* end badly for me? "I'm not going to propose to Laila in the finale," I declare. "Not for any amount of money."

Nadine doesn't speak for a long moment, but I can hear her wheels turning over the phone line. Finally, she says, "I was hoping for a different answer from you, Savage. The truth is, in the absence of a confirmed proposal in the finale, we're going to need to shake things up a bit."

Goosebumps erupt on my arms and neck. "Shake things up *how?*"

"You and Laila are going to break up this week. And we're going to terminate her contract."

Fucking bitch. Laila was right. "You can't do that, Nadine."

"Actually, I can. There's a buy-out clause in Laila's contract. And in the absence of a confirmed proposal on the horizon, we're going to exercise it. We might bring Laila back for the finale. In fact, we hope to do that. But we'll have to play it by ear and see how the new storyline unfolds."

"Laila was promised a performance slot in the finale, in her *written* contract. We relied on that and wrote a song to perform together."

"I'd be happy to show you Laila's contract. Invocation of the early-termination clause expressly renders all other promises in the contract null and void. So, technically, if we were to terminate Laila, we'd be released from our promise to give her that performance slot. We'd love to give her that slot, regardless. Which we'd do, if you were to call me, at least two weeks before the finale, and say you've 'gotten back together' with Laila and now plan to propose to her in the finale. Of course, you could avoid that entire rollercoaster ride by agreeing now, in writing, to propose to Laila in the finale."

I argue Laila's case for a while—talking passionately about Laila's incredible talent and charisma. I talk about how good she is with people, and insist the contestants on her team, as well as the audience, will love her. And as I say that last bit—about the contestants and audience loving Laila—my heart swells and solidifies with my *own* love for Laila.

But it's no use. No matter what I say, Nadine has made her decision. She's hell-bent on getting that proposal out of me, one way or another. Or if not, making people tune in to watch me overcome my supposedly broken heart on national TV.

"Okay, Nadine," I finally say. "You've made an offer to me. Now, let me make one to you. I'll let you keep a half-mill of my salary, if you'll promise, right now, to keep Laila on the show for the rest of the season and leave us alone to be happy. In that time, I promise I'll consider proposing to Laila in the finale. If I do, you wouldn't need to pay me any bonus. I'd do it for nothing."

In truth, I won't be proposing to Laila on reality TV, no matter what. But by then, what could they possibly do to me if I don't get down on bended knee like they want?

I add, "That'd be a net positive to you of a million bucks, Nadine. You'd keep the bonus you just offered me *and* keep a half-mill of my salary, too."

Nadine pauses, which means she's considering my offer. She says, "Let us keep a *million* bucks of your salary now, and you've got yourself a deal."

I close my eyes. *Fuck.* "Do you promise to leave Laila

and me alone—no more demands for 'Vintage Savage and Laila'? No attempts to create any kind of love triangle?"

"Ah, Colin told Laila about our offer to him, and Laila told you? I *knew* he'd run and tell her."

I press my lips together. My "love triangle" comment was purely hypothetical. I was grasping at straws. But clearly, my instinct about why they hired Colin as Laila's mentor was correct. Were they planning to create the storyline in the editing room? I'm sure there's plenty of footage to allow them to stitch together a saucy little narrative. Hugs and smiles between Colin and Laila. Daggers between Colin and me. Not to mention, Laila and I delivered a whole lot of spicy "trouble in paradise" footage on Draft Day.

"Yeah, Laila told me everything about your plans with Colin," I lie. "And one of my conditions, if I pay you that million bucks, is that you stop chasing any 'love triangle' storyline that involves Colin or anyone else."

"Well, that's a moot point now, seeing as how he said no."

No to what? "Yeah, but you guys are geniuses in the editing room. I don't want you to stitch something together to create even the suggestion that Colin or anyone else has come between Laila and me."

Nadine sighs. "Look, I'm going to need you to pledge your full salary as collateral, in order to agree to this side deal. If you wind up proposing in the finale, then I'll release a million back to you. If you don't propose, then we'll keep the full two mill."

Fuck, fuck, fuck! I run a palm down my face, my mind whirring, but quickly decide I've got no choice. "Okay, Nadine, but only if you meet three conditions. One, you'll call Laila within the next twenty minutes to tell her she's doing a bang-up job on the show, better than your wildest dreams, and you want her to know you're going to keep her on for the entire season. You'll say, 'We're tearing up that early buy-out clause. We can't imagine doing the show without you.'"

"Fine."

"Two, I hope this goes without saying, but Laila and I will be performing our duet in the finale, as planned."

"Yes."

"Three, you'll never tell Laila about this side deal of ours. *Ever*."

"Wouldn't you want Laila to know you're her knight in shining armor?"

"No. She already feels guilty enough she's getting half my initial salary. She doesn't need any reason to feel even guiltier." I hear footsteps in the hallway, getting closer. "So, do we have a deal or not?"

Nadine sighs. "Yes, we have a deal."

"Great. I've got to go. Don't forget to make that call to Laila."

"Will do. Happy holidays."

"Bye, Nadine."

The door opens as I'm saying "Nadine," and Laila steps into the room. As she approaches, I toss my phone onto the nightstand. "Hey, baby. Is Mimi ready to see me now?"

Laila sits on the edge of the bed next to me and takes my hand. "No, Sasha is in there. You were talking to Nadine?"

My heart lurches. "Yeah, she called to wish me happy holidays and tell me how thrilled everyone is with us. Apparently, our 'fight' on Draft Day quenched their thirst for drama, and now, they want us to go back to being a happy couple for the entire rest of the season."

Laila's jaw drops. "Nadine said that?"

"She did. Oh, and she also said she's looking forward to our performance in the finale."

Laila looks flabbergasted. "And I was so positive they were going to fire me during the break! I wasn't going to tell you this, but when Colin and I were alone in my dressing room, he told me something confidential—something that made me all the more certain my days on the show were numbered." She tells me her story, which makes my blood boil, and wraps up with, "See? I told you Colin is a good guy. He came straight to me with the information, rather than ambushing me for an easy hundred grand."

"That was cool of him," I admit. "I'm a little surprised you didn't march outside with him, right then and there, and kiss the hell out of him for the cameras, just to get back at me for the Charlie thing. You were so pissed at me."

She looks shocked. "Adrian, I would *never* do that to you, no matter how upset I was about the Charlie thing. That would have been way beyond the pale for me to do to you. Plus, why would I do that to *myself*? Forevermore, I'd have been The Girl Who Cheated on Adrian Savage. God help me if ever I ran into one of your diehard fans on the street after that."

I pause for a long time, before saying, "I feel like I owe Colin a phone call. If I'm completely honest with myself, I think Colin and I were a bit more than acquaintances when I hooked up with his ex. I see Colin all the time. We have mutual friends. Colin isn't like Kendrick or Kai to me, obviously. Not even close. But he was a friend, and I did betray him. But, despite that, when he had the chance to take that bonus, and use you to get back at me, he didn't do it. He looked out for you, no matter what."

"And for you, too, indirectly. Even if that wasn't his motivation, he did save both of us from quite a bit of humiliation."

"True." I process everything for a moment, and then ask, "So, what did Mimi say to you? You two looked as thick as thieves."

Laila smiles. "She just wanted to give me some advice about you. She's so happy we're 'engaged' and wants to make sure we have a long and happy marriage." She squeezes my hand and smiles. "But guess what? I already knew pretty much everything Mimi told me about you, all on my own."

"What'd she tell you?"

"She didn't phrase it this way, of course. This is my own interpretation. But, basically, she told me you're a prince who was sadly turned into an unruly beast a long time ago by a mean woman who held a grudge, for no good reason."

My heart skips a beat.

"Again, that's not how Mimi put it, but listening to her, I felt like everything she was saying was basically a retelling of *Beauty and the Beast*."

"Well, aren't you clever."

"I'm a genius." She grins. "So, did Nadine mention that bonus they've offered to you?"

"She did. I told her it's a non-starter. I'm not going to propose on national TV. Making Mimi happy was the only thing that made me consider it. But now that we've told Mimi the deed is done, and Nadine is so happy with you on the show, there's no reason for me to even think about that."

"A quarter-million bucks is a lot of money. Especially when you're giving half your salary to me, and you've bought houses for Sasha and Mimi."

"Please, Laila, don't feel guilty about the salary thing. You negotiated your share, fair and square."

"I wish I'd said yes to ten percent, like you first offered. I think that was fair."

"Stop, please. We're going to make bank on the duet. And my album is releasing next week. Honestly, I don't want to talk about the money again. We've pressed the 'reset button,' remember? The money is part of that."

Laila sighs. "You promise you're not secretly mad about the money?"

I kiss her cheek. "Baby, I'm not even capable of being mad at you."

As I'm saying that last sentence, there's a knock at the door.

"Adrian?" Sasha's wobbly voice says. My cousin sniffles behind the door, making my breathing halt, before adding, "Honey, Mimi is ready to see you now."

TWENTY-SEVEN
SAVAGE

As I enter Mimi's bedroom, I nod at the caregiver, Felicia, in the corner, lay my laptop on a table, and slide into a chair next to the bed. "Hey, Mimi," I whisper, taking her hand. She looks impossibly frail under her covers. Exhausted like I've never seen her before. "I'm here, Mimi. I'm right here."

My grandmother opens her eyes and purses her lips, asking for a kiss, and I lean forward and give her one, before settling back into my chair and cupping her slender hand in both of mine.

"Would you like me to carry you around the house, so you can tell me stories from when you and Jasper were young?" I whisper.

Mimi shakes her head, turning me down. And I realize talking has become difficult for my sweet grandmother.

Swallowing hard, I gently squeeze Mimi's frail hand. "Would you like me to sing to you?"

This time, Mimi nods. So, I launch into singing the

lullaby that's become part of our ritual, and when I reach the end of that simple song, and Mimi is still awake and attentive, I sing another. This time, one of my all-time favorites by one of my favorite singer-songwriters: "Grace" by Jeff Buckley. Buckley was a genius, if you ask me, who died way too young, well before he'd graced the world with the full extent of his gifts. And the song of his I've chosen is about accepting mortality in the face of true love—a song about letting go gracefully. Frankly, I can't imagine a better song for this moment.

Grace.

It's the word, more than any other, that describes what Mimi has always shown to me. The gift of unconditional love and acceptance.

When I finish singing, Mimi whispers, in a barely audible voice. "I'm ready, Ady."

Tears flood my eyes. Sasha warned me last night that's what Mimi's been thinking, but I didn't expect Mimi to say it to me so bluntly. So starkly, without warning or lead-in.

The words "Not yet, Mimi!" form on my lips. But I bite them back and swallow them down. Of course, I want my grandmother to stay here with me. I can't imagine a world where she isn't here to chastise me with a gentle *"Adrian"* when I'm being a shithead. To smile at me when I'm being goofy. And most of all, to love me, no matter what stupid thing I do or say. But I know all of those desires are selfish— that now it's my turn to show Mimi *grace.*

Still cupping Mimi's slight hand in mine, I rest my elbows onto the mattress and say, "If you're ready to go, then go. Cross the bridge to Jasper and Frank. Have a picnic with them. Give them lots of hugs and kisses. I'll miss you so much—more than I could ever say in words. But I promise I'll be okay, and that I'll spend the rest of my life doing my best to be the man you've tried to teach me to be." I wipe a tear from her cheek. "Oh, how you've tried to teach me. I was quite a project, huh?"

Mimi smiles weakly.

"You did good, Maria Savage," I whisper, caressing her white hair. "I'm going to be okay, thanks to you. You taught me how to love with all my heart and soul. You taught me, Mimi. And I listened and learned. I know it didn't seem like it sometimes, but I promise I did. I understand everything now, Mimi, so you can go now, without worrying about me."

Mimi smiles, letting me know my words have touched her, and then she looks at her caregiver in the corner.

"Now?" the woman says. And when Mimi nods, her nurse walks to the dresser, pulls out a tiny box from the top drawer, and brings it to me, its lid opened. There's a simple ring inside—a band with the tiniest of diamonds at its center.

"Your grandfather slipped this ring onto your grand-mother's finger the day they got married," the nurse says. "Mimi wants you to take the diamond out of this ring and use it somewhere in the setting of Laila's engagement or wedding ring."

"Oh, Mimi," I say, feeling overcome with guilt. I felt justified in lying to Mimi about my fake engagement with Laila yesterday, given the situation, but accepting Mimi's treasured wedding ring from Jasper today, to give to my fake fiancée, feels wrong. "I shouldn't accept this," I say reflex-ively, but add quickly, "Sasha should have it, in case she gets married one day."

Mimi looks exasperated with me—which, I must admit,

makes me grin. How many times have I seen this same look of exasperation on Maria Savage's face over the years, when talking to me? Too many to count. And every time, it makes me smile.

The nurse says, "Mimi's already talked to Sasha about this ring, and told her she wanted you to have it for your future wife one day. This was weeks ago, before she knew about you and Laila. And Sasha said that sounded like a lovely idea. Mimi's given Sasha all her other jewelry, and Sasha is thrilled with that."

I exhale, feeling a bit better about the situation. If Mimi wanted me to have this ring before I'd lied to her about Laila, *and* Sasha's not bummed to miss out, then I suppose I can take the ring, as Mimi wishes. "Thank you, Mimi," I say, slipping the box into the pocket of my hoodie. "This means a lot."

She nods weakly.

Once again, I stroke her white hair. "Do you want to see me as a judge on *Sing Your Heart Out*? I've got the first episode cued up on my laptop over there."

Mimi nods and smiles.

I ask softly, "Should I call Sasha and Laila to come in here and watch with us?"

Mimi shakes her head and whispers, "Just you and me, Ady."

My heart squeezes. "Okay. That sounds good, Mimi. Just you and me."

Trembling, I grab my laptop and connect it to the large television on the far wall. And when I've got the show cued up, I crawl into Mimi's bed alongside her, reposition her frail body until she's lying comfortably in my arms, and press play.

The familiar theme song of *Sing Your Heart Out* begins and Mimi makes the tiniest cooing sound in my arms. It's a far cry from the whooping and laughter and shrieks I expected to hear from my grandmother when I've imagined this moment. I never envisioned Mimi watching me on the show while lying in my arms, unable to speak without significant effort. But even so, that little cooing sound was enough. It tells me she's conscious, able to understand what she's seeing, and thrilled about it.

At the end of the day, all I wanted was for Maria Savage to get to see that the little twelve-year-old asshole she took into her home—and into her heart—has grown up and made her proud. I wanted her to see that, thanks to her, and her ability to dream so fucking big for me, that little asshole is now sitting at the judges' table on her all-time favorite show. I wanted her to see *she* did this. *She* took an angry and distrustful pile of shit and turned him into something golden. Someone people actually care about. All because *Mimi* cared first and so fucking well.

About fifteen minutes into the show, I glance down to find Mimi's eyes closed. I look in panic at the monitor next to the bed and exhale with relief when the neon line marking her heartbeat is still bouncing up and down, albeit slowly.

"Is this it, Felicia?" I ask the caregiver. "Will she wake up?"

"I think she will," Felicia says. "But she's close now, Adrian. Very close."

I swallow down the lump in my throat and kiss the top of Mimi's head. I whisper, "You can go now, Mimi. Have a picnic with Jasper and Frank. I'll be right here the whole time, holding you, so you won't be alone as you cross the bridge." A sob catches in my throat, but I take a deep, halting breath that somehow chases it away. I clear my throat. "Felicia, will you do me a favor and let Sasha and Laila know I've had my alone-time with Mimi, and they're welcome to come in now? In and out, if they want. Any time. But tell them I'm going to stay right here with my grandma, without letting go of her, for as long as it takes."

TWENTY-EIGHT
SAVAGE

Los Angeles, California
Two weeks later

I stop my car in front of Reed Rivers' iron gate, roll down my window, and press the intercom button.

"Adrian!" a female voice says.

"Hey, Abu!" I say, recognizing Amalia's sweet voice. I smile into the camera on the box. "What's shaking, woman?"

Amalia giggles. "Reed isn't here, Adrian. He and Georgina are out to dinner. Was he expecting you?"

"Nope. I came to steal you away from Reed, as a matter of fact. So pack a bag and let's *gooo!*"

Amalia laughs. "I've told you I'll never leave Reed. But I can offer you some tea and conversation."

"I'd rather steal you away, but I guess some tea and conversation would be a nice consolation prize."

The gate buzzes and slowly begins opening, and I drive

through and park near the front door—and by the time I get out of my car, Amalia is already standing there waiting for me.

I hug Amalia in greeting and squeeze her tight, and as I do, every bit of pain I've been holding in and stuffing down since Mimi died surges inside me.

When the time finally came the day before Christmas, Sasha, Laila, and I were at Mimi's side. After that, Laila remained in Chicago with me through Christmas and beyond, as Sasha and I threw together a small funeral for our grandma, which my bandmates attended, as did some of Mimi's old neighbors, her caregivers, and Sasha's mother.

After that, I insisted Laila take the trip to Cabo we'd originally planned to take together, but with her mom, sister, and baby niece. I told Laila I could use a few days to grieve with Sasha in Chicago, and then on my own in LA. And it was the truth when I said it. But the minute Laila left Chicago, I felt like I was missing my right arm. And when I walked into that stupid reality TV mansion in LA, all by myself, I felt like I was missing not only my other arm, but both legs, too. As it turned out, I didn't want to be alone, like I'd thought I would. *I wanted to be with Laila.*

I release Amalia from our warm hug, made even warmer by the cool night air.

"My grandma, Mimi, died," I say softly. "The day before Christmas."

Sympathy washes over Amalia's elegant face. "Oh, Adrian. I'm so sorry." She hugs me again and then guides me inside. In Reed's kitchen, I sit at the table while Amalia puts the kettle on. And we talk, every bit as easily as we did the last time, even though I'm not shitfaced this time.

As we drink our tea, we talk about Mimi, at first. After a

while, however, we talk about spirituality, in general. The fact that we both believe Mimi is still with me, and always will be. And, finally, I tell Amalia about Laila. Specifically, I admit I've fallen desperately in love with her, but haven't had the nerve to say the magic words to her, just yet.

"I guess I'm waiting for the perfect moment," I say.

"Don't wait for a 'perfect moment,'" Amalia advises. "Just let it blurt out of you, whenever you can't hold it in any longer."

"Maybe I'll get lucky and she'll say it first."

Amalia looks at me the same way Mimi always did whenever I'd said something stupid. "Don't worry about being first, Adrian," she says. "Tell Laila you love her whenever you're ready, whether Laila has said it or not. Better to have spoken what's on your heart and risked it all, then wonder 'What if?' later."

I nod. "That's good advice, Abu. Thanks." I bite my lip. "I've got a favor to ask you. Laila is out of town until Tuesday, and all my friends are scattered for the holidays. I don't want to spend the night, all alone, in the huge house I share with Laila. So, I was wondering if I could stay here with you?"

"Of course, you can."

My heart leaps. "You don't think Reed will mind?"

"Reed would insist on it."

My shoulders soften. "It'll only be two nights. And I won't bug you. I'll just say hi to you, here and there, in between whatever you're doing."

Amalia smiles. "You can stay as long as you like."

"Thank you. I've got a bag in the car. If you'd said no, I was going straight to a hotel."

Amalia scowls. "No more hotels for you, Adrian, unless

you're on vacation. If ever you need a place to stay, you'll *always* come here. Do you understand?"

My heart bursts. "Yes, ma'am. Although I'm sure Reed will have a slightly different opinion."

"No, he won't. I've mentioned to him how much I adore you, and he was highly supportive of me taking you under my wing."

"He was?"

"Of course. Reed thought it was very sweet that we bonded when you stayed here with the show."

I run my finger over the rim of my mug for a moment, trying to imagine Reed and Amalia's conversation about me, but it doesn't compute. The Reed Rivers I know would cut off my balls, dip them in eggs and breadcrumbs, bake them at four hundred degrees, and eat them with a nice aioli sauce. "Reed must be a lot nicer behind closed doors than he seems, huh? I mean, if you like him so much."

"Reed is a prince among men and also a shrewd businessman. A man can be both."

"I wouldn't know. I'm neither."

She chuckles. "I don't know about that. You seem like a prince to me. At least, a prince in training. I'm sure Laila would agree."

I smile shyly. "Laila calls me The Beast, actually. You know, like in *Beauty and the Beast*?"

Amalia's dark eyes sparkle. "I'd bet anything that's Laila's highest compliment."

"Yeah, when she says it, she gets a naughty little gleam in her eye that gives me a little zap where it counts, if you know what I mean."

"*Adrian.* That's not what I meant."

I laugh. That's exactly how Mimi used to say my name

when I'd said something kind of naughty. I ask, "Will you say that again for me, Abu?"

"Say what?"

"My name. Like I've gravely disappointed you."

Amalia pauses, looking lovely. But, finally she humors me and repeats my name. This time, looking positively charmed by me.

"Thank you. I like hearing you say my name like that. You sound just like Mimi."

Amalia lays her hand on mine. "I'll always be here for you, Adrian."

"Thank you." I look down at my mug of tea. "I realized something after Mimi died. Even if you're lucky enough to leave this earth with white hair and wrinkled skin, there's still far too little time. And I don't want to waste mine. Not a second of it." I run my fingertip over the rim of my mug again. "Last week, I was able to sell a house I'd bought for Mimi for a tidy sum. So, I've decided to use that money to buy a place of my own and ask Laila to move in with me, when the show is over."

"How exciting. Congratulations."

"Hopefully, I'll get the courage to say the magic words to her before then. If not, that'd be pretty awkward, huh?"

Amalia chuckles.

"I don't want to ask if I can move in with Laila at her condo. That'd feel like me mooching, you know? Like me asking Kendrick if I can sleep on his couch, rather than The Beast turning into The Prince and inviting Belle to live at his castle."

Amalia puts her palm on her heaving chest. "Maybe you're not a prince in *training*, after all."

I shrug. "I'm a little nervous Laila will turn me down,

only because she loves the little condo she bought herself. She's super proud of it. So, I think I should buy a place that'll knock Laila onto her ass, you know? Some place that's a huge step up from her condo, where she'll be excited to live with me."

"I'm confident Laila will say yes to you, and it will have nothing to do with the house itself. She'll say yes because she wants to be with *you*."

"Well, that would be preferable," I admit. "But I'm not taking any chances. You should have seen her excitement when she saw the fancy mansion we're living in now. I don't want a place as big as that. I don't like big spaces. But I do want whatever house I get to have some kind of 'wow' factor. Maybe an ocean view. Laila said she loves the ocean. I'd want a home gym and hot tub, too. Oh, and a living room that's big enough for a baby grand piano."

"You play piano?"

"No, but Laila does."

Amalia smiles. "That sounds lovely."

"So I guess what I'm asking is will you help me find a house like that? My manager gave me the number for a real estate agent, but the whole thing feels overwhelming to me. I've never bought a house for myself, and certainly not one I'm planning to surprise my girlfriend with."

"Oh, you're not going to ask Laila to help you look for the perfect place?"

"No. Going house hunting with my girlfriend feels like way too big a *thing*. I just want to find the perfect house and surprise her with it. And when she's feeling blown away by my new digs, I'll surprise her by asking her to live there with me."

"That sounds wonderful. But I'm not the right person to

help you buy a house. Reed, however, is an expert when it comes to real estate. I'm sure he'd—"

Movement at the entrance to the kitchen attracts our attention, and speak of the devil, Reed enters the room, along with his fiancée, Georgina, both of them dressed to kill.

"Savage," Reed says, sounding surprised, but not upset, to find me sitting at his kitchen table.

"Adrian needs a place to stay for a few nights," Amalia explains. "His grandmother passed away recently and Laila is out of town. He'd rather not be alone."

"Of course, you're welcome here," Reed says. He and Georgina offer their condolences about my grandmother and take seats at the kitchen table.

Amalia says, "Adrian, do you mind if I tell Reed about your house hunting?"

"Feel free."

Amalia gives Reed the scoop, after which Reed enthusiastically offers his assistance, even without any prompting by Amalia.

"Wow, Reed, thanks," I say. "I appreciate that."

"Don't look so surprised," Reed says. "I told you in New York I'd owe you a personal favor if you appeared in Alessandra's music video. Well, consider this that favor."

"Don't tell Laila about this, okay? I want to get a kickass place as a surprise and invite her to move in with me when the show is over."

"Aw," Georgina says. "That's so sweet."

I bite my lip. "Hey, Georgina, I feel like I should mention . . . I didn't *actually* hit on you at that party. I mean, I did. But on a dare. It was Kendrick's birthday, and Kendrick, Kai, and I have played 'Birthday Truth or Dare' for years now. We all knew Reed wanted you, even back then, so

Kendrick thought it'd be funny to make Reed want to murder me."

Reed chuckles.

"Sorry," I say to Georgina. "That's in no way meant to imply you're not worthy of being hit on. But I know better than to step on the big boss's toes. Plus, regardless of Reed, I'd already seen Laila that night. And from then on, she was the only one for me."

"Oh my gosh," Georgina says, swooning with Amalia. "That's so lovely."

"Reed," Amalia says. "May I ask a favor of you?"

"Anything."

"When Adrian has found his new home, could you spare me once a week for a few months, so I can get him and Laila nice and settled?"

"Sure," Reed says. "As long as he doesn't try to steal you away from me."

"I've already tried, repeatedly," I admit. "And she keeps saying she'll never leave you."

"Never," Amalia confirms.

"That's a loyal woman right there," Reed says.

"And wise, too," I say. "Why do you think I keep trying to steal her?"

We sing Amalia's praises for a bit longer, until, finally, Reed gets up from the table and extends his hand to Georgina.

"Make yourself at home," Reed says to me. "Stay as long as you like."

"Thanks. I'll be heading back home the second Laila is back in town."

Reed stops in the doorway with Georgina. "Hey, I could

move a few meetings around tomorrow so we can check out some places, if you're free."

"Free as a bird. I'd love it."

Reed looks at Georgina. "Are you free tomorrow?"

"I can make myself free."

"Please do. You make everything more fun." Reed flashes his fiancée a beaming smile, the likes of which I've never seen on his face before. And in reply, Georgina pats Reed's scruff playfully, causing the huge diamond on her finger to sparkle under the kitchen lights.

Out of nowhere, the sparkle on Georgina's finger has me imagining me slipping a similar rock onto Laila's hand. Not only asking Laila to live with me in whatever fancy house Reed helps me find, but to *marry* me, too. Suddenly, I realize the idea of proposing to Laila doesn't even freak me out! Actually, whoa, yes, it does. But only a little bit. Not as much as I would have thought. And that's a pretty mind-blowing development.

". . . or in the hills?" Reed says from across the kitchen.

"Huh?" I say. "Sorry. My mind was wandering."

Reed says, "I asked if you want to live by the coast or in the hills."

"Coast."

"Okay, I've got the perfect real estate agent in mind. I'll text her now and tell her to drop all her silly plans for tomorrow."

"Thanks so much, Reed."

"What's your budget, so I can tell her?"

"You know my financial situation better than anybody. What should my budget be?"

"With all the exposure you're about to get from the show, the new album and your duet with Laila will both be smash hits. So, even if it doesn't feel like it right now, in the near future, I think it would be very realistic for you to get a place in the range of seven to nine mill."

"*Whoa.* Seriously? I bought a house for my grandma in Chicago for five mill, and I had to take out a huge loan."

"You won't have to do that this time. How much is the show paying you?"

"Zippo."

"What?"

"They're not paying me a dime. They were initially going to pay me four mill for the season. But through a series of events I don't particularly want to talk about, I'm now making exactly zero dollars for being a judge on the show."

Reed looks flabbergasted. "What the fuck, Savage?"

I laugh, realizing I'm not mad in the slightest about the money I've paid to Laila, or about the money I'm letting the show keep to ensure Laila remains on the show. In fact, I'd do it all again, if it would ensure I'd be right back here in my life, head over heels in love with Laila, wanting to move in with her. "What can I say? I traded money for love," I say. "And I'd do it again."

Reed chuckles. "Goodnight, Savage."

"Goodnight."

Reed and Georgina exit the kitchen. And when they're gone, Amalia turns to me and says, "Adrian, I don't know what you did to 'trade money for love,' but whatever it was, I know Mimi is smiling down on you, feeling very, *very* proud of you for doing exactly that."

TWENTY-NINE
SAVAGE

"Savage!" Laila shrieks happily from the foyer of our massive reality TV mansion.

At the sound of Laila's voice, the ache that's been ravaging my heart since Mimi's death and Laila's departure on her trip feels instantly soothed. In fact, as Laila gleefully screams my name again, my heart feels as gleeful as she sounds. I feel *happy*. Relieved. And certain of the path I've been sprinting down the past couple days in Laila's absence.

Having returned to this house from Reed's only a few minutes ago, I've been sitting here on the couch, excitedly skimming the offer Reed's real estate agent just submitted for me on the house of my dreams. It was a dream I didn't even know I had a week ago, but now that I've seen *that* house, and Laila is back, and I can so clearly envision how happy I could be with Laila, I know in my bones Mimi was right all along. *This* is what I've always needed and wanted. Love. Acceptance. Trust. Family. Stability. *Grace*. And I'm going to have it all with Laila.

Quickly, I slam my laptop closed and sprint through the

house toward the foyer. When I get there, I find a tanned and sparkling Laila, surrounded by far too many pieces of luggage for her short trip to Mexico. When she sees me, she barrels to me, and then launches herself into my waiting, open arms like a missile. Somehow, I catch her without falling over, and as she wraps her legs around my waist and peppers my face with kisses, I squeeze her tightly, clutching her to me, groping her ass, breathing her in, and, finally, kissing her deeply, without holding back. For the first time since Mimi died, I suddenly, in this moment, feel like *me* again. Only better. I feel at peace now. I feel whole, despite the Mimi-sized hole in my heart.

I love you, I think. But what I say is, "I missed you." Once I start saying the magic words to Laila, I'm sure they'll pop out of my mouth as easily as "good morning" and "good-night." I certainly had no problems saying them to Mimi. And I say them to Sasha all the time, too. But saying them to Laila feels different. Monumental. I want to be sure, totally sure, when the words come out of my mouth, they'll be met in kind.

"I missed you, too," she gasps out.

We've got plenty to talk about. I'm sure she'll tell me all about her trip and show me photos. And I'll tell her that I've been doing a lot better, in terms of handling my grief about Mimi. I'm sure I'll tell her some of the cool stuff Reed's got lined up for my band's album release next week. But right now, I don't want to talk. I need to get inside her.

I put her down where we're standing, pull up her sundress and yank down her undies, grab her hot little ass, and indulge in the pussy that owns me. When she's wet and moaning, even before she's come, I back her up to the nearest wall, pull my cock out of my jeans, pick her up, and impale her. I'll make sure she gets hers before we're done. But in this moment, I feel a primal, urgent need to get inside her and fuck her hard. To claim her by leaving my load inside her and marking her as mine.

My thrusts are animalistic and raw. With each hard thrust of my body, we both growl and grunt. Moan and groan. She takes my bottom lip between her teeth and grits out, "Yes!" And I fuck her with everything I've got. With each movement of my body, I'm slamming into the farthest reaches of hers. Invading her. Conquering. With each thrust, I'm leaving a piece of myself behind. Giving all that I am to her. All that I could be, if only she'll promise to love me in return. Now that my walls are down and my heart is bare and vulnerable—beating, totally unprotected, in Laila's palms—I realize just how guarded and scared I was before now. How much I held back, for fear of rejection. The same rejection I *thought* I'd suffered during the last month of the tour.

"Laila," I grit out, impaling her against the wall with every ounce of force I can muster. I've fucked her against a wall before. And those times, I've whispered into her ear, "I'm pinning you against the wall because you're a work of art." But this time, there's no way I could make a quip like that. In this moment, I can't be smooth or funny. Dirty talk isn't a possibility. I'm raw. Wrecked. In love. Desperate. I need her to understand I'm hers now. Mind, body, and soul.

"Adrian," she replies. And the tone of her voice, the fact that she's used my first name, for some reason, that one word has said it all. She's mine. Every bit as much as I'm hers.

"I love you," I choke out. "I love you, Laila."

She bursts into tears. "I love you, too." I feel her body rippling around mine. Milking mine.

A sensation of white-hot ecstasy consumes me, as my body quakes and convulses. When my body quiets down, I set Laila on her feet and kiss the hell out of her.

"How have you been doing?" she asks softly, cupping my face in her palms. And it's plain from her tone she's referring to my grief about Mimi.

"I'm a whole lot better, now that you're here."

"I shouldn't have left you."

"I insisted, remember? And, honestly, it was for the best. Being without you . . . it made my feelings so obvious. So *indisputable.* I don't only want you, Laila. I *need* you. I love you. I can't live without you. I can't be happy without you. I can't be *me* without *you.*"

Her eyes water. "I feel the same way. And it became so clear to me when we were apart. I realized . . ." She stops herself. "Actually, I have a much better way of telling you what I realized. During my trip, I wrote a little song that will tell you exactly what I realized."

I smile. "You wrote a song for me?"

"Yes and no. I wrote a response to 'Hate Sex High'—a slowed-down version with new lyrics. It's your song, done my way."

"Oh my God, Laila."

"There was a piano at the hotel and I'd go down there every night and play for a bit before bedtime. You know me. My favorite way to unwind. And one night, when I was missing you so much, I started playing 'Hate Sex High,' just to feel closer to you. And when I got to my name in the song, I switched things up a bit. And, suddenly, all new lyrics for the entire song started flooding me. I jotted them down on my phone, so I could maybe sing you my version of the song one day, if ever I mustered the courage." She chuckles. "I didn't think in a million years I'd be playing the song for you right after returning home from my trip. But now, I can't stand the thought of this moment passing without me playing it for you."

"I can't wait to hear it."

She grabs my hand and leads me into the living room. While Laila takes a seat at the baby grand, I stand next to the piano, watching her, my heart crashing with anticipation.

Smiling, Laila lays her fingers onto the keys. "Wow. This feels even more nerve-wracking than performing on *Sylvia*."

"Take your time."

She looks into my eyes for a long beat, apparently mustering her nerve. "I can't believe I'm about to play this for you. I'm so happy, Savage. I love you so much."

"I love you, too."

We share a huge smile. Until, finally, Laila begins to play her song:

True Love High

Yeah, yeah

I've fallen, fallen deep into love with you
I'm feeling something so beautiful

You saw me with him at the show
I was a liar

I played it cold to your face
I was on fire
I said I was his all along
Knew you wouldn't like it
I wanted you desperately
But wanted you only on your knees

I've fallen, fallen deep into love with you
And I'm feeling something so beautiful
I've fallen, fallen deep into love with you
And I'm feeling something so beautiful

La la la la la I love you, I love you
La la la la la la I love you, I love you

I saw you so clearly that night
Like it was the first time
You made me a bowl of fish soup
And sang with a sweet smile
I swore not to catch any feelings
But couldn't resist
Now I'm a slave to you, boy
And you're stuck with this bitch

I've fallen, fallen deep into love with you
And I'm feeling something so beautiful
I've fallen, fallen deep into love with you
And I'm feeling something so beautiful

La la la la la I love you, I love you
La la la la la I love you, I love you

You fucked with my body, baby
Then stole my heart
I said you meant nothing to me
I was yours from the start
Yours from the start
Yours from the start
All along, been chasing a
True Love High

As Laila sings out the last high note of her song, I feel a tsunami of love and certainty crashing into me. Pure euphoria. But even more than that, I feel a deep sense of completeness. I've found the great love of my life. The woman I'm going to spend the rest of my life with, without a doubt. I've found true love, exactly the way she just sang to me.

I scoop Laila up in my arms and kiss her deeply. And then, as words of love and adoration flow from my lips, as the last remnants of fear and indecision leave my body, as certainty and peace and grace flood me, I pick my woman up like a bride, carry her up the staircase and to our bedroom, and worship her body for the next two hours, stopping only when we're both too physically exhausted to keep going.

Go to
http://www.laurenrowebooks.com/laila-f-true-love-high
to hear Laila sing True Love High to Savage

THIRTY
SAVAGE

"Wake up!" Laila shouts. She taps on my forehead. *Tap, tap, tap.* "Time to wake up, Adrian! Wakey, wakey!"

I squint at her. "What the fuck are you doing?"

"I have a surprise for you!"

I look at the clock on the nightstand. It's just past eleven in the morning. Which wouldn't be an unreasonable wake-up time, normally. But, in this instance, Laila and I stayed up until sunrise, talking and making love. Rummaging through the refrigerator. Sharing a contraband bottle of whiskey while soaking naked in our hot tub. Basically, reveling in our true love high.

"Laila, go back to sleep," I mutter. "You can give me this 'surprise' later."

"I can't wait." *Tap, tap, tap.* "The most important part of my gift finally arrived a minute ago and I *cannot* wait another second to give it to you!"

I rub my eyes and yawn. "You got me a gift?"

"I did."

"Why?"

"Because I love you and you sent me and my family to Cabo and treated us to the fanciest vacation, ever. Because paybacks are a bitch, bitch! So get up!"

I sit up. "I don't need a present from you."

"Too bad. I already had a little present in the works for you, when I left for Cabo. But while I was there, I realized it wasn't nearly enough, so I started making some other arrangements. And now, I've finally got all of it and I can't wait to give it to you!" She grabs my face and kisses me. "Stay right here and don't move a muscle and don't you dare go back to sleep!" She rustles my hair, squeals, and sprints out of the room, leaving me feeling dazed and confused and highly intrigued.

A moment later, Laila returns to the bedroom, carrying a large cube wrapped in bright paper, as well as a book-sized wrapped gift lying on top of the cube. She tosses the small gift onto the mattress and shoves the large cube at me. "Open this one first."

"You shouldn't have gotten me anything," I say.

"Fuck right off with that. I have more money than I know what to do with and a man I love with all my heart. Of course, I'm going to buy you a gift or two, especially after you sent me and my family on such an extravagant trip."

"Laila, it was Cabo. Let's not overstate the extravagance here. Plus, I sent you on that trip as a *gift*. Gifts don't require *payback*."

"Would you shut up and open my gift, motherfucker? I can spend my money any way I see fit, whether you like it or not. And what I want is to give my man this *gift*."

"*Jeez.* So feisty." Chuckling, I take the large gift and begin unwrapping it and soon discover it's an old-school guitar amp.

"Oh, wow. This is so cool!"

Laila shrieks, "*It belonged to Jeff Buckley!*"

My jaw drops. I don't think I've mentioned my near-obsession with Jeff Buckley to Laila. Not that I was keeping it a secret. It just never came up. Did she hear about it from Kendrick? "Laila," I breathe, my heart pounding. "He's one of my all-time favorites."

"Yes, I know. Hence, the gift."

"Laila," I say stupidly, feeling overcome. "Wow. Thank you." I hug her tightly and sputter, "This is the best gift I've ever gotten."

"Check it out," she says. "It's super cool."

I turn my attention to the amplifier, running my hands over it. Twisting its knobs, each touch of my flesh on places where Jeff Buckley's hands also touched giving me goose-bumps. All traces of sleepiness gone, I hop up from the bed, shouting, "I'm gonna get my guitar and plug it in!"

"Not yet!" she yells. "Wait, Adrian! There's more to the gift!"

I dance around like I've got ants in my pants. Like I'm four years old, wearing my Christmas jammies, and just got a toy train that needs its caboose. "Babe, I want to get my guitar. *Please.*"

She giggles. "Before you do that, there's more to this gift." She motions to the spot I just left. "Please."

"Whatever more there is, take it back," I say, shuffling toward the bed. "It's only downhill from here. This is *literally* the best thing you could have gotten for me, in the history of time." I resume my seat on the mattress next to her. "Did Kendrick tell you how much I love Jeff Buckley?"

"No, *you* told me, without actually telling me." She winks. "You always sing Jeff Buckley in the shower."

"I *do*?"

She nods. "All the time. And, of course, besides that little lullaby you always used to sing to Mimi, you often sang little snippets of Jeff Buckley to her, too. I could tell how meaningful his songs were to you."

My heart is bursting. "Still, though, it's a giant leap that you'd think to shell out the kind of money it'd take to buy one of Buckley's *actual* amps. I'm blown away."

"I love you. That's worth more than all the money in the world."

I grin broadly, thinking about the money I've given up to keep Laila on the show. And once again, like I told Reed the other night, I'm positive I did the right thing. In fact, I'd do it again and again, every single time, if my life were *Groundhog Day*. If it meant I'd be here with Laila this morning, with "True Love High" still ringing in my ears, and Jeff Buckley's amp sitting on my bed . . . and, most importantly, Laila's beautiful smile lighting up my bedroom.

Laila points. "The amp's got papers certifying it was Buckley's. I taped them to the bottom of the amp. Check 'em out."

I turn the amp over, as requested, and I'll be damned, there's a folded-up piece of paper taped to the bottom. I detach the paper and unfold it, excited to see Buckley's name in black and white. Which I do. But I also find a small envelope with the certificate. I open the envelope and find a USB flash drive inside. I hold it up to Laila, a question on my face, and she smiles as big as the Grand Canyon.

"Adrian Savage, my love," she says. "On that flash drive, you will find . . . a rare treasure." Against all odds, her smile somehow finds a way to widen even more. She says, "That flash drive is loaded with the pro tools multi track stems . . ."

"No."

"Of the entire album . . ."

"Oh my God, Laila."

"Of *Grace!*"

"Laila!"

"Every single track from every single song on *Grace*, your favorite album by your favorite artist, the original owner of that guitar amp."

I feel like I'm going to faint. Or have a heart attack or stroke. All while being simultaneously shot out of a cannon. It's unthinkable that she's acquired this impossible treasure for me. It's beyond my wildest dreams or fantasies or imaginations. In my palm, I'm holding something priceless. Something that can't be bought on the open market: the *actual* raw files from the recording sessions which were then layered and edited and seamlessly woven together to create the songs on my all-time favorite album. In other words, she's given me the Holy Grail. A magical gift only a fellow artist would ever give—a gift only a fellow artist would possibly *understand* to give.

I thought the amp was the best gift, ever. And it was, a moment ago. But now, this is, by far, the most boner-inducing, heart palpitating, perfect, mind-blowing gift Laila could ever, ever, ever have given me. And to think she did it not only because she loves me. But because she knows me, so well. Because she's figured me out, without anyone, not even Kendrick, telling her this would be the best gift I could receive. Honestly, I don't think even Kendrick would come up with this idea, if tasked with finding the perfect gift for me. Only Laila could or would do something so magical for me. So amazing. And the effect on me is like she's given my very soul the most amazing blowjob in the history of time.

I swoop her into my arms and kiss the hell out of her, thanking her profusely. I tell her I love her, over and over again, as I take off her clothes. And she tells me she loves me, too, over and over again, as she slides her naked body onto my cock and rides me like there's no tomorrow. I devour her breasts and nipples. Massage her clit. We fuck and laugh and kiss, our euphoria palpable. I didn't know love could feel like this. I thought love like this was a fairytale. And love songs about it were bullshit. But now I know this kind of love is not only real, it's the only thing that matters.

When we're done making love, we lie in bed for a bit, kissing and laughing. But soon, I can't resist grabbing my laptop and inserting the flash drive, as Laila cuddles up to me and lays her cheek on my shoulder. As the files unfurl on my screen, I "ooh" and "aah" like I'm watching a fireworks display on the Fourth of July, and Laila giggles at my reaction.

"How did you get your hands on this?" I ask, clicking around through the files like a madman.

"Reed said he owed me a big favor for doing the music video for Alessandra. So, I called in the favor."

"I could weep."

She laughs, not realizing I'm not joking.

I pull her to me and silently hug her close for a very long moment, long enough to gather myself. Finally, I feel in control of myself enough to pepper her gorgeous face with kisses, before taking her face in my palms. "Laila Fitzgerald, if I'm ever so much as cranky toward you, if I'm ever even remotely close to being an asshole in your presence, ever, please, *please*, say 'Buckley multi track stems' and I promise on my life I'll instantly stop whatever shitty or immature thing I'm saying or doing, drop to my knees, and kiss your feet."

She makes an adorable sound of pure joy. "I'm gonna hold you to that."

"And rightly so."

We kiss again. But, suddenly, Laila says, "Oh! There's one more gift you need to open."

"No. Stop. No more."

"This one is a small token. It cost me approximately twenty dollars."

She grabs the book-sized wrapped gift from the corner of the bed, and hands it to me. "I had this made for you when we were in Chicago. But I decided to wait a little bit to give it to you."

My heart thumping, I open the wrapping paper to find the inside of an old birthday card, given to me by Mimi on the first birthday I spent with her. My thirteenth. Laila's gotten the card framed behind glass like it's an exquisite work of art. Which it is, to me.

The handwritten note on the card from Mimi reads:

My dearest Adrian,

Happy 13th birthday, my love. I thank God everyday he brought you to me, so you could light up my life like a shooting star. Whenever you get frustrated or angry, if you're feeling like the world is against you, take a deep breath and remember you're never going to be alone again. You've got me now. And I'm not going anywhere. Even when I'm gone from this earth, my love for you will remain. You're the light of my life, Adrian. I love you, forever and always.

Love,
Mimi

THIRTY-ONE
LAILA

One month later

It's around nine in the morning on my twenty-fifth birthday. I'm sitting at the baby grand in the corner of the living room while Savage sleeps upstairs. For the past hour or so, I've been working on a song for my third album that came to me in a dream.

Ever since I got back from Mexico a month ago, and Savage and I shared that incredible, magical night, during which we must have said "I love you" to each other a thousand times, I've been flooded with musical inspiration. All of it, about love. Or if not that, directly, happiness and joy. And it's no surprise, considering how great everything has been going in my life. Not only with Savage, but with the show, too. When it started airing, the ratings hit record numbers and never dipped. Which, thankfully, has insulated Savage and me from any more meddling from Nadine. In fact, she's left Savage and me alone to be happy and authentic on-camera, exactly the way she said she'd do when she called me in Chicago. And now, I can't write one of my usual "fuck you!" kind of songs to save my life.

"Happy birthday," Savage says, entering the living room, and I quickly stop playing the song I was working on—the passionate love song about Savage that came to me in my sleep.

When Savage reaches me, he kisses me in greeting and then makes me scooch over on the piano bench so he can join me. "The big two-five," he says, settling himself next to me. "I should have gotten you a walker for your birthday."

"You didn't? Darn."

Savage tickles the ivories playfully. "Nope. Unfortunately, all I got you was a baby grand, just like this one, that'll be delivered to your place when we're booted out of here in a few weeks."

I gasp. "*No.*"

Savage grins. "Happy birthday, baby."

Squealing, I hug him and thank him profusely, and we talk about my exciting gift for several minutes. "So, hey," I say, "speaking of us being booted out of here in a few weeks." I take a deep breath. I've been wanting to broach this topic with Savage for a few weeks now. He's told me in the past he hates feeling "tied down" or "locked in," but we've been so happy together, I can't stand the thought of not waking up to his face every morning after we leave here. Savage couldn't possibly want to live apart when our contractual relationship is over, could he? I walk my fingers up the piano keys, mustering my courage. "When we leave this house, where are you planning to live?"

When he's silent, I gather the courage to peek at Savage's face and find him red and flustered.

"A hotel?" I ask, returning to the piano keys.

"Uh . . . yeah. A hotel."

"I figured. I've been thinking, though . . . maybe it would be fun if you came to live with me at my condo." Savage says nothing, so I peek at him again. This time, he looks like his mind is racing. Like he's been caught with his hand in a cookie jar. "Uh oh, did I scare you away?" I've tried to make my tone sound light and bright. Like this is no biggie. Ha, ha. Just a wild idea. But, truthfully, I feel disappointed he hasn't replied with a quick and simple yes. But oh well, at least he hasn't given me an immediate no. So, that's something.

Savage's features soften when he sees whatever look of anxiety has crept onto my face. "Of course, you didn't scare me away, Fitzy," he says. "Nothing you could say or do could possibly scare me away. I just don't want to be a mooch, that's all."

I sigh with relief. "Don't think of it like that, babe. I have a place and you don't. This makes sense. One plus one equals two."

Savage bites his lower lip. "You know what? You're right. Of course, we should live together after the show, since I don't have a place of my own."

"Exactly."

"It makes perfect sense."

"I couldn't agree more."

Savage snickers.

"What?"

"Nothing. I'm just excited. Thanks for asking me to live with you."

"Thanks for saying yes." I shudder with excitement. "This is going to be so *fun*!"

Savage smiles broadly. "Yes, it is. 'A grand adventure,' as Mimi always used to say."

"Indeed."

We seal the deal with a kiss, after which I squeal again and say, "I can't wait to play my new piano in my condo! It'll be a tight fit, but I can get rid of a couple chairs and make it work."

"What were you working on when I came in? I heard a snippet. It sounded amazing."

I shake my head.

As Savage knows, I don't reveal my works in progress until I'm certain the song is worthy of being born. And that's especially true of the song I was just working on about Savage. It's the most honest, passionate song I've ever written in my life. A song I'm nervous might freak Savage out a bit, to be honest, if I play it before its time, since it contains some lyrics that will express things to Savage we haven't yet said to each other. I've told Savage I love him many times. But telling him I'm going to love him *forever*, that my love is "infinite and everlasting," as this song does, repeatedly, feels like taking our relationship to the next level, and I'm not sure he's ready for that yet.

"Okay, then, if you won't play me whatever you were working on when I came in," Savage says, "then play me *something*. You can't whet my appetite like that and then leave me hanging."

"Sure. Any requests?"

"How about one of your cool Laila Fitzgerald covers?"

I can't help smiling. Savage loves it when I transform one of my favorite songs by another artist into a slowed-down, piano cover. I pause, considering my options, and then start playing the intro to "Fireflies" by our friends, 22 Goats—one of my all-time favorite songs to sing. But since I'm playing the song much slower than the recorded original, and also on nothing but piano, Savage only recognizes the song when I start singing the famous first line: "Fireflies, you've got me feeling 'em/never before or since."

"I've got goosebumps!" Savage blurts. "Just like the ones I got when I heard you singing this song with Aloha and the Goats at Reed's party!"

I stop playing on a dime, my jaw hanging open. "You heard me singing this song at Reed's party? But you told me you didn't come inside and see the performance."

"I didn't. I was standing outside on the patio and could hear the first part of the performance from there. Don't stop. Sing me the whole thing. I love your voice on this one."

"Your wish is my command." I return my fingers to the keys and start from the beginning again, turning "Fireflies" into a piano ballad, with a few tweaks to the original lyrics, especially for my love:

Fireflies
You got me feelin' 'em
Never before or since
All my life
Been chasing butterflies
And in
Just one night
One perfect night . . .
Boy, you made butterflies your bitch

. . .

Oh, Fireflies
Oh, In your eyes

Don't know if you're feeling it
These wings and lights
Or if everything's all in my head
But there's one thing I know
One singular truth:
I need you
I need you
Boy, I need you so bad
In my life
In my bed

Oh, Fireflies
Oh, in your eyes
Oh, Fireflies
Oh, in your eyes

Fireflies
Fireflies
You got me feelin' 'em
With you
And nobody else
You're a savage
A puzzle
My destination
Would give my soul to the devil
My soul to the devil

To never stop feeling
Those
Fireflies
With you

When I finish singing my version of "Fireflies," Savage looks absolutely blown away, the same way he always does whenever I sing for him. He kisses and hugs me, whispering, "You sound even more amazing on that song than you did at Reed's party. I love it when it's just you and your piano, and no other instrumentation."

"I can't believe you heard me singing this song at Reed's party. I thought for sure you hadn't."

"I heard half of it. I left midway through the song."

"I looked for your face in the audience during the entire performance! And when I didn't see you, I decided, 'Screw it, when I'm done performing, I'll put my ego aside and find him, and be the first one to say hello.' But when I got offstage, and did a lap of the party looking for you, you were nowhere to be found."

Savage chuckles. "I heard you singing 'Fireflies' and couldn't stay at the party a second longer. Your voice was so gorgeous, so mesmerizing to me, it made me want to cock-block Kendrick the second you walked offstage. So, I left the party, right then, to keep myself from hitting on you."

"Oh my gosh," I say. "I was positive I couldn't find you because you'd left the party with whichever lucky lady you'd decided to bang that night. Georgina, or the woman you'd been talking to by the pool, or whoever else."

He shakes his head. "I didn't want to be a dick to Kendrick. By the way, I didn't hit on Georgina that night. I mean, I *did*, but only because that was Kendrick's birthday dare for me. Although, admittedly, I was thrilled to do it to get you back for flirting so brazenly with Cash in front of me."

I snicker. "I wasn't remotely interested in Cash." I wink. "But I sure did enjoy the look of molten jealousy in your eyes when I flirted with him."

"You're an evil woman," he says with a lopsided grin, but his tone feels like he's giving me his highest compliment.

I shrug. "I wanted you to hit on me, and you weren't. All's fair in love and war."

"Hell yeah, it is. Too-fucking-shay, Fitzy."

I bite my lip. "Speaking of 'Birthday Truth or Dare' . . . Will you let me play tonight at my birthday party?"

Savage shakes his head. "Only Kendrick, Kai, and I are allowed to play. We've never even let Ruby and Titus play on their birthday—and trust me, Ruby's held a grudge about it for a long time."

"Well, that's a simple fix. Let me play tonight and let the twins play on their next birthday. The more the merrier, right?"

Savage pauses. And for a second, it's like his hard drive is rebooting. Like, he's truly never considered it could be just that simple to change a longstanding tradition.

"I mean, no worries," I add quickly. "I'm cool with not playing. I'm just saying you *could* let me play, if that's what you want to do. The past is the past. The future is whatever you want it to be."

Savage stares at me, dumbfounded, making me laugh.

"Don't worry about it, honey," I say, patting his hand. "It was just an off-handed remark. You don't have to change a thing."

Savage's face is flushed. I don't know what just happened inside his brain, but I know him well enough to know he's having some deep thoughts. "You know . . ." he begins. "You don't need to be playing 'Birthday Truth or Dare' to get me to do something for you—or *to* you. Whatever you want, your wish is my command, every day of the year. You know that, right?"

I grin. "Yes, I do. I'm not sure it works that way when it comes to getting you to tell me the truth, but, yes, I know I don't need a birthday dare to get you to do something for or to me."

"Well, if 'Truth' is what you want, then you wouldn't get that, even if we let you play. There's no 'Truth' option in our game."

"But it's called 'Birthday *Truth* or Dare.'"

"That's a misnomer. We deleted the 'Truth' option years ago, when we realized truth is boring as hell."

"I don't think it's boring. In fact, if you ask the right question, then 'Truth' is far more interesting—and scary—than any dare could possibly be."

Savage considers that. "Huh." He looks at me blankly for a long moment. And then, "Well, either way, you don't need the game because I always tell you the truth."

I snort. "No, you tell me whatever truth you're ready to share. I'm not calling you a liar, babe, just saying I think I could get a whole lot more out of you if you *knew* you had no choice but to tell me the whole, unvarnished truth, so help you God, about a particular topic." I raise an eyebrow. "You want to try it now—play a private little game of 'Birthday Truth or *Truth*,' just you and me?"

"I can't think of anything I'd like to do . . . *less*." He

laughs. "But you know what I *would* like to do, as a private little game for your birthday? Can you guess?"

"Eat the Birthday Girl's Pussy?" I ask coyly. Because I know that gleam in my man's eyes. The swipe of his tongue over his lower lip. It's what Savage *always* does when he's got a boner and his tongue is craving the pleasure of a pussy well eaten.

"Ding, ding, ding!" Savage shouts. "We've got a winner!"

With that, my hot boyfriend stands, guides me onto my back on the piano bench, pulls off my panties, and with dark, burning eyes, proceeds to kick off my twenty-fifth birthday in the most delightful, toe-curling way imaginable. *Happy birthday to me.*

Go to
http://www.laurenrowebooks.com/laila-f-fireflies
to listen to Laila's cover of "Fireflies" along with Savage.

Go to
http://www.laurenrowebooks.com/22-goats-fireflies
if you're curious to hear 22 Goats' original version of "Fireflies."

THIRTY-TWO

"What do you mean you're not *drinking?*" Rhoda, the junior producer from *Sing Your Heart Out* who's become my friend—the one who gave Savage and me a tour of our love nest on day one—gasps out. She's just arrived at my birthday party and found out I'm drinking club soda tonight. I'm standing with Rhoda in the already-crowded living room of the reality TV mansion I share with Savage—and Rhoda is beside herself with exasperation to find out I'm not drinking tonight in solidarity with Savage. Rhoda yells above the din, "But it's your own damned birthday party! You at *least* need to sip a glass of champagne on your own freaking birthday!"

I shake my head and hold up my glass. "I promised Savage I wouldn't drink while he's contractually not allowed to drink."

Rhoda looks surprised.

"You don't know that's one of the terms of Savage's employment?" I ask. "That he can't drink during the season?"

"I had no idea."

"Nadine doesn't want to see Savage's dick trending on Twitter again."

Rhoda snorts. "It's nothing the world hasn't already seen."

"Tell that to your boss."

"I will." Rhoda pulls out her phone. "With the ratings you two have been pulling in, Nadine should at least give Savage a one-night dispensation to get drunk off his ass, at his own fake house, to celebrate his very real girlfriend's quarter-century."

"Make it happen, Rhoda!" I shout. "I believe in you!"

"I'm going in!"

As Rhoda begins tapping on her phone, I look around the crowded party and notice a group coming through the front door: Fish and Alessandra, Dax and his wife, Violet, and Colin with a pretty date. I race over to the group and exchange greetings with everyone. I meet Colin's date, who seems sweet. And, of course, everyone wishes me a happy birthday.

For a few minutes, I stay and chat with the group, glancing occasionally at Savage across the room. At present, he's doing that thing I love the most: belly laughing with Kendrick and Kai. All of a sudden, a feeling of delicious *déjà vu* washes over me. I can't believe my celebrity crush, whom I watched laughing with those very same bandmates across Reed's crowded party months ago, has now become the great love of my life.

"Okay, Laila, I made it happen," Rhoda, the producer, says, diverting my attention from Savage across the room. She says, "Nadine said Savage can have a *one*-night dispensation to get shitfaced for your birthday, as long as you *personally* guarantee his dick won't make a single new appearance on Twitter."

"Woohoo! Tell Nadine thank you and I accept her terms." I turn and shout into my party, to no one in particular. "Somebody get Savage and me some booze! *Savage!*" Someone taps his shoulder and says something to him, and he looks at me from across the party, just as Rhoda is handing me a champagne glass. I hold it up and point, since the party is noisy, and then motion to him and me, him and me—and then to Rhoda. For her part, Rhoda holds up her phone by way of explanation and nods, and that's all Savage needs. With a loud whoop, my boyfriend grabs a full drink right out of Kendrick's hand, throws it back in one fell swoop, and shouts something I can't make out above the loud music.

Someone turns the music up, even louder, drinks are poured, and less than an hour later, I'm buzzed to perfection and dancing like a fool in the middle of my living room with Savage and a rowdy group of our best friends—Savage's bandmates, some of my musician friends, and, of course, Aloha and her entire crew: her husband, Zander, and the guys from 22 Goats with their dates.

I can't help noticing there's been a complete lack of tension between Colin and Savage tonight, and I'm glad about it. In fact, I've caught the men sharing a laugh here and there. Perhaps, Colin showing up to my party with a date has put Savage at ease. Or maybe the therapist Savage started seeing last week, with plans to see her once a week, has already rubbed off on him. Or maybe Savage finally feels secure enough in our relationship to trust our love for what it is: rock solid.

When the current song on Alessandra's party playlist ends, none other than "Hate Sex High" begins blaring. And of course, the entire party goes ballistic. When Fugitive Summer's album released a few weeks ago, this particular song, which was released as its leadoff single, went straight to number one. And not just in the United States—in countries all over the world.

It was a first for Fugitive Summer to have a leadoff song capture that much global success, and Savage and his fellow band members have been thrilled about it. And not just for the pure accomplishment of it, but because of . . . the *money*. Oh my God, the *money*. Savage isn't a particularly money-driven person, but, still, money means freedom, and it's now clear Savage will be free as a bird for the rest of his life, along with his bandmates, provided nobody does anything too stupid. The one-two punch of "Hate Sex High," along with Savage's high profile on the show, has caused interest in Fugitive Summer and its entire catalog to skyrocket, which, in turn, has launched Fugitive Summer to a whole new level of success.

As "Hate Sex High" hits its first verse, the members of Fugitive Summer find each other on the dance floor and sing the song together loudly, throwing their heads back and jumping around like lunatics, while the entire party sings and laughs along with them. There are a whole lot of musicians and music industry types here tonight, so we all know the success Fugitive Summer is currently having is lightning in a bottle—quite possibly, never to be repeated, no matter how successful they might be in the future—and we're all thrilled to celebrate this amazing time with them. Nobody more than *me*. The muse for the song. La La La *Laila*. The woman who came three times while chasing a "hate sex high."

Fugitive Summer has never confirmed or denied the

widespread belief that the song is about *me*. But it's awfully hard to miss my name at the end of those "la la" lines, no matter what Savage has always stupidly insisted. And so, when the song blaring in the party gets to that part in the song, everyone in the room screams my name at the tops of their lungs, making Savage pick me up and spin me around, while singing along with his own blaring voice. "Laila, Laila."

Even if someone hearing this song for the first time had never heard of Laila Fitzgerald, or had never seen that viral video of Savage and me fighting on a sidewalk or watched my interview on *Sylvia,* they'd know this song is about some chick named *Laila.* Some chick named *Laila* who wanted to "ride" Savage, and did. Some chick named *Laila* who came *three* times in hot pursuit of her "hate sex high." And now, finally, by singing along with the recording at the top of his lungs along with all of our friends, Savage is finally tacitly admitting what the world already knows: yep, he's most definitely singing "Laila" and not "la la" on those parts.

Of course, when the line "You came three times" comes up in the song, the party sings it even louder than anything else, and then goes ballistic around me. When Savage speaks that same line in the middle of the song in a smug, sardonic tone—"You came three times"—the entire party shouts it along with him, while looking straight at me, every single person playfully chastising me along with Savage's snarky voice for claiming sex with Savage had meant "nothing to me."

If my party guests think they're going to make me blush by serenading me on that line, however, they're dead wrong. I'm too drunk to be embarrassed about my sexual appetites at this point. Too in love. In fact, I'm so in love with the man dancing with me right now, the man who threw me this party and earlier today agreed to live with me at my condo when the show is over, I can't do anything but raise my arms in victory and celebrate joyfully. Fuck yeah, I came *three* times with my hot boyfriend, bitches! And since then, I've come a whole lot more! What, *you* don't come three times, or more, with *your* man? Well, that's a pity, sis. I guess my boyfriend is a whole lot hotter, and a whole lot better at putting his fingers, tongue, and dick to use than yours. Ha!

When the song reaches its last, spoken lines: "Did *he* make you come *three* times? Yeah, didn't think so," the party yells the line, yet again. And as they do, my drunk boyfriend bends down and motorboats my rack on the outside of my dress, claiming his prize. Making it clear *he* made me come three times, and *nobody* else. In response, I throw my head back and laugh hysterically, reveling in the fact that Savage feels every bit as unleashed and in love in this moment as I do. I'm in love with Adrian Savage. Riding a true love high. And I'm positive, even when the booze that's coursing through my bloodstream is gone, I'll never *ever* come down.

When "Hate Sex High" ends, and Savage is done motorboating me, he lays a deep kiss on me, making the party cheer and whoop. As his tongue slides into my mouth, I slide my arms around him and devour him, the whiskey on his tongue reminding me of our first kiss at Reed's house.

"I have a birthday present for you," Savage says, grabbing my hand. "Come on."

I hold my breath as he leads me through the crowd. *Is he going to propose?* I can't believe it, but that's the first thing that's popped into my head. That's a crazy thought, right? An unthinkable one. But I've thought it, distinctly, and now, as Savage leads me through the crowded room to parts unknown, I can't *stop* thinking it . . . and *hoping* for it.

When Savage stops, we're standing in front of Kendrick and Kai. He says, "Guys, I demand we let Laila play 'Birthday Truth or Dare' tonight. I won't take no for an answer."

Oh.

Well.

That's incredibly sweet. And I should be thrilled. It's a romantic gesture, considering our conversation this morning while seated at the piano. But I can't help feeling vaguely disappointed, even though there's no logical reason for me to feel that way. Savage once told me he's not boyfriend material. So, come on, Laila, give the guy credit for how far he's come and leave it at that.

In response to Savage's "demand," Kendrick and Kai look at each other like, "What the fuck?"

Kai says, "If we say yes to Laila, then Ruby and Titus will never forgive us. Especially Ruby." He looks at me. "It's nothing personal, Laila, but we've never let *anyone* but the three of us play the game."

"Oh, I understand," I reply.

But Savage is determined. A dog with a bone. "You have to admit we've been running out of good ideas for a while now," he says. "The best Kai could come up with for me last time was a naked swan dive into a swimming pool? I mean, come on! The whole world had already seen my dong by then. And yet *that's* what he thought would humiliate me? *Please.* I vote we invite not only Laila, but Ruby and Titus into our game, too, from now on. But if you can't handle that much change, all at once, then at least let the three of them in for one year, as a test-run, to see if it makes the game more fun. If not, they're out again. We'll make that clear to them up front so there are no hard feelings if we wind up booting them."

Kendrick and Kai consult briefly, before declaring their verdict.

"Okay, but only this year on a probationary basis," Kai says. He looks sternly at me, "You understand the terms? This is a one-shot deal, for now."

"So you'd better make it good," Kendrick adds with a wink.

"I understand. Thank you!" I whoop and do a happy dance. "Are there any rules or limitations?"

"Hold up," Kai says. "Let's get Ruby and Titus over here to give them the good news. Ruby's been demanding to be included for years."

Kendrick retrieves the twins and brings them to our group. And when Ruby hears the good news, she loses her ever-loving mind, like she's just found out Fugitive Summer has been nominated for a Grammy—which, by the way, is something I predict is in Fugitive Summer's near future. When she finishes hugging all three of her benefactors, Ruby hugs me and we laugh and squeal together, while Titus looks at us like we're lunatics. Obviously, Ruby and I are overreacting here. But what I've learned in life is this: overreacting to good news is a whole lot more fun than underreacting to it. Plus, we're drunk and happy and surrounded by a whole lot of happy people, so why not wring every drop of fun out of the situation?

"Okay, Laila, let me tell you the rules," Kai says. "Ruby, Titus, listen up. You won't be performing dares tonight. You'll be admitted into the game, officially, on your birthday."

"You think we don't know the rules by now?" Ruby mumbles, but when Kai nonverbally chastises her, she mimes zipping her lips.

"Rule number one," Kai says. "Your dare can't be something that would maim, kill, or send any of us to prison."

"Shoot," Ruby says, snorting, while I think to myself, "You're assuming I won't pick *Truth*?"

"Two," Kai says, counting off on his fingers. "The dare has to be something the person can do, right here and now. You can't demand we perform some complicated prank that would take hours or days to perform. We have to be able to do it, spur of the moment."

"Dang it!" Ruby says. "There goes my idea of making all of you bitches get a Brazilian wax."

Rolling his eyes, Kai addresses me again. "As long as you follow those two rules, Laila, then the third rule of the game is that your minions have no choice but to do *whatever* you say. We're your loyal subjects, Birthday Queen. Powerless to say no."

Ruby raises her arms to the ceiling. "My prayers have been answered!"

"Dude," Titus says to his sister. "Why are you so excited? Only Laila is doling out dares this time."

"No shit, Sherlock," Ruby replies to her brother. "I'm *vicariously* excited for Laila. For what this means for *womankind*." She turns and massages my shoulders, like she's my cornerman in a prizefight, about to send me into the ring in a title bout. "Okay, Laila. You gotta *represent*, girl. Make womankind proud."

"I'll give it my all, coach!" I say, dancing from foot to foot like a boxer. And when Aloha happens to walk by, an idea pops into my head. Kai Cook is a "too cool for school" type.

The last person in the world who'd ever "fanboy" over *anyone,* least of all a Disney-star-turned-pop-princess. I remember Kendrick once telling me about the time he made his big brother "fanboy" over Keane Morgan, the actor from Alessandra's video shoot, during a game of "Birthday Truth or Dare," so, I decide to follow Kendrick's expert lead for my first foray into the game.

"Kai, you're up first," I say. "I dare you to fanboy over Aloha, until you get her to sing the theme song to 'It's Aloha!' for the entire party. If you can't convince her to sing it, then *you* have to do it."

Our entire group, other than Kai, breaks into raucous laughter. As we all know, Kai doesn't sing. *At all.* He's a fantastic bass player. One of the best in the business. But God did *not* bless him with dulcet vocal cords. Which is why, fun fact, Kai is the only member of Fugitive Summer who never supplies background vocals on any of their songs. Not even the singalong "la la's" in "Hate Sex High."

Predictably, Kai looks tortured as the rest of us laugh with glee. Scowling, he says, "You're girlfriend's a savage, Savage."

Savage smiles at me. "She sure is. It's my favorite thing about her."

In the end, though, as torturous as the dare sounds, it turns out to be a softball. Not surprisingly, Aloha wound up refusing to sing the theme song to her long-running Disney show—after ten years of hearing it everywhere the poor girl went, she now *hates* that song with the passion of a thousand suns. But when Kai finally dragged himself to standing on a chair, poised to sing the hideous song for the entire party, and Ruby turned off the blaring music and got everyone's attention while I sat at the piano to accompany Kai, my victim didn't get two words into the first verse before the *entire* party started singing loudly along with him. In fact, thanks to the iconic theme song being burned into our generation's gray matter, everyone at the party couldn't help singing along with Kai, the same way a knee can't help kicking forward when batted by a doctor's rubber hammer. In fact, by the song's end, even Aloha had started singing along with Kai and the crowd, despite herself. Which tells me she's drunk as hell or an awfully good sport.

When the singalong led by Kai finishes, the entire party applauds and whoops and asks for another singalong. And so, seeing as how I'm sitting at the piano, and 22 Goats is here at the party, I play one of my all-time favorite singalongs —"Fireflies"—the same one we performed at Reed's party. The song I performed for Savage this morning, before he gave me some mighty fine birthday oral sex. And, immediately, it's clear I've picked well. On the iconic line, "Girl, you made butterflies your bitch!" the crowd sings at the tops of their lungs. And in each easy, singalong chorus, the party practically blows the roof off our reality TV mansion.

When our collective performance ends, the crowd demands *another* song. But this time, I stand on the piano bench and tell everyone to put a cork in it because I'm playing my first ever game of "Birthday Truth or Dare" and won't be distracted from it a moment longer.

"That performance from Kai kicked off our game," I explain. "And now, it's time for my dare for Kendrick!" The crowd cheers, apparently already feeling as invested in the game as I do. With a wide smile, I address Kendrick. "KC, I dare you to hit on Reed Rivers over there, to the very best of your abilities, stopping only after you've successfully made him *smile*."

Everyone but Reed claps and hoots in response to my edict. Reed shouts, "Leave me out of this, Fitzgerald!" But his tone is playful.

"Aw, come on, Reed," Savage yells. "It's her birthday!"

The crowd goads Reed on, enthusiastically, until, finally, the music mogul relents.

"Okay, fine," Reed says, and, in response, the crowd cheers like their team just scored a goal at the World Cup.

"Don't go easy on him, Reed!" I shout across the room. "You have to make Kendrick work for that smile!"

"I know of no other way," Reed deadpans.

And away we go. To the great pleasure of the crowd, Kendrick saunters over to Reed. But he doesn't stop when he reaches him. He walks right on by. Immediately, though, Kendrick doubles back, looks Reed up and down lasciviously, and says, "Oh, hey there, baby. Do you believe in love at first sight . . . *or should I walk past you again?*"

Of course, the crowd loves it and reacts accordingly. But Reed doesn't look even tempted to smile. In fact, Reed replies flatly, "No, you can keep on walking with a piss-poor line like that, motherfucker."

Kendrick snorts. "It's not gonna get much better than that, unfortunately." As the crowd laughs and applauds, Kendrick puffs out his cheeks, contemplating his next attempt. But when it's clear Kendrick is ready to try again, the crowd goes quiet with anticipation. "Hey, baby," Kendrick says to Reed. "Do me a favor. Feel my shirt."

"Because it's made of 'boyfriend material'?" Reed supplies. "Sorry, you're gonna have to do better than that."

"Fuck."

Everyone in the room, other than Reed, guffaws again.

But Kendrick won't be denied. Squaring his shoulders,

Kendrick flashes Reed an incredibly hot smolder and says, "Hey there, sexy . . . I seem to have lost my phone number. Can I—"

"Have mine?" Reed interrupts. "No. Fuck off."

There's another round of laughter, before Kendrick swipes his thumb over his nose, winks at Reed, and says, "Hey, gorgeous, are you a parking ticket? Because you've got—"

"*Fine* written all over me." Reed shakes his head. "Amateur. Bush league. Weak. Try again."

And on and on it goes, pretty much just like that, through four more rounds. Until, finally, Reed breaks. But not in response to anything *Kendrick* has said—but in response to something *Reed* himself has said. Kendrick asks, "Can I follow you wherever you're going, Reed? Because my *momma* always told me to—"

"*Follow your dreams,*" Reed interjects, his expression set in stone. And then, he takes a step forward, getting into Kendrick's handsome face, and says, "Do me a favor, KC. Tell your momma I said, 'Fuck Kendrick. Fuck his dreams. And thanks for sucking my cock last night.'"

"Reed!" Georgina shouts, as the party explodes with shocked laughter. And that's when Reed throws his head back and guffaws at his own inappropriate joke.

"That doesn't count!" Kai shouts, as his brother raises his arms in victory. "Kendrick didn't make Reed smile! *Reed* made Reed smile!"

But the rest of the party agrees it did, indeed, count. And, quickly, the group's attention turns to Savage. *My last victim.*

Someone yells, "Make him show us his cock!"

"Just google him if you want to see that," I fire back, and the party hoots with laughter.

"No more dick pics from Savage!" Rhoda, a producer from *Sing Your Heart Out,* yells.

I quickly assure Rhoda, and the boisterous crowd, I've got no desire to add to Savage's online dick pic collection tonight. "Actually . . . ," I say from my perch on the piano bench. I smile at Savage below me. "For Savage, I pick *Truth.*"

"Truth isn't an option," Savage says quickly. But his bandmates desert him instantly, with all of them saying I can pick any damned thing I want, since I'm the Birthday Queen.

"*We* never pick Truth because we know everything there is to know about you," Kendrick explains to his best friend. "But as the Birthday Queen, Laila is all-powerful."

I return to Savage and realize anything worth asking him, I'd want to hear his answer in private. Also, like Savage said to me this morning, there's no need to "dare" the man to do a damned thing, since, one, he'd do any important thing I asked, whether it's my birthday or not, and, two, any not-important thing I might dare him to do, in order to humiliate him in front of a crowd, wouldn't be fun for me. I have no desire to humiliate my sweet boyfriend, even for fun. And even if I did have that urge, it wouldn't outweigh my desire to ask Savage an important question and *know*, without a doubt, he felt required to tell me the *whole* truth, without spinning or half-truthing it.

"I tell you what," I say. "I'll pick Truth *and* a rain check. We'll finish this game later, behind closed doors, when it's just you and me, as long as you agree that Truth is an option."

The crowd boos.

Ruby is beside herself.

The Cook brothers tell me that's not allowed.

But I'm firm in my decision and can't help noticing Savage looks deeply relieved.

"You've got yourself a deal, Fitzy," Savage says, his dark eyes sparkling.

The faux-angry crowd begins throwing napkins and empty Solo cups at me, but I don't care. I hop off the piano bench, straight to the love of my life, and kiss his sensuous lips.

"Don't think I'm letting you off easy," I murmur. "Whatever I ask, you'll need to tell me the whole truth, so help you God."

"That's the game," he says. "All I can say, though, is be careful what you wish for."

Go to
http://www.laurenrowebooks.com/hate-sex-high-music
if you'd like to listen to Fugitive Summer's number one hit,
"Hate Sex High" again.

The house is finally empty. All partygoers have left. It's the wee hours of the morning on the day after my twenty-fifth birthday—the best birthday of my life—and I'm presently sitting on my boyfriend's face on our couch, having an intense orgasm.

When my body stops warping and rippling, and my groans come down, Savage guides me off him, flips me onto my hands and knees, and fucks me from behind like I'm nothing to him but a blow-up doll he purchased online. *And I love it.* He calls me his "dirty birthday girl" and grips my hair. He tells me I'm hot, and his, and that watching me dancing to "Hate Sex High" earlier tonight, and owning that shit like a boss, turned him on like crazy. Until finally, Savage is coming hard inside me, followed by him fingering me until I do, too.

When both our bodies are spent and we're way too exhausted to keep going for now, we cuddle naked on the couch for a long moment, catching our breath. For a fleeting moment, I have the impulse to spring up from the couch and play him the song I've been writing for him. "Savage Love." But I quickly decide, no. First off, I'm not finished tinkering with the song. But, more importantly, I'm not ready to say all that "infinite and everlasting" stuff to Savage, just yet.

When I spoke to Mimi in private, during those last days of her life, she explained that Savage has always suffered from extreme anxiety, though the world would never guess that about him, based on his swagger and showmanship. She told me the thing that helps him keep his anxieties in check is taking things one day at a time. Not making firm commitments about the future. Not feeling tied down.

"That's why Savage proposing to you is especially wonderful," Mimi said to me. "It's a huge breakthrough, to know he loves you enough to be able to envision, and promise, *forever* to you."

Obviously, it wasn't true. Savage had promised no such thing to me. And the weight of that lie hit me like a ton of bricks at the time. But nonetheless, that conversation with Mimi has helped me understand Savage better, which has helped me keep my expectations about him in check. For now, the boy has agreed to move into my condo with me when the show is over in a couple weeks. Surely, if Mimi were here and somehow found out we aren't actually engaged, she'd nonetheless feel Savage's agreement to move in with me, on its own, was a huge breakthrough for him. A massive commitment, standing alone. And I'm determined to be satisfied with only that, without also dreaming about exchanging promises of "forever" with him, as well.

"So, what 'Truth' do you want to know, Fitzy?" Savage asks, pulling me from my thoughts.

"Hmm?"

"Birthday Truth or Dare," he says. "What's this all-important question you have that's more important than getting to watch me make a fool of myself in front of all our friends?"

I pause, considering my options, and finally settle on the one thing that's been nagging at me the most lately—actually, ever since the press conference, and then even more so after our conversation in Chicago, when Savage admitted he hasn't slept with anyone else since first laying eyes on me at Reed's. *What's the whole truth about what Savage said to that Instagrammer at Kai's birthday party?*

I haven't talked to Savage about that, since those very first days when he swore, up and down, he didn't mention my name to her, simply because I've been certain he wouldn't give me a straight answer, even if I asked. Or maybe I haven't asked Savage recently about this because I've been afraid the truth wouldn't be as romantic as I've come to hope. If Savage *did* tell that woman he had to "lay low" for the show, and nothing more, I'd rather not hear that now. On the contrary, I'd rather continue fantasizing about a fairytale where my gorgeous Beast told that Instagrammer he couldn't sleep with her that night because he had his sights set on someone named *Laila.*

I stroke Savage's naked chest and the grooves in his abs for a moment, keeping him in suspense. And finally say, "Okay, here's my question—and I want the whole truth. Tell me whatever you can remember about your conversation with the Instagrammer at Kai's birthday party. I know you were drunk and don't remember *everything,* especially now that so much time has passed, but—"

"I remember every word of that conversation. At least, every word *I* said to *her.*"

My breathing hitches. I look up from his chest and something in his moonlit expression makes me sit up, all the way on the couch, and brace myself for whatever is going to come out of his gorgeous mouth next.

Following my lead, Savage sits up, too. "You want the whole truth? Well, here it is. When I saw her video the next morning, and heard her tell the world I'd said your name *twice,* I was scared shitless she'd outed me—but also relieved as hell. I felt like I'd dodged a huge bullet. Because the *full* truth is that I said your name at least *ten* times to that woman during our short conversation."

"*What?*" I whisper.

Savage's dark eyes flicker with heat. "I was totally and completely obsessed with you by that point. Tortured you hadn't answered any of my texts during the tour, or after it. Tormented you hadn't come to my room in a single city, despite how much I'd begged you. I'd been dreaming about you, pretty much every night. Pulling out my hair, trying to understand how the night of the hot tub wasn't as big a game-changer for you as it had been for me. So, when I saw that woman, and she looked so much like you—although, to be clear, you're *way* hotter than her—I lost it. I told her she looked like you—that she reminded me of *Laila.* And finally saying your name out loud to someone broke the seal on my madness, so to speak. And, suddenly, I couldn't stop myself from confessing everything. *Laila, Laila, Laila.* I poured my heart out to her. Told her how obsessed I was with you. How tortured I'd been. But I guess she didn't hear most of it, due to the noise at the party. When she asked me to take her upstairs, I was shocked. I'd just told her, in no uncertain terms, that I only wanted *you.* And this bitch's response was to think I'd fuck *her* as your stand-in? It pissed me off to think she, and the whole world, assume I'm *that* big a player. So, I told her no, I didn't want to go upstairs with her or anyone else. I told her I'd made a *promise* to myself not to have sex with anyone but *Laila*, ever again. Until the end of time. And that she should feel free to tell the whole world I'd said so."

I gasp.

"I knew who she was the whole time. I'm not stupid. She was constantly tagging me and the band in her posts and videos. So, I drunkenly *told* her to post a video outing me because I wanted *you* to see it. Because I wanted you to know how much I wanted you. Because I wanted you to finally put me out of my misery and contact me, even if only to tell me why you didn't want me the way I wanted you."

I can't speak or breathe. My jaw feels like it's resting in my naked lap. The world feels like it's warping around me.

Savage says, "When I woke up the next morning, my sober brain realized how stupid and reckless my drunk brain had been. So, when Eli gave me a plausible interpretation of what I'd said the night before, I ran with it. But it was *Eli* who said I must have said I had to 'lay low' because of the show. Not me. I didn't use the word 'promise' in relation to my contract with the show, Laila. I said everything that Instagrammer claimed I did and much more. I wanted you so badly, it physically hurt by then, and I couldn't figure out, for the life of me, why you didn't want me, too."

"Oh, Adrian."

I kiss him, passionately. And when our kiss ends, he strokes my cheek and looks deeply into my eyes. "You want to hear a few more Truth bombs?" he asks, his dark eyes on fire. "Because now that I'm confessing the whole truth to you, I don't want to stop."

I nod furiously. "I'll take as many Truth bombs as you've got."

Savage drops his hands from my face and takes one of mine in his. "I watched your set every night during the tour. I sneaked into the wings and hid behind this huge speaker at stage right so you wouldn't see me, and I watched every minute of every performance. Unless, of course, I left a little early to drag some random groupie into your dressing room at precisely the right time for you to walk in and find me."

I bite my lip. "I did the same thing, basically—minus the groupies. I could have left the venue every night after my set was finished. But I never did. Half the time, I listened to your set in my dressing room, with a glass of wine. I'd touch myself and listen to your voice singing 'Come with Me.' And it never failed to make me come, no matter how much I hated you."

"Oh, my God, Laila. That's so hot."

"Other times, I'd creep into the wings during your set and hide behind that same huge speaker at stage right, so you wouldn't see me. And your performance never failed to blow me away. It's how I knew, deep down, I didn't hate you. If I did, you never could have given me goosebumps—which you did every time I watched you."

Savage's chest heaves. "The Video Music Awards. I bet you thought we got put together as presenters, by chance? Or maybe by the producers on purpose, thanks to that viral video of us fighting on the sidewalk in New York?"

I nod, as a mischievous grin spreads across Savage's gorgeous face.

He shakes head. "*I* did that. When the show called to ask me to present an award, I said I'd only do it if they paired me with *you*."

I bite my lip, feeling turned on by this latest revelation.

"I was desperate. You weren't answering my texts and I had to see you again. By then, I'd convinced myself you were in love with Charlie. It was the only thing that made sense. And I had to know."

"The chorus in 'Hate Sex High'?" I ask, breathlessly. "Was the 'something' you didn't want to feel a kernel of truth or a popcorn lie?"

"You already know the answer to that, Laila. The 'something' I was feeling was straight-up obsession, which wasn't something I wanted to feel—and definitely not something I wanted to admit to you."

I kiss him fervently, but abruptly break free of his lips, my breathing ragged. "I already know the truth about this next thing, but I want to hear you say it. You're singing 'Laila' at the end of those 'la la's.' Admit it."

Savage chuckles. "Of course, I am. As a matter of fact, I was hard as a rock the whole time I was recording the vocals to that song. I closed my eyes and thought about you and practically came in the recording booth."

"That's so hot." I kiss him again. And when my clit begins pounding too insistently to ignore, I stroke Savage's cock to hardness, and then slide myself down on it. I fuck him, slowly, while kissing his gorgeous lips. And as our bodies move together, I whisper that I love him. That I'll *always* love him. I've never used that word before with him. Never confessed the endlessness of my love for him. Never been brave enough to pledge my forever in words. But I do it now, as my body moves with his. And to my thrill and joy and relief, Savage whispers that he'll love me "forever," right before coming beneath me.

THIRTY-FOUR
LAILA

Two weeks later

"How's that?" my makeup artist, Susanna, says.

I open my eyes and look at myself in the mirror. "Gorgeous. Love it."

"I added a little extra glitter to your lids this time, so your eyes will sparkle like crazy as you look lovingly into Savage's eyes during your duet."

"Brilliant. The glitter gives off a 'fairytale princess' vibe."

"Along with a little splash of 'He's all mine, bitches!'"

I giggle. "Well, with this face, that's unavoidable."

We've made it to the last episode of the season—the "live taping" of the finale, during which this season's winner will be crowned. I'm in my dressing room with Susanna, awaiting my cue to perform with Savage in about fifteen minutes. Currently, the top ten contestants of the season, other than the two finalists vying for the crown—my quirky, blue-haired crooner, Addison, and Savage's powerhouse belter, Glory—are onstage with Aloha, performing a cheesy group rendition of Aloha's latest hit.

I look at a large clock on the wall of my dressing room and realize I've got a solid ten minutes before I'll need to hit my mark. "I think I'll watch the show from the wings," I say. "I'm too amped to sit still." For more reasons than one, if I'm being honest.

Yes, I'm nervous to perform the duet for the first time. But Savage and I have rehearsed relentlessly, so I'm pretty confident our performance will go off without a hitch. Plus, the song is fantastic—catchy and swoonworthy—a textbook hit, even if it's far more about Fish and Alessandra's uncomplicated love story than mine and Savage's. No, I think the true source of my nerves is the fact that, since Chicago, Savage has never again mentioned that bonus the show offered him. The one where he'd earn a cool two hundred fifty thousand bucks, merely for *faux*-proposing to me after our performance. And I can't help thinking maybe, just maybe, he hasn't mentioned it because he's decided to do it . . . *and maybe even for real.*

I know I'm crazy to think it. To *hope* it. But I can't help myself. Even if the odds are low, I think there's a small chance he'll get down on bended knee the minute we stop singing, and the very thought makes every cell in my body electrify with giddiness.

When I arrive at the wing of the stage, I look around for a PA, or someone with a headset, to make sure the production staff knows where I am. These "live taping" shows are an intense juggling act for the crew, since they're shot precisely as the show will air, with no editing or re-dos. So, given my upcoming performance, it's critical everyone knows where to find me at all times.

As I'm looking around for someone in a headset, I spot Nadine, the executive producer, standing with her back to me alongside Rhoda, the junior producer who's become a good friend. Given that Rhoda and Nadine are both wearing headsets, I head over to the duo, intending to tap one of them on the shoulder and wave, as if to say, "Here I am." But when I get close enough to overhear the women's conversation, I stop short and listen in.

"Who knows if Savage will do it?" Nadine is saying as I come to a stop behind her. "Unfortunately, his contract states he can decide, yes or no, if he wants to earn that bonus, right up to the last moment. So now, all we can do is wait and cross our fingers."

"I'm betting he'll do it," Rhoda says confidently. "And not for the bonus—but for *real*."

Nadine snorts. "I wouldn't hold my breath on that, Rhoda."

"You didn't see him at Laila's birthday party. He's head over heels in love with her, Nadine, for real. Anyone could see it. But, hey, if his love for her doesn't convince him to propose to her on national TV, then maybe a quarter-million bucks will tip the scales for him."

"Try a *million* bucks."

"*What?*" Rhoda gasps out, as I clamp my hand over my mouth to keep my own gasp from becoming audible.

"I made a secret side deal with Savage," Nadine says. "But don't worry, I'm not stupid enough to have agreed to paying him a million bucks out of pocket. He let me keep his full salary, two million, in exchange for me promising *never* to terminate Laila and to leave them alone to be 'happy' without any meddling. If he proposes tonight, like a good little boy, then he'll get a million bucks of the money we've withheld from him."

I clamp my palm over my mouth again, this time to keep myself from screaming.

"Did you give him the ring?" Rhoda says.

"Yeah, a few minutes ago," Nadine replies. "I told him to put it in his pocket, so he'd have it, just in case. And I'll be damned, he took it. So who knows? I'm hoping that's a good sign." Nadine scoffs. "Or maybe he's just fucking with me."

"No. I'd bet anything he's going to give her that ring. A million bucks, a free ring, *and* the chance to propose to the woman he loves on national TV? What rational man *wouldn't* leap at a deal like that?"

"I think we both know Adrian Savage is anything but rational."

I've heard enough. Plus, now that the group song onstage is wrapping up, I'm scared to death these two women will turn around and catch me crouching behind them in the dark. I turn on my heel and sprint away on my tiptoes, as Sunshine Vaughn announces a commercial break.

When I reach my dressing room, I shut the door behind me and lean against it, my eyes wide and my chest heaving. There's so much to unpack here, my brain feels like it's exploding. Out of every shocking thing Nadine just said, however, the thing that's rising to the top of the heap is the part where Nadine said Savage forfeited his *entire* salary in exchange for Nadine's promise not to fire me. *When the hell did that happen?*

I pace circles in my dressing room, too freaked out to sit. I'm insanely grateful Savage swooped in to protect me like that, but I wish he hadn't. I already felt bad enough that he had to give up two million bucks to get me onto the show, in the first place. And now I find out he gave up two million *more* to *keep* me on the show?

All I can hope and pray is that Savage realizes his best bet is to get down on his knee after our performance is done, and fake-propose. Obviously, I'd love to hear those amazing words out of Savage's mouth one day, for *real*. And, selfishly, I'd love to hear them tonight, even if it's only for pretend, solely to have a beautiful, false, fairytale moment with Savage, however fleeting and fake. *Laila, will you marry me?* Just imagining those words coming out of Adrian's mouth gives me goosebumps, even if it's only for show. But, truly, the main thing here is that I want Savage to get himself paid.

I stride toward the exit of my dressing room, determination flooding me. I'm going to hunt Savage down and tell him I know everything. I'm going to demand he fake-propose to me in a few minutes to earn that bonus, and *also* tell him I've decided to return every penny he's paid me this season. I've felt guilty about taking half Savage's salary for a while now, and what I overheard from Nadine was the last straw. It's not like I don't have the ability to make an incredible living on my own now. Thanks to my exposure on the show, I've become a household name, which my agent, Daria, has already started leveraging for all sorts of new projects and ventures. Regardless, though, even if I'd be penniless after returning Savage's two million bucks, I'd do it, anyway, simply to get this elephant off my chest, once and for all.

Before I get to the door of my dressing room, however, someone knocks on it. "Laila?" a voice I recognize as belonging to a PA shouts. "Time to take your mark for the duet!"

"Coming!"

As I follow the production assistant through the back-stage area to the spot where I'll await my cue to walk onstage, I look around frantically for Savage, so I can tell him every-thing that needs to be said. *But he's nowhere to be found.*

Finally, when the PA and I arrive in the wings, I see Savage standing across from me in the wings on the other side of the large stage. Crap. I forgot the director decided at the last minute he wants Savage and me to start singing from opposite ends of the large stage, and then walk toward each other during the first verse. I'm sure that blocking will make for a delightfully dramatic performance and all, but, unfortu-nately, it means I won't have a chance to talk to Savage before we start singing.

"Okay, Laila, stand by," the PA whispers, a hand on her headset. "Three, two . . ." She gestures toward the outer edge of the stage, and I take my mark in the dark, my heart thrum-ming. I accept a live mic handed to me by a crew member and inhale deeply, just as Sunshine Vaughn bellows, "And now, it's Savage and Laila, performing the world premiere of their duet, 'Perfect for Me'!"

The audience applauds wildly, the lights come on, the band kicks off, and Savage and I begin walking slowly toward each other across the large stage, as planned. I sing first in the song—a line about Savage being imperfectly perfect. Blah, blah. And he replies that I'm a "Picasso"—a bit of a mess, with my colors bleeding outside the lines, yet always a "work of art" to him. Blah, blah. And by the time we sing in unison in the chorus about being imperfectly perfect for each other, we've both reached the middle of the stage.

I'm giving the song my all, which thankfully quiets the raging storm in my head. And I can tell Savage is giving it his all, too, even though he's been clear he thinks the song is a "gigantic cheese-fest." And by the time we reach our final, soaring notes, there's no doubt the audience is transfixed.

After we sing our last note together, the band plays the song's melodic outro, and, just like that, everything I was thinking before the music started playing crashes into me, all over again. I lean forward, intending to say, "Get the bonus, Savage!" . . . but freeze when Savage touches his pocket like he's about to slide his hand inside and grab something.

I wait. Hold my breath. And as the music ends, Savage touches his pocket *again* . . . and then unceremoniously drops his empty hand to his side.

Fuck!

I lean in and whisper to him through my smile, like I'm a ventriloquist who's speaking through a dummy, "Bonus. Now." But Savage remains frozen and smiling at me as the audience applauds wildly.

I lean forward, intending to repeat my command, but when I do, Savage goes in for a kiss, making the audience applaud even more wildly. Flustered, I break away from his lips and whisper into his ear, "Get the bonus!" And in reply, Savage grabs my hand and raises it with his, like we're actors executing a Broadway curtain call.

When the audience roars again, Savage puts his arm around me and pulls me close, making it pretty damned clear he's *not* about to kneel before me.

I'm shocked at how long the lights and cameras have remained trained on us, without turning off or the show cutting to commercial. The director is letting this post-performance moment go on for much longer than usual, isn't he? But finally, the bright lights in our faces fade to black. The little red light on the camera directly in front of us turns off. And the director yells, "And we're clear!"

So, that's it.

In the end, Savage decided not to propose. Not even for pretend. Not even to recoup a million bucks out of the four million he forfeited because of me. Not even when he was offered a free freaking ring from some fancy jeweler. I have no doubt Savage loves me with all his heart. For crying out loud, the man secretly paid two million bucks to keep me on the show, netting him literally *nothing* in salary for three months of hard work. But the fact remains, no matter how much Savage loves me, proposing to me—even if only for pretend—was a bridge too far for him.

I shouldn't feel disappointed about that. But if I'm being honest, I do. I desperately wanted Savage to earn that bonus. But even more so, I want Savage to want to marry me! Yes! My feelings are so clear now. More than any amount of money or fame or success in my career, I want to marry Adrian—and I want *him* to feel the same way.

When the lights turn off, a PA immediately escorts Savage and me offstage, before I've had a chance to say a word to him. She compliments our performance and instructs us to wait with her in the wings while Sunshine announces this season's winner. "Once Sunshine makes the announcement," the PA explains, "the winning judge will run onstage to congratulate their contestant for a moment, before the remainder of the cast joins the winning judge and contestant onstage for the 'big celebration.'"

"It's gonna be Addison," Savage whispers to me, referring to the blue-haired cutie who's amassed an unprecedented army of fans since the first audition episode aired.

I take a deep breath. That's what he wants to talk about, after what he just decided *not* to do out there—who's going to be crowned this season's winner on the show? "It'd better be," I whisper, even though there are a thousand other things I want to say, if we were alone. Or maybe, if only I had the courage.

"And the winner this season is . . ." Sunshine, says onstage, as the two finalists—mine and Savage's—huddle together next to the host, both contestants looking like they're going to barf. Sunshine looks up from the opened envelope in her hands and shrieks, "*Addison Swain!*"

As streamers and glitter burst from the ceiling above the stage, I feel swept away in my excitement for Addison and forget about my own concerns for a moment. I hug Savage standing next to me, crying tears of joy for my blue-haired favorite, and a moment later, the PA nudges me and says, "Go congratulate Addison now, Laila! *Go, go, go!*"

As the house band begins playing an upbeat, celebratory dance song, I stride gleefully onto the stage to my darling pixie and take her into my arms. For a long moment, we cry together. I don't know about Addison, but this feels like the finish line of a legit marathon to me.

Out of nowhere, Sunshine shoves a microphone in Addison's face, and she breaks from our hug to thank me profusely for making her win possible. She goes on to thank the audience at home for voting for her, week after week. And her family for their support, too. She thanks the writer of every song she's ever performed, and Sunshine and the producers of the show, and I laugh and cry with her, through it all.

When it's my turn to take Sunshine's microphone, I tell Addison she was already a star the minute she walked onstage that very first time and blew me away. "Your victory today has nothing to do with me, honey," I say, and I mean it with all my heart.

Once I've made my little speech, the whole cast descends onto the stage—the other three judges and all four mentors—and we commence a not-so spontaneous dance party in celebration of Addison's win, as well as yet another successful season of the show. The most successful season yet, as a matter of fact, in terms of ratings and popularity. In fact, from what Daria has told me, Nadine has already indicated her fervent desire to have Savage and me return next season. And not only that, to sign both of us to a multi-year deal.

As music and dancing and laughter continue swirling around me onstage, I glance at Savage across the crowd to find him laughing with genuine abandon with Kendrick, Fish, and Colin, and my heart skips a beat at his easygoing demeanor. It's especially gratifying to catch him, once again, looking comfortable and friendly with Colin. After my birthday party, I asked Savage if he'd said something to Colin to bury the hatchet, and Savage confirmed he had, and that Colin had been extremely receptive and appreciative.

While I'm still looking at my boyfriend, his gaze finds mine. For a moment, time stops as we smile at each other from across the crowded stage, both of us basking in not only our love, but also our newfound freedom from the pressure-cooker of the show. The constant social media posts we've been required to make. The fishbowl nature of it all. On the one hand, it's been the happiest three months of my life, living and working with Savage. And I know Savage feels the exact same way. But I'm also more than relieved to move onto the next phase of our relationship, a much more private one that's not for show, but only for us. I can't wait to find out who we are when we're living together in my tiny condo, rather than a sprawling reality TV mansion. I can't wait to find out who Savage and Laila are when nobody is watching.

The director yells, "We're clear!" and a loud cheer rises up onstage.

Without hesitation, Savage beelines over to me, weaving in and out of happy people. When he reaches me, he swings me around, whooping with joy.

"Free at last!" he booms, before pulling me into him for an exuberant kiss.

"I love you!" I shout amidst the din. And he returns my words, as well as my beaming smile. In the midst of our canoodling, Savage and I are interrupted by Aloha and her husband, Zander, both of whom hug me, and then Savage, and congratulate us on our first season.

"Have you signed on for next season yet?" Aloha asks, putting her palms together in prayer. "Daria told me they're rabid to have you."

I look at Savage and say, "We're still thinking about it." But, in reality, I know it would take a miracle to make Savage say yes to another season—an offer he truly can't refuse. I add, "Our agents are haggling with Nadine, probably as we speak."

"Well, don't sell yourselves short, guys. They had their best ratings, ever, this season. And that certainly wasn't because of *me*. It was because of you two." Aloha addresses Savage, specifically. "Laila and I share an agent, Daria, so she already knows what I make on the show, since Daria's the one who negotiated my deal. But if it helps your agent in negotiations for you, tell him or her I've got a five-year deal, ten mill per season. You and Laila are both worth the same as me now. So, tell your agent not to accept a penny less." She looks at me. "That goes for you, too, girlie. Get yourself paid."

"Holy fuck," I blurt, simply because it never occurred to me to tell Daria to demand what Aloha makes. Aloha is already a legit icon in the industry, after all, and I'm still a relative newbie next to her.

To my surprise, Savage reacts calmly to Aloha's suggestion. "Thanks for the intel," he replies smoothly, his tone tacitly admitting he agrees with Aloha's assessment. "I'll pass it along to my agent."

My chest tightens at the idea of me ever being *that* rich. Growing up, my mom, sister, and I saved our spare change in a jar to afford my piano lessons! But, regardless, it's a moot point because Savage has told me repeatedly he's got *zero* desire to continue as a judge, and I'd never continue as a judge without him. Not that the show would want me without Savage, anyway.

"Are you going to the wrap party now?" I ask Aloha and her husband, eager to change the subject.

"No way, dude, I'm outta here," Aloha says. She snuggles her gorgeous husband. "All I want to do is go home with my man, crank up the fireplace, and have a quiet night, just the two of us."

"That's our plan, too," I say, snuggling into Savage's side in the same way Aloha is doing with Zander. "It's our last night at our fancy mansion. Tomorrow, we're moving into my little condo. So, I've asked our chef to make our favorite meal —cioppino—and get a nice bottle of champagne for us. We're going to eat and drink and relax in our hot tub."

Aloha shoots me a little wink, letting me know she's well aware I've ended my sentence before getting to the best part of all—the part where Savage makes me scream the way she overheard that night, from across the hall. It's crazy to think that drunken night at Reed's house was only three months ago on the calendar, considering it feels like a lifetime ago. Savage and I have not only fallen deeply in love since then, which is earth-quaking news, in and of itself, but we're also *irrevocably* in love. Committed to nurturing and safeguarding our love, always. No matter what. *Forever*. If I'd had a crystal ball three months ago, and saw where our relationship would end up, I never would have believed it. Not in a million years.

After a bit more conversation, Aloha and Zander head off, hand in hand, while Savage and I do the same. We change clothes in our respective dressing rooms for the last time and gather our stuff. We say goodbye to staff and crew and administer hugs here and there. We thank Nadine and a couple other producers we run across, all of whom say basically the same thing: they're eager to put together a multi-year deal with us for many seasons to come. And what does Savage say to that? A noncommittal, "Send your offer to our agents and we'll have them take a look."

Finally, we head to the back of the studio and slide inside our usual SUV to begin our drive to our reality TV love nest for the very last time. As our car pulls away from the curb, Savage looks at me and exhales a long, slow, deep breath. "We did it, Fitzy. Hallelujah."

Leaning my head on his broad shoulder, I whisper, "What a ride."

"Baby," Savage says, kissing the top of my head. "I promise the best of our ride is yet to come."

L aila and I are sitting in the backseat of our SUV
with our usual driver and bodyguard, supposedly
heading to our reality TV mansion in Malibu for
the last time. In actuality, though, we're headed a few miles
down the road to my new, kickass pad—the fully furnished,
four bedroom, cliffside home Reed helped me find and
purchase, and which Amalia and Georgina helped me
personalize and perfect. *And I'm losing my fucking mind.*

When we arrive at my new house, I'm not only going to
tell Laila the shocking news that the place is mine, and that I
want her to move in with me, I'm also going to get down on
my knee and ask Laila to be my wife. Not for pretend. Not
for a bonus. And certainly not with a ring supplied to me by
a sponsor of *Sing Your Heart Out*. No, I'm going to ask Laila
to marry me for *real*, with a million-dollar rock I personally
paid for and picked out for her, although I admit I made my
final decision about which ring to purchase with the help of
Amalia, Georgina, and Sasha on FaceTime. Because, for
fuck's sake, a guy's got to put it *all* on the line when he asks

the woman of his dreams to marry him, including laying down his own goddamned money. Plus, I never would have forfeited the chance to see Mimi's little diamond shining like the most beautiful star in heaven in the setting of my future wife's ring.

". . . during the celebration," Laila is saying, pulling me from my thoughts.

"Hmm? Sorry. I was zoning out."

Laila smiles. "I said I liked seeing you having fun with Fish and Colin during the celebration. It seems like you've buried the hatchet with Colin."

"Yeah, you were spot-on about that whole thing. Plus, Dr. Reynolds told me I should mend fences whenever I can, so . . ."

Laila's smile broadens. She's already made it clear she's beyond thrilled I've started seeing a therapist once a week.

"I think you'd like seeing someone, too," I say, reacting to Laila's smile. "After only a few sessions with Dr. Reynolds, I'm already realizing my childhood has affected me far more than I've ever understood. I bet it'd be the same for you."

Laila nods. "Aloha has a therapist she adores. I'll ask her for the name."

"Good."

Our phones buzz at the same time, and we look down to find a group text from Reed, sent not only to Laila and me, but to Fish and Alessandra, as well, letting us know our cheeseball duet is now sitting at number one on the daily singles downloads chart.

"*Yes!*" Laila says, laughing.

"I have a feeling that sappy love song is going to make us a boatload of money, Fitzy."

"Woohoo!" Laila says exuberantly, and we high-five. She

bites her lip, contemplating something for a moment. "Is it weird I don't feel any emotional connection whatsoever to that song?"

"I feel the same way. That's because the song isn't about us."

"I'm glad it's not," Laila replies. "I wouldn't have wanted to bare my entire soul and the deepest depths of my love for you for the first time on national TV."

I furrow my brow, as the implication of what Laila just said hits me. "You're saying you haven't bared your entire soul to me yet?"

Laila shakes her head. "I've told you how much I love you in *words*. But telling you how I feel in a *song* would be a whole other level." She smiles shyly. "I've actually written a love song to you. I've been working on it for a while now, but haven't felt ready to play it for you . . . until now." She bites her lip. "Now that we've finally got the duet behind us, I'm suddenly dying to play it for you when we get home."

My heart skips a beat as tingles skate across my skin. I've been feeling close to positive Laila will say yes when I propose to her tonight, but, somehow, hearing her say she's written a love song to me, and is now ready to play it for me, obliterates any last irrational shreds of doubt I've been harboring. Laila is a true artist. Which means, although she's damned good at expressing herself in words, it's when she sings and plays her piano that her truest voice can be heard.

I take Laila's hand and squeeze it. "I can't wait to hear the song."

My phone buzzes in my lap and I look down. This time, the incoming text is from my manager, Eli. When Laila and I first got into the car, I relayed Aloha's message about her compensation package, and now, Eli is telling me he's already in the midst of a back-and-forth with producers that makes him feel confident their next written offer, which will be coming shortly, will be in line with Aloha's deal.

I plop my phone onto the car seat. "Eli says he's sure the producers are going to offer me a deal in the range of Aloha's."

"Holy shit," Laila gasps out.

"Have you told Daria what Aloha said?"

Laila shakes her head. "There's no need. Daria is the one who negotiated Aloha's deal. I trust Daria to get me whatever I'm worth."

"No, babe." I motion to Laila's phone in her lap. "Text Daria and tell her you won't take a penny less than what Aloha makes. Make that clear to her."

Laila scoffs.

"Yes, Laila. Tell your agent to coordinate with mine before she responds to any offer. Tell her I'm instructing Eli not to take any deal unless the exact same package is offered to you."

Laila's eyes are wide. Her chest heaves, but she doesn't pick up her phone.

"*Laila*," I say, picking up her phone and shoving it at her. "Do it. Tell Daria not to respond to any offer until Eli gives her the green light. I'll instruct Eli to get the best possible deal for me, nothing less than Aloha's, and *then* tell the producers I'll only take their offer *if* they give the exact same one to you."

Her face flushed and her hand trembling, Laila takes her phone from me. "So . . . does that mean you're willing to say *yes* to doing the show again—and for multiple seasons—if they pay you the same as Aloha?"

I shrug. "If they were to agree to pay me and *you* the

same as Aloha, and also to leave us alone and not require any social media from us, then, yes. That is, if doing the show again, and for multiple seasons, is something *you*'d want." That last part is a bit of theater. I'm one thousand percent certain Laila wants to continue doing the show. But why not give her the chance to talk it through?

Laila's face is the portrait of a woman going out of her mind with excitement who's pretending she's not. "Well," she begins, "I had a blast working with you this season. And I loved getting to spend time with Aloha, too. I thoroughly enjoyed working with my contestants."

"You were a natural with them."

"When Addison won, it was one of the best moments of my life."

"I could tell."

Laila sighs happily, apparently reliving the joy she felt for Addison when the young singer's name was called. She continues, "Aloha loves doing the show and says it's the easiest money she's ever made. So, I think if we just had to show up each week and do the judge thing, the same way Aloha does, without having all that other crazy stuff hanging over our heads, we'd probably have a great time. The shooting schedule wouldn't get in the way of our music. I've written my entire third album this past month, while still doing the show."

I take in her sparkling blue eyes and hopeful expression. I'd never stand in the way of Laila getting to do this, and the producers have already made it clear they want *both* of us, as a package deal. Plus, if the producers truly do come back with money in the range of what Aloha gets, I'd be a fool to turn it down. Not only for myself, but because my continued exposure on the show will wind up lining my bandmates' and manager's pockets, too.

Laila adds, "I'd never want to force you to do something that would make you miserable, though."

I squeeze her hand. "I could never be miserable doing anything, if I was doing it with you." I pick up my phone and begin tapping out a text to my manager. "I'm telling Eli to be sure to coordinate with Daria on this. And not to bother me until they've offered everything I want."

"Sounds good," Laila says. She starts tapping on her phone. "I'm telling Daria to sit tight until she hears from Eli." When she puts her phone down, she looks beside herself with excitement. In fact, she can barely sit still. "Well, damn," she says, "I feel a whole lot better now about you not earning that bonus tonight. If we get this deal, that bonus will feel like chump change, huh?"

Shit. I was hoping Laila wouldn't mention that stupid bonus tonight. Not when, unbeknownst to Laila, I'm going to propose to her for *real* in a matter of minutes.

When I say nothing, Laila fills the awkward silence. "Were you even tempted to earn the bonus tonight?"

Damn. She's obviously not going to magically drop the subject, without me responding. "Uh, no. Once we told Mimi we were engaged, proposing to you on the show was a moot point."

Laila presses her lips together for a long moment, during which I literally pray she drops the subject. But nope. A moment later, Laila says, "Did the producers give you a ring to give to me? I thought I saw you touching your pocket a couple times, right at the end of our song."

Fuck. "Yeah, they did. Some jeweler supplied a ring for promo, and Nadine made me put it in my pocket before I walked onstage, in case I suddenly became overcome by the impulse to get down on bended knee." I chuckle. "I knew Nadine would be watching me with bated breath when our song ended, so I touched my pocket a couple times, just to fuck with her." I flash Laila a wicked smirk, thinking she'll laugh along with me, but she doesn't. In fact, she looks downright stressed. "Aw, come on," I coax. "Nadine deserved that. She's a master at messing with people's emotions. Two can play at that game."

Laila shoots me a tight smile but says nothing, which tells me she's got something big on her mind.

"What is it, Laila?" I ask.

She pauses an eternal beat before blurting, "I know what you did, Savage! I know *everything*."

Every hair on my body stands on end. What, *exactly*, does she know? Does she know about my new house? About the engagement ring in my pocket? Thankfully, Laila speaks again before I've stupidly started confessing everything to her.

"I overheard Nadine talking to Rhoda before we went onstage," Laila explains. "Nadine told Rhoda she'd made a side deal with you that let them keep your *entire* salary—two million bucks!—in exchange for them not firing me."

Well, shit. I wasn't expecting that. I didn't want Laila knowing about any of that, ever. I open and close my mouth, feeling tongue-tied, and Laila forges ahead before I've choked out a single word.

"Nadine said she thought there was a good chance you'd propose after the song, in order to get back half the money you'd let them keep. She said they gave you a free ring *and* promised you could earn back a million bucks by proposing to me. But you didn't do it!"

I'm still opening and closing my mouth like a fish on a line, incapable of forming words.

"You gave up an easy *million* bucks, Savage!" Laila shouts. "How could you do that? I don't care how much you might be making on the new album or on future seasons of the show, that's still a *ton* of money. Especially when you've already paid *me* two million bucks! I wish so badly you'd told me you'd forfeited your entire salary for me, because I never would have let you do that. Thank you so much. Thank you from the bottom of my heart. But I was already feeling so terrible about taking half your salary—"

"Laila, stop. We agreed not to talk about the money, remember?"

"No, *you* agreed. When did you make that side deal with Nadine?"

"In Chicago. Right before Mimi died. And I'd do it again. I have zero regrets."

"Why didn't you tell me what was going on?"

"Why make you feel stressed and guilty, when it was something *I* wanted to do, for my own happiness? Don't you see? I made that deal with Nadine for the same reason I bought that house for Mimi. For the same reason I bought a house for Sasha. Because I love you and want to take care of you. And, also, because, selfishly, I couldn't stand the idea of being stranded on that stupid fucking show without you."

"*Selfishly?* Savage, what you did is the most *selfless*—"

"Please, don't make this a thing, Laila. I did it because I love you and wanted the best for you—because I knew Nadine would be making a huge mistake to get rid of you. And I was right! The show had its best ratings *ever* and now they're *begging* you to sign a multi-year deal. Fuck Nadine! We got the last laugh, baby!"

Her nostrils flare. "Well, I hope you know I'm going to pay you back every dime you paid me this season. That's non-negotiable, Adrian."

I trap my lower lip between my teeth. Laila looks incredibly beautiful right now. Fierce and determined. Feisty and self-righteous. It dawns on me there's no need to argue with her about this right now, considering that, before the night is through, Laila will be my fiancée. And soon after that, my wife. Which means everything I have will be hers, including the two million bucks she's now insisting on repaying me.

"Okay, baby," I concede. I bring her hand to my mouth and kiss it. "Pay me whatever makes you feel good, as long as your repayment buys me the freedom of never, ever having to talk about that two million bucks again."

She grins. "Deal."

We shake on it.

"I'm grateful for what you did for me," she says, her eyes pricking with tears. "Thank you."

"Laila, did you hear a word I said? *I did it for me.*"

She chuckles, and a tear falls down her cheek. She wipes it and sighs. "Would you ever have told me what you did for me, if I hadn't overheard Nadine and Rhoda tonight?"

"No. Never."

"I don't understand."

"Would you have done the same thing for me, if the situation had been reversed?"

"In a heartbeat."

"Then, you *do* understand."

We share a huge smile, and two seconds later, our car takes a different turn than our usual route.

"Where are we going, Mike?" Laila calls to the driver.

"I've asked him to take a detour, so I can show you something," I interject. "I've got a little surprise for you."

"How long will the detour take?" she asks. "I've arranged for dinner to be waiting for us at home."

"Only a few minutes," I say, even though I'm thinking, "*Only the rest of our lives.*"

The car makes a turn, and then another, before coming to a stop in front of my new house.

"Surprise," I say, gesturing out the car window.

Laila follows the trajectory of my gesture and looks straight at my house. But it's clear from her facial expression she has no idea what she's seeing. "Where are we?" she asks. "Who lives here?"

I try not to smile too big. "Let's go inside and find out."

Laila's jaw drops. "Did Kendrick buy a house?"

I chuckle at Laila's shocked reaction. If she's this excited for Kendrick to buy himself a new, beautiful house in Malibu, she's going to have a straight-up aneurysm when she finds out the true owner of this beauty. "You guessed it," I say. "Nothing gets past you. Do you like it?"

"I *love* it. It's *gorgeous*. Wow. Good for Kendrick."

"Let's go inside and say hi."

"Yes! How exciting!"

We get out of the car and walk, hand in hand, toward our new home, as Laila babbles happily about the beauty of the house and its spectacular location. As she rambles, it takes all my willpower not to interrupt her to scream, "The house is ours, you fool! I want you to live here with me, forever!"

My new house isn't huge, like Reed's place. It's not small, by any stretch. But nobody would ever call it a mansion. Which suits me perfectly. As far as I'm concerned, the place is the perfect size for Laila and me and our needs.

We've got enough room for ourselves and any guest we might have—Sasha or Laila's family. Plus, some extra rooms for music- and pottery-making. And best of all, there's a perfect place in the living room for Laila's baby grand—a spot in a corner overlooking the ocean. The house is so perfect for Laila and me, in fact, I wanted it the second I walked through the front door. The minute I entered the house, I said to Reed and Georgina and Reed's real estate agent, "We're done for the day. I'm home." And that feeling only grew and solidified as we visited subsequent houses throughout the day, just in case, none of which held a candle to the cliffside house that had instantly felt like home to me.

When Laila and I arrive at the front door of our new house, she rings the doorbell. And when I punch a code on the box by the door, she rolls her eyes and says, "Of course, Kendrick gave you the code. You two are so cute."

I open the door and follow her inside, and while she gushes about how gorgeous it is, how spectacular the view, how much she loves the furnishings, I say, "I'm glad you like it. Because it's not Kendrick's new house. It's *ours*."

"*What?*" she shrieks.

"I bought it for us, baby. So we could live here together. Please say yes."

She throws herself at me and screams, "Yes!" And I laugh and hug her to me.

We kiss and hug for a long moment. She asks me a thousand questions about when I bought it, how long I've kept this secret. Until, finally, I laugh and say, "Come on, baby. Let me give you a tour of your fancy new house."

THIRTY-SIX

SAVAGE

"**O**ur living room. Obviously." I gesture toward the room we're standing in. "You won't believe the ocean view in the daytime. It's a little slice of heaven."

Laila rushes to the floor-to-ceiling windows on the far side of our living room, and when she gets there, she presses every inch of her body against the glass, like she's one of those rubber lizard toys that adheres to glass with suctions cups. Of course, I can't help belly laughing at her exuberance.

"It's *gorgeous*," she whispers. "Oh my God. I can see so many stars!" She turns around, her face aglow. "I can't wait to sit out on the balcony and watch the sunset with you!"

"My thoughts exactly."

She sprints across the room and flings herself at me, almost knocking me over. "I love it!" Her eyes land on the baby grand piano in a corner behind me and she gasps. Squealing, she disengages from me and lopes over to it, bounding across the room with exaggerated movements, like she's a gazelle bounding through tall grass. And, once again, I belly laugh at her enthusiasm.

"I hope you don't mind I had it delivered here, rather than to your condo," I say, even though her body language makes it clear she's thrilled.

"Thank you!" she shrieks happily, hugging and kissing her beautiful new instrument like it's her long lost child. "I love you, baby!" she coos. But she's not talking to me. She's talking to her new piano.

Without hesitation, Laila slides onto the piano bench and whips off the introduction to one of her biggest hits. "Listen to that sound! It's glorious!" She gasps. "Should I play you the song I wrote for you?" I open my mouth, but before I've said a word, she answers her own question. "No, let's wait. I'm way too excited to see the rest of the house. I won't even remember my lyrics. Come on!"

She leaps up and takes my hand and drags me into the adjacent kitchen. And then proceeds to hug the island and every professional-grade appliance. She opens cupboards and drawers and fawns over every little detail. She holds up a cheese grater. And then a can opener. A couple pots and pans. All of which make her "ooh" and "aah" like she's watching a spectacular fireworks display.

"How do you have *all* this stuff already?" she says.

"I bought it fully furnished, with Reed's help, and then Amalia and Georgina helped me with the finishing touches." I tell her the story of how I wound up staying a couple days at Reed's house after Mimi died, while Laila was still in Cabo. "Great news," I say. "Amalia said she'll come over once a week to hang out with me. I mean, *technically*, she said she'll come over to 'help me with the house.' But I'm going to make her sit down and hang out with me whenever she comes."

Laila giggles. "I can't believe you've kept this secret from me, all this time."

"It's been excruciating," I admit. "I've almost blown it, like, a thousand times." I kiss her cheek. "Sorry about the meal we're not eating back at the mansion. I'll text the chef and tell him to take it home to his family."

"Why don't we order cioppino to be delivered from Salvatore's?" she asks.

"I already did."

Laila laughs at that coincidence, that we've both planned the same celebratory meal for tonight, while I pull out my phone and send a text to our chef. We finish the tour of the house, with Laila reacting to each and every room with even more excitement than I'd hoped. And, finally, when the tour is done, I realize it's time. *This is it.*

"While we wait for the food to arrive," I say, "I have a little surprise for you, out on the balcony."

"So many *surprises!*" Laila gushes, taking my hand and letting me lead her.

When we get to the balcony, I tell her to stay put at the railing. And then, with my heart crashing even louder than the waves in the nearby ocean, I grab a rectangular, wrapped box from behind a chair and bring it to her.

"For you," I say, handing her the wrapped box.

After thanking me, Laila rips open the paper . . . and immediately bursts into tears when she beholds the token of my affection inside. It's a rose encased in glass. The real-life version of the enchanted rose from *Beauty and the Beast.*

"Oh, Adrian."

"Laila," I say, my voice becoming thick with emotion.

"Thanks to you, I've learned to love and to be loved, before the last petal has fallen. Thanks to you, I've transformed from The Beast into your prince. Hopefully, the kind of prince who won't disappoint you."

She touches her heart and whispers, "You could never disappoint me."

"I hope this goes without saying, but I promise to keep fucking you like a Beast, forevermore, even if I'm going to be the Prince now, in all other ways."

Laila laughs and nods with tears in her eyes. "I love you so much."

I inhale a deep breath, take the box from Laila and put it down, and then take both her hands in mine. "Laila, what I'm trying to say with this Beast metaphor is that, from this day forward, you're not only 'allowed' to go into the West Wing, it's *yours*. Because the entire castle is *yours*. Literally and figuratively. Everything I own, everything I *am*, it's all *yours*. Forever."

"Oh, Adrian. I love you."

Shaking, I pull a ring box from my pocket—the one containing the million-dollar rock I bought for Laila with my own money. The one *I* chose for her, that wasn't supplied to me by some jeweler looking for a promotional opportunity.

When Laila sees the box, she gasps. And when I open the lid and she sees the rock nestled inside, she lets out a garbled sound of excitement and shock, the likes of which I've never heard from her.

I swallow hard. "I didn't propose to you on the show tonight because I didn't want you thinking, even for a second, my proposal was fake. And I didn't want to do it for *real* for a TV audience. I'm sick of sharing our love story with the world, Laila. I'm not doing this for money or fame. None of that stuff matters to me, if you're not there with me, enjoying it all, right by my side, forever."

With that, I sink to my knee, making Laila burst into sobs. I hold up the ring and smile up at her, emotion turning into a hard lump in my throat. "Laila Fitzgerald," I whisper. "Not too long ago, I felt coerced into a fifty-fifty partnership with you. But I want you to know, I'm now one hundred percent yours, voluntarily. With this ring, I give you all of me. I want you to take everything I am and everything I'm going to be. It's all yours, just as long as you say yes to being my wife." My hopeful smile broadens. "Laila Fitzgerald, will you marry me?"

"Yes!" she screams. "Yes!"

Tears threaten my eyes, but, somehow, I swallow them down while standing and sliding the ring onto her finger. The ring in place, and our agreement made, I pull my fiancée into me for a deep kiss, and then wrap my arms around her and hold her tight.

After a moment, when I've gathered enough control of myself to speak again, I take Laila's hand and point at a cluster of diamonds nestled around the central rock. "See this little diamond here? That's from the ring Jasper gave to Mimi—the diamond that was in her wedding ring."

"Oh my gosh." She physically convulses with emotion.

"Mimi wanted you to have that diamond in your ring, so you'd always know she was smiling down on us from heaven."

Laila throws her arms around me. "I love it. And I love you. Thank you so much." She pauses. Pulls back. "But what about Sasha? Shouldn't Sasha have Mimi's diamond?"

"No, Sasha wants you to have this."

Laila returns to hugging me and loses herself to sobs.

I hold her shaking, quivering body for a long moment, feeling happier in this moment than I've ever felt in my life. I feel Mimi's love and guidance all around me. I feel certain I'm on the right path, with the great love of my life—a woman I'm going to love and protect, forever. I pull back and look into Laila's tear-filled eyes. "I love you, Laila, and I always will. I can't wait to spend the rest of my life with you."

"I love you, too." She wipes a tear. "I've got a savage love for you, Adrian Savage. It's infinite." She touches my cheek. "And *everlasting*."

EPILOGUE

LAILA

Kendrick, as Savage's best man, raises his champagne flute to Savage and me, and everyone in attendance at our small wedding, which we're having at Reed's sprawling home, follows suit.

"To Savage and Laila," Kendrick says. "You two are perfect for each other. I sincerely believe that. Laila, you make Savage a better man." Kendrick looks at his best friend, the groom, and smiles. "And, Savage, you make Laila make you a better man."

Everyone laughs.

Raising his glass even higher, Kendrick bellows, "Cheers to the bride and groom!"

The party erupts and Savage and I kiss.

We're outside on Reed's large patio, underneath twinkling lights. Savage and I both have shiny new rings on our third fingers and perma-grins on our faces. Our wedding this evening has been a fairly simple affair, attended by our closest friends and family. And it's been perfect. Straight out of a fairytale.

We pulled our wedding together a bit faster than we maybe envisioned when Savage proposed four months ago, once we realized how busy we were going to be in the coming year. My third album just released and it's already soaring. "Savage Love" is my biggest hit, by far, and I've been hard at work on designing a makeup line, too.

Savage and his band are working on their next album. And I have no doubt it's going to be another smash hit. Soon, my husband and I begin shooting the next season of *Sing Your Heart Out*. Our first of four seasons we signed on to do. And once shooting on the show ends, Fugitive Summer and I are going to participate in a "festival style" tour with a slew of other artists, including 22 Goats, Aloha, and Alessandra—a new touring concept that will make the process of bringing live music to our fans a whole lot more fun and less of a grind for everyone involved.

All things considered, Savage and I realized we had to get married pretty quickly, and in a relatively simple fashion, or else wait another year and a half to do it in grand style. So, here we are. And, frankly, I wouldn't have it any other way. The past four months in our new house have been magical for us, to the point where we've both felt an urgent desire to call each other "husband" and "wife," sooner rather than later.

If you ask me, it's not necessary to be married to someone to love them wholeheartedly. Unconditionally. Or even to commit to them "forever." One need only say those words, and make those sacred promises, in quiet moments together, with nobody else around, to make them real and unbreakable. Certainly, based on what I saw of my mother and father's marriage, I'm not a believer that marriage turns a bad relationship into a good one. But, still, I must confess, the little girl in me has always wanted to marry my prince. And today, that's exactly what I've done.

As simple and small as our wedding has been, it's turned out to be as magical as I've ever dreamed it would be. Standing face to face with Savage, looking into his soulful, brown eyes, and hearing him say, "Laila, I promise to love and cherish you, forever, through sickness and health, and richer or poorer," felt every bit as soul-stirring and beautiful as I'd dreamed the words would sound. Even more so, actually, thanks to the look on Savage's face when he said them. He looked so beautiful in that moment. So overcome with love and happiness. I could barely hold it together to say my own vows.

I've decided to take Savage's name, though not professionally. My stage name will always be Laila Fitzgerald. But on all legal documents, I'm now, officially, Laila Savage. And it feels even more awesome than I could have predicted. Now, whenever Savage picks up his guitar and serenades me with his rendition of my song, "Savage Love," which he often does, it'll feel even more like he's singing a love song *he* wrote for *me*.

When Kendrick finishes his best-man speech, Kai and Titus get up to say a few words. And then, my bridesmaids: my sister, Aloha, Sasha, Alessandra, and Ruby. Savage made fun of me for having so many bridesmaids, especially for such a small wedding. But I told him, "It's like 'Birthday Truth or Dare.' As long as I don't maim, kill, or send anyone to prison, nothing is off-limits at my own wedding." And, of course, Savage replied to that, "Knock yourself out, Fitzy. It's your day." To that, I replied, "No, it's *our* day." And Savage replied, "Mostly yours, though." I didn't continue arguing the point, because I knew he was right. Savage would marry me on the beach in front of our house, if given the option, and then throw a party in our living room to celebrate. Anything more than that has pretty much been for me. The girl who grew up enchanted by *Beauty and the Beast*.

My mom takes the mic from Sasha and tearfully tries to tell Savage and me how happy she is, but she can't get more than five words out. Which, honestly, is even more meaningful to me than whatever words she's got written on that little scrap of paper in her hand.

I head over to my weeping mother and hug her as she cries. I understand her emotion completely. The magnitude of this occasion for her. She's not only weeping about my marriage to Savage, although she's obviously over the moon about it. Even more than that, though, I know my mother is crying because I didn't follow in her footsteps. Because I didn't wind up married to a man like my father, or to one of the many assholes I dated before my husband. My mom is crying because I've married a man who'll love me and treat me right, forever—which means all her dreams for me have now come true, every bit as much as Mimi's dreams for Savage have, as well.

As I'm comforting my mother, the familiar first notes of "Savage Love" begin blaring through the reception. I pull away from my mom, wiping my eyes, and instantly notice Savage standing on the edge of the dance floor, grinning at me. He gestures to the dance floor, clearly inviting me to dance with him. So, I take my husband's hand and let him guide me to the middle of the floor for our first dance as husband and wife.

As Savage holds me close, my own voice serenades Savage and me, and I'm struck by the unbridled truth of my words. I've got a savage love for this man, and I know he loves me the same way—because our love is, and always will be, infinite and everlasting.

Savage Love

One for the money
Two for the show
Three cuz you're so good givin' Os
Ooooooooooh

Four for the cameras
Five for the fame
No catchin' feelings, only a game
Ooooooooooh

But then six came along when we had our first kiss
Six made me swoon, yell out "I call dibs!"
Six watched you sleep, whispered, "I want this."
Six held you tight in a white knuckled grip
Ooooooooooh

And now I've got a savage love for you
I've lost count of all the ways you've made me a slave to you
There's no doubt my love is here to stay, I'm addicted to you
I've got a savage love for you, infinite and everlasting

. . .

Six hit the road, now it's long gone
Seven came along, now you're second to none
Ooooooooooh

Cameras are off and our love remains
Eight, nine, and ten, our love never fades
Ooooooooooh

Fake became real and want became need
Can't live without you, I need you to breathe
You're swimming in my bloodstream, enmeshed in my
heart
I dream about you, in pain when we part
Ooooooooooh

I've got a savage love for you
I've lost count of all the ways you've made me a slave
to you
There's no doubt my love is here to stay, I'm addicted
to you
I've got a savage love for you
Infinite and everlasting

Take my heart, take my soul,
Take my blood, bones, and flesh
Take the air from my lungs, every pound, every inch
Take it all, every ounce, I give everything
Savage love, my sweet addiction

Oooooooh

And now I've got a savage love for you
Infinite and everlasting

When the song ends, Savage kisses my cheek and whispers into my ear, "I've got a savage love for you, Mrs. Savage."

I kiss him, but I don't need to say a word in reply, since the song has already said it all for me. I've got a savage love for my husband, too. This beautiful, generous man. A love that's unbreakable and sacred. Unconditional and true. *Infinite and everlasting.*

Go to
http://www.laurenrowebooks.com/savage-love-wedding-dance
if you want to listen to "Savage Love".

THE END

If you want to hear Laila's acoustic version of "Savage Love," the one she played for Savage on her new baby grand during their first night together in their new house, go here: http://www.laurenrowebooks.com/laila-f-savage-love

To read a **bonus scene**, featuring Savage and Laila on their honeymoon, then go here: http://www.laurenrowebooks.com/hate-love-honeymoon

Check out all the music from *The Hate - Love Duet*, as well as tons of magazine articles, music, and extras from the world of River Records, here: http://www.laurenrowebooks.com/river-records

The original song "Hate Sex High" was written by Lauren Rowe and David The Optimist, produced by David The Optimist, and performed by Aiden Chance as Savage.

All songs performed by "Laila" in the duet were written and produced by Lauren Rowe and performed by Jessica Schneider as Laila.

"Fireflies" by 22 Goats was written by Lauren Rowe and Hunter Levy, original version performed by Hunter Levy as Dax Morgan.

Do you want to read about Fish and Ally? Their romance *Smitten* is available now.

If you want to find out how feisty Georgina Ricci brings stubborn Reed Rivers to his knees, start with *BAD LIAR*, the first book of The Reed Rivers Trilogy.

AFTERWORD

Music Playlist for the Hate-Love Duet

"Hate Sex High"—Fugitive Summer
   "Something I Can Never Have (Still)"—Nine Inch Nails
   "Grace"—Jeff Buckley
   "Fireflies"—22 Goats (as covered by Laila Fitzgerald)
   "True Love High"—Laila Fitzgerald
   "Savage Love"—Laila Fitzgerald

Acknowledgments

Special thanks to Sophie Broughton, my beta readers: Sarah Kirk, Lizette Baez, Selina Washington, and Madonna Blackburn.

Huge thanks to David The Optimist (Baby Cuz) and Matthew Embree (Cuz), for being my favorite rock stars, forever and always.

Thank you to Letitia Hasser for the kickass covers.

And thank you to Melissa Saneholtz for your unending help and support.

And most of all, thank you to my incredible, devoted readers! I love you all so much. I'm honored and grateful at the way you love my stories and spread the word about them. Thank you from the bottom of my heart.

BOOKS BY LAUREN ROWE

Standalone Novels

Smitten

When aspiring singer-songwriter, Alessandra, meets Fish, the funny, adorable bass player of 22 Goats, sparks fly between the awkward pair. Fish tells Alessandra he's a "Goat called Fish who's hung like a bull. But not really. I'm actually really average." And Alessandra tells Fish, "There's nothing like a girl's first love." Alessandra thinks she's talking about a song when she makes her comment to Fish—the first song she'd ever heard by 22 Goats, in fact. As she'll later find out, though, her "first love" was actually Fish. The Goat called Fish who, after that night, vowed to do anything to win her heart.

SMITTEN is a **true standalone** romance that will make you swoon.

The Reed Rivers Trilogy

Reed Rivers has met his match in the most unlikely of women— aspiring journalist and spitfire, Georgina Ricci. She's much younger than the women Reed normally pursues, but he can't resist her fiery personality and drop-dead gorgeous looks. But in this game of cat and mouse, who's chasing whom? With each passing day of this wild ride, Reed's not so sure. The books of this trilogy are to be read in order:

Bad Liar

Beautiful Liar

Beloved Liar

The Club Trilogy

Romantic. Scorching hot. Suspenseful. Witty. The Club is your new addiction—a sexy and suspenseful thriller about two wealthy brothers and the sassy women who bring them to their knees . . . all while the foursome bands together to protect one of their own. *The Club Trilogy* is to be read in order, as follows:

The Club: Obsession

The Club: Reclamation

The Club: Redemption

The Club: Culmination

The fourth book for Jonas and Sarah is a full-length epilogue with incredible heart-stopping twists and turns and feels. Read *The Club: Culmination (A Full-Length Epilogue Novel)* after finishing *The Club Trilogy* or, if you prefer, after reading *The Josh and Kat Trilogy*.

The Josh and Kat Trilogy

It's a war of wills between stubborn and sexy Josh Faraday and Kat Morgan. A fight to the bed. Arrogant, wealthy playboy Josh is used to getting what he wants. *And what he wants is Kat Morgan.* The books are to be read in order:

Infatuation

Revelation

Consummation

The Morgan Brothers

Read these **standalones** in any order about the brothers of Kat Morgan. Chronological reading order is below, but they are all complete stories. Note: you do *not* need to read any other books or series before jumping straight into reading about the Morgan boys.

Hero.

The story of heroic firefighter, **Colby Morgan**. When catastrophe strikes Colby Morgan, will physical therapist Lydia save him . . . or will he save her?

Captain.

The insta-love-to-enemies-to-lovers story of tattooed sex god, **Ryan Morgan**, and the woman he'd move heaven and earth to claim.

Ball Peen Hammer.

A steamy, hilarious, friends-to-lovers romantic comedy about cocky-as-hell male stripper, **Keane Morgan**, and the sassy, smart young woman who brings him to his knees during a road trip.

Mister Bodyguard.

The Morgans' beloved honorary brother, **Zander Shaw**, meets his match in the feisty pop star he's assigned to protect on tour.

ROCKSTAR.

When the youngest Morgan brother, **Dax Morgan,** meets a mysterious woman who rocks his world, he must decide if pursuing her is worth risking it all. Be sure to check out four of Dax's original songs from *ROCKSTAR*, written and produced by Lauren, along with full music videos for the songs, on her website (www.laurenrowebooks.com) under the tab MUSIC FROM ROCKSTAR.

Misadventures

Lauren's *Misadventures* titles are page-turning, steamy, swoony standalones, to be read in any order.

- *Misadventures on the Night Shift* —A hotel night shift clerk encounters her teenage fantasy: rock star Lucas Ford. And combustion ensues.

- *Misadventures of a College Girl*—A spunky, virginal theater major meets a cocky football player at her first college party . . . and absolutely nothing goes according to plan for either of them.

- *Misadventures on the Rebound*—A spunky woman on the rebound meets a hot, mysterious stranger in a bar on her way to her five-year high school reunion in Las Vegas and what follows is a misadventure neither of them ever imagined.

Standalone Psychological Thriller/Dark Comedy

Countdown to Killing Kurtis

A young woman with big dreams and skeletons in her closet decides her porno-king husband must die in exactly a year. This is *not* a traditional romance, but it *will* most definitely keep you turning the pages and saying "WTF?"

Free Short Stories

The Secret Note

Looking for a quickie? Try this scorching-hot short story from Lauren Rowe in ebook FOR FREE or in audiobook: He's a hot

Aussie. I'm a girl who isn't shy about getting what she wants. The problem? Ben is my little brother's best friend. An exchange student who's heading back Down Under any day now. But I can't help myself. He's too hot to resist.

All books by Lauren Rowe are available in ebook, paperback, and audiobook formats.

Be sure to sign up for Lauren's newsletter to find out about upcoming releases!

AUTHOR BIOGRAPHY

Lauren Rowe is the USA Today and international #1 best-selling author of newly released Reed Rivers Trilogy, as well as The Club Trilogy, The Josh & Kat Trilogy, The Morgan Brothers Series, Countdown to Killing Kurtis, and select standalone Misadventures.

Lauren's books are full of feels, humor, heat, and heart. Besides writing novels, Lauren is the singer in a party/wedding band in her hometown of San Diego, an audio book narrator, and award-winning songwriter. She is thrilled to connect with readers all over the world. To find out about Lauren's upcoming releases and giveaways, sign up for Lauren's emails here!

Lauren loves to hear from readers! Send Lauren an email from her website, say hi on Twitter, Instagram, or Facebook.

Find out more and check out lots of free bonus material at www.LaurenRoweBooks.com.

CPSIA information can be obtained
at www.ICGtesting.com
Printed in the USA
LVHW111640220721
693425LV00005B/785